NEPHILIM

Also by L.A. Marzulli

The Unholy Deception

NEPHILIM

THE TRUTH IS HERE

L.A. MARZULLI

ZONDERVAN™

GRAND RAPIDS, MICHIGAN 49530 USA

ZONDERVAN™

Nephilim
Copyright © 1999 by Lynn Marzulli

Requests for information should be addressed to:
Zondervan, *Grand Rapids, Michigan 49530*

Library of Congress Cataloging-in-Publication Data

Marzulli, L.A. (Lynn A.), 1950-
     Nephilim / L.A. Marzulli.
         p. cm.
     ISBN: 0-310-22011-4 (softcover)
         I. Title.
     PS3563.A778N46 1999
     813'.54—dc21   99-35509
                                                                                    CIP

Interior design by Laura Klynstra

Printed in the United States of America

04 05 06 07 08 09 /❖ DC/ 19 18 17 16 15 14 13 12 11 10

To my loving wife, Peggy

Acknowledgments

First I would like to thank my close friend, mentor, confidant, and amazing writer, Bill Myers. Without his involvement from the onset, this book would never have come to fruition. Bill would listen to chapters and give me honest feedback. He was and is a constant encouragement and a source of spiritual inspiration.

Next I would like to thank my editor, Dave Lambert at Zondervan. It is his ability to hold an overview of an entire book simultaneously that leads to his insightful critiques. He has goaded, jarred, and pushed this writer out of any resemblance of a comfort zone. Thanks, Dave, for believing in the project and in me!

My father, Lynn Q. Marzulli, proofread the book. His enthusiasm and support coupled with the support of my mother, Lee, are greatly valued.

Marie Irvine, my friend, also proofread and helped keep the book on track.

Gary Schultz was a source for UFO literature and history and served as a technical advisor. Yes, it is the same Gary Schultz who's in the book. Check the website out and look at the picture: www.spiraloflife.com.

Dr. I.D.E. Thomas's book *The Omega Conspiracy* served as a primer, and almost all of the theology has been borrowed from his book. I am indebted to this godly pioneer.

Chuck Missler has been a source of inspiration. His book *Alien Encounters* is a must read for anyone wanting an indepth study of the alien phenomena from a biblical perspective.

Vera Schlamm provided firsthand experience about concentration camps. Her book *Pursued* is an insightful look into the horrors of the camps.

Grant Shamamoto was really helpful in explaining how DNA works. It was his suggestion to have a fifth nucleotide.

Simon from Israel served as my live model for the accent that Uri uses throughout the book.

Thanks, Barry Yates, for the help with the Citabria.

Thanks to Bill McGee for endless encouragement and the lunches at Tom's . . . more ketchup please!

Thanks to Lori VandenBosch for her editing prowess and encouraging e-mails. To Sue Brower for her marketing skills at Zondervan. To Tina Jacobson at B&B Media. And to Mike Hoffman for his help with the website.

A special thanks to all off you who helped and encouraged: Wolf & Christine Marshall, Clint and Lori Smith, Kevin and Laura Smith, Jim and Paula Huffman, Harper and Connie Wren, Jim and Debbie Riordan, Steve and Donna Blinn, Tony and Janey Marzulli, Carrie Rudiselle, Barry and Terry Santavy, Nate and Shirley Lyndsay, Manolo and Virginia Lopez, Fin and Adrian Johnston, Kelly and Kathy Higgins, Brian and Suzy Neuman, David and Terri Schaal, Seth and Karen Semkin, Andy Flamard and special thanks to my manager Kathy Horn!

A special thank you to my loving wife and helpmate who read and reread, typed and proofread, prayed and cheered me on every step of the way. Thank you, Peggy.

Also my two daughters, Corrie and Sarah, for their prayers and support. Thanks, kids.

When men began to increase in number on the earth and daughters were born to them, the sons of God saw that the daughters of men were beautiful, and they married any of them they chose. Then the LORD said, "My Spirit will not contend with man forever, for he is mortal; his days will be a hundred and twenty years."

The Nephilim were on the earth in those days—and also afterward—when the sons of God went to the daughters of men and had children by them. They were the heroes of old, men of renown.

—GENESIS 6:1–4

1

* O *

Alone in the dark, Art MacKenzie slouched on a torn sofa in his disheveled studio apartment. His bare feet rested on the single piece of furniture from his marriage he still possessed: a coffee table with one leg missing. He sipped slowly from a dirty glass and felt the Grand Marnier warm its way down his throat, adding to the fire that already burned in his belly.

He took another sip, this time a longer one, closed his eyes, and relived it all one more time.

* O *

He runs frantically down a hospital corridor and slams into the door of the emergency room. It bursts open, crashing against the wall, the noise reverberating, startling doctors, patients, and nurses who look up at him, wide-eyed.

He steps into the room and stops. His eyes dart wildly from person to person, one hand pushing his hair off his forehead as he tries to catch his breath. His chest heaves—to get here, he has run faster and harder than he has ever run in his life.

He knows he must appear crazy, but he doesn't care.

He draws a deep breath, so deep it hurts, and bellows: "Maggie!"

No one answers.

His heart hammers in his chest, feeling as if it will burst through the bone and muscle as it pounds.

"Mr. MacKenzie?" someone asks.

His muscles tense. "I'm MacKenzie," he blurts out.

A nurse rises from her chair behind the nurses' station and scurries to him. She grabs his hand and rushes him down a hallway.

And there is Maggie, his wife. She doesn't see him at first. Her hands and tear-stained face are pressed against the observation window, as if she were trying to melt through the glass.

Mac touches her shoulder; she jumps, and then they look at each other for an agonizing second, neither saying a word.

Mac takes her hand, and together they watch a team of doctors and nurses working desperately on a young boy.

Their son, Art junior.

The sheets that cover him are soaked with his blood. His short brownish hair is matted and wet with blood and perspiration. His hand hangs limply over the side of the table. He is fragile, helpless, alone, and defenseless against what has happened and is happening to him, and Mac wants only to rush in and hold him, to wash away the blood from his forehead, to see his hazel eyes and crooked smile.

He can imagine the scene, so comforting: he would simply walk into the operating room and tell the doctors that everything is all right, it's just a slight bruise, no need for all of this. Everyone can go home now.

A faint but alarming sound reaches Mac through the window, shattering his daydream. It comes from a monitor at the head of Art's gurney. Mac has seen the movies, the television shows—he doesn't need to be a doctor to know that his son's heart has flat-lined. The doctor who appears to head the team grabs a syringe held out to him by a nurse. He plunges the needle into Art's chest and pumps its liquid in.

He stares at the monitor and looks for a change.

The heart doesn't respond.

Mac is tortured by "if onlys." If only Art had been sitting in a different seat in the family's van, there might have been less damage. If only the firemen had been able to free him from the twisted wreck more quickly. If only the rush-hour traffic hadn't been so heavy, delaying the ambulance on its way to the hospital. If only he hadn't lost so much blood.

So much blood . . .

"Come on . . . Come *on!*" The doctor shouts, pressing Art's chest with such power Mac is surprised his son doesn't fall through the table.

Maggie squeezes Mac's hand; when he looks at her, he sees that she is biting her lower lip with such force blood runs down her chin.

There's panic in the operating room now; the monitor's long, droning, monotone note seems to be terrifying everyone. There's cursing and yelling. Instruments are flung to the floor; people rush back and forth, undoubtedly carrying out logical, preassigned tasks, but to Mac it merely seems the pointless, random scurrying of panic, back and forth, from one end of the room to the other. Mac can't see his son now because of the crowd of milling, frantic doctors and nurses, ten people trying with all the skill they collectively possess to bring Mac's son back.

And still the note drones on.

＊ ◦ ＊

MacKenzie took another sip of Grand Marnier. He was almost numb . . . ready to pass out. The liquor worked like it always did, numbing the pain, the wound that festered in him.

Two years since little Art died. Two years, and the pain lingered.

He felt the room spin as he sipped again. Hovering on the verge of consciousness, he sometimes fell into a dreamlike state, then came out of it, back into a waking stupor, back to watching meaningless images on the TV.

His line of consciousness blurred, and as he slipped away, he heard a quiet voice that he at first assumed came from the TV. "I'll take your pain. I'll take your pain."

His last thought as he tumbled into the oblivion of sleep, only vaguely aware of the half-full glass falling from his hand, was to wonder how he could hear the TV when the sound was turned down.

2

＊◯＊

Mac groaned, wrapping the pillow tighter over his head, fighting to stay in his alcohol-induced oblivion and to ignore that shrill, insistent sound that slowly registered in his mind as a ringing telephone. He moaned, rolling across the lumpy mattress that sagged like an old horse, testifying to the weight and girth of its previous owner.

The phone erupted again, and his head throbbed in unison.

"Already?" he mumbled into the sheets.

He extended an arm and groped for the phone on the cluttered nightstand by the bed. He lifted the receiver and tried to pull it toward him. It wouldn't budge. The cord was a tangled jumble of knots, coiled serpentlike around its base. Mac yanked—and the phone flew off the nightstand, bringing with it an unread paperback, a dish full of change, an empty bottle of Grand Marnier, an unopened letter from Maggie, and a past-due telephone bill.

"For crying out loud," he mumbled, and put the phone to his ear. "Hello."

"Mr. MacKenzie?" The voice of a female operator crackled through the tiny speaker.

"Yeah." He exhaled.

"Good morning, sir. It's 6:45 and this is your wake-up call. Have a nice day, sir."

MacKenzie sat up in bed and slowly rubbed the two-day growth of stubble on his face. How had he gotten into bed last night?

"Oh, my head," he moaned, and forced himself to get up. He stretched slowly, took a deep breath, kicked some dirty clothes out of his way, and shuffled toward the bathroom.

After his shower, he grabbed a large bath towel, still slightly damp from the day before, and dried himself. He wiped a clean spot on the fogged mirror with the palm of his hand and attended to a razor cut on his chin, dabbing at it with a piece of toilet paper. Then he left the bathroom in search of something clean to wear.

He stared at the eclectic variety of clothing in his closet, everything from three-piece suits to worn Levi's with seasoned holes at the knees. He found a pair of slacks that didn't look too bad and opted for those. The choice of a shirt, however, was more difficult. He finally settled on a blue pinstripe, which he matched with a bold electric-blue tie, secured with a flawless Windsor knot.

The phone rang. His desk, unlike the rest of the apartment, was fastidiously maintained. His computer and fax machine all sported dust covers. His files, papers, and resource material were neatly stacked and arranged, habits left over from better days. MacKenzie went to his desk and switched on the speakerphone.

"Glad to see you're up," the voice of Jim Cranston, his editor, echoed through the apartment.

"Yep. Thanks for the bone," Mac answered.

"Well, it's not much . . ." There was an awkward silence, then Jim continued, "But it'll pay the rent. And it *is* an assignment."

"You don't have to tap dance, Jim. Don't worry. I won't drink a drop until after I write the story," Mac said, with a touch of self-conscious sarcasm.

"Look, the deadline's tomorrow night. That new wing cost millions."

"I'll treat it seriously, don't worry," Mac said.

"Fax it in tomorrow?" Cranston sounded annoyed.

"Yep. Promise."

"Write it like the old Mac?"

"Yep."

"Okay. I'll look forward to seeing it."

"Yep."

Cranston hung up.

Mac switched off the speakerphone and glanced at his watch. About time to leave.

Looking around the apartment to find his keys, his eyes settled on the picture of his three children on the corner of his desk. An old picture—taken before the accident. Little Art would have been celebrating his twelfth birthday two months from now. Pain washed over Mac anew as he stared at the smiling face of his oldest boy.

He turned away and stared blankly out the large, wood-framed window in front of the desk. Then, in need of comfort, he turned and looked at the partially emptied case of Grand Marnier by the bed. *Not now.* He forced himself to look away. *I've got an article to write.* Feeling guilty and disloyal, he forced the painful memories from his mind.

He picked up his appointment book, grabbed his keys, and walked out of the apartment. He took every other step going down the two flights of stairs that led to the small vestibule. He opened the weathered stained-glass door—one of the pieces was about to fall out of its lead lining—and stood for a moment on the front steps. Patches of blue shone through the mist; the sun was beginning to burn away the fog along the coastal California town of Venice Beach.

He hurried to his jeep, parked in front of the large gable-roofed house, now converted into apartments.

At one time, Venice had been a prime resort. But the community had diminished as the inner city pressed in on it, leaving much of it to the addicts, gangs, and homeless. The current owner of the house Mac lived in had inherited it at his grandmother's death and had converted it, illegally, into four apartments.

Mac opened the jeep's door and slid onto the worn seat, adjusting a folded beach towel under him. He slid the key into the ignition, rolled his eyes toward heaven, and turned. The starter hesitated, clicked—and then kicked the engine alive.

"Thank you," he said, as he patted the dash reverently.

The drive to Westwood bogged down on the predictably crowded freeways. What should have taken a half hour turned into a fifty-minute, stop-and-start crawl. He switched on the radio; a catchy country tune came on. When the singer reached the chorus and twanged the lyrics, "I'll take the pain away, darlin'," Mac gave the radio an odd, surprised look. *Interesting coincidence,* he thought, remembering the phrase that had come unbidden into his alcohol-drugged consciousness the night before. He turned the dial to another station so he wouldn't have to hear the chorus again.

Once he got beyond a stalled car in the fast lane, traffic began to flow again. Finally Mac steered the jeep off the freeway and began inching his way along the congested streets to the hospital.

The construction of the hospital's new wing must not yet be completed, Mac realized as he pulled into the freshly paved parking lot. A large construction trailer bearing the faded sign of Viking Construction sat in the far corner of the lot, with a few pieces of machinery and equipment camped around it. A lone security guard sat on the metal steps of the trailer, cigarette dangling from his mouth. He watched Mac suspiciously.

Mac parked between a Porsche and a shiny new BMW with the dealer sticker purposely left on the rear window.

"Mental health business must be doing well," he smirked as he slid out of the jeep. The towel followed and fell to the ground. He picked it up and threw it back onto the worn seat, covering several springs that showed through the tattered upholstery.

The security guard shook his head and blew out a long stream of smoke.

Mac grinned back and started across the newly planted sod. He immediately regretted it; his shoes were soaked after two or three steps. He reached the main walkway, stomped his feet on the concrete, and looked up at the mirrored glass building that rose six stories above him.

At the main entrance, two oversized glass doors silently slid open to reveal large squares of rose-colored marble in the foyer. Mac walked to the reception desk, consciously putting on his "objective eyes," a phrase he used to describe a journalist's ability to size up situations, people, and events, to sift through what might appear obvious and find the extraordinary. Mac had spent years training himself to pick up on the little things of life, subtleties most people never noticed.

"Good morning. May I help you?" a well-dressed young black man said, as he smiled at Mac.

"I have an appointment with Ms. Kennedy. I'm Art MacKenzie from the *Times*."

"Just a moment. I'll ring her for you." The man picked up the phone and dialed.

As he did, Mac scrutinized him. Close-cropped hair, athletic, long bony fingers, small scar on the back of his left hand—maybe a graduate student from nearby UCLA.

"Good morning, Ms. Kennedy. This is Thomas at the front desk. A Mr. MacKenzie is here from the *Times*." He nodded his head as he listened, then put the receiver down. "She'll be right down. You can have a seat by the elevators if you'd like." He motioned to a cluster of comfortable looking, floral patterned couches.

A few minutes passed. Mac watched a steady stream of doctors and nurses vanish into one elevator or appear from another.

The elevator opened again; a woman exited and glanced around, her eyes quickly alighting on Mac. Late twenties, attractive, professional, self-assured, assertive—probably the positive personality winner of the year. Mac smirked.

"Mr. MacKenzie?" She smiled and leaned her head to one side. A lock of blonde hair bluntly cut to chin length fell in front of her face; she quickly brushed it behind her ear.

"Call me Mac."

"I'm Evelyn Kennedy. Welcome to the Westwood Center."

Mac followed her into the elevator. While they ascended, she apologized that the construction wasn't yet completed, rattling off financial figures and lamenting unforeseen delays. Even so, she assured him, the new wing was fully functional—the only work that remained was essentially cosmetic. The doors opened and he found himself on the fourth floor.

"The old wing is to our left, new wing to the right," she informed him as they stepped out and she guided him into the new section. "This is where we treat our outpatients. Twenty psychologists and psychiatrists practice here on a daily basis. There is also a fully staffed pharmacy on the floor directly below us," she informed him proudly.

Mac glanced at the polished floors and sterile acoustical ceiling tiles. Words like *antiseptic, institutional,* and *non-threatening* crossed his mind.

They walked down the hall. Kennedy pointed overhead to the air-conditioning ducts, explaining with delight how the air circulated through a filtering system before it was pumped through the building. "No Legionnaires' disease here," she laughed.

Mac forced himself to focus on her endless stream of facts and figures.

"Fascinating," he replied insincerely as she finished informing him of the special acoustical properties of the overhead ceiling tiles. He cleared his throat. "Do you treat any serious cases here?"

"Well." She paused. "There are varying degrees of mental illness, of course. Some of the more serious cases we receive are sent on to other locations."

"How serious are they? Why are they treated somewhere else?"

"I'm glad you asked that." She brushed her hair back from her face. "If one of our doctors believes a particular case is serious enough that the patient should be institutionalized, then there are facilities better equipped to handle that patient's long-term needs. So we refer that patient to those institutions."

Mac stopped walking. "Wait. So you don't treat anything really *serious* here? Say, uh . . . multiple personality disorders?"

Kennedy thought a moment. "We could treat that, providing the patient was nonviolent."

"Is that some sort of criteria for being treated here—lacking a tendency toward violence?"

"That would be one."

"Oh." Mac stared at one of the ceiling tiles overhead, then said, "Well, surely some of your patients must occasionally get violent?" He was hoping for something more interesting for his article than the endless series of facts and figures.

Kennedy shifted her weight from one high-heeled shoe to the other and said offhandedly, "Occasionally, but it's rare."

Mac sensed her uneasiness. "How often is occasionally?" he pressed. "Is any of the staff ever injured? Do the patients hurt themselves?"

She folded her arms in front of her, smiled, and said, "Mr. MacKenzie, I'm afraid that I can't give out any information that specific about our patients. But let's say that we are prepared for that eventuality."

Mac pursed his lips and frowned. "So do you isolate the more violent patients?" he asked.

"We have designated areas for them, yes."

"Would you show me one of them?"

Kennedy's cheerful expression faded. She stared at Mac. "I was informed by your editor that you were here to do a story on the overall construction cost and the special features designed into this wing of the hospital."

"That's true." Mac shrugged in acknowledgment. "But I'm a reporter; reporters ask questions."

"Even so, I don't see the connection between that assignment and your questions about the behavioral patterns of our patients here," she said tersely.

Her reluctance piqued his interest, but he knew he'd get no information from a well-disciplined, hostile PR professional. He decided to back off. "I suppose you're right."

"So would you please limit your questions to the construction of the new wing?" she asked, accenting her demand with a phony smile.

Mac nodded in acquiescence. "Is there anything unique about the, uh . . . water system?"

"I'm glad you asked," Kennedy replied and launched into a monologue, informing Mac how incoming water was filtered, bath water was recycled and used to irrigate the grounds, and so on—for another half hour.

Mac drifted in and out of her monologue, trying his best to nod at the appropriate times. He even took a couple of notes, just to make it appear that he was really listening.

She guided him into a large office where he was introduced to hospital administrators who boasted about how well the new wing of the hospital was functioning.

The rest of the tour was uneventful, and eventually Mac found himself back in the lobby. He watched with satisfaction as the elevator doors closed, grateful to see the last of Kennedy and her phony smile.

Mac walked quickly through the foyer, involuntarily shuddering as he stepped outside and felt the warmth of the sun hit him.

He walked briskly down the tree-lined walkway into the parking lot and climbed into his jeep. He slipped the key into the ignition, closed his eyes, and gave the key a turn.

Nothing.

"For crying out loud!" He exhaled angrily, and tried again. Still nothing.

He got out, struggled to find the hood latch, and popped the hood. He stared at the oil-grimed motor, chagrined that after all these years of driving he still didn't have a clue as to how it really worked. He cautiously reached in and jiggled the battery cable, encrusted around the battery terminal with a salt-like deposit of green crystals. He got back in and tried to start it again.

This time the engine responded with a clicking noise. Encouraged, he climbed out to try again and noticed the security guard walking toward him.

Mac ignored the man and stuck his head under the hood, trying to look like he knew what he was doing. He knew when the man reached him by the sudden smell of nicotine and unchanged clothes.

"Trouble?" the guard asked.

"Yeah . . . won't start. I think it's the cables." Mac nodded at the corrosion.

The guard's eyes narrowed shrewdly and he poked at the green pile of flakes with a long, grease-darkened fingernail. "There's your problem. No juice comin' from the battery." Before Mac could reply, the man produced a worn Swiss army knife from one of his pants pockets. "Handy little thing," he said, as he placed it on the radiator. He reached into his faded blue uniform shirt pocket, grabbed a pack of Marlboros, and gingerly pulled a cigarette out and placed it between his lips. He let it dangle there, unlit. He picked up the knife and selected one of the blades.

"All that green stuff keeps the juice from the starter," he said as he pulled the cable from the battery's post. He scraped away the flakes encrusted around the cable's clamp and forced it back onto the post. "Give it a try."

Mac climbed back into the jeep and turned the key. The engine fired up. The guard closed the hood, winked at Mac, and lit his cigarette.

"Thanks," Mac called out.

"Better get some new cables."

"It's on the top of my list," Mac lied.

"You got a relative in there?" The guard nodded in the direction of the new wing.

Mac laughed, and shook his head.

"Good thing, too," the man said sagely.

"What do you mean?"

"You don't ever want to spend the night in that place."

"Why?" Mac turned off the motor, his curiosity piqued.

The guard took a couple of steps closer and put his foot up on the running board of the jeep. He inhaled for what seemed like a minute and then began talking as he slowly let the smoke out of his mouth.

"I have a lady friend that works there. Does the night shift, been there since the place opened up."

"Nurse?"

He shook his head. "Maintenance. Changes the sheets, cleans the toilets, tidies up the place."

"It's honest work," Mac replied, reaching for the ignition key.

The man's eyes narrowed and he leaned closer to Mac. "She gets up to the sixth floor."

"What's so important about the sixth floor?"

He took another long drag. Mac watched the ash glow red, crawling up the length of the cigarette.

"It's where they keep the real crazies. All sorts of weird stuff up there. Run by the military."

"The military?" Mac repeated. Kennedy hadn't said anything about the military. But then, she hadn't said much about anything at all. Mac looked at the guard skeptically. "What goes on up there?"

"You wouldn't believe me."

"I make my living by not believing what I hear."

"What's that mean?"

"I'm a reporter."

"Newspaper reporter?" The guard looked shocked.

Mac nodded. "I'm here to do a story for the *Times*."

"Sixth floor is where your story is. Bet they didn't let you anywheres near there." The guard chuckled knowingly.

"Right about that. But what's so special about the sixth floor?"

"Aliens."

Mac's stomach flipped and his fingers gripped the steering wheel. A flood of unwanted memories flashed in his mind. "Aliens." He forced himself to say the word.

The man nodded, took one last drag, and flicked the butt onto the asphalt.

"UFO stuff. Ab-duc-tions," the man said, with an attitude, enjoying his role as an "insider."

"Abductions," Mac heard himself repeat.

"The aliens kidnap 'em and do experiments, and after they're done experimenting the poor slobs wind up here."

"What kind of experiments?"

The guard shrugged. "Mostly with the women. My friend I told you about? She says most of the women are so doped up they sleep most of the time. But she hears pieces of the same story out of each of 'em."

"And do the pieces make a picture?" Mac asked.

The man thought for a moment, then said slowly, "My friend's shift starts at seven. Be here just before that and see for yourself."

Mac looked at him. Was this guy telling the truth? *That could explain Kennedy's reluctance to discuss what kinds of treatment the hospital is involved in,* Mac thought. *On the other hand, maybe this guy's seen too many episodes of the X-Files.*

"What time did you say?" Mac asked.

"Be here before seven. We'll sneak you in. Make you up like a maintenance man."

"Okay. See you before seven." Mac fired the engine. "But this better be good." He backed the jeep up, nodded at the guard, and sped out of the parking lot. He glanced back once in his rearview mirror.

"Aliens," he scoffed.

But his mouth went dry.

3

⚫

Later that evening, Mac pulled his jeep into the hospital parking lot. The overhead lights cast dim pools of light on the asphalt. He parked and hurried toward the security guard's trailer.

Lights shone through the tiny windows, and he heard a man and a woman talking as he rapped on the battered aluminum trailer door.

"Just a minute," rasped a voice, which he recognized as the guard's.

The door opened, and a cloud of cigarette smoke billowed from the trailer.

"See you decided to check it out after all," the guard said. "Come on in." He motioned Mac forward.

Mac climbed the steps and entered a wreck in progress. Dishes were piled in the sink; stacks of newspapers and magazines littered the floor. A TV sat precariously on a table with a broken leg; a coat hanger substituted for its antenna. Layers of smoke permeated every nook and cranny of the cramped quarters. *My place is a palace compared to this,* Mac thought.

At the rear, an emaciated woman sat on an unmade double bed in a wrinkled white uniform. One skinny leg clothed

27

in support hose dangled over her other knee. Her stringy hair, piled loosely on top of her head, was held in place with bobby pins. She looked at Mac, then exhaled a stream of smoke that slowly added itself to the growing haze. With long, bony fingers, she flicked an ash into an overflowing ashtray; her ashes slid off and fell to the floor.

"This him?" she asked.

The guard nodded.

She looked at Mac and asked, "You the reporter Harry told me about?"

Mac opened his mouth to reply and immediately choked on the smoke; he erupted in a fit of coughing, then finally cleared his throat and said, "The very same. And you are . . . ?"

"Linda," she said. "Harry says you want to go to the sixth floor." She glanced at the guard who leaned against the shower stall.

"I do, if what Harry tells me is true."

"Well, it's off-limits. Military people run it. You need special clearance." She paused, then added, "And what Harry here told you's true all right." She uncrossed her legs and rested her elbows on her knees. "I oughta know, I'm up there every night. Least the nights I'm working my shift. What you gonna write about, anyway?"

Mac leaned against the tiny Formica counter that was part of the trailer's kitchen. "It depends on what I find out. There may be nothing at all to write about," he said flatly.

"There's plenty to write about, all right. Harry told you about the . . . the aliens then?"

"He mentioned them. So what? Crazy people make up crazy stories. That's why they're here, isn't it?" Mac challenged.

Linda glanced skeptically at Harry, then stubbed her cigarette out.

"Look, Mister. I clean up there, make the beds, keep everything tidy and hospital-like. So I see everything. And I tell you, there's something going on in that place. Why else they have them cameras everywhere?"

"Cameras?"

"You come up there with me and see for yourself."

"Linda got you a uniform to wear," Harry interjected.

"I could lose my job for this, if they ever found out," she grumbled.

"Don't worry," Mac said. "I wouldn't be much of a journalist if I didn't protect my sources. Nobody has to find out anything."

"Put 'em on," Harry said, and handed Mac a rolled bundle of white clothes. "You can change here." He opened the shower stall door.

After struggling for several minutes, his body banging against the fiberglass walls of the tiny stall, Mac finally succeeded in putting the uniform on. He emerged from the stall.

"Pants are too small for him," Harry said, pointing to the bottom hem of Mac's pants, which fell just short of his ankles.

"That don't matter. Nobody cares whether his pants are too short, just as long as he's got some on," Linda laughed, reminding Mac of the sound of a crow. "You just follow me on my rounds and do as I tell you. This time of night is slow, and most of them that's up there's all doped out anyway."

That didn't sound hopeful. "Will any of the patients be coherent enough to talk to me, then?"

Linda thought for a moment, then replied, "There's one woman, kinda new, came in early this week. She's a wild one. They had to restrain her the first couple of nights 'cause she was yellin', screamin', makin' a racket, disturbin' all the other patients. But they settled her down, all right. I was cleanin' her room when the nurse come in to give her some pills. I saw her put those pills into her mouth and pretend to swallow. But after the nurse left she spit 'em out and put 'em under her mattress."

"What's wrong with her?" Mac asked.

"Same as the others. Says she was abducted by the aliens. But she's more afraid of the people who locked her up. We'll work our way to her room and you can see for yourself."

Mac nodded.

Linda rose from the bed. "Just stay close by me."

"Promise," Mac said.

She looked at Harry and said, "I could lose my job over this."

Harry shrugged. "Nothin' gonna happen, so stop your worryin'."

Linda mumbled something and left the trailer; Mac followed. They walked across the parking lot, down the driveway to the truck dock at the rear of the hospital, and entered through the service garage.

Linda punched in and set her time card back in the plastic rack.

"*Hola*, Linda," a Latino woman called out from across the large room.

Linda squinted as she tried to identify the person, then replied, "Hey, Theresa. How'd your shift go?"

"Just like always," the woman answered. "You breaking in a new man?"

Linda nodded toward Mac. "Yeah. Gonna show him the ins and outs of keepin' the place tidy and all." The crow-cackle laugh erupted from her throat again.

Theresa nodded and went back to work stacking sheets and supplies on her cart.

Mac kept his head turned down and away from Theresa as he followed Linda across the gray-painted concrete floor. She got her cart. "Filled it at the end of my shift last night, so's I don't have to start work by workin'." She winked at Mac and pushed the cart past a stack of boxes with medical markings stamped on the side, then meandered slowly toward the service elevator at the end of the room.

When they reached the elevator, Linda produced a ring of keys. She selected one and slipped it into the lock at the side of the closed elevator doors. She put them back into her pocket, folded her arms, and sighed as they waited for the elevator.

"What do you want me to do?" Mac asked, wondering whether he was expected to be more than a spectator tonight.

"Nothin', just tag behind me and hand me what I ask for."

The elevator doors opened. Linda pushed the cart inside and hit the number five button on the control panel.

The doors closed and the elevator began its ascent.

"I thought we were going to the sixth floor," Mac said.

"I got to make my rounds on the fifth first."

"How long is that going to take?"

"Depends on how messy the patients is."

Mac shook his head. This could take all night. And in the end he might have nothing to show for it.

For the next hour and a half, Mac obediently followed Linda around the fifth floor like a well-trained dog, providing a never-ending supply of towels, sheets, cleansers, and disinfectant—and wondering why he had ever decided to be there at all.

"Last one, then up to the sixth," Linda informed him as she went into another room.

Mac perked up, and actually began to respond faster in the hope of expediting his arrival at the sixth floor.

"Hey, you're gettin' the hang of this," Linda praised him genuinely.

"Thanks," Mac mumbled, and handed her the disinfectant, feeling more like a maid than a reporter.

They finished cleaning the last room. Mac pushed the cart to the elevator.

"Special key," Linda stated proudly, holding up a red key. "Lets me get to the sixth floor."

"Why you?" Mac asked. "How come you have the run of the place?"

"Somebody gotta clean up."

Mac pushed the cart into the elevator and they rode up. When the doors opened on the sixth floor, Mac whispered, "Why is the lighting different?"

Linda shrugged. "Beats me."

The entire corridor was lit with dull amber, in contrast to the bright, white, fluorescent glow on the floors below.

"This way." Linda jerked her head and walked down the corridor.

The first room they came to was empty. So was the next. The occupant of the third room was bound to her bed at the wrists with cloth straps. She lay on her back, openmouthed, breathing deeply. There was a fresh scar at her temple.

My God—she's had a lobotomy, Mac realized, and his stomach flipped. He wasn't yet ready to buy into Linda's story that this floor represented some kind of military covert op, but whatever was happening here, it didn't seem to match up with what the glib Ms. Kennedy had told him.

Linda went into the bathroom and washed down the toilet and the sink.

"Get the bed pan, will you?" she called.

"What?" Mac asked, surprised. "I thought only nurses did that."

"Yeah, the nurses help the patients use 'em. But then they leave 'em for me to clean up." She pointed and said, "It's by the bed."

Mac found it and carried it into the bathroom.

"She's not the one I was tellin' you about," Linda whispered as she took it from him and emptied its contents into the toilet. "The one you want's in the next room."

Back in the hallway, Linda locked the wire-reinforced glass door behind her and pointed to the camera attached to the ceiling a few feet above the door. "They got them things everywhere," she whispered. "They're always watchin'. But not so much at night."

Mac glanced at the camera and pushed the cart to the next room. When Linda unlocked the door and opened it, Mac saw a woman who appeared to be in her early thirties standing listlessly by the barred window, gazing out at the city below her. Even though she must have heard them come into her room, she remained at the window and gave no hint that she knew they were there.

"Is this her?" Mac whispered.

Linda wiped her nose on her sleeve "You got till the bathroom's clean."

Mac nodded.

The patient at the window turned and looked at him. Mac felt the hair on the back of his neck stand up as he felt the intensity of her gaze. She crossed her arms in front of her and grabbed her hospital smock with both hands as she began to walk slowly toward him.

As she approached, Mac's journalist's eye took in her disheveled hair, the dark rings around her eyes, the nervous twitch at the corner of her mouth, her chewed fingernails.

She stopped a few feet away and stared at him with troubled, unblinking eyes.

Mac reached into his shirt pocket and clicked his tape recorder on.

"You're not one of them, are you?" she asked. Her voice was a surprise, for although it sounded pained, there was a natural melody to it that contrasted sharply with her appearance.

Mac hesitated, then replied, "I'm not sure what you mean."

"You don't work here."

"Why do you say—"

"Because you're not helping the cleaning woman. If you worked here, you'd be helping her. Did my husband send you to spy on me?"

"No."

"Why are you here then?"

Mac thought for a moment, then answered truthfully. "I'm a reporter."

Her eyes sparked with sudden interest. "Will you listen to me—please?" She glanced at the camera in the corner of the ceiling. "Will you help me get out of here?"

As she spoke, she became increasingly emotionally agitated, and Mac reminded himself that he was dealing with a mental patient. "Sure," he said reassuringly, and tried to smile.

"Don't humor me," she said. "I'm not crazy."

"I'm sorry. I just don't know—"

"They took my baby." Tears appeared in the woman's eyes. "That's why I'm in here."

Mac frowned and waited for her to continue.

"They took my baby from me. They take whatever they want. They're horrible."

"Who's horrible?"

The woman shook her head. "What's the use? You won't believe me. You're just like my husband and everyone else. You think I'm making it up. Well, I'm *not!*" she shouted.

Linda appeared at the bathroom door, shaking her head and holding a finger to her lips.

"It's all right," Mac told her. "We're okay." He turned back to the patient and replied softly, "I don't think you're making it up."

"You don't?" She wiped the tears from her eyes, took a step closer, and began again, "They're not human. They come from somewhere else, somewhere far away . . ." Her voice dwindled and her eyes focused somewhere outside the room. "They come at night. Always at night. With the darkness. They come to my room and take me. My husband, he's always asleep, and I cry out to him but he doesn't hear, and they carry me out of my house." Her words came faster, in a rush. "I try to struggle but I can't move!" She started to sob again.

What have I gotten myself into? Mac wondered, feeling the goosebumps rising on his arms.

"I lie on a table and they do something to me, something sexual, and I can't do anything about it. They put something inside me and it hurts and I'm alone and afraid, so afraid . . ." Her voice trailed off, and she seemed to withdraw inside herself.

I'm losing her, Mac thought. "Who took you?" he prompted gently.

"They're not from here."

"Where are they from?"

"Outer space," she whispered.

Well, there it was. Mac had known what he was likely to hear tonight, but that didn't lessen the hollow fear in the pit of his stomach when he actually heard the words. *Here we go again.*

"My husband and I were trying to have a baby, and when I got pregnant we were happy. We were actually *happy*. That's because they do something with your memory so you don't remember, you think everything is normal. Then the next thing I know I'm on the bathroom floor and it's night and I'm bleeding and my . . . my . . ." She bit down hard on her lower lip, and as the blood trickled down her chin Mac felt a gut-kick memory of another night, a trickle of blood down Maggie's chin . . .

Another baby taken away . . .

"And my baby's gone!" She stared through Mac for a moment, and Mac found himself nodding, understanding perfectly.

"The doctor says I did something to the baby, that I caused a miscarriage and that they don't know what I did with the baby. 'Where's the baby?' they say, over and over, and I don't know, don't remember anything, and they search the house but they don't find anything and then when I'm in bed, suddenly I remember what happened—they came and took my baby from me." She stopped and wiped the trickle of blood from her chin with her wrist. "I tried to make them stop, I screamed at them, but it doesn't do any good, they can do whatever they want and you can't stop them. I could feel them down there, taking the baby out of me, and then they hold it up and show it to me . . . they show it to me . . ." Trembling, she wrapped her arms around herself.

He wanted to comfort her, wanted to put his arms around her and hold her close, but he couldn't move. He was frozen, standing there feeling a mixture of compassion, fear, and denial.

"They take the baby," she continued in a whisper, "and they show it to me. And I can't believe it—it's not human." She looked at Mac with the most haunted expression he had ever seen in another human being. "And when I look at them, I realize that they are enjoying it—showing me that it isn't . . . isn't . . ."

Mac cleared his throat and gently asked, "Where did they take your baby?"

Still holding herself, she moved her shoulders from side to side, rocking.

"I don't know. Up there . . ."

"What did they look like?" Mac asked. "These—" He had to force himself to finish his thought. "These beings from outer space?"

The woman closed her eyes, shook her head, and continued to rock back and forth.

"We got to get going," Linda called from the bathroom door.

"What?" Mac answered.

"We gotta leave now," Linda said, and she pushed the cart toward the door.

Mac walked slowly backward toward the door, not taking his eyes off the woman, mentally photographing every detail.

A bony hand pulled at the shoulder of his borrowed smock. "Come *on*," Linda insisted. She pulled him out of the room and quickly shut the door. "Satisfied?" she asked with a look of triumph as she turned her key in the lock.

Mac reached into his pocket and clicked off the tape recorder. He rubbed the back of his neck and nodded slowly.

Linda grinned. "I told you."

"It doesn't mean she's telling the truth," Mac whispered as they went to the next room.

"What?"

"She might just be crazy. That is, after all, what this place is in business for." He gestured toward the room they had just left.

"Well, that don't explain the others, does it? And why does the *military* have them locked up here?"

Mac shrugged. "There's no way to corroborate her story."

Linda stopped pushing her cart and looked squarely into Mac's eyes. "I spend a lot of time around crazy people, and these women who seen the aliens is different. And sane people don't tell stories like she did if they ain't true. Why would they? Look where it's gotten her."

Mac was about to answer when footsteps sounded in the corridor.

Linda's eyes opened wider, startled. "Security making their rounds. Get in here." She hustled into the next room. "Take this and scrub the toilet in there." She handed him a sponge and some spray disinfectant.

Mac took them and hurried into the bathroom. He knelt down next to the toilet and began to scrub vigorously. As the footsteps grew louder, Mac felt his heart beating faster. He was about to get busted. By the military, no less. And was it worth it? How could he possibly get a story out of what he'd just heard?

"Hi, Linda," a tenor voice echoed in the hall.

"Hi, Carl. Just about wrapped up, this is the last room," she answered.

"Okay, you know the way out," the man chuckled. The footsteps continued down the corridor. Mac stood quietly and listened to them fade.

"It's all right, he's gone," Linda whispered. "Let's get you out of here."

"I'm all for that," he said.

They wheeled the cart quickly down the corridor and boarded the elevator. When the elevator doors opened after their descent, Mac found himself back in the service area of the hospital.

"You can find your way back up to the trailer," she said when she had taken him back to the door to the outside. "I still got work to do. You gonna write the story?"

"We'll see. I have to listen to the tape again, see what's there."

She nodded then asked, "You won't use me and Harry's name, will you? I could lose my job."

"Promise," Mac answered. "Thanks for getting me up there." He stuck out his hand.

Linda shook it. "You better get goin'."

Fifteen minutes later, in his own clothes again, Mac climbed into his jeep and looked at the watch he had hung from the rearview mirror. Close to midnight. He fired up the jeep and sped out of the parking lot, making the tires chirp as he shifted into second gear.

4

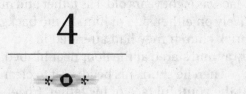

Slouching at his desk, Mac stared at the blank screen of his computer monitor. The glow emanating from it—along with the always-on television—were the only light sources in the room.

Next to him lay a notepad with a dozen scribbled ideas crossed out. He glanced at his watch: two-thirty in the morning. Still plenty of time before he had to fax the story about the Westwood Medical Center to Cranston.

He looked at the half-empty case of Grand Marnier next to the bed. *My reward when I'm finished,* he thought, tapping a pencil on the edge of his blotter.

Restlessly, he changed positions in his chair. If he stuck strictly to his assignment, all he would have is a bunch of boring figures regurgitated by Kennedy and the rest of the bean counters.

Then, as they had dozens of times that night already, his eyes strayed to the small tape recorder sitting next to the monitor. What he really wanted to write about was in there.

He didn't work at the *Times* anymore. What was the worst that could happen? The story wouldn't go to ink. And if it didn't, he wouldn't get paid. And he needed the money.

He put the pencil in his mouth and bit down on it.

His eyes drifted toward the corner of the desk where the picture of his children rested. He picked it up and studied their faces. Then, turning the frame over, he unhooked the plastic fasteners that held the back on and removed two photos stashed there.

The first was black-and-white and grainy, taken when Mac was eight years old. His father and mother stood protectively on either side of him. In the background was the tiny brick church they had attended in New Mexico. He turned away and stared at the floor near his bed, lost in thought.

Then he shook his head, as if to clear it, and looked back at the youthful face of his father, frozen in time. "You were crazy," he said out loud, and flipped the photo onto the desktop.

He hesitated a moment, looking at the ceiling, and then forced himself to look at the second photo. It showed a much older Mac, an adult, with three children and his wife, Maggie, standing under the spreading canopy of an ancient, gnarled California oak. Behind them stretched Maggie's parents' vineyards in Paso Robles. Beams of sunlight streamed through the foliage and surrounded the family, creating a magical weave of light and shadow. In the distance, trellised rows of grapes ripened in the sun.

Different days. A different life.

He put the photo with his wife and kids back into the frame but kept the one of his parents out, leaned it against the tape player, and clicked the play button.

He closed his eyes and listened to the recording he'd made at the hospital, envisioning in detail the woman's haunted features as her chilling account of alien abduction and impregnation crackled over the small speaker.

You're all crazy, the bunch of you, he thought, and that was what he really wanted to believe. It would be such a relief to dismiss the woman as just another wacko, fringe-dwelling, conspiracy-theorizing nutcase.

He opened his eyes and stared again at the picture leaning against the recorder, feeling rising anger and resentment even all these years after the man's death. He'd been fairly successful in recent years in putting his father—and his father's beliefs—out of his mind, or at least buried so far within him that they never came to the surface. Talking to that woman tonight had brought it all screaming back.

But isn't that the real reason I went back to the hospital and subjected myself to Linda and the inside of a toilet bowl—to somehow come to terms with the past and overcome it?

The voice on the tape recorder caught his attention: "They show it to me. And I can't believe it—it's not human . . ."

He shivered.

Did he want to spend the rest of his life in fear, avoiding things, hiding? Wasn't it time to face this thing?

He grabbed his notepad and scribbled a title: "The Abduction Phenomenon: Fact or Fiction?"

He stared at it. There were possibilities here.

He jotted down a couple of ideas, refined those and added a few more, liking what he saw.

He chuckled grimly. None of this had anything to do with his assignment. Worse, it hinted at a possible secret floor in the newly constructed wing of the Westwood Medical Center, operated by the military. "And especially designed to deal with UFO abductees, at that! Cranston's going to have a cow. Maybe two!" he said to himself, laughing.

He looked one last time at the rough outline, then tore that sheet off and rearranged the ideas on a clean sheet. He pinned it with a paper clip to the lamp next to his monitor and began to peck away at his keyboard. He hunched over his work, totally absorbed, for over an hour, and knew that he had the beginning of a good story. Half an hour later he finished the second draft and read it.

Mac straightened in his chair and arched his back, making the bones in his spine crack. He grinned as he read the story one last time, then opened his fax software and selected Cranston's number. *Why do I do things like this?* he asked himself, shaking his head. *Bucking the system, playing the wild card—Cranston's going to be ticked.*

But besides that internal warning, Mac also felt a degree of satisfaction.

Or was it just that he was being deliberately spiteful? Into his awareness swam another thought he'd been trying to suppress for two days, since Mac first heard from a friend that Cranston was seeing his ex-wife. Was there something going on there? Had Jim been biding his time, waiting for Mac and Maggie to split up so that he could move in on her?

Mac shook off the thought. He didn't even know if it was true. What was more interesting was that Cranston happened to be on the board of directors at the Westwood Medical Center. Of course that didn't mean he was implicated in anything. In fact, Mac's article didn't directly accuse anyone of anything.

Mac double-clicked Cranston's number and waited for the linkup, smiling as the machines talked to each other.

When the transmission was complete, Mac slipped the dust cover back over his computer, turned off the ringer to his phone, and bounded over to the case of Grand Marnier to select a bottle. He slipped off his tennis shoes and sank onto the worn, lumpy couch, staring at the soundless screen. An old John Wayne movie was on. He broke the seal around the neck of the bottle and gently eased the cork out. He looked around for a glass. The one he'd used the night before was on the floor a few feet away. But getting up would be too much effort. He tipped the bottle back and let the first taste of the liquor swirl around in his mouth before it trickled down his throat. He stared at the silent action on the television. He sipped again, a little longer this time. He felt his body relax into the couch and adjusted a pillow against the small of his back to get comfortable. Another hit from the bottle, and he began to feel lightheaded. The thoughts he had held at bay rushed in on him:

My dead father.

My dead son.

My dead marriage.

The crazy woman at the hospital who might as well be dead.

Linda's bony hand pulling me out of the room ... rescuing me?

He guzzled from the bottle, spilling some of it on his shirt. His eyes rolled in his head, and he felt the bottle slide out of his hand—and with it, the thoughts plaguing him began to slip mercifully away ...

* ○ *

At his desk early the next morning, Jim Cranston tried his best not to yell into the receiver. It was bad enough that his paper was involved in a libel suit. Now it was starting to look as if they might actually lose. In the middle of trying to explain to one of the paper's lawyers why losing wasn't an option, he was interrupted midsentence by a knock at his door. He squeezed the worn golf ball in his hand, threw it a couple of feet in the air, and yelled, "Come in!" Then he caught the golf ball and finished his sentence to the attorney.

An attractive woman entered and walked briskly toward his desk. He looked her over appreciatively and made a mental note: *Ask this woman to lunch.* Meanwhile, he toyed with his perfectly clipped white mustache.

She stopped a few feet from his desk and held up some kind of manuscript, pointing at it with her free hand. Cranston squinted at it—which reminded him he needed to get his eyes checked—then shrugged. It was Art MacKenzie's piece. "What?" he blared into the telephone receiver. Had that lawyer just said what Cranston thought he'd said? He waved her away.

The woman shook her head adamantly and pointed again to the article.

"That's impossible and you know it!" Cranston yelled into the phone. "Hold on a second, will you?" He exhaled wearily and loosened his tie.

Seeing her opportunity, the woman quickly said, "You need to read this."

"What?" Cranston said absently, taking a quick hit from the glass bottle of imported water sitting on his desk. "Just handle it, Rita. I'm tied up. Is it written well?"

"It's not *how* it's written. It's *what* is written." She took a step closer, holding the article out to him.

But Cranston had already retreated into his telephone conversation again. "We're not paying that amount! No way. *No way!*" he yelled into the receiver.

Rita shook the article to get his attention, but Cranston waved his hand in dismissal and swiveled his chair so that his back was to her.

"I wash my hands!" he heard Rita call as she closed the door behind her.

Free of distraction, Cranston concentrated on doing what he loved—bending his opponent to his point of view by yelling, cajoling, threatening to hang up, or using any of a number of other tricks he had perfected over the years. Rita and the article were quickly forgotten.

5

* ◯ *

General Nathan sat comfortably cloistered in his private study and reread the documents before him on his desk.

An eclectic assortment of pictures crowded the walls, reflecting a lifetime of military service: spectacular shots of warplanes banking and diving, of rockets spewing clouds of billowing smoke at their launch pads, of weightless astronauts floating eerily high above the earth. Others showed him shaking hands with various presidents. One faded picture revealed a grinning young man in a leather flight jacket climbing aboard a fighter plane during World War II.

Nathan had been only sixteen when he'd enlisted—he'd lied about his age, of course—just as the Americans entered World War II. He had not only learned to fly, he had also found that military life suited him. He'd made a career of it, rising steadily through the ranks in a succession of gradual promotions until he attained his present rank: two-star general.

Nathan pushed the documents away from him, then closed his eyes and rubbed them with his fingertips. He winced in pain and tried to adjust his position in the chair. It didn't help.

There was a knock on his door. "Daddy, it's time for your pills." The muffled voice of his daughter filtered through the steel-plated reinforced door.

He opened his top desk drawer and pushed the button that controlled the electronic bolts on the door. There was a slight clicking sound, then the door opened and Laura, his daughter, came in. With her long brown hair and vibrant smile, she was a wonderful contrast to dusty documents and war planes. "Already?" He feigned annoyance.

"You know what happens if you don't take them," she said. "You're so stubborn." She skirted the desk and stood next to him, holding four pills in one hand and a small glass of water in the other.

"You look more like your mother every day," Nathan said wistfully.

She smiled. "Thanks, Daddy. But please take your pills—now."

Nathan grabbed two of the pills, popped them into his mouth, and swallowed them without water.

"I hate when you do that." She grimaced. "You know that bothers me." She studied him for a moment, then asked, "Is there a lot of pain today?"

He shook his head, lying. The pain, although dulled by the morphine pills he took at regular intervals, was ever present. He had learned to live with it.

"Two more," Laura said, holding the remaining pills out in her hand. "Your Lupron."

"I'm not taking them."

"The doctor told you to—"

"I'm starting to grow breasts from those stinking things," he growled.

"It's just a side effect. These pills are part of your therapy. The radiation won't be as effective if you don't take the Lupron too."

"Well, it's a side effect I can do without," he shot back. "Hang it all, those idiots wanted to castrate me!"

"Dad, prostate cancer is—"

He cut her off. "I don't have to be reminded. But I'm not going to die looking like some freak in a sideshow."

"I'm sorry. You're right." She glanced at a picture halfway out of its folder on his desk. "He's good-looking," she said, trying to change the subject.

He relaxed and said, "Don't go looking at these reports or I'll have to shoot you."

She looked at the picture again. "Too bad you can't introduce me."

"He's not your type."

"Well, I'll leave you to your work," she said. She kissed him on the cheek and turned to go.

Nathan touched her arm and she stopped. He looked into his daughter's face and softly said, "It's going to be all right, Laura. Don't worry."

She nodded, then flipped her waist-length brown hair behind her back and left the room, closing the door behind her.

He pulled the picture the rest of the way out of the file and stared at it. He turned it over and read the information on the back: "Arthur MacKenzie, taken at Venice Beach, California, July 12, 1999."

Leaning back in his chair, he rubbed his bare knuckles on his thick mat of gray hair. Then he grabbed the telephone and dialed a number. His gaunt face was expressionless as he listened to it ring.

"Hello," a thin, raspy voice answered.

"It's Nathan, sir. I've finished reading it. I think he might be our man, especially with the link to his father's past," he said.

Nathan could hear the man struggle to breathe. "You mean his father's participation in '47?" The man fought for his next breath, which Nathan heard as a wheezing, hollow metallic sound.

"Yes. That could be the key to gaining his attention and, eventually, his commitment."

"I'm worried about that. If he knew the truth . . . about his father . . . there's no telling what he would do," the airy voice said.

Nathan swiveled in his chair and stared at the horrific picture of the Challenger rocket, exploding seconds after lift-off. "It does make him somewhat unpredictable."

There was a brief silence on the other line, and then the voice suggested, "Why don't you feel him out and see how he responds, then get back to me. How much are you going to tell him?"

"Enough to hook him. That part should be easy, with his reporter's nose."

The man gasped for breath, tried in vain to clear his throat, then managed to say, "Call me when it's finished."

"Yes, sir."

Nathan placed the phone back on its cradle. Sitting upright in his chair, he looked at the picture of Art MacKenzie on his desk. He opened the manila folder and secured the photo with a paper clip. He flipped to the first page, which contained the basic facts of MacKenzie's life: name, marital status, age, birthday, license number, parents, schools, personal friends, jobs held, church attended. Next to each item was a page number for more detailed information.

A searing pain in Nathan's lower back made him wince. *Thank goodness for the drugs,* he thought, suddenly glad of his daughter's diligence.

He looked again at the photograph and wondered.

* ○ *

The phone rang in Art MacKenzie's apartment. It was after eleven in the morning, and his head pounded as he lay on the couch. The Alka-Seltzer wasn't working fast enough.

"Hello," Mac mumbled into the receiver.

"Is this Arthur MacKenzie?"

Bill collector, Mac thought. "Who wants to know?"

"Mr. MacKenzie, I read your article the other day in the *Times*, found it very interesting."

"Thanks." Mac relaxed.

"I was wondering if you would like to discuss it further."

"What's to discuss? It's just a story. One reporter's opinion."

"What if I were to tell you that I have information you might find interesting?"

"What kind of information?"

"Corroborating the woman's story. The abduction story."

"Who is this? This Michael?" Mac said, thinking it might be one of the guys from the paper playing a joke on him.

"No, I'm not Michael. And my name isn't important."

"Okay, I'll play along. Whatcha got?"

"Can you meet me in an hour?"

"What? Come on, who is this?" Mac said.

"Your ninth grade teacher's name was Mr. Sibly, and he was also your track coach."

"Mr. Sibly?" Mac hesitated. "How did you—"

"Your mother's maiden name was Kemberton and she was born in South Bend, Indiana. She died when you were seventeen. Your father was stationed in Roswell, New Mexico, and witnessed—"

"Who is this?" Mac demanded, his stomach tightening.

"Would you care to hear more? I have pages full of it," the caller said calmly.

Mac stared blankly at the soundless rerun of *The Andy Griffith Show*. "What do you want? My father's been dead for years. He died when I was just a kid. Are you from the IRS or something?"

"I'd like to give you some information. Can you meet me?"

"Why don't you just say what you want to now?"

"Would you rather watch a movie or have somebody tell you about it?"

"Okay, I get the point."

"Meet me in an hour and see for yourself."

Mac hesitated, then answered, "Where?"

"The corner of Barrington and Third Street. There's an abandoned factory. I'll meet you there."

"How will I know it's you?"

"One hour from now, at 12:00."

"All right, Third and Barrington in an hour."

The phone went dead and Mac stared at it in disbelief. He ran his hand through his hair a few times, brushing it back off his forehead. *What am I doing? This guy sounds like a nutcase.*

Mac went over to his desk, opened the top drawer, and took out a map book. He thumbed through the index, found Barrington, and turned to the corresponding page. He followed it on the map until it intersected Third.

"Great part of town," he muttered sarcastically.

He thought about calling Cranston and asking if this was some sort of retaliation for writing the article about the hospital. Then he decided against it. Cranston wouldn't waste his time with something like this, and besides, the caller knew information that wasn't in the public record. Maybe there was something to it.

* o *

Mac parked his jeep next to the litter-strewn curb on Third Street and looked around. The street was deserted except for two men walking in the other direction a couple of blocks away. He looked at the weather-worn address on the dirty brick building that had once been a furniture manufacturing plant. Then he got out of the jeep and stood next to it for a minute, unsure what to do, his hand still on the door handle.

Slowly, he let go and walked around to the side of the building. The loading docks and parking lot looked long abandoned; two burned-out car chassis surrounded by bits of broken blue glass sat on the cracked, weed-infested asphalt. Mac walked up the rusted metal steps onto the loading dock. He expected to find the massive wooden door locked, but when he turned the knob and pulled, it opened easily. He let it swing all the way back against the building. Standing at the threshold, he allowed his eyes to adjust to the dim interior of the building. Whitewashed square posts rose from the wood plank floor, creating two aisles that ran the length of the building. They supported massive beams that disappeared into the brick walls twelve feet above the floor. At the far end of the room, light streamed in from a row of large windows, some of which were broken and had shards of glass dangling from them.

"Hello," he called, and listened to his voice echo slightly.

No reply. He ventured a few feet further into the room but kept his body turned so he could see the doorway.

"Hello," he called again.

He walked further into the building, kicking a beer bottle that lay in front of him and watching as it bumped and skidded across the floor, finally splintering into pieces against the wall. He looked around the empty warehouse, shrugged, and turned to leave.

"Mr. MacKenzie?" a voice called out from the other end of the building.

The voice startled Mac. He spun around and saw a man standing next to one of the posts. Mac took a step closer to the door and called back, "Who wants to know?"

"I'm the man who called you. You can call me Roswell."

The hair on the back of Mac's neck stood on end. "Roswell, as in New Mexico?" he managed to say.

"Yes, New Mexico. Where your father was stationed."

Someone had gone to a lot of trouble to pull off whatever sick joke they were playing here. "That was years ago." His anger rising, Mac said, "Look, what's this all about? And how do you know about my father?"

"Roswell" began to walk quickly toward him, stopping less than a yard away. He was taller than Mac, which put him well over six feet. His face was pale and lined, and he looked at Mac with an unreadable deadpan stare. He reached into his coat and produced a large manila envelope and handed it to Mac.

Mac took it, angry with himself for not seeing the obvious bulge sooner. It could have been anything.

"Read this. I'll be in touch."

Mac took the envelope and looked at Roswell, hoping for an explanation.

None came. The man simply sidestepped Mac and walked toward the door. Mac spun around to watch him exit through the same door Mac had entered. He heard footsteps on the metal stairs, followed by the sound of a car pulling into the parking lot. Mac ran to the door and peered cautiously around the frame. Roswell got into a black Lincoln with government plates. The car lurched out of the parking lot and sped down the deserted street. Mac ran out onto the loading dock and watched as the Lincoln swerved sharply down a side street and disappeared.

Mac examined the unopened envelope as he slowly walked to his jeep. He climbed in and threw the packet on the passenger's seat. Then he gassed the jeep, pulled a U-turn, and looked one last time at the warehouse in his rearview mirror.

* o *

At his desk, Mac inserted a worn letter opener into the manila envelope, pulled out a plain white folder, and set it in front of him. He slowly opened it and whistled as he read the heading on the first page: "For Your Eyes Only. Top Secret!" On the following page in large type and all capitals was the single word *MAJESTIC*.

I wonder what that means, he thought.

A half hour later, shocked and frightened by what he'd read, Mac reached the last page and found a round-trip ticket to Israel along with the name and phone number of a contact there, a Uri BenHassen.

Mac's hands trembled as he closed the folder. This was nothing more than an elaborate joke. A hoax. It had to be. Mac's father was long dead, and all of this—he waved the folder with annoyance—had been buried with him long ago.

But another feeling nagged at him, one he wished he could ignore.

What if it were true?

He inhaled deeply, almost as if he had forgotten to breathe, and looked again at the ticket to Israel. He slowly picked up the phone and dialed the number.

"Shalom," a voice answered, sounding like it was next door.

"Is . . . ah . . . Uri there?"

"This is Uri," a thickly accented voice said.

"Is this . . ." Mac quickly checked the information in the folder. "Uri BenHassen?"

"Yes. Can I help you?"

"Uh . . . This is MacKenzie. Art MacKenzie."

"Art MacKenzie, the American reporter?" Uri asked.

"That's right."

Another pause. "We were hoping you would maybe call. You read the material?"

"Yes. Very interesting."

"You are coming then?"

"Why would I? What's so important that I need to fly there?"

"Mr. MacKenzie, I am an archaeologist here. What we have discovered may fit the information that General Roswell gave you."

"So Roswell's a general?"

"A two-star general in your Air Force."

Mac raised an eyebrow, surprised.

"When are you coming?"

"I don't know," Mac answered, his mind reeling. "I've been given a folder full of very strange and probably false information, but I haven't been given one good reason why I should come to Israel."

There was a pause, then Uri answered, "Mr. MacKenzie, archaeology is sometimes many surprises. In the Rabbinical Tunnel someone discovered accidentally a hidden chamber."

"What's the Rabbinical Tunnel?" Mac asked.

"Sorry. You know, in Jerusalem, the Temple Mount?" Uri asked.

"Isn't that part of the Wailing Wall?"

"They are the same. It is all that remains of the Temple, where my ancestors worshiped their God of Abraham, Isaac, and Jacob. Underneath the Temple Mount is the Rabbinical Tunnel. One night, after a dig at the tunnel's far end, a man and woman who were part of a survey team heard something fall from behind the tunnel wall. They tapped the wall with a digging tool and it sounded hollow. They reported it."

"Okay. So what happened?"

"You know what? They found a hidden room. You must come to Israel and see for yourself."

"Drop everything and fly to Israel just because somebody finds a secret room? Who cares?"

"Mr. MacKenzie."

"Call me Mac."

"Okay. Mac, I can maybe promise what might be the story of the century."

Mac was silent.

"General Roswell believes you are the man to tell it," Uri coaxed.

"Story of the century," Mac huffed, then raised his voice. "I hate airplanes! I hate to fly!"

"I'm thinking, you won't be disappointed."

Mac looked around the room at his unmade bed, the pile of unpaid bills, and the empty bottles of Grand Marnier—a sad commentary on his life. It's not as if he had a lot to leave behind. He looked at the dates on the tickets.

"All right. I still have a couple of days before the flight. I have to see my kids first."

"I am understanding," Uri replied.

"What do I do when—"

"Everything is taken care of. Just come. I meet you at the airport in Tel Aviv. Something else: Don't tell where you are going and don't tell what you received from Roswell."

"What does this tunnel have to do with . . . with what Roswell gave me?" Mac asked.

"Maybe everything. You will see for yourself. Shalom, MacKenzie." The phone went dead.

Mac opened again the document Roswell had given him. Then he cursed himself for writing that story about the woman in the hospital. And then he cursed his father.

6

Mac drove his jeep north on the Pacific Coast Highway. On his left, the expanse of the Pacific Ocean shimmered and sparkled like radiant silver in the late afternoon sun. The top was down and the warm ocean air blasted his face as he cruised slightly over the speed limit. The radio boomed a popular song, and he banged alternately on the steering wheel and his thigh, in time with the pulse of the music. For once it felt good to be alive.

He was headed toward Paso Robles, where his ex-wife Maggie and their two remaining children lived on Maggie's family vineyard. He had always thought of it as a farm but Maggie had corrected him many times; *vineyard* was the appropriate term.

Its name, "Creek Walk Vineyard," came from the creek that meandered through the vineyard's two hundred acres of fertile land tucked into the gently rolling hills of Paso Robles. When Maggie's great-great-grandfather, Robert Dunning, cleared the land, he let stand as many native California oak trees as possible, creating a majestic border around the property. He planted Chardonnay grapes on the choicest parts and

Merlot and Cabernet for his private use on the remaining acreage. The vineyard produced some of the finest grapes in California and had the distinction of almost always placing first in local wine contests.

Mac glanced at the sign pointing inland to Paso Robles and turned off the highway. He cut the radio and eased off the accelerator. Having traveled this road dozens of times, he knew it was a bumpy, potholed, poorly maintained stretch of ancient asphalt. He adjusted the towel underneath him for the millionth time and wiggled in the seat to avoid the protruding springs.

Mac hadn't called Maggie to let her know he was coming, and now that he was almost at the vineyard, he began to regret his oversight.

Too late to turn back now, he thought. *Well, it'll be a surprise; the kids will love it.*

The problem was that Maggie hated surprises.

Okay. But still, it'll be good for the four of us to be together again, he argued. But he also knew that the moment he saw his two remaining children without his oldest son, Art, he would—*no, don't want to go down that road right now.* He gripped the steering wheel tighter and shifted his weight in the seat, trying once again to avoid the springs—which caused him to overlook a particularly large pothole. The front left tire fell into it, and the jeep shuddered and somehow jolted loose one thought that Mac was doing his best to ignore.

Child support.

He couldn't remember the last time he had sent Maggie a dime. He had lost count of what he owed, and was clueless as to how many months he was behind. Turning the jeep onto the long gravel driveway that ran through the heart of Creek Walk Vineyards, he began to rationalize a myriad of reasons he had been negligent, and almost succeeded in believing them.

Still far from the house, Mac turned the engine off and let the jeep coast until it came to rest under the spreading oak from the picture he had resurrected from the back of the frame a few nights before. Leaning his head on the back of the seat, he stared overhead at the quiet green canopy. He relaxed, content to let his mind wander for a few moments.

Turning his head, he looked across the neatly trellised rows of grapes that spread in every direction, riding the contour of the land. He pretended to hear the grapes growing.

That was an expression Maggie's father had used habitually throughout his life. "Can you hear 'em growing?" he would ask, and then put his hand to his ear as if he could actually hear the grapes stretching in their skins. The phrase always brought a smile to Mac, and it did so now, as he wistfully remembered his father-in-law. A heart attack had taken him in his sleep, a year before little Art's death. *It was a merciful death; he never knew what hit him,* Mac thought gratefully—and then found himself wondering for the thousandth time how much pain his son had endured as he lay in the twisted metal remains that had once been the family car.

Enough of that. He fired the jeep, and its engine coughed to life, then roared as sound erupted from the worn muffler. Startled, a covey of quail burst into flight from among the vines.

He continued up the drive under the canopy of oaks. Ahead, he saw the house elevated majestically above an expanse of well-manicured lawn. It was a monument to the craftsmanship of another century. Decorative rafters formed the steep, gabled roof, adorned with dark green slate quarried and shipped west from Pennsylvania. Large, wood-framed windows graced the second story; below, several sets of French doors joined the interior with a roofed porch that encircled the entire house. Twin rocking chairs sat like ancient sentinels at the front doors.

The driveway continued around the south side of the house toward the large barn where the family parked their cars and trucks. Mac's stomach churned when he recognized one of the parked cars. It belonged to his ex-boss at the *Times*, Jim Cranston. There were many BMWs in California, but there was no mistaking the ever-present set of golf clubs resting in their habitual spot against the rear seat of the car.

Some golfing rendezvous up north? Mac wondered. *So maybe the rumors are true after all.* He thought about turning the jeep around. Just the thought of Maggie and Cranston together made him angrily slap the steering wheel.

"Daddy!" squealed a high, familiar voice. Mac saw a small blur scoot off the porch, sail down the steps, and run across the yard toward him with her arms flailing over her head. He turned the motor off, jumped out of the jeep, and took a step toward his daughter as she flung herself into his arms.

"Daddy! Daddy!" Sarah laughed as she buried her head against his chest.

"Hi, honey, I missed you." Mac held her, rocking her in his arms, running his fingers through her blond curls. "Where's Mom and Jeremy?" he asked softly.

"Inside, with Grandma."

He hugged her close as he climbed the three wooden steps up onto the porch.

"I love you, Daddy," she giggled.

"I love you too, honey," he answered, holding her tightly.

Mac opened the screen door and stepped inside. His daughter's cry heralded his arrival, and the rest of the household hurried to meet him.

"Dad!" Jeremy cried as he ran down the wide hallway.

Mac dropped to one knee; still holding Sarah, he embraced his son.

"Hello, Mac," his mother-in-law said warmly.

Maggie appeared from the kitchen, followed by Jim Cranston. Mac stiffened as he saw them together.

"Mac, what a pleasant surprise," Maggie said, the edge of annoyance in her voice belying her smile.

Mac gently pried Sarah and Jeremy away and slowly rose to his feet. "Maggie, Jim," he said, and looked only at Maggie, deliberately avoiding any eye contact with Cranston.

She looks great, he admitted, feeling a tug at his heart. She was dressed in a T-shirt and cutoff jeans whose frayed white edges encircled her tan, athletic legs. Her thick, sandy-brown hair hung loosely around her shoulders. Bangs that were always just a little too long almost covered her hazel eyes, which stared at him, silently asking, *What are you doing here?*

"I was in the neighborhood and just dropped by." He shrugged.

"I wish you'd called first," Maggie said, folding her arms in front of her.

Cranston moved closer to her. *If he puts his arm around her,* Mac thought, *I'm going to pop him one in the nose.* Immediately, another thought followed. *She isn't yours anymore— get over it! What do you care anyway? Besides, she could do a lot worse. Cranston's not such a bad guy.*

"Nice to see you, Jim," Mac said, as Cranston was about to speak.

Silence menaced the little group, freezing everyone in a tableau of awkwardness that seemed to last forever. Jeremy grabbed Mac's leg and yelled, "Foot ride! Foot ride!"

Sarah echoed the chant and wrapped her arms tightly around his other leg while planting her little bottom firmly on his tennis shoe, hanging on for all she was worth.

Everyone laughed, glad of the distraction.

Mac staggered from side to side, lifting one foot, then the other, and planting them firmly on the floor in front of him, accenting each movement with a throaty, "Boom! Boom!" He clumped and stomped his way into the living room, glad to be away from Maggie and Cranston.

"Do you want some lemonade?" Doris, his mother-in-law, called from behind him.

"Sounds great!" Mac replied as he *boom-boomed* around the living room.

Cranston tactfully followed Doris into the kitchen, leaving Maggie in the doorway. She looked at Mac and grinned. Mac pretended he didn't see her as he continued stomping. But he did. He saw her watching him, and then he saw her eyes drift toward the mantle, and he saw the pain on her face. He followed her gaze to where a picture of his dead son rested in the center of the mantle. Next to it sat a small vase of fresh-cut flowers.

"Mom, do you need any help?" Maggie called, and disappeared down the hall without waiting for a reply.

It struck Mac that she shared the same tormenting memories as he did. Despite their divorce, they were bound together by a tragedy that neither of them could completely reconcile or heal.

"All right, you guys, my legs can't do this anymore," he pleaded, and stopped for a moment.

"Just once more around the room, please!" Jeremy said, tilting his head back to see Mac.

"Come on, Dad! *Please!*" they cried, in unison.

Mac sighed, clumped around the room again, then headed for the couch and collapsed onto it, moving it a couple of inches from its intended place on the carpet.

"Just once more!" the kids pleaded.

"No. That's it. I mean it. No more! That's it! Okay?"

Sarah and Jeremy reluctantly unwound themselves from their father's legs, climbed onto the couch on either side of him, and snuggled close.

"So how are you guys doing?" Mac asked, putting an arm around each of them.

"Do you want to see my new dolly?" Sarah asked.

"What's her name?" Mac replied.

"Julie."

"That's a nice name."

"Hey, Dad! Hey, Dad, we killed a rattler a couple of days ago," Jeremy interrupted.

"Really? How big? Who killed it?"

"Manolo, and it was *this big*," Jeremy said, holding his hands as far apart as he could.

"Manolo chopped its head off with a shovel," Sarah added, scrunching up her nose in disgust.

"You guys have to be careful out here. Your mom doesn't let you go out into the vineyard by yourselves, does she?"

"No, we have to be with a grownup," Jeremy lamented.

"Good thing. And what do you guys do if you see a snake?" Mac asked.

"We scream and run. No, I mean run and *then* we scream," Sarah corrected herself.

Mac laughed and nodded.

"Daddy, can I show you how good I can read?" Sarah pleaded.

"You're reading?" Mac asked, surprised.

"Yep," she answered proudly, as she slid off the couch and bounded out of the room. She returned with four or five books under her arm and wiggled her way back into her spot next to Mac.

"What's this one?" Mac asked.

"*The Tickle Bugs*," she replied.

"And what are tickle bugs?" Mac asked seriously.

"They're stupid," Jeremy interjected.

"Are not," Sarah shouted back.

"Are too," Jeremy returned.

"Hey! Come on, I just got here and you guys are fighting." He waited for them to settle down, then said, "Let me see how good you read." He opened the book and set it on Sarah's lap.

She began to read, slowly sounding out each word.

"That's great, honey," Mac said, surprised and delighted.

She finished the story, then picked up another book.

"This is my favorite," she announced. "It's about Noah and a whole bunch of animals."

Mac put his arm around her and drew her close as she began to read again. He helped her with some of the more difficult words. She pointed out her favorite animals and then skipped to the last page and showed Mac the big rainbow. "It's the best part," she said. Then she set the book on Mac's lap and picked up another. "This is my favorite one."

"I thought Noah was your favorite," Mac said.

Jeremy rolled his eyes and looked the other way.

"It is, but this is too," she said.

"Oh," Mac smiled. "What's this one?"

"David and Go . . . Gol . . ."

"Goliath!" Jeremy blurted out, clearly exasperated with his sister.

"David and Goliath," Sarah repeated.

"Where did you get these?" Mac asked.

"From church," Jeremy answered. "Grandmom takes us every Sunday."

"Every Sunday?" Mac asked, remembering when regular attendance had been a routine part of his life.

Jeremy nodded. "She wants us to know about God. She says Art's up in heaven with him," and he pointed toward the ceiling.

"Daddy, *listen,*" Sarah insisted, ignoring her brother.

"Okay, honey, go ahead," Mac answered, glad for the interruption.

After struggling through the first page, Sarah set the book down and asked, "Dad, what's a giant? Like in David and Go . . . Goliath?" she asked.

Mac thought about it for a moment, then answered, "They're really, really big people. But there's no such thing."

"Well, Grandma says that David killed the bad giant with a stone."

"It's just a story, honey, that's all."

"Well, Grandma says it really happened. Do you believe in giants, Dad?"

"No, honey. Not anymore."

"Grandma says that God helped David kill the mean giant."

"Here's the lemonade," Doris called pleasantly, carefully balancing the tray in front of her as she walked into the living room. Maggie and Cranston followed a few steps behind and seated themselves opposite the sofa in two identical wingback chairs. Doris placed the tray on the corner of the polished dark mahogany coffee table and held it with one hand while the other moved pictures and assorted keepsakes, clearing a place for the tray.

"Let me help you," Mac said, as he moved a small silver chest holding a sachet of dried rose petals.

Doris handed out the drinks. "It's fresh squeezed from our own trees," she said proudly. "Not too much sugar added either."

Mac took a sip and nodded approvingly.

"So what brings you up here?" Maggie asked bluntly.

Mac took another sip, leaned forward, and set his glass carefully in front of him on the leather coaster. He turned it twice around and stared at the condensation on the outside of the glass. He looked at Maggie. "Well," he began, "I'm going on an assignment."

"Oh, that's great, Mac," Maggie said, not hiding her surprise.

Cranston lifted his eyebrows.

"I'm going to Israel," Mac stated, secretly glad his announcement had surprised them both.

"Where's Israel?" Jeremy asked.

"On the other side of the world, across a big wide ocean," Mac said, putting a bit of mystery in the inflection of his voice.

"What's the assignment?" Maggie asked.

"Can't really talk about it," Mac said and folded his arms across his chest. "It's confidential."

"Confidential," Cranston repeated. "I wish you'd been more confidential in that article you wrote for me. I trust you to write a simple story and you go off the deep end. I only wish I'd taken the time to read it before it went to print."

"You mean you didn't even look at it?" Mac asked, delighted.

"No. I should have, though." Cranston stroked his white mustache. "One of the other editors called my attention to it, but I was just too busy with a phone call. So I gave it the okay based on our last conversation."

"Oh," Mac said, his face broadening in a grin. "You should have read it. There's some pretty far-out stuff happening there—on the sixth floor, particularly."

"By the way, that sixth floor is a military psych unit. They weren't at all pleased by your article."

"Then you know all about women being abducted by little gray men who come from somewhere beyond our galaxy." Mac spread his arms out as if to encompass the universe.

Cranston shifted in his chair and chuckled patronizingly. "That's preposterous. Who'd make up a ridiculous story like that?"

"I have my sources."

Cranston laughed. "It *is* a nuthouse, after all." He waved his hand in dismissal.

"Well, I'm sure you can check the story. You *are* on the board of directors, right?" Mac said, relishing the moment.

"Your trip sounds exciting," Maggie interjected, hoping to ease the tension between the two men.

"So when do you leave?" Cranston asked, impatience edging his voice.

Mac avoided him, looked at Maggie, and said, "I leave tomorrow."

"You mean you're leaving already?" Sarah asked, and her face collapsed in disappointment.

"Yeah, you just *got* here," Jeremy protested.

"Yes, but I'll be back before you know it," Mac said, and hugged both of them to himself, knowing full well that he was lying.

"I'm glad for you, Mac," Maggie said. "Whatever it is it sounds like a fabulous opportunity."

"Thanks."

"Well, I think that's just wonderful," Doris said, adding her approval.

Mac took another sip of his lemonade, looked directly at Maggie, and rose from the sofa.

"Well, I better get going."

"Oh, Dad," the kids whined.

"Can't you at least stay for dinner? Fried chicken and honeyed yams!" Doris baited.

"No, I really have to get going. I have to pack and all," he said.

"Mac, stay for dinner," Maggie pleaded.

Her request caught Mac off guard and for a second he actually considered it. But then he thought of all of them sitting at the table with Cranston. "Maybe when I get back," he said, and he walked toward the foyer.

The children followed, but Maggie called to them, "Kids, give me a minute with your father alone, okay?" and she hurried to catch up with Mac.

"Mom," Sarah began to whine.

"Just a minute, Sarah," she said firmly.

"Honey, come sit with Grandma," Doris said, holding her arms out to Sarah.

Mac waited for Maggie by the front door, resting his hand on the doorknob.

"What gives you the right to just barge in here and disrupt everybody's life?" she whispered under her breath angrily.

"I'm not disrupting anything, am I?" he said, feigning innocence. "And if by everybody you mean you and the wannabe golf pro, I offer no apologies. Besides, they're my kids, too."

"Mr. Sarcasm returns. I can't even have a normal conversation with you."

"You started it."

She sighed, then pleaded softly, "I don't want to fight. The kids really miss you, that's all. They want their dad."

Mac looked at her. "I'm doing the best I can."

"You have to get over it, Mac," she said, avoiding Art's name.

"Like you," he countered, with a pointed look.

"At least I have a life," she shot back defiantly.

"Playing golf is a life? I thought you hated golf."

"Is it against the law to change what I like?"

"The kids told me they almost got bit by a rattler. Maybe you should spend more time watching them and less on the golf course with Casanova, for crying out loud!"

"What are you talking about!" she whispered angrily. "You know—I don't even know why I bother with you, Mac. You can show yourself out!" She spun around and walked down the hall, disappearing into the kitchen. "And send the child support!" she called, as the rear door slammed.

Mac headed for his jeep, glad to be out of the house and away from Maggie, from Cranston—and even glad, in a way, to be leaving his children.

Jeremy and Sarah burst through the door behind him. He stooped and gave them each a hug.

"Bye, Dad," Sarah said, trying not to cry.

Jeremy hugged Mac once more, then grabbed his sister's hand and the two kids ran back into the house.

Mac already had the jeep started when his mother-in-law walked up beside him and gently rested her hand on his arm.

"You know—they're just friends," Doris said.

"Oh?" Mac took a deep breath, trying to calm down.

Doris nodded. "Maggie's still young. Living way out here ... well, he takes her to dinner. Who can blame her for wanting to get out every now and then? But I think her heart's still here." And she touched Mac's chest.

"Thanks," he said, cracking a smile. "Tell her I'll write as soon as I get a chance. Better yet, tell her I'll call."

"You be careful, Mac."

"I'll be careful, Mom. And thanks."

Doris stepped back from the jeep. Mac threw it into gear and started down the gravel driveway.

7

Mac hunched pensively over the leatherette bar rail of the Jolly Roger lounge. Less than ten feet away, a steady stream of passengers hurried to their gates at Los Angeles International Airport.

A world within a world, he thought, gazing at the multiethnic variety of rushing commuters and travelers.

He turned back to the bar and eyed the tumbler that the bartender, dressed in cheap imitation pirate garb, had ceremoniously placed in front of him a moment ago. His third. Or maybe fourth. He wasn't keeping track.

He picked up the glass, raised it to his lips, and squinted through the bar's dim light at the plastic porthole clock. *Another hour of this and I won't care if they volunteer me for the space shuttle, for crying out loud.* He sipped from his drink.

He patted the ticket inside his jacket for the tenth time, reassuring himself it was still there. He hated to fly. No, that wasn't strong enough. He despised it. At best, it was a loathsome convenience. Just the thought of flying 35,000 feet above sea level, helplessly suspended over the frigid waters of the Atlantic, made him shiver. This would be the longest flight, by far, in his deliberately stunted flying career.

He sipped again.

An impeccably dressed, portly man sat down at a barstool next to Mac. His hair was slicked straight back, covering a small bald spot on the rear of his round head. Pinkie rings rested snugly on the fleshy, manicured fingers of each hand.

"Coming or going?" he asked, leaning in Mac's direction and smiling affably.

"Gloing," Mac slurred as he lifted his glass toward the man.

"Me too. Overseas," he stated.

Mac sipped the Grand Marnier and felt obliged to say something. "Europe?" he asked, unable to think of anywhere else at the moment.

"Algiers. And I'll have a gin and tonic, huh?" he added to the pirate bartender, then turned to Mac and confided, "Business."

"Oh . . ." Mac nodded, staring vacantly at his half-drained drink.

"Where you headed?" the man asked.

Mac drained the glass, set it back on the bar, and motioned to the bartender for another. "Israel," he replied.

"Tourist?" the man queried.

"Sort of," Mac mumbled, and wished the guy would stop asking questions.

"Fascinating place, Israel. In fact, the Middle East in general, huh?" the portly man said, twisting one of his pinkie rings. "Seems there's always a war starting or ending or somewhere in the middle, and I'm never sure who with." He laughed, then slurped a generous sip of his drink. "The place is no bigger than the state of New Jersey! Right? Let the Jews have it and be done with it. Or blow them all to kingdom come. Either way's all right with me."

"I'm overwhelmed at your sensitivity," Mac said.

The man became serious for a moment. "Oh, I value human life." Then he chuckled and placed his hand over his heart. "My own. Hey, I bet we're on the same flight. El Al? Seventy-four?"

"No, that's not mine," Mac answered, relieved, imagining what it would be like sitting next to this Grand Inquisitor for fourteen hours.

The portly man began to talk about sports. He rattled off an impressive series of scores and statistics. Probably prompted by Mac's obvious disinterest in the topic, he changed subjects, prattling on about the government, taxes, the national debt, and the upcoming elections. Mac was in no condition to respond.

He switched topics again, discussing strange diseases coming from Third World countries: ebola, Lhasa fever, and Brazilian meningitis. Mac tried to follow along.

Time ticked by. The man with the rings bought Mac another round.

Maybe I'll go to the men's room, Mac thought groggily. *Anything to get away from this guy. If he says "huh?" one more time I'm going to lose it.*

Before Mac could excuse himself, the conversation slid to a new topic, this time focusing on escaped Nazis hiding out in South America. Mac rolled his eyes and chuckled.

"You really believe all that? About the Nazis?" Mac asked.

"Huh?"

Mac shrugged and sipped his drink. *Will this guy ever leave?*

"Hey, look at that!" the man exclaimed, pointing toward the television tucked up near the ceiling.

Mac glanced up. It was an old science fiction movie.

"Isn't that *War of the Worlds?*" the man asked.

"Yeah . . . I think so." Mac watched as an alien ship fired a death ray at fleeing civilians.

"Wonder if they really do exist, huh?" The man nodded toward the screen. "You know, other life-forms—extraterrestrials or whatever you want to call 'em."

Mac almost choked on his drink. The guy's comment seemed innocent enough—but what a coincidence. "The subject's never interested me," he stated dryly.

But Pinkie Rings continued, ignoring Mac's answer. "Hey, the universe is a big place. Besides, too many people have seen them."

Mac shrugged, hoping the man would change the subject.

"UFOs are practically a fact of life." The businessman waved his hand. "Almost everybody has seen one, huh? Even Jimmy Carter said he saw one." He leaned closer to Mac and confided, "I saw one once myself."

"Hmm?" Mac feigned boredom.

"Yep, I have. When I was a kid, maybe twelve or so. Huh?"

Through the haze of alcohol, Mac thought, *Why is this guy pressing this on me?*

The man whispered, "So you don't believe, then?"

Mac stared straight ahead.

The man began again. "I was about twelve. I was at Boy Scout camp. There are four of us walking up this little ravine, taking a shortcut back to where our troop's camped. It's around noon because I remember the reason we were taking the shortcut was so we wouldn't be late for lunch, huh? We're in single file, walking up the ravine, when one of the other kids shouts and points to the sky. The other two kids see it too and they start yelling and screaming. I'm last in line, so at first I don't know what it is they're looking at. So I ask one of the kids next to me, 'Jimmy, what is it?' He points to the sky and I look up where he's pointing and there it is."

He paused dramatically, then continued. "The sky was big and blue. Not a cloud in it. There, off to my right, hovering, is this silver disk. Just hovering. Sittin' in the middle of the sky without a sound. We all stare at it, for, I don't know . . . thirty seconds or so. Then all of a sudden this thing just takes off, straight up into the air. Without a sound. One instant it's there and the next it's gone. Just like that." He snapped his fingers and rolled his eyes upward.

The story was uncomfortably familiar, and Mac shifted uneasily in his seat. "Then what happened?" he finally asked.

"Well, we all ran back to camp as fast as we could. We told everybody what we'd seen. Here's the part I'll never forget, though: Six hours later everybody but me denied that we had seen anything."

"What do you mean?" Mac asked.

"I mean all the other kids made so much fun of us that we felt like outsiders. So the three other kids denied the story. In fact, by dinner that evening, they all said it was just a joke, that we'd just made it up. I didn't go along, though."

"You didn't change your story?"

"Nope. And that got me in a lot of trouble." The man's face grew dark and angry. He reached over and grabbed Mac's arm and pinned it to the bar. "And if you know what's good for you, you'll forget everything you've seen, too—MacKenzie."

How does this guy know my name? Mac wondered. *Did I tell him?* He yanked his arm away and tried to stand, his head reeling from the alcohol. Some instinct screamed for him to run—but run from what? Mac swayed on his feet.

Pinkie Rings slid off his stool. He was bigger and quicker than he'd seemed, and now he suddenly loomed inches from Mac's face.

"Now you listen and you listen good," the man's voice rasped in Mac's ear. "Go home and forget all this stuff. Just forget it."

Mac heard a dull thud and felt a stabbing pain above his stomach. He was most of the way to the floor before he realized he'd been slugged in the solar plexus.

"Hey, what's going on here!" Mac heard the bartender yell.

The portly man suddenly loomed over Mac's face, and Mac felt himself being hoisted upward by his jacket collar. "Just go home."

"Hey, let the guy go!" the bartender's voice insisted. "I'm callin' security!"

The portly man dropped Mac back to the floor and hurried out of the bar, disappearing into the endless flow of commuters.

"You all right?" the bartender called out, waving the phone with one hand.

Mac held his stomach and struggled back to his feet.

"Yeah. Hey, don't call anybody, okay? I'm all right. The guy's just a jerk, that's all."

Mac leaned on the barstool, closed his eyes, and tried to catch his breath. Suddenly he felt a hand on his shoulder. He jerked upright and blindly swung at whatever, whoever, was there—but checked his swing as he spun and saw that it was a woman.

"Are you all right?" she asked. She was almost as tall as Mac, with striking blonde, almost white, bobbed hair, carefully painted red lips, high cheekbones, and dark sunglasses. When she removed her sunglasses, Mac stared into the most striking green eyes he had ever seen. *Must be those new colored contacts,* he thought.

"Are you all right?" she repeated.

"Yeah, I guess so," he answered, and slumped onto the stool.

"Why did he punch you?" she asked.

"You saw him punch me? Where were you?" Mac asked slowly.

"I've been tailing you. Roswell sent me to make sure you got on the plane safely. He knows you hate to fly."

Mac brushed his hair vigorously back from his forehead with both hands. "Roswell sent you?" he asked incredulously.

She nodded. "Did the guy say anything to you? Have you ever seen him before?"

Mac shook his head. "Never seen the jerk. I wasn't really listening to what he was saying. He blabbed about a bunch of things. The guy wouldn't shut up. There was some old sci-fi movie on the television and the next thing I know he's telling me some crazy story about UFOs."

"Why did he hit you?" she asked again.

Mac looked at her. "He threatened me." Mac was far from sober, but he was at least conscious enough to know one thing: whoever the guy was, he'd known way too much about Mac. The attack had been deliberate.

The woman watched him as if trying to read his thoughts. "Did he try to discourage you from going to Israel?"

Mac nodded.

"Did he succeed?"

Mac looked tight-lipped at her, then asked, "Who *are* you people?"

"People who want to know the truth," she said.

"Maybe I should just go home and forget about all this. This is way over my head."

"Don't *you* want to know the truth?" she asked, then added, "I know about your father."

Mac took a deep breath and rubbed his aching solar plexus. "Listen. Right now I don't give a flip about my father or about the 'truth,' as you put it, if it's going to get me killed."

"You could help, you know. With all of this."

Mac shook his head, "Why me? Why not send someone else?"

"Because unlike most people, you're linked to what's going on, through your father. Because of your past, you're special—you've been in it from the beginning. You've just chosen to ignore it."

Over the loudspeaker came the announcement for his flight. Mac stared at her, unblinking.

"That's your flight," she said, her eyes locked on his.

"You sure you're all right?" the bartender asked again.

"Yeah. Thanks. I'll be okay." Mac managed a smile. Turning back to the woman, he asked, "What's your name? Do you have a real name, or is it a code name like Aurora or something equally stupid?"

She smiled. "Laura ... for real."

"Let's get out of here," he mumbled and took a step toward the exit. She walked next to him. They made their way slowly, staying next to the wall to allow for the frantic racing of late commuters in the crowded walkway. Mac became aware of her perfume. He looked at her as she walked next to him, matching his stride. Who was she—really? She seemed assured but wary, confident, calculating, and intelligent. She was also drop-dead gorgeous.

"Here's your gate," she said, nodding in the direction of a crowd of people clustered around an El Al boarding tube. The crowd slowly formed itself into a semblance of a line and began to board the plane.

"Why should I go?" he asked. "Give me one good reason, after what just happened back there."

She folded her arms in front of her. "Okay, here's your one good reason. MacKenzie, the man who hit you wants to keep you away from something. What is it? What could be so important? Don't you see? Somebody is trying to hide something."

"Why can't you just tell me what it is and save me the plane ride?"

"What kind of talk is that from a reporter? You have to see for yourself, form your own opinion."

"Why does my opinion matter so much?"

"Somebody had to be chosen; Roswell chose you. After all, you were a great reporter—once."

Great—she knows everything about me, Mac realized.

"You could bring a viewpoint to the story that few people could ever hope to have."

"Because of my father."

She nodded.

Mac studied the handful of people who hadn't yet boarded the flight to Israel. He looked back at her, surprised to see how calm she was. There was no pleading, no whining, no coercing. She'd done her job. Now it was his move.

"Flight number 757 with service to Tel Aviv is now finished boarding and ready for take off. All ticketed passengers should now be on board. El Al Flight 757, leaving for Tel Aviv, gate number 3 . . ." The announcement echoed through the terminal.

"All right. I'll go." He patted his jacket pocket. "Besides, I already have the ticket."

"Good. Now listen." She grabbed him by the arm and started him in the direction of the gate. "I'll inform Roswell of your assailant. We'll also notify Uri. You have nothing to worry about. Try to relax and get some sleep during the flight."

"You make it sound so simple."

"Here you are," she said as they reached the boarding tube. He handed his ticket to the agent at the mouth of the boarding tube.

"Have a nice flight, Mr. MacKenzie." The agent smiled as she handed his ticket back.

"Thank you," Mac said mechanically.

As he entered the tube he glanced quickly over his shoulder and scanned the crowded gate area. She was gone. He thought he saw a blond head weaving in the crowd, but it vanished.

8

In his dream he bursts into the hospital emergency room, but instead of the nurse calling his name, the guy from the bar who slugged him blocks his way.

He plows into the man with his shoulder and the guy falls against the wall, hits his head, and slumps to the floor.

Mac runs down the hallway and sees Maggie. She is pressed against the glass. As she turns to look at him it's not Maggie at all. It's the woman from the hospital. The woman whose baby was abducted. She points to the operating room. Mac turns and sees his son Art, lying on a table. The head doctor turns to look at Mac, and he realizes that it is not the doctor at all but his father. "You can't do this . . . you're *dead!*" he screams as he tries to get to the door. His feet become welded to the floor and it takes all his effort to move them. He stares down at them expecting to see Sarah and Jeremy clinging to them, but instead there are two hybrid children, with large elongated black eyes . . . alien eyes. They stare at him. Mac realizes that he can't move and he looks again at the operating table. His father lies on it instead of Art.

He struggles to free himself but can't because of the two children entwined about his legs. He screams for Maggie. The woman next to him ignores him and continues on about her abducted baby. The man with the pinkie rings has recovered and runs down the hall. He grabs Mac's head and pushes it against the glass. Mac is forced to stare at the operation in progress. His father is gone from the operating table, and it is little Art who now lies there. None of the doctors or nurses is doing anything to help him. They are standing to the side of the operating table. He hears the man's angry voice hiss in his ear. "Go home! Go home! Go home!" The machine monitoring Art begins to drone in the next room. There is no heartbeat.

The head doctor takes up the chant. "Go home!" Soon everyone in the room is repeating it. "Go home! Go home!"

Mac screams again, "Maggie!"

"Mister! Mister! Wake up."

"Maggie . . . Maggie."

"Mister, you're having a bad dream . . . wake up!"

"What?" Mac mumbled, as his eyes blinked open. He saw a girl with blue hair. His seatmate. He slowly realized where he was. On the airplane. Flying to Israel.

"Are you okay?" she asked with genuine concern.

"Yeah." Mac rubbed his perspiring forehead with the back of his hand.

While she went back to her Walkman, he stared out the window at a group of thunderhead clouds in the distance. He rubbed the back of his neck, trying to clear his mind, but the image of his father kept returning.

What a crazy dream, he thought.

He wondered if by some remote chance his father might be alive. Three years after his father disappeared, hikers had found a body just outside of the ten-mile search radius the police had conducted in the Angeles Mountains. The body was badly decomposed and had been disturbed by animals, and the dental records didn't match up exactly. But everyone—including the police and his mother—assumed that the body was that of his father and that he had been murdered. They had never found the perpetrator, however. But Mac had always suspected it had something to do with his father's work at Roswell.

He thought about the picture in the document Roswell had given him and shifted uneasily. There was no mistaking a much younger version of General Roswell with his arm around Mac's father. Mac had scrutinized the picture looking for signs of forgery, but it seemed to be genuine. On the back side was a faded date: *July 1947*.

Why then, when he'd met Roswell at the warehouse, was he so reticent to talk about his father? Why would the government need to cover up anything that happened in 1947?

He thought again about the incident at the bar. Why should he trust Roswell or BenHassen? Why should he trust any of these people? Who did they work for? Who wrote their paychecks?

If things don't add up when I get to Israel, I can always return on the next plane to the U.S., he reassured himself. He let the questions drift away unanswered in his mind.

* ○ *

Mac woke again to the pilot's voice announcing their descent into Tel Aviv, Israel. An hour later, after going through the passport and customs check and collecting his luggage, he emerged into the bustling terminal.

He spied a crude cardboard sign with the word "MacKenzie" scrawled on it, held by a rugged-looking man with wavy black hair and a thick bushy mustache.

He went over and introduced himself. "I'm Art MacKenzie."

"Shalom! Welcome to Israel. I'm Uri BenHassen." He extended a dry, thick calloused hand, which Mac clasped in return.

"You are looking better than your picture," Uri commented.

Mac laughed, surprised by the backhanded compliment. "How was your flight?"

"Long and boring," Mac replied wearily.

"I am sorry." Uri grabbed Mac's bag and headed for the door.

Hot, dry air hit Mac's face as they stepped outside the terminal. He breathed deeply. *Not too bad,* he thought. *Almost like California, but without the pollution.*

"My van." Uri pointed to a white Ford covered with a veneer of yellow and brown dust. He opened the back door and Mac peered in at an assortment of shovels, picks, digging bars, ropes, stakes, markers, brushes, and other accoutrements used in archaeology. On one side of the van a row of metal shelves held an assortment of boxes with pieces of pottery. Each was carefully tagged and numbered.

"First century," Uri said as he picked up an artifact, set it into one of the boxes, and placed it on one of the overburdened shelves. He set Mac's bag on top of the tools. "Here, look at this." He reached into one of the boxes, pulled out a coin in a plastic zipped pouch, and handed it to Mac.

Mac turned it in the light. Even through the plastic there was no mistaking the worn image of Augustus Caesar.

"From a *tel* we are excavating," Uri explained.

"Fascinating," he replied, giving the coin back. They climbed into the van, and Uri started the engine that spurted noisily to life. "Hole in the muffler," he explained as he shifted into reverse and backed out.

"Yeah, I thought it sounded familiar," Mac said, thinking of his jeep.

As they left the airport Mac was awed to see the ubiquitous presence of the military. Armored jeeps, some mounted with machine guns fastened in the rear, cruised the parking lot and were stationed at intersections. Helmeted soldiers with automatic weapons seemed to be everywhere. "It looks like a war zone," he commented.

"It is! Unfortunately, it is our way. If we relax for even a moment, our neighbors will push us to the sea."

"How so?" Mac asked.

"Remember Six Day War? Or Yom Kippur War? Who attacked first?" Without waiting for Mac to reply he continued, "You see, we are small country just over three hundred miles, tip to tip, and maybe fifty at the widest place. Small country. We are surrounded by people who think we have no right to the land. But our claim goes back thousands of years. Before Muhammad and his hordes, Jews were here. We built the first Temple. When it was destroyed by the Babylonians and we were carted off to slavery for seventy years, our ancestors vowed to return. We did and built the second Temple. When Titus and his legions came and burned everything and killed a million people, new generations promised that one day they would be returning to Jerusalem and rebuild the Temple. Now the Muslim shrine, the Dome of the Rock, rests on top of what is left of Temple Mount. Its presence certainly is a big problem. We Jews believe the Temple Mount is ours, but . . ." And his eyes twinkled. "I'm thinking in a way it offers a solution to the problem . . . They built on *our* foundation! So who was here first?" And he laughed good-naturedly.

"Are you religious?" Mac asked.

"I am not. I am a Jew, and what Jew doesn't know of these things? It is our history."

They drove by an armored personnel vehicle with troops gathering around it. "Look at this." Uri motioned at the armored car. "We live in tension, between the constant threat of war and very fragile peace. But that is what makes us strong. We depend on one another in a way you Americans haven't done since World War II. Every day the threat of surprise attack looms over us. This day could be the one our enemies decide to attack us. We have learned to pull together. To be strong together."

Uri pulled his van out onto the freeway that connected Tel Aviv with Jerusalem, and they began their slow ascent. The six-lane road was in excellent condition, and Uri pushed the van five miles over the speed limit, which was a modest fifty-five.

"You keep going up slowly, up and up, and then you come to Jerusalem," Uri informed him.

"How far is it?" Mac asked.

"Maybe one hour. You've never been here? The Middle East?"

"No. I thought about it once, right after college. You know, travel, see Europe, Istanbul . . . I got married instead."

Uri nodded toward a picture of a woman with long dark hair that dangled from a necklace of colored braided twine from his rearview mirror. "Rebecca. We've been fourteen years married . . . three children. You?"

Mac shifted in his seat and leaned forward, pretending to look at something. "Well, I'm not anymore. It would have been . . . ah . . . fifteen years. But . . . we're divorced."

"Sorry." Uri concentrated on his driving for a moment, then said, "I'm sometimes thinking, you came quickly, Elisha wondered if you would come at all."

"Elisha?" Mac asked.

"My grandfather, Elisha BenHassen." Uri smiled proudly.

"Oh . . . I still don't understand what the big secret is."

"It is what you say . . . a big secret," Uri said, and laughed.

"Well, tell me about the room. Who found it?"

"Like some discoveries here, it was an accident. Two workmen were coming back from another area under the Temple Mount and one of them thought he heard something fall from behind the wall of the tunnel. He took a tool and knocked on the stone. It sounded hollow. The workers reported the incident, and a few days later an archaeological team was sent to investigate. They used a special device. It is called, I think, 'ultrasound'?" Uri said, momentarily troubled with his Hebrew-to-English translation.

Mac nodded. "Yeah, that's right. Ultrasound."

"They used the ultrasound and discovered that there was a room behind the tunnel wall. Once they knew, they brought in equipment to remove the stones and opened it."

"And I suppose you don't want to tell me what's in the room. Presuming of course that there is something," Mac pressed, hoping for the slightest inkling.

"Elisha said to not tell you anything . . . he wants you to look first. Believing is seeing?" Uri grinned.

"You mean seeing is believing," Mac corrected.

"Oh!" Uri smiled.

"Why all the mystery?" Mac asked.

"Because not everyone is ready to come to understand what is going on," Uri answered.

"And what is going on?"

"The briefing packet Roswell gave you. How did it make you feel? Were you disturbed, realizing that we might not be alone in the universe? Did it cause you to doubt your origins or your god . . . assuming you believe in one."

"I thought the pictures were fakes," Mac said, not revealing what he really thought.

"Think what you like, but Roswell has been with all of this for a very long time. He knows what we're dealing with."

"Oh. And what do you think we're dealing with?" Mac asked.

"A superintelligent extraterrestrial life-form that has the ability to travel light years in space in a very short time," Uri replied. "They are centuries ahead of us technologically. I'm thinking . . . from what . . . a dying race. They come here to regenerate their gene pool."

"If that were the case, then why the abductions? Why not just ask for volunteers?"

"I'm thinking they have their reasons which are above us intellectually, as we are above a dog!"

"Come on, you don't just take people against their will," Mac argued. "I saw some of the results of what happens to people who supposedly get abducted! It's not pleasant. The woman I saw was a basket case. Literally!"

"Basket case?"

"You know, she was nuts."

"Well, sometimes people are not ready—"

Mac cut him off. "Not ready? For what? It's not right. I don't care how advanced these ... aliens are. To be taken against your will goes against everything we believe in."

"You see ... you just said it. Everything we ... you ... believe in. That is why all the hush up! People are slow to change what they believe is truth. It is too much threatening. Remember it wasn't long ago people believed the world was flat ... Here, look." And Uri motioned out the front window.

Mac looked and saw the city of Jerusalem sprawled in front of him. It was late in the afternoon and what caught Mac's eye was a large golden dome shining gloriously in the sun: the Dome of the Rock.

Mac recalled a trip he had made to Williamsburg. He had been impressed by how old everything looked there, but it paled in comparison to what he now saw. Here was antiquity. Before him lay the tangible result of thousands of years of history, a legacy of the ebb and flow of a myriad of peoples and cultures.

"Unbelievable!" he murmured.

"A good word for it. The dome you see is the Muslim shrine, the Mosque of Omar. It sits on what is left of our Temple Mount. Below it is the most sacred place to any Jew—the Wailing Wall. Jews come here from all over the world just to touch it, kiss it, wet it with their tears and pray before it. The Rabbinical Tunnel is underneath. That is where we will be in some minutes."

Uri BenHassen guided the van off the freeway into a tangle of side streets in the Christian quarter of the Old City. He parked the van and jumped out. Mac climbed out and stared around him. It was as if he had stepped into another century.

"Be close. Ignore the vendors," Uri said. He walked swiftly, winding his way through the narrow lanes. The ever-present Israeli military displayed themselves on rooftops, in darkened doorways, in the marketplace. Essentially they were positioned in every strategic spot around the Temple Mount.

"Is it always like this?"

"Always. More so during the holy days for Muslim, Christian, and Jew." He looked around the crowded area then said, "Once a few years ago, a story circulated. The Palestinians were going to come with knives and kill Israeli soldiers. The sentries heard about this and became nervous. A few Palestinians happened to show near the Temple Mount. They were detained and started to be searched. One of the men gestured or said something, maybe he moved too quickly. Something went wrong and one of the guards opened fire. The other men shouted. The Arabs that are here in the marketplace heard the shots and then the cries of the men, and what should have been a routine search became a riot. The authorities found out later that the men stopped weren't armed. The rumor had been just that, a rumor. But . . ." He wagged his finger at Mac. "Who is what! People sit at a cafe, here in the Old City, drinking tea, talking, enjoying the sun, the open air. A woman comes along with a baby carriage. No one really notices her. She is a woman with baby carriage, that is normal thing. No one sees her walk away and leave the carriage. A few minutes later—boom! A dozen people are killed, some are maimed for life. You see . . . that is how we live."

They stood at the entrance to the Rabbinical Tunnel. Two armed sentries were posted on either side of the entrance. Other personnel, looking bored, stood near a guard shack. Uri stopped and talked briefly to one of them in Hebrew, gesturing toward Mac as he did so. The sentry glanced at Mac, then nodded to Uri.

"Let's go," Uri said, and they walked into the tunnel.

It was maybe ten feet in height and a little more than that across. Soft electric lights glowed from the walls every fifteen feet or so, casting shadows on the rough quarried stone.

Mac became aware that the floor of the tunnel felt like large slabs of stone, interconnected randomly at different intervals. It was cool and their footsteps echoed slightly as they walked deeper into the tunnel.

"There are more secret tunnels than this one," Uri explained. "They go in all directions under the Temple Mount. Here again is conflict, as the Arabs are afraid we will undermine the Dome of the Rock with all of our diggings. There is even a rumor, a rumor only, mind you, that the lost Ark of the Covenant was found in one of the tunnels."

Mac snickered. "Come on, I'm not some Indiana Jones wannabe you're talking to."

"No, really," Uri insisted, "it has been thought that Solomon had a secret room constructed to hide the Ark. Remember, the Ark of the Covenant was most holy object to the Jews. Solomon reasoned that if invaders overran Jerusalem, they wouldn't find the Ark. After the Babylonians came and destroyed the Temple, the Ark was never seen again. Poof! It vanished!" And he slapped his hands together. "The second Temple did not have the Ark. So there is a chance that it might be lying in a secret room for all of these centuries."

"So who found it?"

"The story is, and I say it is only a story but . . . late one night archaeologists and rabbinical scholars were excavating along the lower level of the Western Wall. They entered a fairly long tunnel. At the end of the tunnel they saw what they thought was the Ark. It had dried animal skins all over it. But they could see one end of it gleam with gold as they held their torches. They went to get the Chief Rabbi. Hours passed. By the time they returned, the Arabs had made a concrete wall."

"Why didn't they just break the concrete wall down?" Mac asked incredulously.

"Good question. The Rabbis say they are waiting to hear from God, and when they do they will get the Ark. The government officially denies the discovery. And the Arabs avoid the topic altogether, choosing instead to caution us about the foundation being weakened by all of the diggings."

"Politics and religion, bad chemistry," Mac blurted.

"Yes, and I'm sometimes thinking if the Rabbis are waiting for God they have a long wait!"

They walked further and then turned into another tunnel that had a slight incline to it. Ahead of them Mac could see a hastily constructed plywood wall that went out into the corridor perhaps five feet and spanned from floor to ceiling. In front of it a sentry slumped on a stool and smoked a cigarette.

"Shalom," Uri called out as they neared him.

"Shalom," the guard muttered, took a drag off his cigarette, and slowly stood up and stretched himself.

He said something in Hebrew and motioned toward Mac. Uri smiled, then translated for Mac's benefit.

"He said he was hoping we were his replacements," Uri explained. "Follow me." He went into the plywood anteroom.

Mac passed through the newly created opening through the tunnel wall and entered the secret room.

"There it is," said Uri as he gestured with his hand.

Mac stepped further into the room and carefully looked about. It was perhaps eighteen feet square and hewn from solid rock. But what caught Mac's eye as he entered was a large stone sarcophagus. Perhaps twelve feet or more in length, it dominated the small chamber. The lid had been taken off and laid next to it on thick blocks of wood.

Directly above it several electric lamps illuminated the sarcophagus and its contents.

"Go. Look," Uri whispered.

Mac grew suddenly aware of his pounding heart, which seemed to echo throughout the room. He took several steps and came alongside the sarcophagus and peered into it.

He gasped. Before him lay the skeleton of a man of enormous size. A giant skeleton, and it was completely intact.

Uri stepped next to Mac and pointed. "Look here, six fingers and six toes on each of the hands and feet."

Mac was stupefied. "What is . . . What was it?"

Uri went over to the lid and pointed to the chiseled arcane inscription at the top of it. They were distracted by the sound of shuffling feet as someone entered the room.

"Nephilim. Anakim. Rephaim," a ragged voice replied, to Mac's question.

"This is my grandfather," Uri said as he went to the man's side. "Dr. Elisha BenHassen." He helped him into the room.

A wizened elderly man with a bushy white beard and a slight stoop to his shoulders presented himself to Mac. He was dressed in dirt-stained khaki pants and a faded white cotton shirt, which hung loosely around his thin body. His white hair crept over his ears, concealing the ends of wire-rim trifocal lenses.

Elisha extended a twisted arthritic hand, and Mac stepped forward to grasp it.

"This is Art MacKenzie . . . the American that Roswell told us about," Uri said.

"It's a pleasure, sir," Mac replied. He studied the man's deeply lined, weathered face.

Uri grabbed one of the crates lying near the wall and set it next to his grandfather. The old man eased himself gingerly down on the makeshift seat.

His crooked fingers traced the letters etched in the lid of the sarcophagus. "Nephilim. Anakim. Rephaim. All different words, uttered by my ancestors thousands of years ago to describe the same creature. The remains of which you see before you. Have you ever heard those words before?"

"No."

"Most people haven't. A handful of biblical scholars are familiar with them, but most have no idea of what the significance is. Have you ever heard of David and Goliath?"

"Of course . . . no, you're not saying that . . ." Mac remembered the last conversation with his daughter and marveled at the coincidence.

Elisha nodded, and a playful smile spread over his face. "Hard to imagine, isn't it?"

"That's an understatement," Mac replied.

"What you are looking at are the bones of a giant, like Goliath, preserved here and hidden away all these years."

Mac looked again at the skeleton and wondered if it could really be true.

"When my ancestors first entered the Promised Land, under the leadership of Moses, they sent twelve men in to spy out the land. When the men returned, they reported giants living there . . . To use their exact words, 'We saw the Nephilim there. We seemed like grasshoppers in our own eyes, and we looked the same to them.' Ten of the twelve counseled Moses and the people not to go in. But two of the spies, Joshua and Caleb, disagreed."

"Excuse me. I'm sorry," Mac interrupted, "but is this the same Moses, as in parting the Red Sea and the Ten Commandments?"

"Yes." Elisha chuckled. His laughter abruptly turned into a hacking cough. He cleared his throat, turned his head, and spat toward a corner of the room.

"One of the souvenirs I carry from the war," he lamented.

Mac waited for an explanation but none came, just a slight shifting of Uri's feet.

Elisha continued, "Because the people believed the ten spies and not Joshua and Caleb, that generation did not enter into the Promised Land. They all perished. Forty years later Joshua crossed the Jordan River, and the conquest of Canaan began. The stories are true, the accounts accurate, and here are the bones to prove it."

"Some of this I remember from Sunday school, but what does finding giant bones, no matter whose they are, have to do with UFOs? I don't see the connection."

Elisha gazed steadily at him through his trifocals. The room grew quiet. "Maybe everything," he said softly. "But this place"—and he gestured wearily with his hand—"is dark and musty. And though an archaeologist I may be, I'm hungry and some things are best said in the light of day."

Uri went over and helped Elisha rise to his feet.

"We'll come here tomorrow," Elisha promised.

They left the room with Elisha leaning slightly on his grandson's arm. Mac followed them.

An electric cart was parked next to the plywood wall. They climbed in. Uri drove, Elisha sat next to him, and Mac sat cross-legged on the makeshift platform in the rear. They drove through the tunnel and soon found themselves at the entrance. Mac squinted as his eyes tried to adjust to the late afternoon sun. Uri parked the cart next to the guard shack and then helped his grandfather get out.

Elisha conversed briefly with the guards, who nodded respectfully, and the three men left for Uri's van.

Mac looked back at the entrance to the tunnel and wondered what a giant skeleton had to do with flying saucers.

9

Uri BenHassen helped his grandfather into the front seat of his van. He then opened the side door for Mac, who crawled in and found a place to sit on a stack of dusty burlap sacks.

Uri maneuvered through a series of circuitous shortcuts through the narrow streets of Jerusalem. On the way he pointed out various points of interest to Mac. The Dung Gate, David's Tomb, the Russian Orthodox Cathedral, the War of Independence Memorial. Mac tilted his head awkwardly and caught fleeting glimpses of monuments and buildings through the front window. He punctuated each one with an obligatory staccato of uh-huhs as the van bounced and rocked along the road.

A while later Uri slowed down and pulled up in front of a modest complex of townhouses.

"Here we are," he said. While he helped his grandfather out, Mac opened his door and carefully crawled out of the van. He stood upright on the sidewalk, arching his back and stretching his legs, thankful to be out of the cramped Houdini-like position.

Elisha leaned on Uri as they climbed the concrete steps that led to a small courtyard. Uri's townhouse was tucked in the rear of the quadrangle, offering the rare luxury of privacy.

Uri produced his key ring, selected a key, fitted it into the lock, and opened the door. He helped his grandfather into the house. Mac followed but paused at the threshold, for he was met with a strong aroma of fresh baked bread that made his stomach growl and his mouth water. He realized he hadn't eaten since his arrival in Tel Aviv.

"Papa! Papa!" The joyous cries echoed through the house as three children burst into the room and swarmed all over the men in a flurry of hugs and kisses, shouting all the while with childlike glee.

Mac stood at the doorway and remembered such greetings before the accident . . . when his son was alive and his family was still together. The scene tugged at his heart.

Another lifetime, he thought.

"Children, this is Mr. MacKenzie," Uri said. "This is my eldest, Moshe." He reached out and patted the head of a boy perhaps ten years of age. "This is Vera," he added, as he hugged his daughter of seven years. "And this is my youngest . . ."

"Our youngest," corrected a lilting, musical voice. "His name is also Elisha after his great-grandfather . . . and I'm Rebecca." She introduced herself to Mac as she entered the room.

Mac thought of the photo in Uri's van and realized it could never possibly relate the qualities that made her not only beautiful to behold but so vibrantly alive. The sound of her voice, her dark shining eyes, her thick long hair tied loosely behind her back, the swish of her skirt as she walked into the room and stood close to Uri's side . . . all of this was so wonderfully feminine.

"My wife," Uri said, and gazed at her lovingly.

"My granddaughter," Elisha added proudly, as he opened his arms to greet her.

She kissed Uri, then went to her grandfather-in-law and pecked him affectionately on his cheek.

Seeing Mac poised in the doorway, Rebecca went to him, took his hand, and escorted him into the living room.

"Come and sit down—you must be exhausted. Knowing my husband, he has not thought anything of what you must feel like after flying in an airplane from America!" She threw Uri a derisive look, then turned to Mac, smiled warmly, and said, "Our home is your home. Our family will be your family while you are here!"

"Thank you," Mac said, allowing her to lead him to the couch where he promptly plopped himself down and let out a weary sigh.

Rebecca went into the kitchen and returned with a pitcher of iced tea on a tray. She poured four large glasses, served the men, and then herself. The children gathered around Mac and began to ask questions.

"Not now. Go and play. Mr. MacKenzie will be here for some days. You will have plenty of time to talk with him," Rebecca admonished gently.

To Mac's amazement there was no pleading, whining, or cajoling from the children. They simply got up and left the room.

"I have only one rule while you are here," she said, assuming a stern air as she looked at Mac. "My husband and his grandfather, and now you, have all day to work. When you walk through the door of this house at night, you must leave your work out there." And she pointed at the door.

Uri nodded. "She means it," he lamented.

"Okay," Mac agreed, realizing he was left with only one appropriate answer.

"Rebecca, what is that wonderful smell?" asked Elisha.

"Oh, the bread!" Rebecca exclaimed and darted for the kitchen.

Mac watched her run out of the room, then turned to Uri and said, "You have a wonderful family, Uri. You're fortunate."

"I'm a lucky man." Uri beamed, spreading his mustache across his face.

"Blessed is the more appropriate term," Elisha added. "I introduced them. Rebecca was one of my students at the university, an exceptionally bright young woman. We were working a new *tel*. I arranged for Uri to be there that weekend, and, well, nature took care of the rest."

"The matchmaker! He loves the story." Uri laughed.

"Does she help you with your work now?" Mac asked.

"With the children, not so much, but she still manages to do most of the reports," Uri replied.

"What does she think of the bones you . . ." Mac began.

"No, no!" Elisha chided. "You mustn't discuss work. It hasn't been more than a minute and see, it's harder to do than you think!" He leaned back in his chair and chuckled.

"Come to the table!" Rebecca called from the kitchen.

The three men rose and walked to the dining room only to be intercepted on the way by the children, who fought to sit next to Mac.

The meal came on large polished silver trays that were obviously a prized family heirloom. Rebecca served chicken cooked in herbs and wine, small new potatoes roasted in garlic, and cold fresh cucumbers and tomatoes in a vinaigrette dressing. The meal was topped off, of course, with a warm loaf of fresh baked bread. Mac had trouble recalling a finer meal.

Rebecca conducted the conversation, weaving an array of questions at those eating at her table. She queried the children about school. She talked with Uri about the upcoming Olympics and Israel's chances of getting a gold in the hurdles. She asked Elisha how his arthritis was and scolded him for not taking his medicine. She then asked Mac what life was like in America.

"Some more bread?" she offered, while Mac briefly related what his life consisted of as a reporter.

Mac took the offering, deliberately cut his story short, and savored the piece.

When the meal was over, they sat and listened to each child tell of their favorite thing they had done that day. Afterward the children cleared the table and helped with the dishes.

The task of kitchen work completed, Mac and Elisha retired to the living room while Uri and Rebecca settled the children down for the night, but not before each child said good night to their great-grandfather and Mac.

"How late will you be out tonight?" Rebecca asked Elisha, as she and Uri came back into the room.

"Not too long," Elisha promised.

She frowned and lamented, "Oh no! That means all night!"

"No, no." Uri started in defense of Elisha.

"No, no?" She mimicked him. "I know both of you well enough to know what that means. Mr. MacKenzie." She turned to Mac. "I'm sure you are exhausted from your travel, but as for these two, huh!" And she glared at them. "They have little concern for that! I hope you don't like to sleep because there will probably be very little of it tonight." She folded her arms in front of her defiantly.

Uri went over and put his arm around her. "We promise not too late," he cooed, trying his best to appease her.

"Oh, I don't know why I put up with you two," she said.

"Because you love us," Elisha answered.

"We should go now," Uri said.

"Wonderful to meet you, and dinner was extraordinary," Mac said, rising wearily from the sofa.

Rebecca smiled and said, "Thank you, Mr. MacKenzie."

"Call me Mac."

"Thank you . . . Mac."

Elisha cleared his throat. "I must agree with Rebecca," he said. "Mac's eyes are rolling around in his head. He is exhausted. And, as I said earlier, some things are best saved for the light of day. Rebecca, why don't you show Mac his room while Uri gets his bags?"

Uri started to protest but after a look at Mac's beleaguered face and a quick glance at Rebecca, he acquiesced. "All right, the bag," he mumbled, and headed out to the van.

Elisha clasped Mac's hand in both of his and said warmly, "Well, Mac, when you awaken in the morning, Uri will drive you out to my house and we'll talk. I pray your sleep will be restful."

Mac nodded, looking forward to it.

"This way," Rebecca said, as she grabbed Mac's hand and pulled him down the hallway. "It's Moshe's room. He was honored to give it to you while you stay with us."

"Thanks, I could have slept on the couch," Mac answered, feeling awkward.

"No, this is better." She opened the door to the room and left him.

Mac was alone for the first time since being in Israel. In the silence of the room his exhaustion overwhelmed him. He looked around at posters of motorcycle racers and rock stars plastered on the walls. An outdated computer sat atop the child's desk next to the window that overlooked the courtyard. Neatly arranged books, with perhaps a dozen comic books interspersed among them, rested on a shelf above the bed.

Uri knocked on the door of the room and entered. "If not for Rebecca I would work . . . what, all the time?" He grinned, then added, "Here's your bag. I'll see you in the morning."

"Good night," Mac replied, as his host closed the door.

Mac changed out of his clothes. *How many hours have I been in these?* he wondered. He tried to do the math but realized his brain was too tired to function properly and he was too tired to care. He left his clothes in a heap on the floor and tumbled into the small single bed. He pulled the covers around his neck and promptly went to sleep.

10

Mac was awakened by giggling children peering through a crack in his door. He kicked the covers in a flurry with his feet, making the children erupt in laughter at his antics. Then he jumped out of bed, stretched his hands high over his head, and growled, taking a step to the door as he did so, which caused the children to run down the hall in a confusion of screams and laughter.

As he entered the bathroom, his mind drifted to thoughts of Jeremy and Sarah. He missed them.

He took a brief but vigorous shower, then found his way out to the kitchen, where Rebecca was serving breakfast. He guzzled two cups of coffee and wolfed down a couple of slices of toast topped with plum marmalade. Then he and Uri left the townhouse and headed toward Elisha's.

Mac bounced in the front seat of the van as they skirted the Old City of Jerusalem.

Uri made a wide turn around a stalled vehicle. "Elisha lives in a house built before the War of Independence," he told Mac. "An Englishman made it. After war, very few English remained. People were certain there would be war with the Palestinians. People panicked, real estate prices went very low, and Grandfather bought the house for a tenth of its value. He raised his children in that house."

"Your father was raised there?"

Uri nodded.

"Where is he now?" Mac asked, curious as to why Uri had never mentioned him.

"Accident. He died a number of years ago from a stray sniper bullet. After his death my mother moved from Israel and went to live with relatives in France. She was tired of wars and killing."

"I'm sorry."

Uri shrugged off the comment, "You know what? It is something we have come to accept. Almost everyone has lost member of their family because of our struggle to be sovereign nation."

Mac's dead son and his father's murder came to the forefront of his mind. He felt numb as he looked out the window at the ruins of the Old City.

They drove a few more miles, then Uri turned on a narrow lane that wound its way up the side of a small hill. Near the crest, they swung into a gravel driveway hidden by tall, stately cypress trees. The trees marked the boundaries of the Ben-Hassen property, creating a cloistered sanctuary.

A white-washed, two-story stucco house with a flat expanse of tended lawn sat toward the rear of the property.

"This is it. He's lived here since the war. It is the same as the day he bought it, but the cypress have grown up," Uri explained as he parked the van.

They walked toward the front porch. Mac felt the solitude and quiet privacy that the towering cypress trees afforded. Like silent sentinels they enclosed the house and grounds from the outside world.

"I see you're both here early," Elisha called, as he swung the massive front door open and stepped onto the small porch of the house.

"He has surveillance cameras everywhere," Uri explained, as he pointed to one mounted near a second-story window.

They climbed the steps and Elisha and Uri embraced.

"Good to see you again, MacKenzie. You slept well?" Elisha asked, as he extended his hand.

"Very well, thank you. You have a beautiful home here."

Elisha smiled proudly. "Yes, I'm fortunate to have obtained this. I think God restored the years the locusts consumed . . . that portion of my life, lived in Germany."

Uri cleared his throat and looked away from his grandfather. Mac sensed uneasiness in Uri and attributed it to Elisha's comment. He made a mental note of it.

"Come in, let me show you our laboratory," Elisha said.

Mac stepped into the foyer, the walls of which were lined with pictures of Elisha's family. Bearded patriarchs with black top hats and phylacteries stared solemnly from dusty frames. At one end were recent pictures of Uri and Rebecca and what Mac assumed to be other children sired by the elder BenHassen. Close to the front door and set apart from the others was a faded black-and-white portrait of a newly married couple that Mac thought might be Elisha and his bride.

"Isn't she beautiful?" Elisha offered, following Mac's eyes toward the portrait. "That was taken so many years ago. I've been widowed almost ten years."

"I'm sorry," Mac replied awkwardly.

He jutted his lower lip and said, "Death is part of life." For a moment he became lost in some private memory, but he suddenly came back and resumed his role as host. "But thank you . . . come in, come in!" And he smiled at Mac reassuringly.

They walked out of the foyer into a wide hall, which ran toward the rear of the house. To the right was a long single step that led to the living room. A cathedral ceiling loomed over bookshelves that lined three of the walls and reached to the base of the dark wooden rafters. Books were stacked in an assortment of ways on the shelves, revealing a working library. Two large tables presented a sizable work area in the middle of the room. Next to piles of notes and stacks of reports were three computers set in a row on one of the tables. A large map of the world sat on an easel with notes and colored flags pinned to it. Mac counted four separate telephones spread throughout the room; next to one was a fax machine, which had spewed a stream of paper onto the floor. Beside it and fastened to one of the bookshelves was a blown-up photograph of what appeared to be a meteor or fireball streaking across the night sky. Mac stared at it for a moment, thinking it might not be the fireball he assumed it to be.

"It was taken by an American, Gary Schultz, near a secret government installation in Nevada. It is a UFO," Uri said, noticing Mac's interest in the photograph.

Mac raised his eyebrows and asked, "How do you know it wasn't faked?"

"Roswell and Schultz were together when the photo was taken. In fact it was Roswell who tipped him off as to when was the best time to take the photograph. And we have had it analyzed ourselves. At this location it seems they experiment with the alien craft midweek, usually on Wednesday after midnight, and go until daybreak."

"You mean they have a schedule for flying these?" Mac asked incredulously.

"You know what? As hard as it is to imagine, they have a schedule," Uri said. "Under Roswell's direction, Schultz positioned himself near what is called the 'Action Zone,' an area just outside the base where the disks would sometimes be flying over. That's where he took the photo."

"Still, it could be faked," Mac challenged.

Uri nodded. "Yes, but this one has been put through a barrage of tests . . . I'm thinking, is the real goods."

Elisha glanced at the photo, nodded in agreement with Uri, then gestured toward the room. "This is where we work. Most of our research is carried on here."

Mac shifted on his feet. "How do the bones in the sarcophagus—the Nephilim—figure into the UFO phenomena?"

"Here, please." Elisha pointed to one of four worn leather chairs.

Mac sat down. Elisha and Uri took seats on either side of him, forming a semicircle.

Elisha rested his hands on the arms of his chair, cleared his throat, and asked, "Are you familiar with the Torah, the books of the Old Testament?"

Mac frowned. "Somewhat," he replied. "I was brought up going to church, but it's been a while since I've actually read any of it, especially the Old Testament."

"Have you read the book of Genesis?" Elisha asked.

"No, not really," and Mac wondered what direction Elisha could possibly be headed with this.

"Then, let's begin there." He leaned forward expectantly, rested his hands in his lap, and began. "In Genesis, in the sixth chapter, the beginning passage states that, 'When men began to increase in number on earth and daughters were born to them, the sons of God saw that the daughters of men were beautiful, and they married any of them they chose. Then the LORD said, "My Spirit will not contend with man forever, for he is mortal; his days will be a hundred and twenty years." Now listen carefully to this next passage," Elisha said. "'The Nephilim were on the earth in those days—and also afterward—when the sons of God went into the daughters of men and had children by them. They were the heroes of old, men of renown.' The term *Nephilim* is the same that you saw on the inscription of the sarcophagus yesterday underneath the Temple Mount."

"I remember, but what or who are the 'sons of God'?" Mac asked.

"Good question. Commentators differ on their interpretations, but I believe the sons of God are fallen angels."

"Fallen angels?" Mac asked in disbelief.

Elisha nodded. "Yes, the Hebrew translation for 'sons of God' is *bene Elohim*, which is only used in reference to the fallen angels. It appears that these fallen angels, also known as 'The Watchers,' came to earth and resided here, resulting in an unholy union between themselves and the earthly women. Their offspring were giants! Men of great strength. But these giants or Nephilim were anathema. Cursed of God. According to other apocryphal texts, they corrupted the entire earth with violence, so much that God had little choice except to destroy them." He paused for a moment and allowed Mac to digest what he had said, then began again. "However, underscoring this is something far more sinister, pernicious if you will. It seems that by corrupting the human offspring, the angels may have altered human DNA so much that the human race was corrupt, tainted, essentially non-human. And if you follow this line of reasoning one step further, this would negate any hope of the promised Messiah being born of men! So God saved those who had not been corrupted by the fallen angels. Perhaps this is why it says that Noah was pure in all his generations. The rest of the inhabitants of earth he destroyed with what has become known in many different cultures as 'The Great Flood.'"

"Noah . . . as in Noah and the ark?" Mac asked, a bit amused by the prospect of this seemingly learned man believing in something as mythical as the flood.

Elisha leaned back in his chair and said, "Most cultures throughout the world have a flood legend. Look at the Gilgamesh legend of the Sumerians brought to light in the earlier part of this century. There are aborigines in Australia and ancient Greeks who have flood legends. There is also a small tribe in your native California, the Chumash, I believe they are called, who have a flood legend that describes an evil race of people who dwelt below the middle kingdom, or the place that men inhabited. I could go on, the legends are numerous, but let me assure you that I don't say these things lightly, nor do I take for granted those who have studied and written about these arcane ideas long before me. One such author, G. H. Pember, wrote an extensive treatise called *Earth's Earliest Ages*. The thrust of his book illuminates the prospect of the return of these beings, or fallen angels, shortly before the return of Christ ... presuming, of course, he was here the first time." Elisha chuckled. "What is interesting are the similarities between their first appearance and what now may be their last."

Mac looked doubtful. "I don't follow you. Do you mean the ... ah ... fallen angels are here on earth? Now?"

"I do," Elisha answered firmly. "I will quote another passage from the Christian Scriptures, the New Testament."

"Oh?" Mac asked, wondering what interest the New Testament could possibly have to this old Jew.

"This is attributed to a famous rabbi," Elisha said, "Jeshua ben Joseph."

Mac shrugged. The name had no meaning to him.

Elisha smiled and said, "You might know him better by his more common Greek name of Jesus."

Mac nodded but was annoyed at Elisha playing linguistic games with him.

"Jesus said, 'As it was in the days of Noah, so it will be at the coming of the Son of Man.' I believe it is one of his most cryptic utterances. You must ask yourself, what is it that differentiates the 'days of Noah' from any other time in history?" He waited for Mac to respond.

Mac shifted uneasily in his chair. He wondered if the conversation could possibly get more bizarre. "I don't have a clue," he muttered.

Elisha continued, "Some believe that the West's moral decay and the frequency of wars or the onset of famine or increase of disease and plagues are indicators that the Second Coming may be imminent. But those factors have always been with us, more or less. But I believe a unique dynamic is with us now—the presence of fallen angels. They are here again and doing much of the same mischief that they were responsible for before, only under the guise of extraterrestrials. And since 1947 the number of sightings, abductions, and people with missing time has grown exponentially."

Mac thought of the mental hospital and the woman who had claimed to have her baby taken by aliens.

"They are impregnating the women and creating a race of hybrids—Nephilim," Elisha finished.

"That's a lot to swallow," Mac exclaimed. "You really see a connection between Noah and flying saucers?"

"Yes, part of an elaborate deception," Elisha explained. "The book of Enoch records that the first time they came they supplied us with technology. They showed us the art of weapon making. In return they gained access to the women. Now leap forward to present day—these aliens also have technology which they have traded or bargained in exchange for the same access . . . to women."

Uri, who had remained silent until then, interrupted and said, "But that is your theory. What if they are from a dying race from a distant planet and have come only to renew themselves with fresh genetic material?"

"Certainly plausible," Elisha agreed, "and of course it would explain the government's willingness to conceal all of this from the public."

Mac leaned forward in his chair. "Look, I'm not saying I believe what I've heard here, but one thing's for sure—if they do exist, can you imagine the repercussions if they revealed themselves?"

"Precisely," Elisha agreed. "What would people do if they realized that we are not alone? Remember Orson Welles's 'War of the Worlds' broadcast, which caused hysteria in some parts of your country when it was first aired? What would happen if the aliens actually made their presence known? The philosophical and religious implications would be enormous."

Uri nodded gravely. "I believe it would cause panic. Information that Roswell has given us is suggesting that the aliens genetically manipulated us, maybe some ten thousand years ago, and in fact are our progenitors."

"Do you believe that?" Mac asked Elisha.

"No, absolutely not," he stated without hesitation.

Mac looked at Uri and waited for him to continue.

"If what they claim is true, then I think . . . You know what. If they did genetically engineer us from primitive humans, then what many major religions teach and millions believe becomes not so good."

"But what if this is an elaborate deception?" countered Elisha. "What if they have lured us in the same way the ancient texts reveal—through the Trojan horse of technology? What if they are who I think they are? The resurgence of the fallen angels." He paused and gathered his thoughts. "Here, if you will, might be a litmus test. How do you discern whether these beings are benevolent or malevolent, good or evil?"

"Good and evil are relative terms," Mac responded.

"Not so relative," Elisha exclaimed. "I believe you would agree that good aliens do not take helpless women in the middle of the night, impregnate them, then remove the fetuses in the third month of development, all against the will of the poor soul who has been abducted."

"Okay, I'll admit that," Mac answered.

"But you make that argument from our perspective—what we determine is good and evil," Uri argued. "What if the aliens are beyond such things?"

Elisha shook his head. "In order to embrace your thought, you have to abandon the very essence of human morality and ethics. Examine the Nazi concentration camp guards. After the war, during the Nuremberg trials, they had a favorite saying, when asked how they could willingly commit such heinous crimes against humanity. Their response? We've all heard it before, so much that the phrase has become almost a joke. 'We were just following orders,' they said. They had abandoned any hint of morality, the ability to discern right from wrong, good from evil. They abdicated that responsibility for the privilege of serving in the Third Reich, which was the mechanism, the catalyst, that helped them transform into the monsters they became."

Mac and Uri sat silent.

"Let me assure you," Elisha began, "there are many similarities between what happened ages ago during the days of Noah and what is happening now. And what is happening is evil."

Elisha paused and the room was silent for a moment. Then he said, "Uri, would you please find the book of Enoch? I want Mr. MacKenzie to see something for himself."

Uri went to the library, found the book that Elisha had requested, and handed it to Mac.

"What is the book of Enoch?" Mac asked, holding the worn volume.

"It is a pseudoepigraphical book . . . meaning a book that has a false author's name ascribed to it, in this case Enoch. It is a book that is not part of the Christian canon, and of course I don't treat it as such. But it was read widely during the time of Christ, and passages of it are quoted in the canon, specifically from the book of Jude. It was also found in Qumran, in the Dead Sea scrolls. We can at least appreciate its historicity." He leaned forward. "Look at the book of Enoch. Go to page thirty-four and look at section six," Elisha instructed.

Mac read the paragraph, then looked up at Elisha.

Elisha summarized, "It says in the manuscript that Semjaza was the leader of the angels, or children of heaven, I believe the text calls them. It continues and says that he required the other angels to swear an oath with him, binding them together. A pact created and formed for the sole purpose of taking the woman of earth for wives . . . because they lusted after them. Now remember all of this takes place during the time frame in which Noah is alive, which may have been ten thousand years ago, or longer. You know the rest of the story. They have intercourse with the women and the offspring is the Nephilim. Then God judges them and destroys the world in a deluge."

Mac looked at Elisha and said, "I've always thought that a bit severe."

"It *is* severe," Elisha exclaimed passionately. "He had little choice, for with Semjaza being a fallen angel, the offspring of that unholy union were demonic."

"But Semjaza could also be an interdimensional being," Uri said.

"What's that?" Mac asked.

"An entity that exists in another dimension but can access ours. We live in what? The three-dimensional space-time continuum. Height, width, and depth. Because of that we are subject to properties and constraints of time. What would a being from another dimension, that was not subject to time as we know it, look like? Could they have the same qualities that Enoch describes? Would they in fact live for thousands of years? I'm thinking, in our ignorance, we might mistakenly call them gods or angels," Uri said.

"But what if they are precisely what the book of Enoch and the book of Jude describe them as," countered Elisha.

"The book of Jude?" Mac asked, trying to keep up with all of the literary references.

"Jude is the book that precedes Revelation in the Christian Bible. Jude echoes the book of Enoch and describes the angels." Elisha turned to Uri. "Why do you have such a hard time believing what these books say about these beings, that they are fallen angels? Beings that were created to be in the presence of the holy and eternal God of light, the Creator of the universe, the holy God of Israel. But they sinned—as Jude says, 'The angels did not keep their positions of authority but abandoned their own home.'"

Uri brushed his mustache down over his upper lip, took a deep breath, then said, "Because to me these books are myths and superstitions that the men living in those times passed down orally and then were written by others maybe a very long time after the events. They are filled with legend and lore, old wives' tales and superstitions. You know what? There may be an element of truth to some of what is said. But I'm thinking the writers were ignorant, unlearned men. And what if what the aliens are saying is true, that we are a direct result of their genetic manipulation thousands of years ago? Maybe these stories are accounts of what happened then. But now I think they are conducting some kind of genetic research. I think to replenish their race through our genetic material."

Elisha leaned on one elbow, pointed his finger at Uri, and said, "Remember, angels are created beings, and for all we know they may have been in existence for millions of years. They are not some cherubic, emasculated, winged beings but were and are creatures of immense power! So much so that men are reduced to lying as if dead during the briefest of encounters with them. They are created to be in the presence of a holy God. And who knows what knowledge they possess, both the good and the fallen?"

Uri shook his head.

Elisha continued, "I believe that they are super scientists. It says in the book of Enoch that the fallen angels showed the men of earth secrets, the art of weapon making. That implies technology. Technology that at the time had not been developed here on earth. Think of what they might be able to dazzle us with now! And the similarity of trading knowledge for access to the woman, to me this is no coincidence. They are back because they know that their time is short here."

Uri rose from his chair, paced a few times, and argued, "I don't agree. We have been through this over and over again . . . a dog who chases his tail . . . No? You argue always from spiritual and I from secular . . . I'm thinking no one really knows.

But that is why we are involved in the research. We agree something is going on. We have different answers to what . . . but we believe. It seems that some governments in the world are not telling everything they know, to keep these things from their citizens. But we believe women and men are being abducted, and disks are seen by people everywhere."

Mac's mind was full of new and unsettling ideas. He needed a break from the conversation. "Do you have a rest room?" he asked.

"Yes, of course," Elisha answered. "And while you're gone I'll fix some coffee."

Mac closed the bathroom door. *What have you gotten yourself into?* he thought, staring at his reflection in the mirror.

Minutes later he made his way back into the living room. The room was empty, and Mac settled back down in his chair. He could smell the coffee and looked forward to drinking a cup.

A short while later Elisha returned, followed by Uri, who held a tray cautiously in front of him.

Mac smiled as he watched Uri pick his way carefully down the single step into the living room and set the tray on a small table. *Not something he does every day,* Mac thought.

"Here, this will be good for you," Elisha said merrily as he poured the coffee from an old ivory-colored pitcher.

Mac quickly rose from his seat and accepted the cup.

"Have a piece of cake," Elisha insisted.

"Thanks," Mac said as he eagerly reached for a piece of cake.

"Did Roswell fax you a copy of the article I wrote?" Mac asked. He took a bite of cake. Spice. Delicious.

"Yes, we both read it," Uri replied.

He took a sip of coffee, washed the cake down, and said, "The woman I wrote about in the article was convinced that something had happened to her. To be specific, she believed aliens had impregnated her. She embraced this to such a degree that she had to be confined to a mental hospital and placed under surveillance. Whatever it was she went through left her disabled and confused. If she was abducted then whoever did this is"—and he nodded toward Elisha—"malevolent. The woman's life was ruined. She was violated in every possible way. That, to me, is evil. Whoever, or whatever, is responsible for her debilitated state, their actions are evil, for crying out loud."

The room grew quiet. Mac realized that Elisha and Uri were staring at him.

"Mac, Roswell also gave us a briefing packet on you . . . and your father," Elisha said softly.

Mac bit his lower lip, balled his fingers into a fist, and stared at Elisha, whose face was poised with patience and passivity.

Mac glanced toward the bookshelves, let out his breath slowly, and said, "All right. All right. What do you guys want to know?"

"Not anything you don't want to tell us," Elisha said gently, "but Roswell informed us that your father was at the 1947 crash in New Mexico, and that he was one of the commanding officers responsible for the retrieval of the craft."

"And the bodies," Uri interjected.

"Yeah. He was there. And being there is what probably got him murdered too," Mac answered.

"You know, of course, that Roswell knew him?" Elisha asked.

"Yeah. That's what he said."

"The only difference between your father and Roswell is that Roswell had the presence of mind to keep his feelings and opinions to himself," Elisha said. "When the military or government covered everything up, he went along with what they instructed him to do. He obeyed orders. This enabled him to wait and climb the ranks until he was in a position to do something."

Mac closed his eyes and muttered, "My father thought that his life might be in danger. He wrote a letter, hired an attorney, and instructed him to keep it until my eighteenth birthday. My mother apparently knew nothing about it. I assumed afterward that he was afraid they might go after her too."

"What did it say? Do you feel you can tell us?" Elisha asked.

Mac straightened himself in his chair, looked at Elisha and Uri, then said, "What I read really, really scared me. The letter was written a few days after my father's initial contact with the aliens at Roswell. It was lucid, desperately lucid, like he was obsessed with archiving his thoughts and feelings so he wouldn't forget them. In it he said he couldn't believe our government would deliberately hide the knowledge of the existence of extraterrestrial life. That realization—that life did exist on other planets—shattered everything my father believed in. God, family, country . . . everything."

"Did he say anything else?" Uri asked.

"Yes. He said that the military created a cover-up story and may have murdered some of its own citizens to keep the truth hidden from the public. He also plainly stated that he was afraid for his life because of his involvement. Reading it made me wonder whether he was murdered by his own government, but I didn't want to know anymore. It was just too crazy, too painful, and I was too young to deal with it, so I buried it and just tried to forget it. Until now."

"Did he talk about the debris field?" Elisha asked.

Mac grew quiet and looked at Elisha, wanting to trust him, wanting to confide in him. Elisha's gaze never wavered. Mac wondered what he saw in Elisha's eyes. *Is it peace? Is it assurance? What makes this old Jewish scholar tick?*

Mac nodded his head a few times, prefacing his response. "He wrote about handling sections of the disk or whatever it was. He also saved a piece."

Uri's mouth dropped and Elisha smiled.

"Do you still have it?" Elisha asked softly.

"Yeah."

"Does any one else know?" Uri asked.

Mac shook his head. "No one. Not even my wife . . . ex-wife."

"Where is it?" Uri pressed.

"In a safe deposit box."

"What does it look like?" Uri asked, his voice not able to conceal his excitement.

"Sort of like aluminum foil. It's about eight by ten inches. I have it in the original manila envelope my dad left me along with the letter. The odd thing about it is that when you roll it into a ball, it unravels itself and is perfectly smooth again. Not a wrinkle or crease. And you can't tear it or burn it."

Uri whistled lightly between his teeth and asked, "When was the last time you looked at it?"

"It's been a while. A couple of years anyway. I try not to think about it. I've never been able to believe most of this—it's always been too incredible. Dragging it all up creates a lot of very unpleasant memories. I believe that my father's involvement with UFOs, or whatever they are, led to his murder."

There was a brief silence, then Uri said, "We believe that the aliens are accelerating whatever their mission is here. With the increase in UFO sightings, abductions, cattle mutilations—"

"Cattle mutilations?" Mac interrupted.

"Cows are found with certain parts of their anatomy removed," Elisha explained.

"So?" Mac shrugged.

"The incisions are so very precise, like that of a laser," Uri added.

"And what is removed is, to say the least, bizarre," Elisha said. "Eyes, reproductive organs, tongues. And the animal is drained completely of blood."

Mac nodded. "I heard something about that a few years back, when I was still a reporter, but dismissed it as sensationalism run amuck."

"We have some pictures and good documentation," Uri said. "But we are feeling that all of this is adding up to something."

"And what do you think is about to happen?" Mac asked.

Uri looked at Elisha, deferring Mac's question to his grandfather.

Elisha looked at the photo of the UFO on the wall, then turned to Mac and said softly, "I call it the 'The Great Deception'—an unholy intermingling between the fallen angels and the women of earth. Of course, part of the deception is that they pose as beings from other worlds."

"But why? For what purpose?" Mac asked.

Elisha frowned, then said slowly, "To deceive men . . . because they know their time is short."

"That's it? Just to deceive us?"

"In the book of Thessalonians—"

"What book?" Mac asked.

"Thessalonians is a letter written by Paul the apostle and is found in the New Testament," Elisha instructed. "Paul says in Second Thessalonians 2 verses 9 and 10: 'The coming of the lawless one will be in accordance with the work of Satan displayed in all kinds of counterfeit miracles, signs and wonders, and in every sort of evil that deceives those who are perishing.'"

"What does that mean?" Mac asked.

"It means that the emergence of UFOs and aliens might be setting the stage for the lawless one . . . the Antichrist. I believe the Antichrist will somehow have an alien connection. Perhaps they will aid him in counterfeit miracles as the passage describes. It seems they have already deceived many. There are those who believe they are here to usher mankind into a golden age. It is a last attempt to seduce the human race into believing the lie that there *is* another god besides the one of the Bible. That is why I call it the Great Deception."

Mac nodded. Elisha had given him much to absorb. Perhaps too much.

11

＊◯＊

Mac spent the rest of the day delving more into the UFO phenomena and would have continued into the night had it not been for Rebecca's phone call to Uri reminding him that dinner was to be served in half an hour.

Mac enjoyed another delicious meal with Uri's family. Then, still feeling some of the effects of jet lag, he excused himself and went off to bed. The next morning, though, he awoke eager to explore and learn more. After taking a shower and dressing, he pulled out his laptop to do some work. First he recorded the facts that he'd learned. Then, pulling up a new file, he began a journal to explore his feelings.

June 4

I find myself in the ancient city of Jerusalem. Upon my arrival here I was shown an artifact underneath the Temple Mount that astounded me—the remains of a massive skeleton well over ten feet sealed for centuries in a hidden room. Dr. BenHassen (see c:/EBH) believes that the skeleton is that of the Nephilim (see c:/NEPH). I cannot imagine coming face to face with such a creature. Dr. BenHassen has hired a lab to test the DNA of the bones. Through this I have been introduced to the disparate theories of "Fallen Angels Versus Friendly Aliens" as an explanation to the UFO phenomena. It is at best unsettling, and given what happened to my father, downright terrifying.

Moments after seeing the skeleton I began to feel tense and apprehensive, as if something wicked was coming. What an odd sensation. It is a physical feeling, a queasiness in my stomach, a sudden tightness of my neck muscles. But what is there to fear?

Watching Uri's kids here, seeing him interact with them, makes me realize how I miss my own children. And if I'm honest, Maggie too. I wonder how involved she is with Cranston. Why should this matter? After all, we are divorced. But somehow it does.

Then there's Laura, the woman with the green eyes at the airport, supposedly sent by Roswell. I find myself wondering what it would be like to see her again.

Today Uri and I will go to get the test results of the DNA. This should be interesting. DNA of what? An ancient extraterrestrial or a demonic hybrid? Both seem equally absurd.

"Breakfast!" Rebecca called, knocking at his bedroom door.

"I'll be right there," Mac said.

Mac saved his work, then shut down the computer and headed out for breakfast. The meal was a hurried affair, with both Mac and Uri eager to get back to their work.

"Let's go," Uri said, pushing back his chair.

"Okay." Mac grabbed one last piece of toast and followed Uri out the door.

"Where are we going?" Mac asked Uri as they walked down the steps of Uri's townhouse.

"To Dr. Fineberg's lab. He is heading up the DNA testing on the bones from the sarcophagus, trying to determine if there's anything abnormal. I'm thinking he is not going to see anything," Uri answered. He unlocked the van and they got in.

"So you don't agree with your grandfather's theory about the origin of the bones being attributed to fallen angels?" Mac said, as the van swerved onto the street.

"You know what? To me, his theory is legend, fables handed down from one generation to another. Each time the story is told, someone adds to it. So there were giants . . . I think what the lab will find is that this is a freak of nature. An overactive pituitary gland. There is nothing to it."

"What if they find something else?" Mac asked.

"If that happens, then I will walk across the bridge."

"You mean cross that bridge when you come to it," Mac corrected, and tried unsuccessfully to conceal his smile.

"Oh, thank you . . . cross that bridge . . ." Uri repeated.

"Your grandfather seems fairly confident that the DNA testing will produce the evidence he is looking for," Mac pressed.

Uri frowned. "I love grandfather, but he is an old man and has been through a lot. He is from the old school. I am a Sabra."

"A Sabra?"

"An Israeli-born and educated Jew. I have lived here all my life. I see the world in a modern way. This is the difference between grandfather and me. He is . . ." He groped for the word and finally said, "Superstitious."

"Because he believes in the stories from the Bible?"

"The Bible," he scoffed. "Where was the God of the Bible in the concentration camps of Europe? Grandfather is much different because of the war and what he has been through. Who is what?" Uri threw both hands in the air. "I only know for me that I am Israeli, a Sabra. This is my country. My land.

Land of my ancestors. We will never be driven out again! I believe what I can see. What my hands can touch!"

They drove for a while in silence, and Mac was content to observe the complexities of everyday life in Jerusalem. Arabs, soldiers, children, and veiled women shared the crowded streets. An ancient, bent Hasidic Jew in a worn beaver hat prayed silently on a corner. Young boys raced through the traffic on bicycles while young Jewish women, looking much like their Western counterparts, walked about in tight jeans and makeup. A man with bowed legs and a faded red fez crowning his head stood in a doorway smoking a handmade cigarette. And of course everywhere tourists, mostly Americans, with cameras dangling from their necks and tour maps protruding from their fanny packs, pockets, or purses.

They drove to a modern section of the town in which office buildings rose several stories overhead.

"Dr. Fineberg's lab is here," Uri said, nodding toward one of the buildings.

They had trouble finding a parking place and finally parked several blocks from the lab. As they walked to the lab, the sun climbed rapidly in the sky and the temperature corresponded accordingly, causing Mac to break into a light sweat.

They entered the building and rode the elevator to the fourth floor.

"This way," Uri said as they walked down the plush carpeted hallway.

They opened one of the doors in the corridor and entered a small, sterile-looking anteroom. Except for a large painting of the double helix, or DNA spiral, in pulsating reds and blues on the wall, the room held no other furnishings.

"Interesting," Mac commented, as they walked past the painting, through a doorway, and into a large laboratory where two men and a woman were busy running different experiments. Computers and an array of sophisticated equipment lined the walls and sat atop benches and tables.

A short, stocky young Israeli woman walked over and greeted them.

Mac caught the habitual *shalom* and after a brief, incomprehensible dialogue with Uri, she led them into an adjoining office, which Mac assumed was Dr. Fineberg's.

"He'll be with us soon. He's looking at data," Uri informed him.

They sat down and Mac surveyed his surroundings. Several educational degrees were displayed in brushed aluminum frames. An oversize black and white photograph of Masada was suspended directly behind the blue-colored glass desk. File cabinets and a well supplied library, filled mostly with medical books and journals, stood opposite a row of tinted, plate glass windows, through which the morning sun streaked in.

"Do you know what DNA is?" Uri asked.

"Not really ... Just what I write in the papers," Mac replied, the sarcasm of which was lost on Uri.

"DNA is the building block of life that ascended from primordial soup millions of years ago. Without it, life wouldn't exist." He rattled off the statement like a litany.

Before Mac could respond, the door opened and Dr. Fineberg entered his office.

Mac and Uri rose to greet Fineberg.

"Dr. Fineberg, this is Art MacKenzie, the American my grandfather told you about."

"I am pleased to make your acquaintance," Fineberg said, in a very slow, thick accent. "Please, gentlemen, sit down. Make yourselves com-for-ta-ble," he said, deliberately accenting each syllable carefully.

Fineberg walked behind his desk and sat down, crossing one long thin leg atop the other, while his hands twitched nervously on the arms of the oversize chair.

"How is the testing?" Uri asked.

"Well, as I informed you last week, we ran the tests and we wanted to make sure before com-mit-ting ourselves to their results. So I had them run again. Let me preface what I want to tell you by saying that there is less than two percent difference between the DNA of a monkey and that of a hu-man be-ing." He paused for effect.

"Really? Less than two percent?" Mac asked.

Fineberg nodded. "Yes, that is correct. Well, when we ran the tests the first time and discovered some great anomalies, we didn't know what to think. So we ran them again, to be certain of the results."

"What did you discover?" Uri asked.

"I want you to come into the lab and see for yourself," Fineberg suggested.

The three men left the office and went into the lab.

"This is Moishe," Fineberg said, introducing one of his lab assistants. "He has been working on the DNA samples taken from the sarcophagus."

Moishe smiled pleasantly, then stated, "The samples, the bones, are in remarkable condition considering they are over three thousand years old."

"That fits the time line that Elisha established for the Israelites' conquest of Canaan," Uri commented.

"Are you certain of the dating?" Mac asked.

"We could be off by five hundred years either way," Fineberg added. "But there is more." And he motioned to Moishe.

"Yes, this part is very interesting. Whoever this DNA belonged to, wherever this came from . . . the test shows that this is not entirely a human being. It is something different . . . something we have never seen, perhaps a hybrid of some sort."

Mac frowned. "What's so different?"

"Look here at the light box," Moishe said, and pointed to the wall.

Mac watched as Moishe slipped what looked like a large piece of film over the box and then switched on the light.

"It's like an X ray, isn't it?" Mac asked.

"Very much so," Fineberg replied.

"You see that?" Moishe pointed to the film.

"Yeah, but what am I looking at?" Mac asked.

"That is the DNA from the sample. From the sarcophagus. It is not complete," Moishe said.

"It is frag-men-ted," Fineberg added.

"You see the four lanes that begin to go down to the bottom of the slide, that look like the rungs of a ladder?" Moishe asked.

"Yeah, but there are rungs missing," Mac replied

"Good, you noticed. Now look," Moishe instructed as he switched slides.

Mac looked closely at the slide. "The ladder goes to the bottom of the slide . . . it continues. The rungs aren't broken."

"This slide is what my DNA looks like," Moishe explained.

"It's our control sample," Fineberg added.

Moishe switched the slides again and put the sample from the sarcophagus back on the light box.

Mac scrutinized it. "Why doesn't the pattern go to the bottom like the control model?" he asked.

Fineberg smiled thinly. "We think there is an undiscovered foreign or ex-ot-ic nucleotide."

"Which creates an exotic pair of nucleotide," Moishe added. "We ran this three times using a dideoxy sequencing gel. This should have allowed us to separate the different DNA according to size."

"And what happened?" Mac asked.

"The control sample sequenced, but the sar-coph-a-gus sample did not," Fineberg said.

Moishe pointed to the slide and stated emphatically, "It won't sequence."

"So why doesn't it sequence?" Mac asked.

"As I said, it must have a different nucleotide or perhaps a defective one," Fineberg stated.

"We've never seen anything like it," Moishe exclaimed.

"Yes, it is very much an anomaly," Fineberg agreed. "But there is more, we did something else to it." And he motioned for Moishe to continue.

Moishe gestured toward the slide. "We cut the DNA into individual nucleotides and analyzed it by high sensitivity chromatic graphic methods. And we discovered two unknown peaks in the readout."

"So we analyzed that by mass spectrometry," Fineberg said.

"What happened?" Uri asked.

"It differs significantly with all known nucleotides," Moishe said.

"It doesn't match up with any of the four known nucleotides," Fineberg agreed.

"So what is it?" Mac asked impatiently, wanting the bottom line.

"We're not certain," Moishe replied. "With what we know about DNA, it is so different . . . Nothing that has its origins on this planet has a fifth nucleotide . . ."

"Nothing that grows and reproduces," Fineberg said. "Simply put, this is a different life-form, and the implications of that discovery are staggering."

"Could there be extraterrestrial connection?" Uri asked excitedly.

"Extra-ter-res-tri-al?" Fineberg repeated.

"Something from another planet or solar system," Uri said.

Fineberg adjusted the glasses on the bridge of his nose, sucked on his cheeks, and replied, "Yes, yes, I know, but how can I possibly tell if it was? I have nothing to compare it to!"

"Children and animals born in and around Chernobyl, where the radioactive fallout from the reactor is very great, have chromosomes and genes that are altered," Moishe offered as an explanation.

"But not a fifth nucleotide," Fineberg countered.

"Would that account for the enormous size of the skeleton?" Mac asked.

Fineberg looked doubtful. "The size could be attributed to many different factors. But yes, size certainly could be affected."

"How could a fifth nucleotide happen?" Mac asked.

Fineberg shook his head, "I don't know . . . As Uri suggests, a commingling with another life-form . . . but . . ."

"Like an interbreeding . . . with something that originated outside our solar system?" Mac asked.

"It is very likely . . ."

"I'm thinking we need to tell Elisha about this. He will be jumping by the news," Uri said. "He is waiting at the Rabbinical Tunnel."

"Yes, Elisha should see this for himself," Fineberg agreed.

Mac looked again at the slide and marveled, realizing he was looking at something that might not be entirely from this earth.

The hair raised on the back of his neck. "Nephilim," he mumbled as he stared at the slide.

12

＊◉＊

Uri was the first to see the roadblock that lay directly ahead. It consisted of two Israeli soldiers who'd parked their jeep so that it blocked the oncoming lane of the road. The soldiers' Uzis hung loosely from their shoulders. One leaned against the jeep and smoked a cigarette while the other listened impassively to the pleas of each new motorist as to why they should be allowed past the blockade.

"Something is happening in the Old City," Uri said, as he eased the van up close to the bumper of a faded station wagon six cars back from the blockade.

"What's going on?" Mac asked.

"The Palestinians! Who else," he said.

"This happen often?"

"Yes, but I'm not getting too excited."

The van inched forward.

Mac watched a battered VW turn around at the blockade. The angry face of an Arab driver glared at him as he gassed the ancient car and passed by.

"Do you think we'll get through?" Mac asked.

"I have high security clearance; we should be going through," Uri replied confidently.

A short time later Mac reported, "That's five for five. The guy's not letting anybody past."

"We will see," Uri said, as he slowly pulled the van up to the soldier and addressed him in Hebrew. He flipped open his wallet, exposed his I.D., and held it out the window. The soldier leaned forward and examined it without touching it.

The man looked at it, then at Uri. He suddenly snapped to attention and saluted. Uri returned the salute. The guard spoke again and pointed toward the Old City.

Uri put the van in gear and rolled past the roadblock.

"What did he say was going on?" Mac asked, impressed by Uri's clout.

"There are Palestinians at the steps to the Dome of the Rock."

"Are they rioting?"

"No, but the soldier said things are getting out of hand soon."

"Oh." Mac looked out the window at the nearly deserted streets. "Why did he salute you?"

"Special card from the Prime Minister's office. It enables Grandfather and me to go almost anywhere in Israel because of our involvement with National Antiquities. There is also an insignia on the card, telling that I served in the thirty-first paratroop brigade."

Mac turned to get a better look at Uri. "Did you see much action?"

Uri's face remained expressionless. Without taking his eyes off the road he answered, "Enough of action. I was in the War of Atonement in '73."

"Oh?" Mac asked, hoping for more.

Uri ignored him.

The van rolled by a shop, and Mac saw a short rotund man in a fez hastily rolling up the awning. Uri continued, "One thing is for certain."

"What's that?"

"If the Arabs have a chance, they will attack again. They say peace for land, but those of us who know don't believe this. To the Arab there can never be peace as long as a single Jew remains in the land. One day they war against us again . . . Now look!" He pointed out the front window.

A quarter mile away, Mac saw a crowd of several hundred men converging near the steps leading to the Muslim shrine, the Dome of the Rock. Fifty feet from them a line of Israeli military personnel in riot gear prevented the mob from moving further toward the Dome.

Mac saw one of the protesters pick up a rock and hurl it at the line of soldiers. It bounced harmlessly off one of the clear plastic shields with which each soldier faced the rioters.

"This will go on for a while. Then one side has enough, and the violence will begin," Uri stated. He slowed the van to a crawl while he surveyed the crowd. "I'm thinking it's good to get out of here. We can enter the Rabbinical Tunnel from the other side near the Western Wall."

A short distance away, Uri pulled the van up to the mouth of a small side street that was not wide enough to drive into. He parked so close to the crumbling stone of an ancient building that Mac had to climb out on Uri's side to exit the van. Uri double-checked the locks.

They walked quickly down the street, hoping to go around the impending riot. Doors and windows were shuttered and barred. Somewhere in one of the closed shops a crackling radio playing Arabic music was suddenly turned off.

In the distance Mac heard the roar of the crowd. *Almost like a football game,* he thought.

An old man with bowing knees, an unshaven face, and a partially unraveled turban hurried by on the opposite side of the street.

Mac could feel the tension in the air. He sensed that something unpredictable, ominous, shifting, and volatile was about to occur.

They came to the end of the street and turned the corner. To the left they could see the gold dome of the second holiest sight in the Muslim world. They heard a rise from the crowd, although from their vantage point they couldn't see what was responsible for it.

A stone wall, perhaps four feet high, ran on the left side of the street and followed the curve of the road as it turned away from the Temple Mount.

"We will go over here," Uri said, as he swung his leg over the wall, sat for a moment, then pushed away. He dropped twelve feet to the street below him and landed on the balls of his feet in a balanced crouch.

Mac followed and sat on the wall. He turned around and lowered himself so that his hands held onto the ledge while his body stretched its full six feet along the rough stones. He pushed out with his feet and fell the remaining distance. He landed, lost his balance, and fell backward.

"Pretty good," Uri said, and offered him a hand.

"Right," Mac said sarcastically, as he grabbed Uri's hand. He got up, brushed the hair from his forehead, and dusted himself off.

Across a large square about a hundred yards away was the entrance to the Rabbinical Tunnel. Mac counted ten sentries guarding the entrance. They were alert and braced for trouble. A sudden cry from the crowd distracted the sentries. They turned as one in the direction of the Dome of the Rock.

"Let's go, quick," Uri said, starting off at a slight trot. Mac followed close behind. At about fifty feet from the entrance, Uri stopped and waved. He was recognized, and a few of the guards waved back. They quickly walked the remaining distance to the mouth of the tunnel.

Uri talked with the captain of the guard about what Mac assumed was the massing of the Palestinians around the Dome. The soldiers were tense with anticipation. They were outfitted in riot gear and, according to Uri, had rubber bullets in their guns. A shortwave radio blared to life. One of the men picked up the receiver and talked into it.

"Let's go. We will be all right in there no matter what happens," Uri said, as he walked into the tunnel.

As they entered, the noise from the crowd suddenly ceased. Mac welcomed the silence. He hadn't realized how tense he was. He rubbed the back of his neck and rolled his head a few times to loosen up.

"It gets to you," Uri said knowingly. "It comes up on you and you get tense . . . You know what? I've lived with it almost every day of my life." He continued walking down the tunnel a few steps ahead of Mac.

They came to the plywood barrier, and Uri and the soldier stationed there exchanged greetings. Mac nodded and mumbled an awkward, "Shalom."

Mac noticed Elisha's electric cart parked close to the entrance. It was fitted with a small trailer used to haul equipment to different sections of the tunnel.

They entered the room. There they found Elisha seated on the same crate as two days before. He oversaw the work of two students as they painstakingly removed bits of debris from the interior of the sarcophagus. Next to the sarcophagus was a large wooden crate with packing material spilling over its sides. Two powerful banks of lights that ran on batteries illuminated the room. A video camera rested on a tripod at the foot of the sarcophagus.

"Shalom, shalom, Grandfather," Uri said, as he embraced the elder BenHassen.

"Shalom. Uri, look what we found as we were preparing to move the skeleton," Elisha said, his eyes bright with excitement. "It was underneath the ribcage. No wonder we've never seen it before." He held up a large stone spearhead. "Vivian discovered it," Elisha continued, introducing the student.

The young woman smiled at Dr. BenHassen and quickly returned to her work.

Uri took the spearhead and felt the weight of it in his hands, then passed it to Mac.

"Put muscle on this skeleton of bone and dress that in armor and I believe you would have a terrifying sight. Imagine him throwing that at you," Elisha said, pointing to the spearhead that Mac held.

"I hope he wasn't too accurate," Mac joked as he handed the spearhead back to Elisha.

"What did you discover at Dr. Fineberg's?" Elisha asked.

Uri brushed his mustache down on his upper lip. "Something is different with the DNA."

"What specifically?" Elisha asked, unable to contain his excitement.

Uri smiled at his grandfather and said, "It has a fifth nucleotide. He said nothing that has its origins on this planet has a fifth nucleotide."

"What does he mean by that?"

"He does not want to commit to anything, but no one in the lab has seen anything like this before."

Elisha pressed his lips together and slapped his thighs with the palms of his hands. "When will he know for certain?"

"Maybe by week's end," Uri stated.

Elisha turned the collar of his shirt up over his neck.

"You are cold?" Uri asked.

"Yes, yes, but also excited. I must call Fineberg this afternoon. But now I want to leave. The dampness slowly works its way into my soul in this place. Let's go," Elisha said as he turned toward the entrance of the room. He stopped at the doorway and was about to say something to the students when he erupted in a coughing spasm which reverberated through the small room. He leaned against the wall to steady himself. Vivian and the other student stopped working and started to go to him.

Elisha held out his hand and shook his head. The coughing subsided, and he cleared his throat and spit on the floor.

"Excuse me," he sighed wearily. "I'm all right. Thank you . . . go back to work."

Uri came up next to him and helped him out of the room.

Elisha allowed his grandson to lead him to the electric cart, where he slumped onto the front seat. Uri assumed his position at the wheel while Mac sat in the rear of the cart. Uri maneuvered the cart through the passageway, and soon they were at the main entrance.

Mac heard the crowd. It sounded angrier now. The roar surged, then quieted slightly, then surged again, like a hellish choir. Uri talked to one of the guards, getting an update, while the elder BenHassen remained in the cart and listened to the seething crowd in the distance.

He looks weary and every bit of his seventy-eight years, Mac thought.

Uri finished, walked over to Mac, and said, "It's too far for my grandfather. We will get the van and come back for him. With all that's going on, it might be taking a while."

"He'll be all right here?" Mac asked.

"I'll be fine," Elisha reassured them. "Remember I fought in the War of Independence . . . I'm used to it."

The crowd roared louder and the cluster of soldiers and men looked toward the Dome. Mac noticed that the soldiers seemed more on edge than when they first arrived.

"We better go now," Uri said.

Mac waved to Elisha and started across the square. Uri walked after him but suddenly turned around and went back to Elisha. The two men conversed for a minute, then Uri started across the square again.

"We must hurry," Uri called.

Mac was about halfway across the open space when the noise from the crowd crescendoed. He heard a few gunshots. He froze where he stood and listened. More gunshots followed by a cacophony of shouts and screams. The riot had begun.

He heard men running. Frantic running, a stampede, and it grew louder.

"They're coming!" Uri yelled from behind him. "Quick!" He ran toward the soldiers at the entrance of the Rabbinical Tunnel.

Mac hesitated for a moment, then began to run for the wall at the other side of the square.

"No! No!" he heard Uri's voice scream.

Mac stopped and looked toward the Dome. White smoke drifted toward him in the hot afternoon air, misting his view of the golden edifice. His eyes darted toward the end of the square. The first man of the mob appeared and sprinted like a gazelle. He was followed by a second runner, then three more clustered tightly together, then came the rest of the pack. He watched as one man tripped, stumbled, and went down. The man directly behind tumbled over him. Two others tried to jump out of the way. One man succeeded and continued to run. The second collided with another, lost his footing, and fell screaming to the ground.

"Go out of there!" Uri yelled.

The fleeing mob of men fanned out in the square. Mac realized he would never make it back to where Uri and Elisha were. The thought chilled him. He looked at the place where he had jumped from the wall and realized it was too far away. He was trapped. With no other choice he began to run in the same direction as the pack.

Something whizzed over his head as he ran. *A bullet!*

A Palestinian ran next to him. The man glared at him, baring his black crooked teeth. He yelled something and lashed out at him with his fist. The punch grazed off Mac's shoulder. He stumbled, barely caught himself, and continued to run.

Something whistled overhead, landed in front of him, and then exploded, spewing a white gas over the square. Mac's eyes began to burn and tear. His lungs felt like a bomb went off in them, and he started to choke. *It's tear gas,* he thought, as someone bumped him from behind.

Another canister exploded to his right. He pulled his shirt out of his pants and held it over his face as he ran.

The pack left the square and ran wildly down a narrow street. Mac squinted through his tears and saw a doorway to the left of him. He tried to get over to it, but a man to his left blocked his way. A little further ahead he saw another doorway. He remembered his freeway trick, slowed his pace, ducked in behind the man, and dove for the doorway. He slammed into the rough wooden door and pressed his body close to it as the pack of men ran by.

He heard the sound of boot-shod feet running toward him. *Thank God, the soldiers,* he thought and relaxed, glad the ordeal was over. He turned his head and tried to see, but his vision was still blurred.

Powerful arms grabbed him from both sides, jacked him up against the door, and knocked the wind out of him.

Something thudded next to his head. A soldier screamed at him. Mac felt the blast of the man's hot breath as saliva sprayed his cheeks. The soldier grabbed Mac by the hair and slammed his head against the door. Something exploded on the wood next to his face. A sharp splinter tore into Mac's neck. *He's got a blackjack . . . he's going to split my head open!* he thought. "American, I'm an American," he yelled.

The soldier screamed in Mac's face and brought the blackjack down against the door panel.

"American . . . American," Mac screamed.

Mac heard someone yelling. It was Uri. *Thank God,* Mac thought.

Still holding Mac by his hair, the soldier faced Uri, who managed to talk calmly to the soldier.

The man snarled a reply to Uri. He let go of Mac's head but then placed the tip of his blackjack on Mac's cheek. Mac's knees almost buckled and he felt like he was about to pass out. He forced his eyes open and looked at Uri, who continued to talk to the soldier. Uri took a step closer. The soldier lowered his blackjack and barked an order. The soldiers who pinned Mac to the door let him go. Uri took a few more steps toward Mac, reassuring the soldiers as he did.

The soldier with the blackjack curled his lips and shouted a final order. The three soldiers left and hurried down the street in the direction of the fleeing Palestinians.

"You all right?" Uri asked.

"Yeah . . ." Mac replied, as he rubbed his arms.

"Your neck is bleeding," Uri said, as he pointed to the spot.

Mac dabbed at the trickle of blood. "The guy was going to bust my head open," he said.

"He thought you were a Russian or Iraqi."

"An Iraqi?"

"He suspected you were one of the leaders. Lucky I got here when I did. Can you walk?"

"Yeah, I'm all right. My eyes are killing me."

"Tear gas. Don't rub it. Makes it worse. Are you sure you're all right?"

Mac squinted and looked at Uri. "Hey, thanks," he muttered.

Mac took a couple of steps out of the doorway. His legs were wobbly and his hands trembled. He opened and closed his fists a few times, trying to stop them from shaking. Slowly they headed back up the street.

As they entered the square, Mac saw Israeli military personnel everywhere. At the other end of the square five Palestinians lay facedown on the stone pavement. Soldiers with guns stood over them. The square was littered with fragments of clothing. A tear gas canister spurted a wisp of smoke.

They walked to the guardhouse at the entrance of the Rabbinical Tunnel.

"Is he hurt?" Elisha called out.

"I'm okay," Mac called back.

"One of the soldiers thought he was an Iraqi. One of the leaders," Uri said.

"Crusader blood." Elisha smiled wanly.

"Crusader blood?" Mac asked.

"You'd be surprised how much of it shows up in the Arab population," Elisha replied. "With your dark hair . . . and you were running from the soldiers . . . well?"

"I'll get the van and be coming back for you," Uri said as he left them.

Mac shuffled over to the guardhouse and collapsed on a rickety stool. He leaned back against the structure, closed his eyes, and let out a deep sigh. He felt a hand rest on his shoulder. He slowly opened his eyes and saw Dr. Elisha BenHassen standing next to him.

"Nothing just happens," the old man stated.

Mac frowned. "What do you mean?"

"Nothing *just* happens. Unseen forces were trying to destroy you . . . but a greater power prevented them from doing so."

"What are you trying to say?"

"Have you ever considered that God might be guiding you, protecting and separating you from the evil of this world? I don't believe that luck prevented you from getting hurt in the riot . . . The hand of God is upon you . . ."

In spite of his efforts to control them, Mac's hands trembled. He rubbed them together and stared at Elisha, not knowing what to say.

13

Mac spoke softly into a portable telephone while he leaned against a bookshelf in Dr. Elisha BenHassen's library. He faced a row of books, keeping his conversation from Elisha and Uri, who worked at the computers at the other end of the room.

"Maggie, the bullets went flying over my head, for crying out loud."

"This happened today? It's lucky you didn't get killed!" she said, the anger rising in her voice. "How would I have explained that to our children?"

Our children, Mac thought. For a moment he softened. Then, hiding behind sarcasm, he said, "Well, you don't have to explain a thing, because I'm still breathing."

"Come on, Mac, really . . . something horrible could have happened."

He was about to tell her about the soldier who almost clobbered him with the blackjack but figured she was upset enough. "Why so worried?"

There was silence on the phone, then she answered, "I am . . . about you . . . more than you think."

"Nice to know somebody cares."

"I've always cared . . . you know that."

Mac started to say something but stopped when he heard someone call, "Maggie?" in the background. There was no mistaking the voice of Jim Cranston.

He listened as Cranston called out, "Maggie, the food's getting cold."

"That's Cranston? He's having dinner with you?" Mac asked.

"And if he is, what business is that of yours?" she said.

"You're right, it's none of my business. Why don't you go. After all, the food is getting cold."

"Mac, it's not like—"

He cut her off. "Oh, come on, admit it, for crying out loud. You're in love with the guy. Just stop leading me on with all the phony 'I care' business."

"I wasn't lead—"

"What?" He pretended that someone was calling him away from the phone. "Hey, I have to go—I'm tying up the phone lines. Say hi to the kids."

"Mac, don't hang—"

"Okay. Bye. I'll call whenever." And he clicked the phone off.

Immediately he regretted what he'd done. *I'm an idiot,* he thought. He brushed his hair off his forehead, then rubbed the back of his neck as he stared with unfocused eyes at the row of books in front of him.

"I want a drink," he mumbled. "No, that's not exactly right, I want several of them." He sucked in his cheeks and looked over at Uri and Elisha.

I'm marooned with a couple of UFO nuts, he thought. He stared at the picture of the flying saucer across the room and snickered to himself. *Guess I'm along for the ride.*

He walked over to the worktable and pulled up a chair next to Elisha.

"Look at this, MacKenzie," Elisha said, pointing to the screen.

Mac pulled his chair closer. On the monitor were the corresponding names and stories of eyewitnesses involved in UFO sightings, abductions, and cattle mutilations.

"Here is a particularly interesting account," Elisha began as he highlighted and clicked the file open. "It is the testimony of a rancher who saw the debris field at the Roswell sight. A deathbed confession."

Mac leaned forward and scanned the article on the screen. "How many of these do you have?" he asked.

"More than we have time to be looking at," Uri answered, as he typed on his keyboard.

Mac read the article, then asked Elisha, "This guy kept all of this to himself for fifty years?"

"Yes. Even from his family. Your government, or what I believe is actually a splinter group, threatened him in the usual way." Elisha lowered his voice and said with mock gravity, "What you've seen is of great national security! If you say anything, you might be putting you and your family in the path of danger."

Mac nodded. "It echoes what my father said in his letter to me . . . about national security. I was afraid to talk about the Roswell crash. My father also warned me not to show the piece of wreckage from the saucer to anyone. Remember when I got this it had been years since his murder. I didn't know what to think. The truth was I didn't want to think about any of it at all."

"There are other witnesses from the Roswell site that have come forward. Are you interested in seeing another?" Elisha asked.

"Always Roswell," Mac said, not concealing his bitterness.

Elisha scrolled down and found the entry.

Mac read the testimony of another witness who had been stationed at Roswell and was a member of the 509th Bombing Group, the only atomic bombing group in the world at that time. He attested that he had seen the alien bodies after they had been retrieved from the crash site. The witness was still alive, only recently breaking his silence, due partly because others had come forward.

"Another wacko loose out there," he said, but inwardly the story made him feel connected to his father. He secretly hoped Elisha would show him more.

"You know what?" Uri said. "Much of what is coming from the witnesses fits other stories . . . even after fifty years."

"Roswell instructed me to show you this when I thought you'd be ready for it," Elisha stated as he typed a command on his keyboard.

Mac stared at the screen and read the title, "Extraterrestrial Entities and Technology, Recovery and Disposal." The date on the title page was 1950. Mac shook his head.

Elisha scrolled to the next page and Mac began to read.

"Lieutenant MacKenzie's contact . . ."

"Hey, this is about my father," Mac stammered.

"Yes, it is," Elisha said, and motioned that Mac should continue.

"Lieutenant MacKenzie's contact with the surviving extraterrestrial continues to be ongoing, beginning in July 1947 at the first point of contact. Communication appears to be in the form of mental telepathy. Lieutenant MacKenzie seems to have been chosen by the extraterrestrials as a liaison between their race and ours.

"The other survivor of the crash died shortly after its arrival at the 509th Bombing Group stationed at Roswell, New Mexico, bringing the total of bodies to five recovered. Four dead, one living.

"MacKenzie along with Lieutenant Nathan were the first officers at the crash site and supervised the handling of the then two live extraterrestrials. Unlike other Air Force personnel who shunned direct physical contact with the extraterrestrials, MacKenzie handled the two injured biological entities and personally lifted them into the transport. This may be the reason for the apparent selection of MacKenzie as a point of contact from the surviving extraterrestrial.

"MacKenzie, along with the extraterrestrial biological entity, or EBE, remains at Wright-Patterson for further study . . ."

Mac leaned back in his chair, took a deep breath, and said, "He mentioned some of that in his letter, but reading it like this . . . in an official report . . ."

"Sobering, isn't it?" Elisha said.

"That's an understatement," Mac replied.

Elisha's monitor flashing grabbed Mac's attention.

"Security breach," Elisha muttered. "Must be the Major."

A moment later a knock rang out from the front door. Elisha typed a command into his computer. The screen changed images, and Mac saw a man standing outside the front door.

"It is good to have surveillance," Elisha said. "A few years ago a close friend of mine was murdered."

Mac was caught off guard by the remark. "Oh?"

"My friend worked for the government. One evening, someone knocked on his door. My friend answered and was gunned down on the spot. Terrorists! They never captured those responsible." Elisha typed another command and the camera closed in the face of the caller. "Good. It's the Major."

Mac waited for an explanation.

"Uri, will you get it?" Elisha asked.

Uri nodded and left.

"We call him Major. A joke name. Officially he doesn't hold a rank, but he is high up in the Mossad, our secret service. He has brought us a video I want you to see."

"About?"

"You'll see."

Elisha went over to the bookcase and pressed a concealed button. The middle part of the bookcase opened, revealing a large television monitor behind it.

Uri and the Major entered. Mac's first impression was of a little Caesar. The major was a short, balding man with wide shoulders, a flat stomach, and a round face. Dark sunglasses concealed his eyes. He and Elisha embraced and kissed one another's cheeks.

Mac was introduced and while the obligatory minute of small talk commenced, Uri arranged the chairs in a semicircle facing the television monitor and dimmed the lights.

The men took their chairs and Uri clicked on the video.

"What you are about to see was taken less than six months ago. This is very much classified," the Major said, in a deep, heavily accented voice.

"He is doing me a favor," Elisha added.

The Major patted Elisha on his leg and chuckled. "Always another favor."

The video began. Mac looked at a blue screen for maybe five seconds. Then the screen burst with light and something streaked by. The film jiggled as the cameraman tried to keep the object in focus.

"This was taken from one of our jets at about twenty thousand feet. The copilot filmed this," the Major said.

The object slowed, then stopped and hovered in the air. The jet accelerated, gaining on its target.

"Now watch," the Major said.

The camera zoomed in on the object. Mac stared at the image. There was no mistaking what he saw. It was a silver disk. Mac could make out something that looked like portholes or windows in the upper section of the craft.

"For crying out loud," he exclaimed.

Something shot out from underneath the jet.

"What's that?" Mac yelled.

"It's a missile ... You'll find this interesting," the Major said.

Mac watched as the missile closed in on the object, leaving a vapor trail in its wake. At the point of impact the disk suddenly hopped straight up and the missile flew by harmlessly underneath it.

The jet closed on the target rapidly and fired another missile. Mac watched as the disk disappeared then reappeared slightly above its last location. The missile streaked by.

"Incredible," Uri muttered.

"Our plane is less than a half mile from the object and closing fast. Here is the best part," the Major announced.

Mac watched the disk turn at an angle and then level off. Suddenly it shot straight at the jet . . . on a collision course.

Mac held his breath. The disk accelerated so fast that it was hard to keep in the camera lens. At the last possible moment it veered and rocketed past the plane.

"That was too close," Uri said excitedly.

"Our pilot reports that the object missed his plane by less than a foot," the Major stated. "We calculate its speed at just over twenty thousand miles per hour."

"Unbelievable," Mac said. "And how does it jump like that?"

"We think it bends the space around it," the Major replied.

"Bends space?" Mac asked.

"We don't know how, but alien technology might do that. It would allow them to travel great distances quickly. From their world to ours."

"There is an American who says he worked for your government . . . He has claimed to be working on the propulsion system, trying to back engineer it, before he was let go," Uri added.

"So my government has been secretly involved in the back engineering of a . . ." Mac pointed to the picture of the disk on the wall.

"Roswell sent us information that one of the alien ships was apparently given to us for the purpose of back engineering," Uri said.

"What? A gift? Some sort of trade?" Mac asked, finding it hard to believe what he was hearing.

"Yes," Elisha said. "Roswell has suggested the possibility of aliens and American military personnel working side by side."

"There is testimony from abductees that they have seen what look like military personnel aboard the spacecraft, as they were being medically examined," Uri said. "We have some of their testimonies in our files."

"Unfortunately, no one sees the whole picture," the Major said seriously.

Elisha frowned and gestured toward his monitor. "But what is the part of the picture we do see? The picture I see is a sinister one. For instance, a case could be made linking some of the abductees with involvement in occult practices. The cattle mutilations are done deliberately, as if to send an ominous signal to us. Finally, when they make contact, the aliens claim to have genetically manipulated us thousands of years ago, which renders moot the creative act by a divine being. A concept which almost everyone on this planet, in spite of their religious differences, believes. No, I don't believe these are creatures from another world. I would propose instead, spirit beings from another dimension."

"Well, whatever they are, they don't seem to be going away, do they?" Mac observed.

"How do you account for the piece of material that MacKenzie's father gave him?" Uri asked.

"Spirit beings don't make flying saucers," the Major added.

"It is a mystery," Elisha agreed, "but if the book of Enoch is an accurate account of their arrival the first time, then we know that they dazzled men with their technology. Remember the account says they showed men the art of weapon making? No matter how primitive we may consider those weapons now, to the men living at the time it was a phenomenal leap forward. Think of the state of world affairs directly after World War II. The Cold War existed between the Soviets and the rest of the free world. The atomic bomb had been dropped at Nagasaki and Hiroshima, ushering in a new era of total annihilation on a global scale. Consider for a moment if one of the super powers had the technology we are talking about, alien or otherwise. What would they compromise in order to acquire it? What would they pay for that kind of power? What would they allow in order to get it?"

The Major cleared his throat and said, "Perhaps the aliens crashed the disks deliberately, knowing that we would bargain for their technology."

Elisha nodded. "A deliberate deception. It does fit a similar pattern. We have the historical record from the book of Enoch, accounting some sort of trade . . . access to the women for technology. As I have said before, the results of that union resulted in the Nephilim. The skeleton we have discovered may establish the authenticity of these abominations."

"The DNA testing at Fineberg's lab is showing something," Uri added.

"Yes, and if what he says is true—about a fifth pair of nucleotides—then we may have established a link," Elisha said.

"Maybe my father wasn't so crazy after all," Mac said quietly.

Elisha leaned slightly forward and said, "Remember much of this has been repressed for the last fifty years. Your father must have felt completely alone. He probably was afraid for you and your mother's life, not to mention his own."

"Did he ever say anything about the crash to you, other than what was in the letter?" Uri asked.

Mac thought for a moment, then said, "No, he kept everything to himself. I don't think my mother ever knew anything. She died before I got the letter."

Uri looked at his watch. "It's late. Rebecca is going to be mad. We should be now going."

"And tomorrow I must go to the remains of the Philistine city of Gath, by way of Masada," Elisha said, as he stretched his arms in front of him. "Mac, I think you would find Masada interesting. The ruins are exceptional."

"That sounds good. But what are you doing in Gath?" Mac asked.

"Goliath, the giant, was from the city of Gath," Elisha said. "The book of Numbers chapter 13 seems to indicate that there was again a commingling, or another outbreak if you will, between the fallen angels and the women of the earth, although it was limited to the land of Canaan. When the Israelites conquered the area, remnants of the Nephilim fled to the city of Gath. Goliath was probably a Nephilim. I'm going there to see if we can start a dig to unearth any more relics."

"Sounds fascinating. And I'd like to see Masada. I've heard a bit about it," Mac said.

"Good. My driver will pick you up at Uri's house at five-thirty tomorrow morning."

"That early?" Mac asked.

"To avoid the heat of the day," Uri explained as he got up.

"The Major and I have some unfinished business to attend to," Elisha said as he walked them to the front porch. "See you at five-thirty." He waved as Mac climbed into the van.

14

June 5

It is late at night and everyone at Uri BenHassen's house is asleep. I am sitting cross-legged on my bed with just my laptop as the only source of light in the otherwise dark room.

In looking back at the events of the day, I can hardly believe all that has transpired.

It seems the people of this land balance precariously on the edge of life and death. They stare into the abyss of uncertainty daily, relying on their leaders and military prowess to protect them and keep their enemies from driving them into the sea and annihilating them. The threat is ever present and because of it, people carry Uzis as casually as Londoners carry umbrellas.

I suppose I take being alive for granted. I think, probably like all men, that somehow I will live forever. Incredibly I could have been killed, or at least maimed in the riot today.

In the quiet of this borrowed child's bedroom, I can see the twisted, snarling face of the soldier glare at me like a mad dog. I can hear the thud of his black-jack slam against the door panel, barely missing my head.

It is the closest brush I have ever had with death. I joked to Maggie about the bullets flying over my head. But I realize anything could have happened. I could have been shot and been standing before my Maker instead of pushing keys on my laptop.

If Uri had not rushed to protect me, I'm sure the soldier would have hit me within the next minute or so. I could see him working up to it, losing patience. To him I was nothing but vermin, utterly dispensable, and certainly at that moment something much less than human in his eyes.

I have never been so completely helpless, my fate hanging on the whim of another.

The experience has had a very sobering effect on me. I don't mean from the standpoint of guzzling a bottle of Grand Marnier nightly. No, something deeper, even spiritual I suppose, is the word I am looking for.

Sobering, for I realize I am mortal, that my time here on this earth is limited and finite. Like my father and son, I too will die. I will leave this shell of a body and go where? To Jesus and heaven like I was taught as a child? Like I used to believe? I don't know.

Here in Israel, Jesus has become more real to me. I can almost see him walking the streets of the old city. Here is the place where Christianity began, and all because of an obscure carpenter's son, Jesus.

Jesus. I have blocked him out of my life since my son's death. I am angry with him for allowing the tragedy to happen in the first place. If that's what God is all about, why believe at all?

I used to be distracted by all the things life has to offer. Caught up, like everyone else I know, in acquiring more and getting ahead and being successful in my career. Now since Art died, I just feel dead to it all. Nothing matters.

Maggie is right—I have never been able to accept his death. It is so pointless. What has it accomplished? What has taking that little child's life, poised on the threshold of manhood, meant in the grand scheme of things?

Where is he now?

Does he exist?

Is he with Jesus or God, if they exist?

I would love to believe that.

I would love to hang my hat on that.

What peace and hope there would be if it were true.

But nobody knows. Not one person. It is, as I was taught, a matter of faith.

And right now I have no faith.

It is dead.

I am dead.

I am only going from one distraction to the next, and when the distraction ceases I find myself trying to escape the pain that surrounds my heart in a shroud of sorrow. There doesn't seem to be a way out of it . . .

The information that the BenHassens have filled me with since my arrival is very disturbing. In sifting through it, I am more inclined, however, to accept Elisha's idea that these may in fact be spirit beings. Although as Uri points out, it is difficult to imagine fallen angels building spacecraft.

Adding to the conundrum are the bones in the sarcophagus, or what might be the remains of the

Nephilim. (How bizarre! The offspring of an unholy union between fallen angels and earthly women.)

Sometimes I can't believe what I am hearing from the two of them. Inter-dimensional beings. Abductees. Cattle mutilations. Bending space.

Of course, most disturbing is knowing that my father was involved in something that happened in Roswell, New Mexico, fifty years ago, and he passed to me a souvenir of what he saw. Something now I wish I had never set eyes on.

I find myself being drawn into this crazy world of UFOs.

The BenHassens are consumed with the enigma of them. I believe my father's involvement with them led to his murder. The idea of little green men, or I should say gray men, is too much to believe. And yet I have my own father's letter telling me that is precisely what they are . . . little gray men. From where? I wonder.

Art MacKenzie
Jerusalem

15

✦ ◉ ✦

Jim Cranston sat at his desk, talking on the phone to "John," his contact at the Agency.

"Well, where is he?" Cranston asked impatiently.

"He's in Israel all right. We traced the call to a Dr. BenHassen, lives just outside of Jerusalem."

"Who?"

"BenHassen. He's an archaeologist, huh? Has a lot of connections in the government. Works for the Department of Antiquities. Apparently he has a recent find under the Temple Mount." Cranston heard the man sorting through papers. "Under the Temple Mount they found a sarcophagus."

"And?" Cranston asked.

"BenHassen found this, and somebody is making a big deal about it."

"Why would MacKenzie be associating himself with this man?" Cranston asked.

"I was hoping you might be able to help me on that, huh?" John said. "Here's what I know so far." More sorting of papers. "The guy was in a concentration camp during World War II. He immigrated to Israel in 1946. Fought in the War of Independence. He teaches at the university. He's a Jewish oddity."

"How so?" Cranston asked.

"His religion is listed as Christian. The guy converted from Judaism."

Cranston didn't reply.

"He makes frequent calls to the States," John said.

"To whom, MacKenzie?" Cranston asked.

"Not sure, I'm tracing it. If he contacts you, inform me immediately, huh? I've got to go. I'll call later."

The phone went dead.

Cranston hung up the phone and looked at the original Rothko abstract, illumined by a single spotlight from the cathedral ceiling overhead.

What's the connection? he thought as he played with the clipped ends of his mustache. *What's the importance of this sarcophagus under the Temple Mount, and what does it have to do with MacKenzie?*

He shrugged. Sometimes he wished he'd never gotten involved with the Agency, Westwood Medical Center, or any of this top-secret nonsense about extraterrestrials. But something—a reporter's curiosity, maybe, or the lure of power, or perhaps just the large sums of money the Agency paid him—kept him going.

Obviously MacKenzie's revealing article and subsequent trip to Israel were disturbing to Cranston's contact at the Agency. He'd never heard John sound so rattled.

He turned the whole thing over in his mind as he focused again on the Rothko painting. For a moment he enjoyed the deep red color that seemed to pulsate against the white wall.

* o *

John used a secured phone and dialed another number.

"It's me," he said.

There was no acknowledgment from the other end.

"You might find this interesting concerning Art MacKenzie." He waited for an answer and when none came he proceeded.

"He's the reporter who wrote the article on the Westwood Medical Center—"

"I know who he is," a low, gravelly voice interrupted.

"The article regarding the abductions," John continued. "It seems he's in Israel, and he's connected with a Dr. Ben-Hassen. What do you want me to do?"

"Where does MacKenzie live?" the voice demanded.

"Near Los Angeles. In Venice. He rents an apartment," Cranston replied.

"Anything there we need to look at while he's gone?"

"What do you mean?" John probed.

"You break in and check his apartment out," the voice ordered.

"National security," John chuckled.

"Of course," came the response. "Where national security is threatened, the law doesn't apply."

"Okay. Oh, there's one other thing."

"Yes?"

"This Dr. BenHassen apparently discovered a sarcophagus underneath the Temple Mount in Jerusalem."

"What was in it?"

"Don't know . . . yet."

"Get back to me if it turns out to be something that might concern us. In the meantime keep your eyes on MacKenzie." The receiver went dead.

John smacked the phone against the palm of his hand, making it sting.

He had never met the man he had just talked to. He knew him only by the name of Abaris and secretly . . . he feared him.

16

✦ ● ✦

Art MacKenzie sat in the rear seat of Elisha BenHassen's car while his driver motored south, toward the ruins of Masada. The barren, rugged desert, faintly illuminated in the rising sun, became even more desolate with each passing mile. Ahead a large body of water, looking more like a mirage, wavered uncertainly.

"The Dead Sea," Elisha said, as he rested his newspaper in his lap and gestured toward the front window of the car. "It has been called many names in the past, 'The Salt Sea,' 'The Sea of the Plain,' 'The East Sea.' The Arabs call it, 'The Sea of Lot.'" His face hinted at the beginnings of a smile as he said, "There is a fable that no bird can fly over it."

"But of course that's just a fable."

"Of course." Elisha chuckled. "It does, however, have some fascinatingly odd formations along its shores due to the minerals and salt content. If we had more time I would show you."

Mac saw the water reflecting the dull pink of the morning sky. It seemed to stretch endlessly in the distance.

"The Jordan River flows into it from the Sea of Galilee, north of us," Elisha explained. He returned to his paper again and with his head buried in it said, "There is quite a write-up about yesterday's riot in this morning's *Jerusalem Post*."

"Oh?" Mac replied. "How interesting. For once I'm being written about instead of the other way around."

Elisha laughed, then read aloud, "'About twenty Palestinians were arrested. One man was seriously hurt.'"

"It was almost twenty-one," Mac said.

"Yes, it could have been but for the hand of God's protection," Elisha said.

Mac avoided eye contact. Yesterday's encounter had shaken him more than he liked to admit. "Uri told me this kind of thing happens frequently."

Elisha put down his paper and peered at Mac through his wire-rim trifocals. "Yes, it does. One becomes hardened to it . . . unfortunately, it is our way of life. Children learn from a very early age to dive to the ground at the sound of gunfire."

Mac thought of the comfort and safety of his children and compared it with the war-savvy BenHassen children living in Israel. It was no place for the weak or faint of heart. Only the strong survived here. He began to have an inkling into the pervasive nationalism expressed by the BenHassens and other Israelis he had encountered.

Dr. BenHassen thumbed through another section of the paper, while Mac wove an introspective tapestry of thought that included the giant bones in the sarcophagus, flying saucers, Maggie, Cranston, and the deaths of his son and father.

Dr. BenHassen looked out the window and announced, "There it is, Masada." High above the desert floor lay the ruins of the ancient citadel. "What you see was once the stronghold of a handful of Jewish zealots who withstood the might of the Roman Tenth Legion for seven years before it fell. Even then the Roman victory was a Pyrrhic one."

"How's that?" Mac asked, as he peered through the window at the ruins.

"Rather than be taken alive by the Romans and sold into slavery, the Zealots chose mass suicide."

"They killed themselves?"

"As hard as it is to imagine, they did. Men, women, and children allowed themselves to be killed by members of their own household, rather then submit to capture and servitude."

"Fanatical," Mac replied, with disgust.

"Yes, it is," Elisha agreed. "A Jewish historian, Josephus, recounts the last days of the Jewish settlement. He writes in a lengthy commentary that Eleazar, who was the Zealots' leader, preferred, and I quote from memory, 'To let our wives die before they are abused and our children before they have tasted of slavery; and after we have slain them, let us bestow that glorious benefit upon one another mutually, and preserve ourselves in freedom, as an excellent funeral monument for us.'"

"Still, I can't imagine killing my own family in order to escape slavery, for crying out loud!" Mac retorted.

"It was more than just slavery, for those Jews it was a deeply religious decision. They chose death rather than bow their knee and honor Rome. They remained faithful to the God of their fathers."

Mac looked at the barren fortress with a growing curiosity.

"The Romans built a six-hundred-foot ramp in order to besiege it. They were just as determined as those inside," Elisha said, as he pointed to the ruins and debris of the ramp. "Titus, the Roman general that razed Jerusalem in A.D. 70 and slaughtered a million of its inhabitants, is responsible for the handiwork you see before you."

"It sounds like the Zealots were the Jim Jones of the first century," Mac replied, as he craned his neck to get a better view of the ramp.

"Not a fair comparison. Jones and his followers were *not* about to be cast into the horrors of slavery. There are some things worth dying for, you know." Elisha shot Mac a sidelong look.

Mac didn't answer. Instead he looked out the window at the ruins.

"There's a lot to explore here. You'll find Masada fascinating," Elisha said.

"I'm looking forward to it."

"I've arranged with one of the guides that works here to give you the king's tour. You will have preferential treatment, see the places the general public is not allowed to go."

They reached the foot of the ramp where there was a cable car in operation for those not inclined to hike up the steep rampart to the fortress itself. As Mac got out of the car, a blast of hot, arid air assaulted him. "It's heating up," he commented.

Elisha chuckled. "Now you understand why we left so early. It will be well over a hundred in less than two hours."

"Dr. BenHassen! Dr. BenHassen!" A large, burly man roughly the same age as Mac ran toward them.

"That is Chaim, an old student of mine from the university," Dr. BenHassen informed Mac.

Chaim reached them and immediately threw his arms around Elisha.

"Easy . . . easy," Elisha laughed as he embraced his former student. "This is Art MacKenzie, from the United States."

Mac shook hands.

"Shalom, Shalom, good to meet you." He flashed a smile at Mac.

Elisha said, "As you know, I am going to Gath to look at some recent work on the *tel* there. Mr. MacKenzie is excited to see the fortress firsthand, and by such an experienced guide."

Chaim's face brightened and he said enthusiastically, "The king's tour. You will see the places that we close to the public."

Mac nodded. "Sounds great."

"I'll return in a few hours. In the meantime, he's in your keeping," Elisha said.

"Don't worry, there are no Romans about. He's perfectly safe," Chaim assured him.

Elisha's driver helped him back to the car. The old scholar waved to Mac and Chaim as he settled in the rear seat.

"I'll see you in a few hours," he called through the open window as the car started to pull away.

An hour later, after Chaim's informative tour, Mac was high atop one of the crumbled walls of the Masada fortress. Below him the desert, barren and lifeless, fanned out in all directions. Horizontal stratas of red granite banded the huge rock formations around the fortress. In the horizon, the deep blue waters of the Dead Sea shimmered, contrasting with the desert that it intruded upon.

Mac was alone in the remains of a circular tower that had probably been used to store grain. He sat recklessly on the outer ledge of the tower wall and let his feet dangle below him as he surveyed the desolate country. The sun inched its way higher in the sky, and Mac could feel the warmth of it penetrate his shirt. A deep silence surrounded him. He could almost feel the stillness. Other than the privacy of his room at night, this was really the first time he had been alone since his arrival in Israel.

He shifted his weight on the wall and looked down again at the remains of the ramp the Romans had built. Closing his eyes, he imagined the siege taking place. Soldiers marching with their shields overhead, creating a turtle formation as they climbed the ramp. Drums thudding a cadence by which the soldiers paced their advance. Shouts and taunts from the Jews in their fortress.

For seven years the finest fighting force in the Western world sought to vanquish what to them were stubborn rebels and, to their consternation, were held at bay. And what spoils went to the victor? The bloated carcasses of women and children? It all seemed so pointless in the end.

He was restless.

Deep within, his emotions advanced like soldiers, demanding his attention. The image of the operating room leapt to mind. He saw his son lying on the table, the doctors frantically working.

"I can't handle this now," he said aloud and picked up a small stone that lay next to him on the wall and hurled it into the air. He watched as it fell silently into the space below him. He lost sight of it as it dwindled away to nothing.

The thought occurred to him, almost like it was placed there by someone else, *Maybe I should throw myself after it.* He looked below him. What was it that a friend of his had said about suicide? "Suicide is a permanent solution to a temporary problem."

But his son's death was not a temporary problem.

The familiar grief and anger welled up in him, and he banged his fist on the ruined wall. The sharp stone cut at his hand. But he didn't care. The cut paled beside the ache inside. The raw, festering wound that never healed.

He moved closer to the edge and put both hands on the ledge so he could push himself off. Drums thudded in his ears. The loneliness . . . Oh, God, the loneliness. He was empty and alone. Always alone.

A new thought entered his mind. He saw himself in church, at his son's funeral, and the minister was preaching. Maggie was next to him, her swollen eyes and tear-stained face turned away from him. Mac saw the polished walnut casket adorned with flowers directly beneath the pulpit. He heard the minister's voice soft in tone yet strong with conviction.

"For he triumphed over the grave when he rose again on the third day. He knows the sting of death. He knows the pain and hopelessness it brings. He knows the emptiness. He knows, and he will take your pain. He will carry it for you. He will heal as only he can. He will take your pain . . ."

Mac forced his eyes open and he saw the precipice below him. Instinctively he moved back. He swung his legs back around to the other side of the wall and stood, holding on to the ledge. He took a deep breath and wiped the sweat from his forehead.

"For crying out loud, I don't want to die," he said aloud.

He made his way to the ruins of what had been the center square of the fortress. Leaning up against the partially collapsed wall, he breathed deeply several times, as if doing so would exhale the pain. Exorcise it from him. He thought about the minister's words and mumbled, "If it were only that simple."

He stumbled down toward the ramp unsure of what he was doing, placing one foot ahead of the other mechanically.

Who can rescue me from this? he thought, as he hung his head and slowly continued to walk alone.

17

Four men in civilian clothes and carrying gym bags got out of a van parked just down the street from the building where Dr. Fineberg's office was located. Their leader, a short stocky man with broad shoulders and a balding head, led the other men quickly down the sidewalk and into the building.

The group entered the elevator. As the door closed and the elevator began its ascent, their leader pressed the stop button causing the elevator to jolt to a halt between the first and second floor. Without a word each man knelt on one knee and began to assemble the automatic weapons concealed in their gym bags. Each also donned a tight-fitting ski mask to conceal his face.

When they finished, their leader switched on the elevator. The men stood poised, in a fighting stance, as the elevator slowly made its ascent to the fourth floor.

It stopped and the doors slid back.

The leader cut the power so that they remained open. He looked down the hallway in both directions. Satisfied that they were alone, he stepped out of the elevator, signaled his companions, and walked quickly down the hall, followed closely by the others.

They came to the door of Dr. Fineberg's lab. The leader opened it and they moved into the anteroom. One man remained by the outer entrance poised and ready to apprehend anyone unlucky enough to enter the office.

The leader threw open the door and moved into the main lab. He walked to a lab bench that had various glass dishes and bottles stored on it. He took the barrel of his gun and smashed it into the glass, sending it exploding to the floor.

The three lab technicians, absorbed in their work, looked up when they heard the commotion.

"Get down on the floor!" the leader yelled, in heavily accented Hebrew.

For a moment no one moved. One woman and her two male coworkers stared dumbly at the intruders.

"I said get down!" the leader yelled, and fired a short burst from his gun.

Glass exploded across the room from him, a piece of which flew into the woman's cheek. She screamed. The other two lab technicians tried to go to her aid but were intercepted and forced to the floor. The woman touched her cheek, felt the blood, and became hysterical.

"Where's Fineberg?" the leader yelled.

* ○ *

Inside his office, Dr. Fineberg heard the shot, then the breaking of glass, then the scream. Fear filled him. His eyes darted around the windowless room. There was no place to go, nowhere to hide. And his people were in danger . . .

He heard the voice. "Where's Fineberg?" And he knew. They were after him.

He went to the door, his knees trembling. Opening it, he found himself face-to-face with three masked gunmen. The leader walked over to Fineberg, jammed the barrel of his gun under Fineberg's chin, and pushed him back into his office.

"Please, I have two children ... a wife," Fineberg whimpered.

"Shut up," the leader shouted, as he pushed the gun barrel further into Fineberg's chin. "Where are the bones?"

"What bones?" Fineberg replied.

"The bones that BenHassen gave you."

Fineberg stuttered, "In the lab. I think they're in the lab. I'll get them for you."

"And I want the testing results," the leader growled. He motioned with his gun for Fineberg to go.

Fineberg forced his legs to move and walked out of his office.

Ruth, his female assistant, had passed out and lay in a heap where the man had forced her to the floor. The other two lab technicians were prostrate but appeared to be alive.

Fineberg walked to the lab bench where he had done most of the DNA testing on the bones from the sarcophagus. "Here are the samples. We received only two small fragments."

The leader took them from Fineberg and slipped them into his coat pocket.

"And the data," he demanded gruffly.

"Well, it's in the computer. And backed up on disk. I ..."

"Pull up the file!" the leader ordered.

Fineberg went to the keyboard, scrolled to the file, and clicked it on.

The leader took a disk from his pocket and inserted it into the computer's A drive. Fineberg stared at the monitor as the information began to lose some of its letters.

"A virus," the leader said, "it will erase all of your files. Now, where are your disks?"

Fineberg hesitated, knowing there were years of research on his backup disks, hundreds of hours of data and hard-won information.

"What if I just give you the disks you're looking for?"

"Where are the disks?" the leader said, ignoring his plea. He pointed his gun barrel back into Fineberg's face.

"Over there in the file cabinet," Fineberg moaned, motioning to the metal cabinets across the room.

The leader walked over and opened the drawer. One of the other men joined him and withdrew a plastic bottle from his bag and squirted its contents into the file drawer. A horrible smelling smoke spewed into the room as it began to eat away at the disks.

"Are there any more?" the leader asked.

"That's everything. You . . . you destroyed my files . . ." Fineberg whined pitifully, as he looked at his ruined lab.

The leader walked over to Ruth and put his gun to her head. "Everything?"

"I swear to you it's everything." Fineberg's voice shook with fear.

The leader walked over to the monitor and gazed at the screen, which by now was a hopelessly illegible tangle of letters and numbers. He scrolled down page after page and checked to see if they were the same. Satisfied that the virus was working, he turned away from the computer and walked to one of the telephones. He yanked the wire out of the wall and motioned to one of his men, who repeated his actions with the other phones around the lab.

"This is everything?" The leader demanded of Fineberg once again, as he spun on his heel and faced him.

"That is everything, I swear!" Fineberg whimpered.

"If I have to return here I won't be so considerate," the leader said.

"I promise you . . . it's everything!"

The leader looked at Fineberg and, satisfied that he was telling the truth, motioned for his men to leave. As they left, one of the men paused by the door. He took a grenade from his bag, casually pulled the pin, and tossed it into the room.

"Don't! Are you crazy?" Fineberg screamed.

The leader closed the door behind him, and the intruders were gone.

Before Fineberg could move, the grenade exploded with a loud concussion, and smoke filled the room.

Fineberg was knocked to the floor by the impact of the explosion but otherwise wasn't hurt. He struggled to his feet and groped his way through the thick haze of acrid-smelling smoke.

"Moishe! Ari!" he yelled.

"I'm all right," Moishe called, his voice strained, "but Ari's passed out."

"Open the windows!" Fineberg coughed and then covered his mouth and nostrils with his hand.

He crawled through the smoke and reached Ruth, picked her up, and dragged her into his office. He slammed the door shut and managed to keep out most of the smoke. He placed his hand on her neck and felt a pulse. She was alive. But her face was bloody and her white lab coat was seared from the explosion.

Fineberg went back out to the lab and kept close to the wall as he staggered toward the window.

Moishe had his arm around Ari, supporting him as the two men leaned out over the windowsill and gasped for air.

"Who would do this?" Moishe managed to ask.

Fineberg shook his head and slowly replied, "I don't know . . . I don't know."

* ◊ *

The leader sat in the back of the van as it made its way through a tangle of traffic. He had removed his ski mask and had lit up a cigarette. He exhaled a long stream of smoke as he talked into the cell phone. "We got everything. I'm sure of it," he said.

"And the virus?"

"It took out the hard drive. I saw it myself."

"Good. Very good. Proceed with the second objective."

"Right." The leader clicked off the phone and tossed it on the seat next to him and took a long drag from his cigarette.

"I'm hungry," he said. "Let's get something to eat."

18

* ⬤ *

Art MacKenzie sat at a small folding table which rested on the pebble-strewn shore of the Sea of Galilee. Dr. Elisha BenHassen was directly across from him, and they shared a picnic lunch that Elisha's driver had spread out.

During the drive from Masada to Galilee Mac had been withdrawn and reticent. Dr. BenHassen attempted to show him some pot shards from the *tel* at Gath, but Mac was far removed from any interest in broken bits of ancient clay. Observing this, Elisha politely refrained from any further attempts at conversation.

As he looked around, Mac couldn't help but marvel at the contrast of the country. Where a few hours ago there had been nothing but barren earth, now verdant rolling hills and meadows surrounded the shore of this vast body of water. A short distance from where they were sitting, fishermen, like their predecessors for millennia, were repairing their nets in preparation for going out to sea.

Mac forced himself to take another bite of lunch which consisted of cold chicken, a vegetable salad, and small bits of dried garlic bread. Elisha reached for another piece of bread that lay in a wicker basket on the table's edge. As he did so,

Mac noticed what appeared to be a faded tattoo on his left wrist.

Elisha saw Mac staring at it and said, "One of my lasting souvenirs from World War II, along with, of course, my habitual fits of coughing."

"How so?" Mac asked, as he put down his fork and readied himself to listen.

Elisha cradled the bit of garlic bread in his twisted arthritic hands, then in a halting voice said, "During World War II, I was interned at Bergen Belsen . . . a concentration camp."

Mac raised his eyebrows and pressed his lips together as he imagined the horror the man must have gone through. There was an awkward silence. Then Mac's journalistic instincts took over and he forged ahead boldly. "I've read about them and seen pictures, but I've never had the opportunity to talk to a survivor."

The aged scholar sat perfectly still, the only movement being his chest rising and falling slightly as he breathed.

He absently fingered the bit of bread in his hand and then, like a man forcing himself up the last part of a mountain even though he is exhausted, he began, "The day we arrived at the camp we were separated, woman and children, from the men. Most families never saw each other again after that initial separation. The men who could work were sent to a building where they were stripped of their clothes and any belongings. We were shaved of all our body hair and deloused. They applied the delousing powder directly to our bare skin. We then dressed in the camp uniform, striped shirts and trousers that for most of us were either too big or too small. And then we received our tattoo." He pulled the sleeve of his shirt, then held his wrist up and turned it slowly so that Mac could see the faded numbers.

"Like cattle, I was branded." He paused for a moment and looked at the faded tattoo on his wrist. "They would have inspections at four in the morning, even in the winter. I would stand in the freezing, cold night, along with endless rows of other men, and wait to hear my number called ... five, six, zero, two, four, two ... And then I would yell 'present.' When all the numbers had been called and the roll checked, which could take hours, we would start the workday."

Mac let his breath out slowly between his teeth, then asked softly, "How did you get through it?"

Elisha sat back in his chair and looked out at the blue water sparkling in the afternoon sun. "God was with me. I never lost my faith in him. Although I did not understand why I was in the living hell I found myself in, I never doubted. I knew that he was not responsible for what the Nazis were doing to us."

Mac shook his head, looked at the half-eaten food on his plate, and keeping his eyes fixed there confessed, "I don't know how you can believe in *anything* after going through something so horrible."

Mac's statement lingered unanswered for a moment. Then Elisha replied, "Would you care to hear a true story ... one from the camp?"

Mac nodded.

Elisha shifted the garlic bread to one hand while he rubbed his bearded face with the other. "There was man who, like all of us, was a prisoner. He had been a great musician, a classical violinist. It was very sad, because in the camp, he lost his faith in God. And because of that he despaired of life. Each day he became more morose. I saw his spirit slowly die ... a little each day. There came a day when in desperation, he threw himself against the electric fence and was killed instantly. The only difference between him and me was that I knew nothing could take away what I believed in, my faith in God. In here." He lay a bony hand on his chest. "The guards could kill me and take my body, but not my soul. Most every-one who survived shared the commonality of faith ... in the

God of our fathers. It is the one deciding factor that got us through the Holocaust. Without my belief in God, I would never have survived that nightmarish place."

Mac toyed with the food on his plate. "Does it haunt you today?" he asked.

Elisha looked steadily into Mac's eyes and said, "Yes. It haunts me even now. I lost much of my family in the camps. Some of the things I saw . . . well, they are the work of the Evil One. When I recall those thoughts I pray, and over time, the memory loses its power. It is still there, mind you, for once you take something into your mind it remains there. But now, it no longer has power over me. It is I who control it . . . through prayer."

"I don't understand something," Mac said.

"And what is that?"

"You and Uri seem to be opposites when it comes to religious things. I have the impression that Uri doesn't believe in God at all."

Elisha popped the bit of garlic bread into his mouth, chewed slowly, and said, "Uri has studied the Holocaust extensively. Because of that, he doesn't believe in God. It is ironic that I am the one who believes in God, having lived through the Holocaust. Yet he is more bitter about it than I. There is also something else . . ."

Mac knew from years of talking to people as a reporter that he was about to hit pay dirt. Elisha was going to confide something very personal to him. He tried not to look anxious while he waited for Elisha to begin.

"I'm not exactly what you would consider an Orthodox Jew," Elisha said. He reached for his glass of water, took a small sip, swallowed carefully, and then continued.

"Not unlike Uri, I studied the Holocaust, but not from books. None were yet written. I talked to others like myself, who had gone through the camps and lived to tell about it. It was during this time, a few years after the war, that I met an old rabbi who had been hidden by a Christian family for two years when the Germans occupied Holland and so had escaped the death camps. He lived with this family in the most intimate way, shared their food and clothing. He was completely dependent on them. His benefactor happened to be a Protestant minister. At night, sometimes to pass the time, the two would talk about each other's religion. The rabbi and the minister. It sounds like the start of a joke, doesn't it?"

Mac smiled and nodded.

"They would study the Scriptures together and talk about them. One night the minister showed the rabbi a passage of Scripture in Isaiah which talked about the coming Messiah. The two discussed the passage at length. Many other topics were bandied about over that two-year period, but the rabbi always came back to that particular passage of Scripture dealing with the prophecy of the coming Messiah. One day shortly before the end of the war and after exhaustively studying other prophecies, the rabbi concluded that the Messiah had indeed come in the person of Yeshua."

"Yeshua?" Mac asked.

"Yeshua, the Hebrew name for Jesus. The rabbi became a believer in Yeshua A Meshiac . . . or Jesus the Messiah. The rabbi became what is considered a Messianic Jew."

Mac finished Elisha's thought and said, "And you talked to the rabbi and you accepted Jesus, Yeshua, as the Messiah?"

Elisha smiled broadly and he said, "Yes, it was the most important day of my life."

"Then you're not a Jew?"

Elisha tilted his head back and laughed. "Always a question."

"Always," Mac replied.

Elisha repeated, "Am I a Jew? Simply answered. I am a Jew by birth and observe the Sabbath and Passover and the high holy days . . . *but* I am also a Jew that believes in Jesus as the Messiah of Israel. So I attend also a Christian church. I am a Messianic Jew."

"A Messianic Jew," Mac repeated the phrase slowly.

Elisha leaned back in his chair, folded his hands in his lap, and asked pointedly, "And you, MacKenzie, what do you believe in?"

Mac glanced toward the Sea of Galilee, shifted nervously in his chair, and replied, "I'm not sure anymore. There was a time when I believed in ... No, let me rephrase that ... I thought I believed in ... Jesus. But probably it was just because I'd been brought up that way. Now I don't think I believe in anything."

Elisha brushed off his hands. "This is a wonderful place to take a walk," he said, changing the subject. "Other than Jerusalem, it's my favorite place in all of Israel."

Mac got up and went to Elisha's side and helped him get out of his chair.

"Thank you ... my arthritis," Elisha said. "I come here as often as I can. Isn't it beautiful?" He gestured at the lush hills surrounding them.

Mac nodded as they began to walk in silence along the lake's edge.

After a while Elisha said, "In the file Roswell sent us ... it mentioned that you lost your eldest son?"

Mac felt his stomach tighten. "Yeah ... I've never been able to ..."

"Release him?" Elisha offered.

Mac looked away and answered, "I don't know if release is the right word ... but yeah."

Elisha nodded slowly, then said, "When my wife died there was a time of grief, of mourning. It was a very difficult period. After almost two years, I realized that it was time to release her, to continue my life without her. I prayed that God would help me because this is something that I don't think we can do without his help."

"And did he help?" Mac asked, the sarcasm rising up in his voice.

"Yes. I prayed and the burden was lifted. There was peace."

"Peace?" Mac asked incredulously.

Elisha nodded, then said, "I still love my wife and deeply miss her, but I am at peace with her death. I am at rest, and this is nothing short of miraculous."

"How does it happen? How does it work?" He hesitated and then stammered, "I can't let go of my son . . ."

Elisha stopped walking and looked at Mac.

"What?" Mac said defensively.

"You said, 'I can't let go,' and that is the point. *You* cannot let go on your own. It's beyond all the strength that you possess . . . to let go. But that is what Jesus will help you do, if you let him."

"I used to believe in Jesus as a kid. Even after Maggie and I got married, we went to church. I went through the motions, but I guess I didn't really believe, I had no real faith, because after my son was killed I grew resentful." He looked away, thought for a moment, then asked tentatively, "So how can God help me let go?"

"The Scriptures say in Isaiah 53:3 that 'He was a man of sorrows, and familiar with suffering.' If you ask him to help you, he will. In place of the pain there will be peace. A peace that passes understanding, in our human terms." He paused and looked out at the sparkling waters, then back at Mac. "But you must come to the end of yourself and finally let go."

Mac recalled sitting on the edge of the stone tower at Masada, a part of him wanting to leap off the edge to escape the pain. He also remembered the minister's words at his son's funeral. Now here he was, the old wound uncovered in the light of day.

He grew angry. Raising his voice, he argued, "It doesn't make sense! Why didn't God take me instead of my son?"

"Why did God allow the concentration camps?" Elisha countered.

"Maybe Uri is right," Mac said, "God doesn't give a hoot about us! He's detached from us, for crying out loud!"

"Remember that same God, who you think is so detached, sent his only Son, Yeshua, to hang on a cross, so that he could save us and reconcile us to him," Elisha offered.

"It's too much like some sort of cosmic passion play," Mac said angrily and kicked the gravel, which sent a spray of sand and stone flying into the calm water.

"It is a passion play, and the stakes are high," Elisha said firmly. "Human souls spending eternity with God, or eternal damnation and separation from a holy God! That is what is at stake!"

"Nothing can take away what I feel! You don't know the helplessness I felt at not being able to save him. If only I could have done something . . . That eats at me, unless I drown it in alcohol to the point where I pass out! And the next morning . . . the next morning it all comes back and it's still there . . . the pain, like a ravenous wolf."

"He'll take your pain," Elisha said quietly.

Elisha's words hit Mac like a hammer. "What did you say?" he asked.

"I said, he'll take your pain, but you have to ask him in here." And Elisha pointed toward Mac's heart.

They stopped and faced one another. Mac looked defiantly at Elisha and said, "I can't do that."

"Why not?" Elisha asked softly.

"I don't need anybody's help," Mac shot back. He pressed his lips together and scowled. He felt like he was being backed into a corner. One part of him wanted to run from this wizened old man and drown himself in a good bottle of whatever he could lay his hands on, and the other wanted to fall on Elisha's shoulder and weep. The battle raged inside him. It felt as if he was being torn apart. Anger and resentment welled up in him like a tempest. He wanted to punch the old man who looked at him with such peaceful eyes. How dare he have what Mac so desperately wanted! Was he flaunting it? Lording it over Mac, saying to him that he was superior?

Mac closed his eyes and wiped away the sweat from his forehead. He opened them and stared at Elisha. *The man means me no harm. What am I thinking?* he thought, marveling at the tricks his mind was playing.

"It's time to come back," Elisha whispered. "Let him take the pain."

Mac saw that the old man was crying silently. Tears ran down his lined cheeks and disappeared into his beard.

Something then broke in Mac. As he looked at the older man, he realized that Elisha was crying for him . . . for his pain . . . for his suffering. He understood that he was reaching out to him, like a man reaches desperately for his drowning friend in a raging sea.

And then the wall of self, that bastion of independence and self-reliance, began to crumble. Mac felt it give way. At first it scared him, for it made him feel vulnerable and weak.

As he stood trembling he heard Elisha say, "His burden is light."

He looked at Elisha and blinked his eyes. Sweat poured from his forehead.

"He'll take your pain," Elisha whispered again.

How did he know to say that? Mac thought.

He felt himself sway on his feet. There was a weathered post that was sunk into the gravelly shoreline near him. He reached out and steadied himself on it. He closed his eyes and fought back the tears.

He felt Elisha's hand on his shoulder. "Come back to him . . . he loves you," the old man whispered.

Mac let go of the post and collapsed on the ground.

Elisha followed him, wrapped his arms around him, and held him fast.

Mac's body trembled spasmodically and his shoulders shuddered uncontrollably. He let out a long cry of anguish. A guttural, primal wail, that seemed to release his soul from a darkened prison.

He wept for his son Art, for his dead father. He wept for Maggie and Sarah and Jeremy. All their faces raced clearly into his mind, in rapid succession.

"Take it from me," he murmured. "Oh, Jesus! Take all of it . . . take the pain!" He said it over and over again. And with each time he uttered those words it seemed that a weight was lifted from him. Falling away, leaving him free!

The two men remained locked in one another's arms.

Mac exhausted himself in what was the only catharsis he had ever experienced. So many people and emotions tucked away. Half a lifetime of thoughts unchecked, left to fester, left to bitterness, buried under the fragile veneer of personality and career.

But there was also something new being born. The beginning of a wholeness. He felt alive for the first time in his life. Like he had been awakened from a nightmarish slumber.

The light had entered into him.

His burden was lifted and in its place was peace.

He knew that a miracle had happened, and that the source of that miracle was Jesus, and that somehow he was present . . .

19

***

Mac and Elisha slowly got up from the ground. "Well, how do you feel?" Elisha asked as he rubbed his own tear-stained face.

Mac looked at a small boat with its single sail catching the wind. "Like that little boat out there ... free ... and with a fresh wind at my back."

Elisha put his arm on Mac's shoulder. "That's a good feeling, MacKenzie." He chuckled. "We should get started back ... there's always more work to be done."

They were interrupted by Elisha's driver. "Dr. BenHassen! Dr. BenHassen!" He ran to them waving a cellular phone over his head.

"Something has happened," Elisha said to Mac as he waved his hand overhead, responding to his driver's frantic calls.

The driver caught up to them and tried to catch his breath while he spasmodically conversed with Elisha in Hebrew.

"Oh no," Elisha groaned.

"What?" Mac asked, with growing concern.

"He says that several men broke into Dr. Fineberg's lab sometime this morning, took the sample bones of the Nephilim, and destroyed much of his lab and data."

"What are you going to do?" Mac asked, trying his best to balance this sudden turn of events with the lingering aftermath of his conversion.

"Get back to Jerusalem as fast as we can. I'll call Uri once we get to the car."

The driver ran ahead of them, gathered up the table and chairs, and hastily threw them into the car's trunk.

Mac steadied Elisha as the old man forced himself to walk faster than he could manage. They reached the car and climbed in.

The driver spun the car around and headed back to the Old City, going well over the posted speed limit.

"I'm going to see if I can reach Fineberg and try to get what happened firsthand," Elisha said as he dialed the number.

Mac wondered how anyone could possibly know about Fineberg's testing on the Nephilim bones. Granted, if what Fineberg's lab discovered about them were true—that they contained a fifth nucleotide, making them for all practical purposes a genetic anomaly—this would indeed cause quite a stir in the scientific community. But nothing had been published yet.

How could anyone possibly have found out? And why destroy the discovery? he thought.

"I've reached him," Elisha said to Mac.

Mac listened impatiently to Elisha converse in Hebrew, wishing he understood the language.

Elisha turned to Mac. "It seems three heavily armed men walked into his lab. They roughed up his assistant, put a virus into the main computer terminal, and confiscated the bone samples from the sarcophagus."

"Was anyone hurt?" Mac asked.

"A woman who works with him has some light contusions and is emotionally distraught. But everyone else escaped serious injury. The intruders seemed to be only interested in the lab work concerning the Nephilim bones. I'm going to call Uri."

"Who do you think is responsible?" Mac asked.

"I don't know. I don't think it's the Arabs, although they might attach some significance to the skeleton being found under the Dome of the Rock."

"What about your secret service? Would they do something like this?" Mac asked.

Elisha immediately shook his head. "The Mossad? No, I would have been notified if we were jeopardizing national security in some way. No, I think this originated outside the Middle East, maybe from your country or the Russians. Somehow, someone has gotten a hint of what we've discovered and is threatened by that information."

"What's so threatening?" Mac asked.

"Fineberg's testing points to a genetic anomaly. Because of that, the skeleton *might* be proof of the existence of the Nephilim ... the commingling of fallen angels and the women of earth." He paused and looked Mac squarely in the eye. "I haven't told you about some very interesting information sent by Roswell."

"Such as?"

"Roswell sent the results of DNA testing on residual amniotic fluid from a woman who claims her baby was taken from her by aliens."

"Like the woman I saw at the hospital."

"Yes. Fortunately one of Roswell's agents happened to be working in the emergency room where the woman was brought. She was hemorrhaging badly. He was able to gather a sample and preserve it."

"And Roswell had it tested?"

"Yes, and the results were the same as Fineberg's."

"A fifth nucleotide," Mac stated softly.

Elisha nodded. "Yes, a fifth nucleotide. Do you see where this is leading?"

"There's a link to the past," Mac answered.

"Yes. And I believe it is the beginning of the Great Deception I told you about, the fallen angels mating with human women."

Mac frowned and tried to put the pieces together.

The cell phone rang, and Elisha picked it up. "It's Uri," he informed Mac. "So you know about Fineberg's lab?" He paused as he waited for an answer.

"He knows about it," Elisha informed Mac. "Are you going to the tunnel?" He listened to the answer and replied, for Mac's benefit, "Good, you're there now. Is the skeleton ready to be shipped? Good . . . Yes, we're on our way. We'll see you in an hour. He sends his greetings," Elisha said, as he clicked off the cell phone.

"Do you think the same people will try to get the skeleton?" Mac asked.

"I'm not sure," Elisha answered, his face taut with concern. "It is possible . . . but I think it's highly unlikely they would try anything at the Temple Mount. It is much too volatile."

* o *

Uri BenHassen called the Museum of Antiquities and reaffirmed his request for transportation to move the skeleton in order to have it properly studied. He then made his way to the secret room containing the sarcophagus.

"You are almost finished the packing?" Uri asked one of Elisha's students as he quickly made a mental note of their progress.

One of the students, a girl, nodded and held up a carefully wrapped bone.

"The transport will be coming soon," he remarked and looked at his watch again.

He began to double-check the numbering of the bones against the rendering of the skeleton as it lay in the sarcophagus, which would enable others to reconstruct it at the Museum of Antiquities.

He saw the spearhead was about to be wrapped and put away. "Let me see that, will you?" he asked.

He felt its cool smooth surface as he balanced it in the palm of his hand. Glancing at the inscription on the stone lid, he frowned.

Nephilim . . . where did you come from? What are you? he wondered, and suddenly the spearhead felt very heavy.

* ○ *

The leader sat alone in a restaurant in the Arab quarter. He had gorged himself so much that he loosened the top button of his pants.

He leaned back on two legs of his chair and leisurely smoked an American cigarette, savoring the flavor.

Outside the restaurant, a van pulled up with the same men he had led in the raid on Dr. Fineberg's lab. One of them exited the van and entered the restaurant, found the leader, and sat across from him at the small table.

"Did you pay off the driver?" the leader said as he exhaled smoke toward his comrade's face.

"Yes, he's been paid. He'll call us just as he's leaving."

"And it *is* today? Are you sure?" the leader asked.

"We monitored his cell phone. It's today, soon," the man answered.

Satisfied, the leader nodded. He took one last drag on his cigarette and crushed the butt out in the blackened tin ashtray. He glanced at the man across from him and asked, "What about the uniforms?"

"He's going to get us two," came the reply.

"Good." The leader lit another cigarette and offered one to the other man, who took it.

He waved his hand, and a rotund waiter in a dirty apron shuffled to his table.

The leader held up an empty glass.

"And one for my friend here," he said.

The waiter jerked his head like a marionette and disappeared.

The leader lit the other man's cigarette, leaned back in his chair, and leisurely inhaled.

✳ ○ ✳

Elisha's driver parked his car near the Temple Mount. Elisha and Mac got out and hurried toward the entrance of the Rabbinical Tunnel. The soldiers stationed there nodded respectfully to Elisha as they entered.

"You drive," Elisha said as Mac helped him into the cart.

Mac climbed into the electric cart and drove it through the cool passageways to the secret room holding the sarcophagus.

"You arrived quickly," Uri said as they entered.

Mac saw that the sarcophagus was empty. Next to it lay two large wooden crates, holding the precious artifacts. Their lids were screwed securely shut.

"Any news from Fineberg?" Elisha asked.

"He's very distraught about the files he lost. The police are investigating, but"—Uri threw his hands into the air—"whoever it was is miles away by now. They're not going to find anything."

Elisha sighed, then examined one of the crates. "Are you ready to load them?"

"We're ready now. The truck from the Museum of Antiquities should be arriving shortly," Uri said.

"I wonder if you could open one of the crates," Elisha asked.

"Of course, I'll do it myself."

Elisha sat on the other crate and watched as Uri and one of the students carefully unscrewed the lid and removed some of the packing material. Elisha got up and went over to the crate. He rested his hands on its side for support and leaned over the bones. Each bone had been carefully tagged and numbered so it could later be reconstructed at the museum. He reached into the crate, moved more of the packing material away, and selected what appeared to be a bone from the rib cage.

"I want you to personally be responsible for this," he said, as he handed it to Uri.

Uri took the artifact from his grandfather and slipped it into a canvas pack that leaned against the stone wall near the entrance.

"Well, let's move all of this, shall we?" Elisha said, and clapped his hands together enthusiastically.

"Insurance?" Mac asked Elisha as the students and Uri began to move the crates.

"Yes," Elisha replied, "considering what happened at Fineberg's, I don't think we can be too careful."

* ✿ *

From the basement of the Museum of Antiquities a small diesel flatbed truck lumbered into the late afternoon sunlight.

The driver stopped just before the security gate. He left the vehicle, unlocked the gate, and slid it open. He looked nervously around. Satisfied that he wasn't being watched, he drove slowly out of the fenced security area of the museum. He set the emergency brake, then hopped out and quickly closed the gate before driving away.

He was being paid almost six months' wages for providing the uniforms and the truck. He didn't care who the man was who had approached him. Nor did he particularly wonder about what the truck was going to be used for. He had been assured it would be given back in good condition. No one would know . . . and for his part, he would be richer.

He drove to the address he was instructed to and left the truck parked in a narrow alleyway. After putting the keys on top of the rear tire, he walked quickly down the street. He looked back once, then hurried on his way.

∗ ○ ∗

Mac helped load the last of the crates on the electric cart. He waved as Uri drove it slowly away, down the tunnel.

Mac lagged behind as the two students began to walk toward the entrance. He went back into the secret room and went to the lid of the sarcophagus, staring for a moment at the inscription . . .

"Nephilim . . . Anakim . . . Rephaim . . ."

Here again on earth? he wondered.

He left the room and walked back down the tunnel.

∗ ○ ∗

A white van was parked directly behind the truck from the Museum of Antiquities.

Inside the van the leader put on the uniform that he had retrieved from behind the front seat of the truck, as was pre-arranged. Across from him, another man was complaining that his uniform didn't fit.

The leader rebuked him, "Shut up and get into it."

The man mumbled something under his breath and forced his muscular arm into the sleeve of the shirt.

Two other men were busy underneath the carriage of the flatbed truck. One of them strapped two large bundles of explosives on either side of the gas tank. The other made sure that the antenna of the detonator was tightly secured and that the radio receiver was activated before he crawled out from under the truck.

"Everything ready?" the leader asked.

The men nodded.

"Good, I'll drive," he said. He got out of the van and climbed into the driver's seat of the flatbed. The other man wearing the uniform got into the passenger side of the vehicle. They appeared to be security for the museum.

The leader started the diesel engine and headed down the street. The two other men followed in the van a short distance behind.

* ○ *

Elisha BenHassen sat on a stool in front of the entrance of the Rabbinical Tunnel. The crates were a short distance away. Uri and Mac were talking to the students, and the soldiers on watch were idle and relaxed.

Elisha stirred at the sound of a diesel truck engine. "I think they're coming," he called to Uri.

Uri walked into the square. "It looks like they're here," he affirmed.

* ○ *

"Let me do any talking," the leader instructed as he drove the truck. "If something happens, don't start shooting people. Remember, there are soldiers here. Play dumb, you're good at that. Remember, let me talk," he repeated.

The other man remained mute.

"That's it ahead of us. Keep your gun under your seat. And don't look so nervous." The leader slapped the man's shoulder and laughed.

The other guy grunted and spat out his open window.

* ○ *

Mac sat beside Elisha near the guard shack on the same rickety stool as the day before and watched the truck cross the square and stop directly in front of the entrance to the Rabbinical Tunnel. He watched Uri point to the crates and say something to the driver. The driver waved to his helper, and the man got out of the truck and walked over to where the crates rested. The students helped the two men lift the first crate and set it gently on the rear of the flatbed.

"Is Dr. Sledzik going to receive these?" Mac heard Elisha call to the driver.

Mac looked at the driver and realized the man hadn't heard Elisha.

"I don't think he heard you, Dr. Elisha," Mac said, as he got off his stool and went over to him.

Mac helped Elisha get up and they walked over to the truck.

"Excuse me," Elisha said. "Is Dr. Sledzik going to be there to receive these?"

The driver hesitated for a moment, then called out over his shoulder, "Yes . . . Dr. Sledzik will be there."

They lifted the other crate onto the truck and tied it with a nylon rope.

The men finished securing the crates and started to get back into the truck.

"Wait just a minute," Elisha called. "You forgot the paperwork!"

"Oh . . . yes . . . the paperwork. I'll get it. Hold on." The driver opened his door and began to look for the paperwork. The other man climbed into his seat, then slouched down in it and stared out the window at Elisha and Mac.

"Here it is," the driver said, as he produced a battered clipboard. He walked over and handed it to Elisha.

Elisha glanced at the document, began to frown, and said, "The paperwork's not correct. This is for another pickup, not ours," and he pointed out the mistake to the driver.

"Oh . . . sorry." The driver apologized.

Uri walked over to his grandfather and Mac. "Is something a problem?" he asked.

"The paperwork isn't correct," Elisha said, exasperated.

"Here it is. I'm sorry, it must have gotten mixed up," the driver said and smiled, as he handed the clipboard back to Elisha.

Uri leaned over Elisha's shoulder and looked at the document. "Looks in order," he said.

Elisha examined it carefully, then took a pen from his khaki shirt pocket, signed the bottom of it, and handed it back to the driver.

"All set then?" the driver said, as he patted the clipboard. He walked to the flatbed, threw the clipboard onto the seat, climbed in after it, and started the engine.

Elisha turned to Mac and said, "Incompetence," as the truck pulled away.

"Yeah," Mac agreed.

"I better call Dr. Sledzik and inform him of it."

"Why don't you call from my house?" Uri suggested.

Elisha thought for a moment and then said, "No. I want to call now while things are fresh in my mind. Can you please get me your cell phone?"

Uri walked to the electric cart and pulled his phone from his pack. He returned and handed it to Elisha.

Elisha turned it on, gave the phone a disgusted look, and said, "The battery is weak," as he pointed to the flashing light.

"Sorry. Do you want me to get yours from the car?" Uri offered.

"No, that's all right," Elisha responded. "I suppose it can wait for later. Let's go. I'll call from your house."

＊ ○ ＊

The white van carrying the other terrorists appeared out of an alley and fell directly in behind the flatbed truck. The leader caught sight of it in his rearview mirror and gave a thumbs-up out his window. The driver of the van honked the horn once in response.

The two vehicles left the Old City and headed across the Kidron Valley. Forty minutes later the leader steered onto a rutted dirt road and parked behind a large outcropping of rock. The van pulled up behind it, and the leader and his accomplice left the flatbed and climbed into it. The leader took a small control box and motioned for the driver of the van to back up. The van raised a dust cloud as it backed away from the truck.

"This is good," the leader said.

He slid off his seat and stood next to the van directly behind the door.

He looked around him. Satisfied that they were isolated and concealed, he pointed the box in the direction of the truck, swiveled the antennae, and hit the flashing red button.

There was a slight pause, then a terrible explosion rocked the van, the force of which slammed the door into the leader's chest and knocked him to the ground. Debris flew high into the air. The crates containing the bones of the Nephilim disintegrated. Where the truck had been only moments before, a newly formed blackened crater burned hotly with gasoline and twisted, unrecognizable parts of metal.

The leader got up and wiped the grime from his face. The other men inside the van laughed. He looked at the crater and his face broke into a devilish grin. He reached into his coat pocket, pulled a cigarette from the package with his teeth, and lit up. After staring at the crater for a few seconds, he gave the signal to leave.

The van pulled back onto the main road and headed for Jordan.

* ✿ *

"What do you mean the truck hasn't gotten there yet?" a frustrated Elisha cried into the receiver.

"I'm sorry, Dr. BenHassen, but the truck never got here," a woman answered.

"Is Dr. Sledzik there?" Elisha asked.

"No, he isn't, sir. He's out of town for the week. I expect him back next Monday," she replied.

"Excuse me, but did I hear you say Dr. Sledzik was out of town for the remainder of the week?"

"Yes sir. Until next Monday," she said apologetically.

"And you are sure the truck hasn't arrived? It was carrying rare antiquities," Elisha pressed.

"I'm sorry, sir, but I've checked this myself, and the truck hasn't arrived. Security has been alerted and they're looking into it. I'll call you personally, sir, as soon as we hear something."

Elisha resisted the inclination to slam the receiver down and instead closed his eyes and silently prayed.

Uri asked, "What did they tell you?"

"Dinner's getting cold!" Rebecca called from the kitchen.

"We will be coming," Uri yelled back, from his study.

"The truck hasn't arrived . . . and Sledzik hasn't been at the museum all week. He's out of town," Elisha answered wearily.

"Then who picked up the crates at the Temple Mount?"

Elisha sighed. "We may never know. There is nothing we can do now. The woman informed me that security has been alerted. She will call as soon as they know what happened. We should go to dinner so Rebecca doesn't get upset."

"I can't believe this," Uri said angrily. "What if the crates are gone? Then all of our work . . ."

"No, we still have the one bone I gave to you," Elisha reminded him.

Uri hit the door with his palm angrily as the two men left his study.

They walked into the living room where they found MacKenzie, who was on all fours in the middle of the room with a pile of laughing children on his back.

The healing has begun, Elisha thought, as he watched them play. For a moment he forgot the missing truck and abandoned himself in silent praise.

20

Mac, Elisha, and Uri sat in Elisha's living room and conversed on the speakerphone with a woman administrator from the Museum of Antiquities.

"And security found the man in his apartment?" Elisha asked, and glanced sideways toward Uri.

"Yes, that's correct . . . with his throat cut. Really very horrible," the woman's voice responded through the small speaker.

"And there has been no trace of the truck?" Uri inquired.

She hesitated, then said, "Well . . . we may have discovered what's left of it, sir."

"What do you mean?" Elisha asked.

"I can only imagine," Uri mumbled under his breath.

"Earlier this evening there was a report of an explosion just outside the Old City. Apparently General Security investigated it and according to their report they believe it was the work of terrorists, probably Palestinians or Hezbollah."

"But was it the truck?" Elisha asked impatiently.

"They're not positive, but they believe it might be."

"Of course, no traces of the artifacts?" Uri said.

"Nothing, sir. General Security is having considerable difficulty identifying what type of vehicle it was."

Elisha put his head in his hands. "Oh well." He sighed. "Thank you for the information. If there's anything else we need to know, you have my numbers."

"Yes, sir. I'm sorry, Dr. BenHassen. Good night, sir."

Uri clicked the speakerphone off, and the three men sat immersed in their own thoughts.

"At least you have one bone from the Nephilim skeleton left," Mac said, breaking the silence.

"True. True," Elisha answered softly. "But I believe the rest of the skeleton has been destroyed ... Whoever these people are it seems they will stop at nothing to destroy the truth."

"Including murder," Mac added somberly.

Elisha agreed, "Unfortunately ... even murder." He lingered in thought for a moment, then said, "Uri, I called Dr. Fineberg before we left your house and told him about the last bone that we have in our possession. He was, needless to say, somewhat reluctant to have anything more to do with it."

"I'm thinking we need to contact Roswell," Uri suggested. "He must need to know what has happened here. Maybe his people will want to do the testing on the artifact."

Mac got up from his chair, walked to the picture of the UFO, and stared at it. He called over his shoulder, "You know, I'm leaning toward your theory, Elisha. There seems to be a link here." He pointed to the disk in the picture. "Otherwise why blow a bunch of bones to smithereens?"

"I'm glad I'm making a believer out of you," Elisha said, "although we're not certain as to who is behind the confiscation of the Nephilim artifacts and the murder of the museum employee. It is like a flare going off on a starless night; suddenly you can see where you're going, even if it is just for a few moments. I feel like we now have been pointed in the right direction. I believe there is a link between the Nephilim and the emergence of the UFO phenomena, and whoever destroyed the artifacts knew that. Only a handful of us know about the significance of the bones . . . Yes? Suppressing that information is important enough to someone to go to such extreme measures to silence their witness."

"How much do you think your government knows about all of this?" Mac asked.

Elisha lightly rubbed the arm of his chair with his thumb while he thought. Finally he said, "I have contacts. The Major, whom you met, for one, and others that I have known since our first days of independence. The Major confides that the Air Force is very aware when an unidentified craft flies over Israeli air space. As you saw in the video, they scramble jets and attempt an intercept. Of course nothing we have comes close to matching the speed of these craft."

"Is your government curious about the research you and Uri do here?"

"Unofficially, very interested," Uri said.

"The Major spends most of his time investigating sightings," Elisha added. "We often exchange information."

"We still have the one bone remaining, and I feel Roswell should get that as soon as possible even if we have to hand deliver it ourselves," Mac suggested as he paced in front of the picture. "It's the only physical link that may validate Elisha's theory. Especially if Fineberg's conclusions about the DNA are correct."

"We can now contact Roswell," Uri stated matter-of-factly.

Mac looked at Elisha and waited for him to respond.

Elisha put his hands on the arm rails of his chair and boosted himself from his seat. He steadied himself, then slowly walked over to his computer and sat down.

"You know what? This is amazing," Uri said to Mac, as he followed Elisha over to the computer.

"It is," Elisha agreed, smiling. "It makes me feel like a schoolboy passing notes." He typed in a command. "Did you know Roswell has a Web page?" he asked.

"A Web page ... you're kidding," Mac replied.

"Under Spiral of Life," Elisha answered. "Here, I'll show you."

Elisha typed in *www.spiraloflife.com* and waited.

Mac watched the screen. In a moment an interesting icon flashed onto the screen. "What is that?" he asked.

"A close-up of Michelangelo's painting from the Sistine Chapel but slightly revised. Instead of the finger of God touching Adam's finger in the act of creation, it is replaced with the double helix spiral of DNA."

"Deliberate," Mac said.

"*Very* deliberate," Elisha corrected.

"Here comes the good part," Uri added.

Elisha took the mouse and clicked. The screen changed to a deep blue color and a quote floated in front of the image.

"Go ahead, Mac," Elisha prompted.

Mac read it out loud, "'And the stars of heaven shall fall, and the powers that are in heaven shall be shaken.'"

"It's from the gospel of Mark, chapter 13, verse 25," Elisha stated.

"I didn't know Roswell was religious."

"He's not anymore, but he collaborates with the people who set up the Web page."

"Who are these people?" Mac asked.

"We know that some of them believe like I do that the world is on the verge of the Great Deception spoken about in the Bible." Elisha clicked on the Scripture and it vanished, leaving an open box with a flashing cursor. "You have to know the password," he said, and typed in a series of numbers and letters.

Another box appeared, larger than the first. It contained a strange cuneiform-like writing with symbols and figures of animals.

"What's that?" Mac asked.

"More security, watch." Elisha typed in a command and used the cursor to rearrange some of the icons. The writing changed into a picture of a bare foot floating over the ground.

"What is it?" Mac asked.

"Jesus descending on the Mount of Olives . . . The Second Coming. It's a close-up of his foot just before it touches the earth."

"These people believe that the Second Coming . . ."

"Might be in our lifetime," Elisha finished.

Mac watched as Elisha typed another password. The screen went black for a moment, then the cursor began to blink.

Elisha typed and as he did, the letters appeared white against the black of the screen.

"That's it?" Mac asked.

"Yes. This is an I.C.Q. linkup. The message I send will activate Roswell's pager."

"How secure is the system?"

Uri folded his arms across his chest and said, "No password . . . you can't get in." He picked up a card next to Elisha's computer which had a series of numbers on it and explained, "The code changes every day. Without this"—he waved the card—"it would almost be impossible to gain access."

"But what if someone lifted it right here from your computer?" Mac asked.

"It wouldn't work because a certain section of digits have to be sequenced in reverse order and only someone who has been instructed by Roswell knows where that section is." Elisha typed his message on the page, pushed the return key, and waited.

The letters vanished from the screen and it became black again except for the flashing cursor.

"He's not there?" Uri said.

"Be patient," Elisha whispered.

The men stared at the monitor and waited.

"I'm going for something to drink," Uri said. "You want anything?"

"Nothing for me," Elisha said.

"I'll take whatever you have," Mac answered.

Uri left them and a short while later returned with cold fruit juice.

"Anything?" he asked.

"It takes time," Elisha repeated. "Look, something is coming in." The excitement clearly showed on his face. "I still can't get used to it," he said, and looked boyishly at Mac.

They stared at the monitor, and all that appeared on the screen was a white jumble of numbers and letters.

"Now what?" Mac asked.

"This is the best part. Watch this," Elisha said cryptically.

The message was finished. He hit "save as" and entered a code. Some of the letters unscrambled themselves, most of the others simply disappeared. The three of them read together.

Have read your note. Sorry you had trouble with the artifact. Fortunate you have sample left. MacKenzie should return with it to the States. Uri should come with him. Things seem to be reaching a climax here. They know about you. Be careful.

Elisha waited with his hands poised on the keyboard and looked up at Uri. "What should I answer?"

"Tell him MacKenzie and I will leave within twenty-four hours. Providing I can convince Rebecca," he said.

Elisha typed the message, and they waited for Roswell's reply.

Good. Uri will be invaluable. Will contact you at MacKenzie's. Wait for instructions, don't talk. Be careful.

With a puzzled expression Mac asked, "Who is 'they'?"

Elisha looked at Mac, his brow knit together. He pointed toward the picture of the UFO and softly said, "The beings that make those fly."

* ○ *

"Dad?" Laura called out. "Dad, are you all right?"

"I'm fine, honey," Roswell answered.

"Did you take your medicine?" Laura asked.

Roswell thought about lying, then answered, "No, not yet."

"Was that important . . . what just came in?"

"Yes . . . BenHassen indicates that the Nephilim artifacts were destroyed."

"I'm sorry."

"They still have a sample. MacKenzie and the younger BenHassen are going to return to the States with it."

"Are we going to pick them up?"

"Too conspicuous—oh, my back," he groaned.

"Daddy, are you all right?"

"Where are those darned pills?"

Laura went to his desk and opened the bottle that was next to the phone. "Here, Daddy, take two," and she held the pills out in her hand to him.

Roswell shifted in his chair, took the pills, and swallowed them.

"I'd give anything to have one day without pain," he mumbled.

21

* ◉ *

On his last night in Jerusalem, Mac stayed up late recording the day's events in his journal.

June 6

So much has happened today that I hardly know where to begin. Without doubt the most significant event was the long walk with Elisha on the shores of the Sea of Galilee. Something extraordinary happened there.

But in contrast, just a few hours earlier, I had been sitting high atop the ruined fortress walls of Masada, contemplating hurling myself to the desert floor far below. It is hard to comprehend, let alone reduce to mere words, the inner turmoil I experienced. A lifetime of emotions, thoughts, and memories boiled up in me. I was, as Dr. Elisha puts it, "at the end of myself." I realized I have been hiding from God ever since Art's death. Hiding out of fear? Hate? Anger? Resentment? A combination of these? I don't know.

Somehow, incredible as it seems, something has changed inside me. I have a sense of being released. I am a different person.

I want to call Maggie and tell her what has happened. I want to see Sarah and Jeremy and tell them I love them. Really love them. I want to hold them close and feel the precious gift of life that surges through their little bodies with each breath they take.

It feels as though I have been given another chance.

I realize that I have been touched by the Spirit of the Living God. All along I have been hearing his voice ... I have tried my best to ignore it for it is unsettling. It isn't an audible voice. But it is definite and clear ... and for so long the same phrase has been repeated, "I'll take the pain." But I have done everything to ignore the offer.

I wonder, How is he capable of projecting thoughts in my mind? How is he able to touch me in such a deep, personal way? I suppose that is why he is God.

Part of me screams that this can't be real. That I have been deluded. That Elisha put ideas in my head and that in a weak moment I became emotional and what transpired isn't valid. That what happened to me was reserved for the apostles or a few select saints centuries ago.

I remember as a child praying and also as a young man. Somewhere in college I lost the connection ... or more accurately, deliberately broke it.

But I know I haven't lost my mind or deluded myself or had a break with reality, for I am more alive than I've been since Art's death. I suppose I have returned to my faith.

Yet this has a new dynamic that I'm as yet testing, getting used to the way it fits.

Yeshua.

The Hebrew name for Jesus. What was that Dr. Elisha said about him? That he was a man of sorrows, acquainted with grief? I remember some of the gospel stories, but Elisha seems to have a much deeper knowledge, a working knowledge, where mine is but a cursory overview.

I know (even though I cannot explain it) that he knows what I have gone through with the death of my son. He understands what Elisha experienced in the camps in Germany. He knows of all the hurt and pain and junk that I carry around in me. He knows this and holds out his hands and says, "Here, let me take this burden from you. It is too heavy for you to carry it alone!"

It seems so simple, and yet I want to make it more complex.

I feel like a small child in Sunday school, uneasy as I am asked to sing "Jesus loves me." But no words were ever more true. Jesus loves me! It is a balm on the wounds and hurts of my life. That love has changed me where I could not change myself. Where I was powerless, he was powerful. Where I was lacking and weak, he was strong. I am grateful for another chance.

How does he comfort? I don't know. But my heart is thankful and I am at peace.

Thank you, Jesus!

Switching topics: Something of utmost importance. It seems that the Nephilim artifacts were hijacked and most likely destroyed. Needless to say Dr. Elisha and Uri are distraught over this. Elisha contacted Roswell and informed him of this. I learned that there seems to be a network of people who are involved in this UFO enigma.

He mentioned the Second Coming. He believes that we might be living in the time frame of the physical return of Christ. I find it fascinating. I'm trying to remember what I've read of this and am having trouble getting the facts straight. I need to get a Bible and find out what it says. How long has it been since I cracked one of those open?

I only hope I'm up to speed in dealing with all of this.

A. MacKenzie
Jerusalem

22

Elisha looked like a man who had not slept well as he stood before Uri and Mac. In fact, he hadn't slept at all, for he had been awake in his bed and praying most of the night.

He now presented himself, draped in a worn prayer shawl and wearing a faded yarmulke on top of his head.

"I only wish I had the strength to go with you," Elisha said, and smiled wistfully.

"Who would take care of all of this?" Uri gestured to their office. "Besides, you must leave the battle to the young men," he teased.

"I might surprise you yet," Elisha said. "But now, I want to pray over you. I want you to know that I will pray as often as I can for your safety. As Roswell has warned, you must be careful." He motioned with his hands. "Come closer."

The old man put his calloused, bony arthritic hands out and placed one on Mac's head and the other on Uri's. He closed his eyes and began to faintly sing in what to Mac sounded like Hebrew. Mac shut his eyes and yielded himself.

Elisha finished and slowly took his hands off their heads. He embraced Uri and then Mac. Tears welled up in the corners of his eyes.

Elisha began to talk to his grandson in a paternal tone. "Uri, I know we disagree as to the origins of these beings. I am certainly being redundant when I warn you that I fear that they are malevolent. But you must try not to be deceived. Remember if they are what I think they are, then they may be able to appear as they wish, even as an angel of light."

Uri nodded respectfully, embraced his grandfather, and kissed him on his cheek.

Elisha turned to Mac and continued, "Mac, you leave with the gift of being renewed. The fire is rekindled." He touched Mac's chest. "Guard your heart . . . And you must make time to read this." He handed him a copy of the Bible and the book of Enoch. "This is my own copy of the book of Enoch. Pay special attention to some of the underlined passages."

Mac nodded and took the book.

"Mac," Elisha warned, "men are trapped by evil times that fall unexpectedly upon them. Don't be deceived."

Mac shifted uneasily.

Uri looked at his watch. "I'm not getting too excited, but we have a plane to catch and if we don't soon leave we might not have the time to get through customs."

"I've made a call to the Major," Dr. Elisha said. "You will have a military escort that will put you on the plane. So there will be no need to go through customs."

"That's convenient," Mac said.

They walked to the front door and embraced each other again. Uri started for the van, but Mac felt Elisha's hand on his shoulder.

"I want you to know something," he said. "A month ago I had a dream. Actually, it was more of a vision than a dream. In that vision I saw you. I knew you were coming here and that he sent you."

"You knew?" Mac asked.

"Yes, the Lord told me."

Mac shook his head. "I don't get it, why me? I'm no saint."

Elisha smiled wistfully. "Neither is anyone else he chooses to do his work. He delights in using the weakest of us to carry out his will."

"For what purpose?" Mac demanded.

"I'm not entirely certain, but his hand is upon your life, and I think he will show you in time."

"We're going to be missing the plane," Uri yelled from the van.

Mac looked intensely into Elisha's eyes ... searching. "It's something to do with the Nephilim, isn't it?"

Elisha held Mac's gaze and nodded slowly. "Go now," he said.

Mac turned on his heels and ran for the van.

"Watch Rebecca and the children!" Uri called to his grandfather as Mac stepped into the van.

"I think it is she who will do most of the watching," Elisha said, and he chuckled.

Mac and Elisha's eyes locked on each other. Mac waved and said under his breath, "God bless you, old man."

Elisha held up a hand and blessed them one last time as the van pulled out of the drive and headed down the hill.

* ◊ *

The plane touched down at the Los Angeles International Airport at two-thirty in the morning. Both men were exhausted.

Uri was carrying a diplomatic-attaché I.D. card, which the Major issued to him before boarding at the Tel Aviv Airport. Yet another benefit of Elisha's connections. This enabled the men to get through American customs rapidly.

They stepped out of the terminal and Mac scrunched his nose distastefully as he inhaled the Los Angeles air. "I had almost forgotten what this place smells like," he said. "Come on, we'll grab a cab and get out of here."

"I'm in America!" Uri said, and he threw his hands over his head and did a little dance.

"Easy, big guy," Mac cautioned. "They'll arrest you for less than that here."

"America! This is wonderful. I've always wanted to come . . . and now." He started to dance again.

Mac let him have his moment and hailed a cab. He gave the driver the address and they were off.

"Where are we now?" Uri wanted to know.

Mac had closed his eyes in the back of the cab and didn't want to open them. "I dunno," he mumbled.

"How far before we come to your place?" Uri asked.

"Pretty soon," Mac answered wearily.

Uri grew excited and exclaimed, "Look at the tiny houses . . . and they have little gardens in front."

"How wonderful," Mac moaned.

At last the cab arrived in front of Mac's apartment. Mac paid the driver and climbed out, followed by an all-too-eager Uri.

"You live here?" Uri asked, as he looked up and down the street.

"Yep, this is it. The Venice Hilton," Mac said, with an edge of sarcasm.

Uri looked puzzled so Mac explained, "I'm being facetious . . . a joke. See how run-down everything is?"

Uri grinned. "What? I think it's looking pretty good."

They stood on the front porch while Mac fiddled with his keys. "All this house is yours?" Uri asked.

"No, the landlord converted it into apartments. I'm on the third floor," Mac explained and for a moment he thought about his former spacious house before the divorce. What had he traded all that for? Living alone in a run-down studio apartment in Venice.

He leaned on the door and forced it open because it had swollen tight against the jamb. The glass rattled in its frame, and the sun-bleached curtains shook out a little dust. The men stepped into what had once been part of an elegant foyer. Mac climbed the staircase that led to his apartment, with Uri following close behind. The hall light was on at the top of the stairs, and Mac went over to his door.

"Oh no!" he exclaimed. "It's open. Somebody busted in."

"Wait, don't go in yet," Uri said, and he grabbed Mac's shoulder and held him back. "Let me go first."

Uri moved cautiously to the door, stood next to it, and listened. He motioned Mac to the other side of the hallway. Mac watched as Uri transformed himself from carefree tourist to stealthy Israeli commando. He bent low, pressed himself flat against the wall, and blended into the shadows. He extended his leg and with his foot slowly pushed on the door. It squeaked on its hinges as it opened. The noise sounded like a train whistle to Mac. He held his breath.

Uri waited, then slowly moved his head to the jamb of the door and peered into the darkness of Mac's apartment. Uri slipped catlike into the apartment and vanished. Expecting some sort of confrontation, Mac listened intently and balled his fists, ready to come to Uri's aid.

The light clicked on and Uri called, "It's all right. Now there is no one here."

Mac hurried across the hall and rushed into his apartment. What greeted him made him first angry and then sick to his stomach as he realized that the little he owned in the world was trashed.

"I can't believe this! Look at this place. Everything's upside down."

Uri let Mac rave for a while longer then interrupted him. "Was anything taken? Look carefully."

Mac looked around the room. His books were strewn about, exposing the bare shelves of his bookcase. His computer and fax were upside down on the floor. All of his floppies were dumped out beside them. The mattress was ripped open and the box spring lay on top of it. His clothes were tossed in a pile in front of the closet. Even the refrigerator had been rummaged through.

"I don't know . . . how can I possibly tell, for crying out loud."

"I'm thinking, people were looking for something," Uri explained.

"What would anyone be looking for here?" Mac asked, the anger rising in his voice as he walked over to the refrigerator and started to clean the mess that was in front of it.

"Information . . . about grandfather, the sarcophagus, Roswell . . ." Uri said. He walked over, bent down on one knee, and began to help Mac clean up.

"There was nothing here they would . . ." Mac's face suddenly blanched and he exclaimed, "Oh no. I really messed up."

"What?"

Mac sighed. "Remember the packet of information Roswell gave me? I forgot to take it with me. I left it in one of the drawers of the desk, and it's not there anymore."

"Are you sure?" Uri pressed.

"I'm positive."

"Now they have that."

"But Roswell's name isn't anywhere on the document," Mac protested.

"Who is what . . . uh? I'm thinking Fineberg's lab, the Nephilim artifacts stolen, and now this." Uri picked up a jar of kosher pickles, read the label, and asked, "Are these really kosher?"

"So what happens to your theory about friendly aliens?" Mac pressed.

Uri's face darkened. "I don't know . . . it doesn't fit what I've been all along thinking."

"Right," exclaimed Mac. "It doesn't fit, so now what?"

Uri looked at the pickle jar and said, "I admit things are not going together as they should . . . I'm thinking maybe there is more to this than when I first thought." Uri unscrewed the lid of the jar, reached in, and took a spear. He nibbled cautiously on one end. "Good." He took another bite.

"Well, you better start thinking real quick, because whoever is responsible for this is upping the ante."

"What?" Uri asked.

"You know, making the stakes higher . . . doubling the bet . . . putting more money up."

Uri nodded. "We should make contact to Roswell, he needs to know what happened here. You think the computer is working?"

"Wait, wait . . . there's something I haven't told you." Mac looked across the room to where the bed had been. "Come here, I'll show you."

Mac picked up a butter knife that was lying on the floor amongst the clutter and crossed the room. On the way he carefully closed the door to his apartment and locked it. He went over to the box spring, picked it up and leaned it against the wall, and moved the mattress.

The intruders had rifled through an assortment of boxes that Mac stored under his bed, creating an odd collage of family pictures and bits of newspaper clippings that lay randomly on the floor. He gathered them into a pile and pushed them to the side. "Here," he said, and he pointed toward the floorboards.

"What?" Uri stared where Mac pointed and knitted his dark eyebrows together.

"Here . . . They didn't find it. Least I don't think so," Mac whispered to himself.

He knelt on his knees and slid over to where there was an electric outlet in the wall. His reading lamp was still plugged in but was missing the lampshade. He set it on the floor in front of him and clicked it on.

He ran his fingers down the wall from the bottom of the plug, and when his hand reached the floor he counted twelve boards over to his immediate right and then followed the boards where they butted ends with one another.

"One, two, three," he whispered, under his breath. "Here it is." He carefully slipped the knife in between the boards and wiggled it back and forth. A colored putty worked its way out of the crack, and the space between the boards began to widen. He set the knife deeper and then pried the board, loosening one end of it. He reached with his other hand, took the end of the board, and pulled it up from the rest of the flooring.

"It's still here," Mac said, and he jiggled another floorboard out. His hand disappeared into the newly created hole, and he reached in so that his entire arm was concealed. "Got it," he said, and carefully retrieved his arm.

He placed a slightly rusted metal box on the floor next to him, then looked at Uri and made an eerie noise by whistling and humming at the same time.

"What? You sound like some old radio," Uri smirked.

"It's supposed to be a flying saucer, for crying out loud," Mac said, and made the noise again.

Uri folded his arms in front of him and looked annoyed.

"Look," Mac said, "this is just too much to deal with. All of this, Roswell, the Nephilim bones being stolen . . . my apartment. I'm just blowing off some steam by goofing off on all of this."

"What is goofing?" Uri asked, and looked curiously at Mac.

Mac covered his eyes with his hand, then patiently explained, "Making fun of something when circumstances get too overwhelming. And right now things are overwhelming!"

"Oh . . . goofing off." Uri repeated the phrase, nodded satisfactorily, then repeated it again under his breath, thrilled to have a new American colloquialism under his belt.

Mac turned to the box on the floor and drew back the catch. He paused and looked at Uri. Then he opened the lid.

Inside was a manila envelope that was folded once. He picked it up, unfolded it, and carefully took out a letter and handed it to Uri. "Read this."

Uri took the letter and read it. His lips were drawn together and his eyebrows were raised like bushy antennae on his forehead.

Mac reached into the envelope again and produced a small piece of what looked like dull gray aluminum foil. He crumpled it into a ball, then held it out in front of Uri who watched, like a child seeing his first snowfall, as the foil unfolded itself and remained in Mac's hand without a trace of a wrinkle.

Uri slowly reached a trembling hand and touched the metal. Mac nodded encouragingly, and Uri took it from his opened palm.

"You said it was locked in a vault."

"I lied," Mac said, and grinned. "I had it in a safe-deposit box for a while, but when I went through the divorce I cleaned everything out of it because I was afraid Maggie's lawyers would subpoena it."

"Did they?" Uri asked.

"No, of course not. I was paranoid ... too much booze. Anyway, here it is. Just like I told you and Elisha. This is what my father left me. It's part of the wreckage that he took from the debris field."

"Amazing! I can't be believing this," Uri said, clearly excited. He rolled the foil into a ball and watched as it reverted to its original shape without a wrinkle or a crease. He did it again, became serious, and said, "We must touch the bases with Roswell. Do you think your computer works?"

"It's 'touch base,' not touch the bases ..."

"What? Touch base? Oh ... Okay."

"Let's check it out," Mac said, as he hastily refitted the boards back into place. He took the letter and slipped it into the manila envelope, put it back in the box, and stood up. "Come on."

Uri remained on his knees, still holding the holy grail of the UFO artifact.

Mac went to his overturned desk and righted it. His computer was lying on its side next to the fax machine. The monitor was facedown on the floor. He set it back on the desk, checked the cables, made sure the connections were good, then set his keyboard in front of the monitor and plugged everything into the power surge protector strip. He closed his eyes, gritted his teeth, and turned the power strip on, expecting the worst. Hearing the hard drive start to boot up, he peeked. The monitor was working, and the computer was going through its normal warmup.

"Hey, I think it's all right," Mac said, surprised and relieved.

"Huh?" Uri mumbled.

"I said it's working. The computer's working. We can call Roswell!"

"Oh," Uri said as he slowly got up and made his way to the desk, not taking his eyes off the foil as he walked.

"Do you have the code?"

"Huh?"

"Will you please focus for a moment?" Mac said. "Do you have the code?"

Uri set the foil reverently on the desk in front of him. "Oh, I forgot . . . the code . . . You're right, it won't work from here. We'll have to call Elisha first and have him contact Roswell."

"So *why* didn't you tell me?"

Uri shrugged lamely and stood with his hands on his hips. "Forgive me, but . . ." He groped for the right word to use. "This is *monumental* for me. Because of this"—he pointed to the scrap of foil on Mac's desk—"I know life is existing elsewhere in the universe. What an incredible moment."

Mac looked at Uri and inwardly compared the difference the foil had made between them. In his life it connected him with his father's death. It was for him something ominous, a harbinger of doom. But to Uri it was the tree of life. Physical proof that we were not alone.

Mac said, "I appreciate that, although I don't agree, but we need to call Roswell and we need to do it soon. I feel like we're on the *Titanic* and I'm trying to get us into a lifeboat while you're admiring the iceberg!"

"I'm sorry, you're right. The telephone is working?"

Mac scanned the apartment and said, "I don't know. I can't seem to find it."

Mac moved some books off the floor by the bed and followed the telephone cord until he reached the phone, which was buried under a pile of clothes. "Here it is. Make the call," and he handed Uri the phone.

"Wait." Mac grabbed the phone back, held it to his ear making sure it had a dial tone, then clicked on the speakerphone. "Now we both can hear," Mac said as he handed it back to Uri.

Uri dialed his grandfather's number.

"Shalom," Elisha's voice erupted over the speaker.

Uri's face lit up and he answered, "Shalom! Shalom! Grandfather."

"Uri? You're in America . . . with MacKenzie?" Elisha asked.

"Hello, Elisha," Mac called out.

"Shalom, Mac. I'm glad you're both safe."

"Yes, we are safe, but we have a problem. I need to speak to *someone* that you know," Uri said, emphasizing the word.

Elisha said carefully, "Someone at Spiral of Life?"

"Yes," Uri replied.

"I can locate that person for you. Stay where you are until your party contacts you."

"We're not leaving anywhere," Uri replied.

"Are you both all right?" Elisha asked.

"All right, yes," Uri said. "Tonight I touched the sky."

"The sky?"

"Yes, the sky. The chariots of the gods," Uri exclaimed.

There was silence on the line and finally Elisha's voice responded, "Fascinating."

"Until we hear from you or your friend, we wait here," Uri said.

"I'll set to work on it immediately . . . and Uri . . . Mac."

"Yes."

"Please be careful," Elisha said.

*   ✳   ⚬   ✳

Elisha went to his computer and called up the Spiral of Life Web page. He squinted through his trifocals as he read the coded sequence of numbers and letters that allowed him access to Roswell. He typed in the necessary information and exited the Web page.

His house was quiet and he felt old and alone as he shuffled to his bedroom in the rear of his house.

He sat on the edge of the bed and reached for his worn Bible that lay open on his nightstand. He turned to the Psalms and read a passage. Afterward he closed his eyes and prayed for the blindness to be lifted from his grandson.

✳   ⚬   ✳

General Roswell's pager went off. He looked at the digitally displayed numerical sequence and recognized the pattern of numbers corresponding to Dr. Elisha BenHassen.

He walked over to his computer and brought up Spiral of Life, then punched in his special access code. He opened up his area and typed in the information necessary to unscramble the message from Dr. Elisha. He read the message, then erased the information. He typed in A. MACKENZIE and after a short pause the computer presented him with the file. He found the telephone number and dialed it.

He felt like it was going to be another long night. But after a lifetime of military service he was used to long nights.

He steadied himself and set his will on remaining alert and aware.

23

✦ ◉ ✦

Mac and Uri succeeded in putting the apartment in some semblance of order. Afterwards, they sat in front of the desk, sipped coffee, and waited for the phone to ring.

"Do you think he'll call here?" Mac asked wearily, his eyes bloodshot from lack of sleep.

Uri shrugged an "I don't know."

"Why don't we get some sleep?" Mac suggested, rubbing his stubble of beard with the back of his hand. "I'll take the couch. You can sleep in the bed."

"If he calls, what?" Uri asked, then shook his head. "No, you sleep and I'll wait."

"You mean take the first watch?" Mac scowled and shielded his forehead with his hand. "All quiet on the western front, sir." He forced a laugh as he saluted.

"Yeah, goofing," Uri said. "I'm thinking this is not a good place to be . . . anything might happen." Uri got up and went over to his bag and unzipped it. He carefully slipped his hand into a side pocket of the suitcase, produced a small round plastic tube, and laid it carefully on the floor next to him. He took out his shaving kit and added another plastic piece next to the first one.

Mac stared for a moment, then exclaimed, "You're making a gun, for crying out loud! You've got all the parts of a gun in there." He pointed in disbelief. "We could have gotten arrested coming through customs."

"I'm not getting too excited because you Americans never do a good search to find this." He held up the magazine and exclaimed proudly, "Plastic bullets." He quickly assembled the gun and slipped the clip into the handle. He looked seriously at Mac and said, "Now let them come, but for me . . . I won't be defenseless."

Mac rolled his eyes and muttered, "I can't believe this is happening. I need some sleep." He went over to the bed, lay down on his back, and closed his eyes.

Just at the point where he began to doze off, the phone rang. He sat up and looked at Uri.

"You get it," Uri said, as he bounded from the chair.

Mac nodded and reached for the phone on the nightstand.

"Hello." Mac made his voice sound tired as if he had just been awakened.

"Listen carefully, I can only talk for a minute."

Mac recognized the voice as Roswell's.

"What's that?" Roswell asked.

"I turned the speakerphone on . . . for Uri," Mac quickly answered.

Roswell spoke quickly in a low voice. "I've been advised of your situation and suggest you move away from your present location. In the morning meet me at the warehouse . . . ten A.M." The line went dead.

Mac and Uri looked at each other.

"You heard him," Uri said with a certain amount of satisfaction. "It's not safe here."

"The warehouse," Mac said, ignoring Uri's comment. "That's the same place I met Roswell the first time. It's in a run-down section of the city."

He got up from the bed and walked over to his suitcase that he still hadn't unpacked. "I guess we should get out of here. I know a cheap hotel not far from here."

"No, we need to get more upscale hotel with its own security. No one will want to be bothering us there," Uri said, as he tucked the gun into his back pocket.

"Uri, this isn't Israel, you can't walk around L.A. like that," Mac protested, as he pointed to the gun.

"It's the middle of the night, what? I'll cover it with a jacket."

"And what if we get stopped?"

Uri shrugged, looked at the floor for a moment, then back at Mac. He smiled broadly and said, "I'll cross that bridge when I come to it."

Mac rolled his eyes. "Let's get out of here."

"What about the artifact? From the crash site?"

"We'll put it under the floorboards again," Mac said absently, as he grabbed his suitcase.

"No. We take it with us. Wherever we go," Uri announced firmly.

"Fine. Have it your way. Only let's go, because I'm exhausted and hungry and I'm really getting tired of all the cloak-and-dagger nonsense. Here." He picked up the manila envelope and shoved it at Uri. "You be responsible for the thing. I've looked after it for sixteen years, and I don't care if I ever see the stupid thing again. It's yours . . . for the keeping."

"Does this mean I have to give it back?" Uri asked.

"It means it's four-thirty in the morning and I want to *sleep* somewhere, anywhere . . . and to top it all off, I, we, have to meet Roswell, or whatever his name is, in less than six hours."

"You sound . . . what's the word? Crinky?"

"The word is *cranky* and yes, right now I'm a prime example. Can we go now? Please?"

"I can really keep it?" Uri held the foil up in front of his face and looked at it wide-eyed.

"Yes. You can keep it, but you have to promise me something."

"Anything. Whatever you want." Uri took a step toward Mac and looked like a man ready to pledge his life for a noble cause.

"Promise me that we'll get out of here and get some sleep, for crying out loud," Mac said, and without waiting for an answer he unbolted the door, stepped out into the hall, and waited for Uri.

Uri reverently slipped the foil back in the manila envelope, placed it in his suitcase, and then zipped it up.

"I'm ready. Do you want anything before we leave?"

"Yeah, but I'm not drinking anymore," Mac answered sarcastically. "Let's go!"

Uri looked one last time around the apartment, went to the refrigerator, opened it, and took a can of 7-Up. "You want one?"

"Nope," Mac replied.

Uri popped it open, took a swig, and joined Mac in the hallway.

Mac locked the door and the two of them hurried down the stairs, through the foyer, and onto the street.

They threw their suitcases into the cluttered back seat of the jeep.

"Not so fast," Mac said as he went around to the front and opened the hood. "I've disconnected the cap on the distributor." He struggled with the cap for a moment, succeeded in reconnecting it, and then closed the hood.

"Let's go," Mac said, and they got into the jeep. "I've got to air this thing out . . . smells musty in here," he complained as he fussed with the damp towel, while he tried to get comfortable in the front seat.

He turned the key in the ignition. There was a clicking sound, like an out-of-balance roulette wheel, but the engine didn't fire.

"What's happened?" Uri asked.

Mac remembered the security guard at the hospital. "It's my cables . . . at least I hope," he muttered as he climbed out of the jeep and went to the front and opened the hood. "You have a knife?"

"No. Why?" Uri asked, as he got out.

"The cables to the battery . . . see how corroded they are."

Uri came around and peered under the hood. A single amber streetlight a short distance away cast just enough light so they could make out the interior. Mac tried to loosen the battery cable, but the corrosion had welded it tight to the post of the battery.

"I don't believe this," Mac complained, as he struggled with the cables.

"Very badly corroded, you should change those," Uri suggested, as he pointed to them, then said, "Let me see at something."

Mac moved out of the way and let Uri take a look.

"We need a screwdriver or a knife," Mac said, "I'll go back in the house and get one."

"Wait, let me try one thing," Uri said. He took a long sip from the can of 7-Up, then wiggled it to see how much was left. To Mac's astonishment he poured the rest of the contents over the battery posts.

Mac looked at Uri, then back at the drenched battery, and cried, "What are you doing?"

Uri motioned for him to look. The 7-Up fizzled around the battery posts. Some sort of chemical reaction was taking place.

"What's happening? What's it doing to the battery?" Mac asked.

"It's eating at the corrosion." Uri jiggled the cables, then said, "Go try it now."

Mac hopped into the front seat and turned the key. Much to his delight the engine turned over.

"Hey, it worked."

"Old army trick. Israelis must be resourceful!"

"Thanks. Now get in," and he gassed the engine.

Uri climbed into the jeep and before he could fasten his seat belt, Mac roared off down the street.

* ○ *

They traveled into Westwood and checked into a room at the Westwood Hilton. Uri had used travelers checks to pay for it. They were ushered to their room on the ninth floor by a bellhop.

"Enjoy your stay, gentlemen," the bellhop said, as they entered the room.

"Thanks," Mac said, as he handed the man a couple of bucks.

The bellhop pocketed the two dollars and left without saying thank you.

"He wants to retire on what I tipped him," Mac said.

"What time is it?" Uri asked.

"The ridiculous hour of five-thirty in the morning. We have to meet Roswell . . . I don't want to think about it. I'll call room service and have them give us a wake-up call," Mac said, and went to the phone.

Uri nodded and went into the bathroom.

Mac called room service and requested the wake-up call.

Uri appeared from the bathroom in only his underwear, holding the gun in his right hand. "I'll take the bed near to the door," he said.

"Whatever." Mac exhaled as he stripped down to his underwear, pulled back the covers, and fell into the bed. He wrapped the pillow over his head, mumbled "Good night," and promptly went to sleep.

Uri switched the light off. The room was plunged into darkness.

* o *

Almost half an hour had elapsed since MacKenzie had offered a quick good night. Uri lay on his side facing the door and listened to Mac's restful breathing.

He held the loaded gun next to his face on the pillow. From his military training he knew he couldn't sleep. Rest, yes, but not sleep. There would be time to sleep another day, but for now he must be aware. He gripped the gun and clicked the safety off. With his other hand he rolled up the piece of foil from the UFO wreckage. He let it go and felt it unravel itself into a smooth, flat surface. He did it again and again in the darkness.

Each time the realization of what he held in his hand helped keep him awake, alert, and, more importantly, alive.

24

✱ ⬡ ✱

The phone rang in the hotel room, and the noise of it penetrated the pillow that was wrapped around Mac's head.

It was eight A.M. and he could hear the shower running. Uri was already up.

He reached for the receiver.

"Hello ... Yes, I know it's eight ... thank you ... Yes ... Good morning to you too. Thank you," he said, with forced politeness. He hung up the phone.

He sat on the edge of the bed and stretched his legs and arms to their limits, making his muscles taut from the strain. *It's a good time to call Maggie,* he thought, as he reached for the phone and dialed her number.

"Hello, this is Sarah," a squeaky voice shrilled over the receiver.

Mac laughed at the sound of her voice. "Hello, honey, this is your dad. I'm back from my trip."

"Daddy's back!" she yelled.

Mac pulled the phone away from his ear and chuckled. He listened carefully as he brought the receiver slowly back. Satisfied that there would be no more ear-splitting outbursts, he asked, "Sarah, honey, is your mom there?"

"Daddy, are you coming here soon?" she asked, ignoring his question.

"Yes, honey. Is your mother there?" he repeated.

He heard a slight commotion as the phone exchanged hands.

Maggie's voice replaced Sarah's. "Mac? Is that you? Where are you?"

"Hi. Yes, it's me. I'm back but I can't tell you where I am . . . at least not yet."

"Are you all right?"

"Look, I'm fine. It's a long story . . . but I can't stay at my apartment."

She hesitated, then asked, "What do you mean?"

"Somebody busted in and trashed it . . . they were looking for something."

"That's horrible . . . what were they looking for?"

"Papers," he said, bluntly.

"Papers?"

"Maggie, I can't explain it right now—"

"Mac, what are you involved in?" she interrupted. "You're shot at in Israel and now somebody breaks into your apartment . . . Jim said he didn't like the sound of what you were getting into."

"What does Cranston have to do with it?" he asked, the anger rising in his voice. *She's confiding in him,* he thought. He got control and said, "Look . . . I'm all right. Maggie, listen, I don't want to get into all of this right now but, honestly, I've never been better."

Silence again, then she asked, "Did you meet somebody . . . in Israel?"

"Well, actually I did . . . but it's not what you think."

"Well, I hope you're happy," she said.

"Maggie." He groped for the right words to say, then blurted out, "I had an experience while I was in Israel. A religious experience."

"Oh?" Her voice softened, and there was no mistaking the curiosity in it.

"Look, honestly, I can't talk about all of this now. I have an appointment I have to get to. I'll call you later tonight and we'll talk."

"Promise you'll call . . . for the kids? They need you, Mac."

"I promise. Say hi to Jeremy," he said, not wanting the conversation to end but afraid to pursue it any longer.

"Okay." She paused a moment then hastily added, "I'm worried about you, Mac."

Her last words caught Mac completely off guard. "Oh . . . I'm okay, so don't worry. I'll call tonight, okay? Bye." And without waiting for a response he hung up the phone just as Uri emerged from the bathroom with a towel wrapped around his waist and another draped over his muscular shoulders.

Uri looked agitated. "What are you doing?" he asked.

"I'm calling my wife. Why?" Mac answered.

"It's not safe. Her phone may be tapped."

"Oh, come on. You really think somebody is going to tap her phone?"

Uri shook his head and walked over to the heavy curtains that were drawn over the windows. He went to where they met, opened one slightly, and peered out.

"What are you looking at?" Mac asked.

"Not anything. I need just to see what kind of day it is."

"Oh, I thought . . . never mind," he mumbled.

Uri dried his hair vigorously with the white hotel towel. He wadded it into a ball and backhanded it through the bathroom door. "You know what, we don't know who is responsible for what happened in your apartment. Right? I'm thinking, it's the people who destroyed Fineberg's lab and took the Nephilim artifacts . . ."

"Over here?"

"Yeah." He frowned. "I'm telling you another thing . . . We are dealing with professionals. Your door wasn't broken . . .

they picked the locks. And what is to be missing . . . the information Roswell sent you. You see the connection?"

Mac nodded.

"Somebody is watching what you do. Your wife's phone is more likely to be monitored."

"Yeah?"

"Remember you were telling about the guy who roughed you up in the airport? How did he know you? Somebody knows that you are probing into something they want to keep very secret. These people don't want us to find out. You see that? As we get closer, everybody is more risky."

"Yeah, I know all that, but my wife's phone?" Mac protested.

"It's the first thing, if I wanted to know what and where you are going to." He grinned at Mac. "And I thought you said she was your ex-wife?"

"All right, ex-wife," he corrected.

"We must be careful. People's lives may be at risk."

"So what about the friendly alien theory?" Mac brought back his challenge of the night before.

"I'm thinking that I don't know, but maybe when we see Roswell he can make things more clear."

"Okay, so for the moment we both admit that we don't know what's going on . . . who's behind all the intrigue . . . huh?"

Uri nodded.

"But I don't think friendly aliens that are here to replenish their gene pool destroy laboratories, steal artifacts, and break into people's apartments, for crying out loud."

"You know what? Maybe you're right about that . . . I don't know . . ."

"Don't confuse you with the facts, right?" Mac chuckled. "I'm going to take a shower," Mac said, as he went into the bathroom.

"Hurry, we don't want to be late," Uri reminded him.

* ○ *

Cranston sat at his desk in his office editing an op-ed piece for the weekend edition of the paper. When the phone rang, he grabbed it and growled a "What?" into the receiver.

"He called her a few minutes ago. He's back in the States," the caller said.

Cranston hesitated and wished that the caller would go away. Reluctantly he asked, "MacKenzie?"

"Yeah. We traced the call and he's at the Hilton in Westwood. Guess we scared him out of his place."

"What do you mean?" he asked.

"We searched his apartment . . . trashed it, huh?"

Cranston's stomach tightened. "Are you sure he's at the Hilton? He can't afford that."

"Hey, that's where he is," the caller assured him. "We also put a bug on his car."

"Why?" Cranston asked.

"Keep tabs on him."

"Why are you involving me in this . . . can't your people take care of whatever you need to do?"

"You're his editor, huh? Besides, the story he wrote has had its repercussions."

Cranston thought of the requests he'd ignored to inspect the sixth floor. Requests from city officials and a few desperate letters from people looking for lost loved ones who had disappeared in the labyrinth of top-secret military bureaucracy.

"Look, I'm supposed to be a liaison . . . I don't want to be involved in your dirty work."

The caller's voice became agitated. "You should have thought of that when the Agency approached you. Your part of the deal is to help keep our presence low-key."

Cranston fidgeted in his chair. "I've done that and you know it . . . I can't be responsible for every prying eye twenty-four hours a day. You have your own security for that."

"Well, relax, we know his every move. Keep the faith, huh?" The caller hung up.

Cranston slowly put down the receiver.

Who's paying for the hotel room ... and why all the excitement over some ancient bones exhumed in Israel? he wondered.

He got up from his desk and went over to a large mahogany bookcase. He selected a putter from one of half a dozen leaning against the lower shelf. Then he grabbed a few golf balls and set them down on the rug. He lined up his first shot and sent it rolling across the floor toward the electronic hole. The ball went into the cup, and in a moment the machine kicked it back toward him.

He lined his second shot up and putted. "Darn you, MacKenzie," he said out loud as his second shot missed the cup by several inches.

* ◊ *

"Are you ready?" Uri asked impatiently, as he slipped his gun and the envelope containing the artifact inside his windbreaker.

Mac nodded.

"Let's go," Uri said and zipped up his jacket.

"Do you have the artifact from the sarcophagus?" Mac asked.

"Of course. I've put it in here." He held up a small duffel bag. "Look at this, I want to show you something."

Mac went over to where their suitcases were. Uri had arranged their luggage side by side. He had taken a small piece of Scotch tape and had carefully placed it in a way that if you didn't know it was there and you opened the suitcase, you would tear the tape.

"Pretty clever," MacKenzie said.

"If they search in the room ... we will know."

"Maybe we should take them with us. What if they rig them with a bomb or something?" Mac asked.

"Here? No, too much exposures," Uri assured him.

They left the room and Uri put the Do Not Disturb sign on the door. "This should keep room service out," he said, as he put another piece of tape on the bottom of the jamb. "What? Simple?"

"Yeah," Mac agreed.

* ○ *

Half an hour later Mac's jeep bounced along the tattered asphalt in a depressed area of the city. Most of the buildings were vacant. The area was a haven for vagrants and homeless people. It also attracted a more dangerous element of gangs and drug users.

"This looks like maybe it's a bad area," Uri said as they slowly drove up the trash-littered street.

"Count on it . . . but I met Roswell near here before."

"How much more?" Uri asked.

"Another couple of blocks."

"Turn on this street, quickly," Uri said.

"That's not the way—"

"Trust me . . . turn," Uri interrupted. "Go a little way, then stop," he ordered.

Mac glanced at him and saw he was serious. "Okay, hang on." He turned the wheel sharply and headed down a small side street, went about half a block, and stopped.

Uri reached out the window, grabbed the side mirror, and turned it so he could see behind him. He watched as a car slowly crossed the intersection.

Mac heard the booming bass of some rap song thudding from the car as it passed.

"You know what? That car was following us for a while."

"You don't quit, do you?" Mac jabbed. He threw the jeep in gear and spun it around, making the tires squeal.

Uri patted his jacket where the gun was concealed and answered, "You know what? I've been trained not to trust so much."

Mac backtracked and got on the street he was on before the detour. He drove through a particularly bleak section where some of the buildings were burned out.

"Looks like a war zone," Mac said.

"It reminds me sometimes of home." Uri chuckled.

"Glad you feel comfortable," Mac said sarcastically.

Mac turned down Third Street then slowed the jeep. "This is it," he said, as they pulled up to the abandoned warehouse. They got out of the car and walked around to the entrance Mac had used the previous time he had met with Roswell.

"Just like before," Mac said. "No car. Nobody, nothing, and then *poof!* He just appears from behind one of the columns."

"Through there?" Uri pointed at the large weathered wooden door.

"Yep." Mac nodded, opened the door, and went in. The interior was unchanged. A few more windowpanes were broken but other than that, things looked the same.

Mac walked the length of the room and looked behind each of the stout wooden posts. "He's not here. What time do you have?"

Uri looked at his watch. "We're early," he said, as he leaned against one of the large columns.

Tires crunched the gravel in the parking lot outside. Uri put his finger to his lips, moved quickly to the door, and peered out.

"It's a big black car," he said, and unzipped his jacket.

"A Lincoln?" Mac asked, and he trotted back from the other end of the building and looked out the door. "I think that's his car."

As they looked, the tinted mirrored glass of the rear window rolled silently down. A tired, pale face looked up at them.

"It's Roswell," Mac said, "but he doesn't look so good."

Mac opened the door and he and Uri stepped slowly out onto the loading deck. Roswell motioned for them to come down. Roswell's driver got out of the car and opened the door opposite where Roswell was sitting. Mac and Uri walked around the front of the Lincoln and got in.

"You must be Uri BenHassen," Roswell said, immediately taking charge of the conversation. "You're bigger than I imagined you. The sword is passed to the younger and stronger," he said wistfully. "I'm Roswell." He firmly gripped Uri's hand and pumped it a few times before letting go.

He turned to Mac and said tersely, "MacKenzie," and shook hands.

"Let's go, Diebol," Roswell ordered his chauffeur.

Diebol turned the Lincoln around and then backed up so that the rear bumper of the car touched the rusted fence at the farthest end of the parking lot. The car faced the street and from their new vantage point they were able to see Mac's jeep and any vehicle that might pass by.

"So what happened at your apartment—was anything taken?" Roswell asked.

Mac glanced at Uri, then blurted, "Look, I'm sorry, but I messed up. I left the information packet you gave me in one of the drawers in my desk. They took that."

Roswell tightened his lips and looked steadily at Mac. After what seemed like an inordinate period of silence he asked, "What did you think of the artifact, the skeleton in the sarcophagus?"

"I think it's very interesting, and it seems to shore up Elisha BenHassen's theory of the existence of a union between the fallen angels and the women of earth." Mac motioned to the bag that Uri held in his lap. "We brought the last remaining piece of the skeleton with us."

"Elisha mentioned that testing showed it to have a fifth nucleotide, making it a genetic anomaly of great proportions," Roswell said.

"It's more than just an anomaly—nothing on this planet has a fifth nucleotide," Mac said.

"He's right," Uri said. "I'm thinking it could be extraterrestrial."

"I understand . . . all too well," Roswell muttered, as he turned in his seat so he could see the two men better. "I want you both to know something of what I think is going on." His pale blue eyes gazed at them impassively from a face that over the years had set into an unreadable mask, void of emotion.

"You both are aware that I have been involved with the alien presence since '47." He looked at Mac. "I want you to know that your father was a good soldier. But he wasn't the only man to crack up over what he had seen. There were others who saw less and couldn't handle it. I know of one nurse who has been confined to a sanitarium for the last fifty years. She was never able to cope with what she saw. The idea of other life-forms in '47 was viewed a lot differently than it is today. At that time the government was afraid the public might panic if they knew about the existence of extraterrestrials. The government was concerned especially with the philosophical and religious implications that might unravel the very fabric of our society. Are you with me?"

Mac and Uri nodded.

"President Truman formed a group of men to study the extraterrestrial or alien problem. They were to deal with any crashed saucers and recovered bodies. And also advise about the back engineering of recovered alien technology. It was a good idea . . . on paper. Unfortunately, there were men who used their position for their own aggrandizement. They managed to split off from the main group and became a sort of rogue element. They worked within the government and yet were accountable to no one. Because of my rank and position I have been able to keep tabs on some of what they have done and continue to do. About ten years ago I was contacted by a group of men . . . The same men who are responsible for the Web site you accessed."

"Interesting site," Mac remarked.

"Yes, it is, although they have a different viewpoint than I do. They're very aware of the alien presence and want to expose it to the public at large. Every inhabitant on the planet has the right to know that we're not alone. But before we can do that, the President and Congress must be informed. That's where you come in, MacKenzie. I want you to write about this from a layman's point of view. Someone outside the military establishment. But more importantly, from the perspective of a man who lost his father because of the coverup."

Mac looked at Roswell for a moment and wondered how much of what he was hearing was true. "How many other people know about this?" he finally asked. "And why hasn't anyone tried go public with this?"

Roswell frowned. "Some have tried . . ."

"And what happened?" Mac asked.

"Most of them are found dead in their cars . . . office . . . or a family retreat. Like your father."

"So what makes you think it will be any different if I try?" Mac said.

"I'm not saying things will be different, but as I said, I am part of a group of people who share the same distaste for the rogue element that has kept this clandestine for so long. There is a commonality of patriotism among us that finds this very un-American and contrary to our way of life . . . There is also another dynamic that I haven't told you."

"I'm sure there's a lot you haven't told us," Mac said sarcastically.

"You're right," Roswell admitted, "there are layers upon layers . . . On the Web page you saw the painting, the close-up of the foot descending on the Mount of Olives?"

"Yes, Elisha said it was an illustration of the Second Coming," Mac said.

"Correct . . . some of those I work with believe that we live in the time of Jesus' return."

"Do you believe that?" Mac asked.

Roswell looked away. "There was a time years ago . . . but no, I don't believe that. I've seen too much . . ."

"How have they managed to keep all of this under wraps?" Mac asked.

"MacKenzie, let me explain how the military can keep something secret for so long. Those who are involved work on a need-to-know basis. For instance, if you want to back engineer a recovered disk to see what makes it tick, you give your people who are working on it only the part that pertains to, let's say, the propulsion system. Nothing else. Their need to know is confined to the propulsion system, and only the propulsion system. They don't know where it comes from. You tell them that it was recovered from the Russians. You never say that it is in fact from an alien ship. Every item they look at or touch is classified above top secret. Your people are kept apart. Compartmentalized. Other groups in the same facility can be working on other technology recovered from the same craft. But because they are separated from each other no one knows the whole story. Only a few people at the top have any idea of what the broad picture really is. We built the atomic bomb in this way. People can keep secrets, Mr. MacKenzie."

Mac shifted in his seat, wishing he was outside in the open air instead of in the stuffy interior of the car. "I understand what you're driving at," he said, "but how could all of this get so out of control?"

"A good question, but it's not important to know *how* the situation got that way. What matters is that *now* there are isolated agencies within the military establishment with black ops budgets who are accountable to no one. Part of what we're involved in is to bring to accountability this rogue element."

"So the United States government sanctions what you're doing?" Mac asked.

Roswell hinted at a smile. "Officially, they won't sanction a thing."

"Unofficially?"

"They're anxious for answers . . . so we're protected to a point."

"How about the group that set up the Web page?"

"Private sector . . . large sums of money . . . with a keen knowledge of Bible prophecy. They're working this thing from another angle altogether."

Roswell bent forward, opened his briefcase, and took out a map. He held it in front of him so Mac and Uri could see it.

"This, gentlemen, is a map of an area that officially doesn't exist. It is a top secret, underground facility hidden deep in the Nevada desert. Although it is staffed by American scientists and military personnel, the rogue element that I spoke of controls the base. They've operated it for years this way. Because of the level of security clearance, no one knows who is actually in control. Not even the president." He looked at them both, his silence underscoring the gravity of the situation. "There are also alien craft and personnel working side by side with our own people."

Mac looked at Roswell and shook his head in disbelief.

"I've seen it, and tomorrow both of you will too." He laid the map on his lap. "Tomorrow morning at four o' clock you'll meet me here." He pointed to an area outside Palmdale. "From here we'll fly to the base along with scientists and other military personnel who are shuttled back and forth to work at the base. I've got uniforms that you'll wear that will enable you to accompany me. You'll pose as new technicians."

"What if someone catches on to us while we're there? Why are you willing to take such a risk?" Mac asked.

Roswell straightened in his seat. "Because I want you to write a story that will change the way people think, and to do that you have to go there and see for yourself. Besides, I've had aides with me before. Also, I have introduced scientists into the workforce at this particular base. Now listen. I want you to go back to the hotel and rest. But change rooms first. Okay?"

Mac and Uri nodded.

Roswell continued, "You need to prepare yourselves for tomorrow. Don't go outside. Order your food from room service. Don't make any calls, and most importantly, be on time at four." He looked at the men and, satisfied that he was understood, called out to the driver, "Diebol, check their car."

"Yes, sir," came the crisp reply.

Diebol got out and opened the trunk. Mac could hear him moving things around. Then the muscular chauffeur—or was he a bodyguard?—headed for the street. He held a small box that had what looked like a microphone attached to it by a cord.

Roswell said, "If there's a tracking device on your car, Diebol will find it and deactivate it."

At Mac's jeep, Diebol switched the box on. Mac watched him hold the microphone out toward the jeep and look down at the box. Diebol slowly moved the microphone back and forth, examining different sections of the jeep. After a moment he set the box down on the ground and slid under the jeep's chassis.

A moment later he emerged with a round metal object about the size of a fifty-cent piece in his hand. He held it up for all of them to see, then walked back to the Lincoln.

"Good job, Diebol," Roswell said. "We'll drop it off somewhere interesting later. Meanwhile, give these two their uniforms."

"Yes, sir." He went to the back of the trunk and reappeared holding two shiny silver tote bags.

"Here," Roswell said, as the men were handed the bags. "Now go back to the hotel and get some rest, and that, by the way, is an order! I'll see you at four. Oh, and Uri, leave the bag with the artifact. I'll have it tested by our people."

Uri reluctantly handed it over and said, "It's the only piece we have left."

"I understand. I'll see that it gets to the right people personally," Roswell replied, setting it carefully in front of him.

Mac and Uri climbed out of the car and closed the door.

"One other thing," Roswell said, through the open window. "Park the jeep a few blocks from the hotel, preferably in an underground garage. That way they won't be able to bug you again."

Mac nodded. "Sure thing."

Mac and Uri watched as the Lincoln moved slowly out of the parking lot and turned up the street. They heard its engine accelerate and then fade into the ever-present din of the city.

Uri looked at Mac as if to say "I told you so."

"All right, so you were right. Who would want to bug my car? No, I know who," he answered his own question. "The same people who belted me at the airport and blew up the sarcophagus and ruined Fineberg's lab and my apartment. This is hardball."

"Hardball?" Uri asked.

"Yeah, an expression that refers to our baseball. When you play in the major leagues for money, you play hardball. It means getting serious, getting tough."

"Okay, hardball. I like that," Uri said.

They walked across the parking lot to the jeep.

"Hardball," Uri repeated. "Hardball."

25

＊◆＊

Mac lay in bed with his hands folded behind his neck and stared into the darkness. In the bed next to him, Uri Ben-Hassen punctuated every breath with a loud assortment of snorts and snores. Uri's commotion, however, was not the reason why Mac was awake.

A short while ago he had been stirred from a deep sleep. It felt as if someone had gently roused him like his mother used to, in his childhood. Now it felt as if there was a hand upon him, an inward pressure making him take notice. It was a strange sensation, mildly unpleasant, so that Mac was very aware of it. He had never felt anything like it before.

He remembered the Bible Elisha had given him that still remained in his suitcase . . . untouched. It seemed as if the pressure or inner hand was directing him to it. Somehow the thought appeared in his mind, suggesting he get up and read.

Is this feeling the Spirit of God? he wondered.

He quietly got out of bed and went to the bathroom and shut the door halfway. He reached inside and turned the light on, then closed the door just enough to let some light spill into the room, so as not to disturb Uri.

He went over to his bag, opened it, and groped a bit before he found the two books he was looking for. One was a Bible, the other was the book of Enoch. He crept into the bathroom and closed the door. Then he leaned up against the vanity and started to read.

He opened the Bible to where Elisha instructed him to look first, in Ephesians. He read the small book of six chapters, not understanding much. One thing that impressed him was the last chapter. The passage about "the spiritual forces of evil in the heavenly realms." It sounded ominous to him, reminding him of what Elisha had said about the abductees and the cattle mutilations.

His eyes fell onto another verse near the end of Ephesians. He read it again. "Put on the full armor of God so that you can take your stand against the devil's schemes." *The armor of God,* he thought. *I need as much of that as I can get.*

He glanced at his watch and decided it was time to get ready. He showered quickly, wrapped a towel around his waist, and left the bathroom.

"Uri, it's time," he called.

Uri opened his eyes and kissed the gun he'd held during the night.

"Do you have to do that?" Mac asked.

"What? Sometime you may be thanking me for it."

"Whatever . . . we're up a little early, but I figure we could stop and get something to eat on the road."

"Well, hey, good for us," Uri said, and he climbed out of his bed and headed for the shower.

* o *

A short time later they left the hotel room and rode the elevator down to the lobby. It was deserted with the exception of a young woman sitting behind the polished granite counter painting her fingernails.

They cautiously went out onto the sidewalk and looked up and down the street. It was deserted. A heavy coastal fog had come in sometime during the night and soaked everything with a layer of marine air. Satisfied that they were not being followed, they quickly walked down the desolate sidewalks of Los Angeles. They arrived at the parking lot and rode the elevator three stories underground and walked to Mac's jeep.

"Looks okay," Mac said, motioning to it.

"Let's make sure," Uri said, as he went down on his knees and looked under the chassis of the jeep. "Okay," he repeated.

They got in and Mac fired the engine. It reverberated deafeningly off the concrete walls, ceiling, and floor.

"I'm thinking you must need to get that muffler fixed," Uri yelled, as he held his hands to his ears and shot Mac a disapproving look.

"I know, it's on the top of my list after I return from a secret alien base," Mac replied.

He threw the jeep in gear, stopped and paid his parking fee, then headed out into the dampened streets of L.A. A few red lights, a couple of turns, up the freeway ramp, and they were on their way to Palmdale.

Well outside the city limits they pulled over at a truck stop and each inhaled a breakfast special. With their stomachs filled and nervous systems wired on coffee, they drove the rest of the distance to where Roswell had instructed them he would meet them.

"We're early again, aren't we?" Mac asked, as he pulled off onto the small service road that Roswell had designated as their meeting place.

Uri glanced at his watch and said, "Yeah, but we can do the changing into jumpsuits."

Mac drove off the road then turned off the motor. The terrain was spotted with small bushes and scrubby trees. He and Uri hopped out of the jeep and began to undress.

"It's freezing out here! We should have changed at the hotel," Mac joked as he pulled the silver jumpsuit out of the bag. "I can see us walking around L.A. in these!"

"It's a free world." Uri laughed as he unfolded his silver jumpsuit.

"Yeah, we'd fit right into the local nightlife."

They laughed and continued to suit up. Finished dressing, they stood by the jeep and waited for Roswell.

"I'm not getting too excited, but do you realize where we are going?" Uri asked.

"Who are you kidding? You're about to burst."

"You know the feeling . . ." Uri replied.

Mac looked overhead at the surplus of stars in the clear night sky and said, "No, I don't. I'll be honest with you . . . I'm scared," he confessed. "The more I get into this thing, the more I find myself leaning toward what Elisha's told us. I think the phenomenon is evil."

"Satan and his hordes," Uri scoffed, "folklore." Uri kicked the gravel on the road, looked up at the stars overhead, and said, "Look at those. If another form of life journeyed here and simply needed to replenish itself genetically, what then? Because men and governments do evil things, that doesn't mean the aliens are evil. Roswell tells us, what . . . that some group has taken control. You know what? If the aliens are with them because they have no other choice . . . what then? Maybe somehow this rogue element are the ones who are pulling strings."

"No, I don't buy that," Mac interrupted. "If they have the kind of technology that the Major showed us, I think they can do just about anything they please—hey, what's that?" He pointed to headlights that had just swung onto the service road.

"Must be them," Uri said.

The car flashed its headlights once, then stopped. "MacKenzie," a woman's voice called out through the darkness.

"Who's that?" Uri asked.

"I don't know," Mac replied.

They reached the car and Mac climbed into the back of the Lincoln followed by Uri.

"Hello, MacKenzie," Roswell said. "This is my daughter, Laura."

Mac looked toward the front seat of the car. Laura smiled slightly and said, "Hello, MacKenzie, still having trouble flying?"

Mac looked confused. "I don't follow."

Her smile broadened and her eyes danced playfully as she looked at him. "At the airport . . . I convinced you to get on the plane."

"You?" Mac gaped.

"I had blond hair and green eyes then," she said as she tossed a long brown braid over her shoulder. "It was a wig," she said and laughed playfully.

"Green Eyes," he said and smiled.

Roswell cleared his throat. "And this is Uri BenHassen."

Laura extended her hand. "Pleased," Uri said, as he took it.

"Let's go, Diebol," Roswell ordered.

Diebol started the car and slowly backed out of the service road and headed toward Palmdale.

Roswell produced two plastic I.D. badges from his briefcase and said, "A few things you need to know. First, put these on. Clip them onto your right pocket, above the top of the flap. There's a little loop especially sewed into the suit to accommodate it."

Mac fumbled with the clip and it took him three tries to succeed in fastening it to the loop. In his frustration he looked up and noticed Laura smiling at him as he fumbled with the tag.

"Now listen," Roswell instructed, "you're not to address anyone no matter what happens. If you are spoken to, you defer to me, immediately, and I'll take care of the rest. And whatever you happen to see, under any circumstances, do not look in the least bit surprised. Is that clear? We're going to board the plane in a few minutes. You will not talk on the flight to each other or to anyone or me. Understand?"

Mac and Uri nodded.

"If by some remote chance we are separated, and I don't anticipate that in a month of Sundays, but if we are, try to make your way to the base canteen, sit down, and eat a meal slowly. Don't look for me, I'll find you. And don't talk to anyone." He shifted in his seat and Mac noticed him wince. "Now here's something you have to understand right from the get-go. There is a strong military police presence there. It permeates everything. You can't go to the bathroom in that place without an escort. You will be watched constantly, which is why I need you to act like soldiers. Discipline yourselves. I'm not worried about BenHassen, I know he was decorated in the War of '73." He gave a quick nod of recognition to Uri.

"Thank you, sir," Uri replied.

The general continued, "MacKenzie, on the other hand, has no military training. And what I'm worried most about is that you are going to see something fantastic and that reporter brain of yours is going to want to ask a lot of questions. You are not to do that."

"Yes, sir," Mac answered.

"There'll be plenty of time after we leave the base to discuss what you see."

"Is Laura coming with us?" Mac asked.

"No, she has another assignment . . ." Roswell said. "Okay, we're almost there . . . let's be careful."

Laura turned around from the back seat and her eyes met MacKenzie's.

She's beautiful, he mused, and for a moment he forgot about underground bases and aliens. But as the Lincoln pulled out onto the highway he felt his stomach flip. *We're not playing around here,* he realized. *We're really on our way to an alien base.*

He shivered.

26

Mac sat pensively in the forward section of a modified 737 airplane. Uri was next to him with his back pressed straight against the padded seat and his hands folded in his lap. Roswell occupied both seats across the aisle. His briefcase lay open on the seat next to him and his laptop computer rested on the tray in front of him. Immersed in his work, he ignored both Mac and Uri.

Although over a hundred men and women sat dispersed throughout the plane, there was no conversation. A quiet somberness hung over the passengers, like a shroud. Mac closed his eyes. *Put on the full armor of God,* he thought. He had a feeling he was going to need it. He squeezed his hands and began to pray.

After about half an hour, Mac opened his eyes again. The plane was heading directly into the dull orange ball of the rising sun, which had just crested the horizon. As if by some pre-arranged cue, the passengers began to fasten their seatbelts on their own initiative. They packed their books and papers and readied themselves for landing as the plane slowed and made its final approach. The wheels hit the tarmac once, then rolled smoothly along the flawlessly maintained runway.

Mac looked out the window. In the early dawn he saw a landing field that was larger than LAX. A huge hangar whose footprint must have taken up ten or more acres loomed ahead of them. The plane was dwarfed by the size of the building as it rolled to a stop near the entrance. The building's opening was at least four stories high, and the plane could easily have entered.

The occupants silently rose from their seats. Some adjusted I.D. tags while others fidgeted with their briefcases. A line formed and everyone began to deplane. The silence was unnerving.

At the door of the plane two yellow-helmeted MPs with walkie-talkies and side arms inspected each person's I.D. tag before allowing them to descend the metal staircase out of the plane.

Roswell was one of the first to disembark. Mac and Uri followed him closely. Mac felt butterflies in his stomach as one of the MPs checked the I.D. on his jumpsuit. He left the plane and felt a warm dry wind across his face as he stepped onto the surface of the tarmac. He hurried to catch up with Roswell.

Roswell looked at him stonily, whispered, "Stay close," then walked into the hangar. Mac and Uri followed one pace behind.

The first impression that rushed at Mac was the over-bearing deployment of MPs everywhere. They were always in groups of twos. One MP handled a walkie-talkie while the other shouldered a rifle and surveyed the personnel. Both were outfitted with holstered side arms. It was all very intimidating.

Mac noticed that the scientists and passengers from his plane deliberately ignored the MPs as much as possible. It was clearly evident that there was a keen dislike between the two groups.

Some of the scientists and workers headed toward what appeared to be a large elevator several hundred yards away.

As Mac walked toward it he noticed that certain areas of the hangar had been sectioned off with black wall partitions that almost reached the curved ceiling high overhead. From the noise that escaped from some of these, he assumed teams of technicians were working on aircraft of some fashion.

The three of them formed a single line with Mac in the middle as they approached the elevator. As they drew nearer to it the presence of MPs doubled.

A line of personnel began to funnel into the elevator, which was large enough to hold as many as a hundred people. Each scientist, technician, or assistant was meticulously checked by an MP and walked through some sort of metal detector. Mac watched two men in blue jumpsuits pass through an eye-scanning device. There was an eerie silence as the group slowly progressed into the elevator.

It was Roswell's turn to be inspected. The only discernible difference between how he was treated and everyone else was that the MPs snapped to attention and saluted him. He returned a crisp salute, then allowed himself to be processed.

"These men are with me, Sergeant," he said to the MP.

"Yes, sir." The MP nodded, then turned to Mac and Uri.

Mac was nervous. His throat was dry and his palms were sweaty. He held himself erect as he walked forward and stopped in front of the MP.

The MP glanced at Mac's silver jumpsuit and then held his I.D. tag in his hand. He looked Mac squarely in the eyes almost as if he were mentally photographing him, and then with a quick motion of his hand waved him forward.

Uri went through the same procedure, and Mac held his breath until Uri was cleared.

They joined Roswell at the entrance of the elevator, then followed him into its interior. Slowly it filled with an array of scientists and technicians, most of whom appeared to be civilians ... and of course the ever-present yellow-helmeted MPs.

Mac noticed an exceptionally tall MP who was the elevator operator. His height enabled him to look above the heads of those occupying the interior of the elevator. He had a key attached to his belt, which was inserted into the elevator's control panel.

Four more MPs entered just before the operator closed the doors. They stood with their backs to the doors and faced the personnel.

The situation made Mac very uncomfortable. All around him people stared straight ahead like zombies. Someone sneezed behind him and out of habit he almost said, "God bless you," but he was able to stifle the impulse at the last moment.

The elevator descended very rapidly with no audible sound.

Roswell had explained earlier that the levels below the hangar floor could withstand a direct hit from a nuclear weapon. He informed Mac that layers of specially formulated steel reinforced concrete, over sixty feet thick, formed the foundation on which the hangar was constructed. Underneath the protective shield of concrete, twenty levels descended into the bowels of the earth. The first of these was probably a minimum of a hundred feet below the surface.

Roswell cleared his throat. Mac waited a moment, then casually turned to look at him. It was a prearranged signal between them, made before getting on the plane in Palmdale.

Roswell slipped his hands behind his back and with one finger pointed toward the control panel operated by an MP. Mac waited a moment, then lowered his head and stole a glance at the panel. It had numbers running to twenty. Where the number twelve should have been there was a red star and the letters MAJ. Mac remembered the briefing packet from Roswell and wondered if MAJ was an abbreviated form of MAJESTIC. He made a mental note to confer with Roswell about it.

Next to the letters MAJ a horizontal slot opened up in the panel to allow the insertion of a specially constructed key card. Mac studied the panel and made a mental note of its buttons and operations.

The elevator stopped on the first level and paused as the operator released the airlock. The doors slid open noiselessly. The MPs negotiated a crisp about-face and stepped off the elevator into what appeared to be an anteroom of some sort. An additional four MPs on that level inspected each person as they exited the elevator.

Mac watched as a scientist in a white lab coat emerged from a solid wall. A panel had simply glided to the side and the man stepped out. Mac glimpsed what appeared to be a small chamber the size of a large phone booth.

Roswell had explained that to allow maximum security and to guarantee total control of certain projects, a system of air locks was created on each level. For example, if you got off on the fourth level, you stepped into the main anteroom. You then would walk to one of the hidden panels, step on the plate in front of it, and the door would automatically open. As you entered the small room, the door would close behind you and once it was shut another in front of you would then open. This allowed complete privacy and isolation between the floors where top-secret research was being conducted. It insured that no one riding the main elevator would just happen to see something that they weren't supposed to. It also maintained isolation to each particular level, in case of viral or bacterial infection or contamination, which according to Roswell was the main consideration for the precautionary measures.

The elevator reached the eleventh level and Roswell motioned that they were to follow him. The doors opened and the MPs exited. Roswell stepped out of the elevator, followed closely by Mac and Uri. The MPs saluted Roswell then got back aboard the elevator. Mac heard the sound of the airlocks as the doors closed. Immediately afterward, another set of doors closed, which sealed off the level from the elevator shaft.

Mac found himself in an anteroom fifty feet wide and twenty in depth. It was constructed of what appeared to be a smooth, lightweight material he had never seen before. Walls, ceiling, and floor were all colored a monochromatic, somber military gray. Light emanated from the ceiling and reflected in little pools on the smooth expanse of floor.

Mac stood in the anteroom and heard the oscillation of a very low-frequency hum that seemed to originate below him. His impulse was to ask Roswell what it was. He restrained himself, remembering Roswell's admonition.

Mac and Uri followed Roswell toward what appeared to be a blank wall. As they drew closer Mac could see faintly the outline of a series of panels spaced about every ten feet.

Roswell stood in front of one of the panels on a rectangular plate. The panel slid quietly to the left. Roswell stepped in and vanished as the panel closed. Uri followed, leaving Mac alone except for the ever-present MPs stationed near the elevators.

For a moment he panicked and felt anxious. Then he stepped on the plate in the floor and the panel opened in front of him. He walked into the small chamber and heard the door close behind him. When it was shut, another opened in front of him. As he stepped out he closed his eyes as Roswell had instructed him to do. Even so a brilliant light stunned him as he entered the room. For a moment he dared not move.

Roswell had explained that this was yet another security measure and also served to decontaminate any bacteria on the person's clothing as they entered this level.

Mac's vision began to clear, and he regained his bearings. He noticed another pair of MPs stationed on this side of the openings. They were positioned behind a dark green tinted glass window.

Mac found Roswell and Uri and they walked down a wide corridor that curved to their left. Laboratories and offices were located to the inside of the curved hall. Thick plate glass windows allowed viewing into each room, although most were covered with black panels to insure privacy and security.

As Mac followed Roswell down the corridor, a small group of men and women filed past. He took special notice of a woman whom he estimated to be a few years younger than he. In spite of her blond hair gathered tightly behind her head and the absence of makeup, she was a very attractive woman.

Their eyes met for a moment and he smiled at her. She quickly looked down at the floor and kept walking on the other side of the corridor.

Her reaction startled him.

Why wasn't she able to exchange a simple greeting? he wondered. The heavy somberness that had enveloped the personnel on the plane permeated the entire underground base as well.

Roswell stopped in front of an opening that led into yet another lab. He waited for Mac and Uri and then entered. It was a large room, perhaps a third the size of a football field. Incredibly, there were only six people in the room. They were huddled around an object on a large table.

Mac wondered what he was seeing. It was a cylindrical object about four feet high and half again as round and appeared to be cast in one piece. They moved within ten feet of it and stopped. There were no moving parts, at least that Mac could see. No wires. No controls.

A middle-aged man with a pear-shaped body and a patchy black and white beard stopped talking and looked at Roswell, who gave no sign of acknowledgment.

The scientist paused, then continued to address the group in a more subdued voice.

Roswell walked past the group and went over to a large blackboard covered with diagrams, equations, and chalky sketches. He pointed to one of the sketches which resembled the object on the table and began to lecture Mac and Uri as if they were newly recruited scientists being briefed for a new job.

"This is part of a recovered spacecraft from the Russians. More precisely, this is a model of the propulsion system of the spacecraft. This team is involved in the back engineering of it."

Mac and Uri looked attentive, acting out their parts as new employees. But Mac had to stifle a small smile. A spacecraft from the Russians . . . the story just as Roswell had said.

Mac heard a slight whirring noise and looked in its direction. On the ceiling a mounted surveillance camera began to turn and stopped when it pointed to where he was standing.

Roswell looked toward the entrance. Two men in white lab coats entered. One man wore white plastic surgical gloves and carried a small metal box in his hand. They walked over to where the group was huddled around the cylinder on the table. The man carrying the box placed it carefully on the table, opened it, and took out something that looked like an orange wafer.

Roswell moved away from the blackboard and walked further into the lab, away from the huddled group of scientists. Mac and Uri followed.

"It's the fuel for the propulsion system," Roswell said, under his breath. "Some of our scientists have labeled it Element 115 . . . it doesn't exist anywhere on the earth."

Mac slowly looked over his shoulder at the table where the scientists appeared to be discussing the orange-looking wafers—Element 115.

"Is it radioactive?" Uri asked.

Roswell shook his head.

"How does it work?" Mac whispered.

Roswell frowned, indicating the termination of the conversation. He walked back toward the group of scientists and deliberately ignored them as he left the room. Mac and Uri followed.

They moved down the corridor with Mac and Uri always one step behind Roswell. As they passed another lab Roswell briefly slowed and motioned for them to look as they passed by.

Mac slowed his pace as he gazed through the opening. He saw a small gray being standing next to a scientist. They appeared to be examining something.

Mac wanted to go into the lab, affirm what he thought he saw. One more step and the scene vanished and was replaced by the corridor wall.

What was that? He began to argue in his mind. *No . . . It wasn't an . . . It was . . . I saw it . . . It moved . . . Its arms moved . . . It was so tiny, almost childlike . . .* He forced himself to think the unthinkable: *I've seen an alien.*

He became nauseous and his legs felt like rubber. He glanced at Uri. The color had drained from his friend's face, and he looked like he was in a trance as he continued to walk.

Oh, God, help me, Mac prayed. *Why do I feel so ill at ease? Why is it that when I saw the alien something repelled me? What was it?*

His mind was a flurry of questions. *What is it that troubles me about all of these people who work here? Why is everyone so detached?*

He searched for a word to define the people. He stared at the back of Roswell's head as he followed him and thought, *These people are detached, but that's only a symptom of something greater. They're afraid. But of what?*

He suddenly felt the strange feeling, the stirring, inside him, and the presence of it jolted him. He forced himself to hold his thoughts in check for a moment. A new thought appeared in his mind. It was a sentence he had read from the Bible that morning, the same sentence that came to him on the plane. *Put on the full armor of God . . .*

He repeated it again silently and realized what he needed to do. His lips moved slightly as he began to pray in earnest for the protection of Uri, Roswell, and himself.

Roswell stopped in front of a thick glass partition. "We're about to access another part—" Suddenly he stopped, wincing in pain. He leaned against the wall and closed his eyes. "I'm all right," he said, though his lips barely moved. "Just give me a minute." He took a couple of deep breaths.

"What was that we saw back there?" Mac whispered.

"What do you think?" Roswell asked, as he grimaced again in pain. He reached into his pants pocket, produced a small yellow pill, and swallowed it.

Mac said, "Uri, did you see it?"

"I couldn't believe it . . . Yes."

Roswell opened his eyes. "Don't talk about it . . . later . . ."

Mac could see him gathering his will . . . to overcome the pain? *He really looks sick,* Mac thought.

Roswell straightened himself and squared his shoulders. He tried to take a step, found his body would permit it, and began to walk slowly toward another set of doors. "I'm all right . . . it's passed now," he said, as he reached out and set the palm of his hand on a scanning device near the door. There was a slight pause, then it slid open.

They walked into the small detaining room and were saluted by two MPs. Roswell returned the salute. The MPs inspected their tags and allowed them to pass.

They entered the platform of a small train station. There was a cylindrical tube perhaps twenty feet in diameter. In the center of it were sets of miniature train tracks. On the platform were benches that were seamless and constructed of a material Mac had never seen before. It appeared that the platform and benches had been molded in place at the same time.

Roswell walked over to the edge of the platform and peered down the tracks. Mac followed him and gazed down the dimly lit tube. He saw it curve inwardly, and he assumed it linked together other areas of the underground base.

Roswell glanced at his watch and said, "The train will be here in less than five minutes. I want to show you two other areas and then we'll go topside."

Mac and Uri nodded.

Mac wanted to continue talking about the alien in the lab they passed in the corridor but forced himself not to, complying with Roswell's prior instructions. As if Roswell could read his inner struggle he looked right at Mac and said, "This next place we are going"—and he pointed down the tunnel where the tracks disappeared—"may have some other life-forms that may . . . ahh . . . prove interesting."

The door to the anteroom opened and two MPs walked out onto the platform. They saluted Roswell, who saluted back. One of the MPs stared at Mac. He looked away and moved closer to Roswell. Thankfully the train arrived after a few minutes.

There was a conductor in a glass-domed car at the front. Behind the control car were four other cars, each having the capacity to carry six people, two abreast. The train was empty.

Roswell got in the first car, followed by Mac and Uri, who sat directly behind him. The MPs climbed in the car behind them.

The train accelerated quickly and raced down the tube. There were other stops similar to the one they had just departed. Most of them, however, were empty. Then two stops further down the line, two more MPs joined them and rode until the next area, where they got off. Both saluted Roswell upon their exit.

Mac realized that being with Roswell put him and Uri in a volatile position. On one hand, it allowed them access and clearance to seemingly anywhere on the base. On the other, Roswell was conspicuous because of his rank. He drew attention to himself and of course to Mac and Uri. Mac couldn't help feeling that maintaining their anonymity would be very difficult.

The train stopped and Roswell climbed out of the car followed by Mac and Uri. They went through a set of doors and found themselves in a small room staffed by two MPs. The repetitive clearance procedure ensued before they were able to enter the new area.

The doors slid open and Mac walked behind Uri. He caught his breath because the place he found himself in was enormous.

"It's a natural cavern that used to be an underground reservoir. They diverted the water source, and this is the result," Roswell informed them quietly.

Mac looked at the roof of the cavern where perhaps one hundred feet above him an intricate series of steel-girded catwalks were erected that supported a maze of powerful lights, thick metal cables, and overhead cranes. Uniformed technicians were stationed on numerous platforms. In the center of the catwalks a glass command post was positioned. From it, the catwalks spread out like the legs of a spider over most of the cavern. At the far end of the cavern was a tunnel that slowly ascended to what Mac assumed was the surface.

Years before Mac had been assigned to cover a breaking story in New York City. He had driven through the Lincoln tunnel, and it had created a lasting impression on him as a marvel of engineering skills. But what he beheld now dwarfed it. This was at least twice its size, perhaps more. It appeared to be constructed of the same material that Mac had seen used throughout much of the underground facility. Large luminous orbs imbedded in the tunnel's ceiling cast a peculiar greenish light in its interior.

Mac was hypnotized by his surroundings. He heard Roswell clear his throat and realized that he and Uri had walked a dozen paces from where Mac stood. He quickly rejoined them.

"Stay close . . . be careful," Roswell admonished sternly.

"Okay," Mac said, awestruck.

They started to cross the cavern floor. Mac was still transfixed. Then he heard Uri exclaim, "What?"

He glanced at Uri, saw the wonder expressed on his face, then sought the reason for it.

A short distance away was a disk-shaped flying saucer. It hovered silently above the floor of the cavern.

Mac wanted to stop and just look at it. But Roswell continued at the same pace, rapidly closing the distance between them and the saucer.

Mac looked overhead to see if any cables were attached from the catwalks above. While there were a few dangling above the disk, it was plain that there weren't any actually attached to it. The disk was hovering on its own power. There was a metal boarding ramp that was next to the craft, similar to the one that they had used in exiting the plane when they had landed.

A technician dressed in the same silver jumpsuit that Mac and Uri wore climbed aboard the disk. He held a small computer-like device in his hands as he ascended into the craft. A portal was open, exposing the interior. Mac could see two men standing in the opening.

They were about fifty feet from the disk when Roswell stopped. Uri and Mac came alongside of him, and they stared at the saucer.

Mac took in every detail he possibly could, his brain acting like a camera. He noticed the seamless, sleek exterior of dull gray metal-like material, similar to the material his father had given him. A row of windows circled the craft near the top. On the bottom were rounded indentations that he thought might conceal lights. As he gazed transfixed, the disk remained motionless, floating noiselessly ten feet above the floor of the cavern.

One of the men standing in front of the portal moved from the interior and walked down the boarding ramp. Mac stole a glance at Uri, who was practically comatose with awe. He then looked back at the craft and what he saw stunned him to the core of his being. There was an alien similar to the one that he had glimpsed a short while before. It looked very much like the one in the photograph that Roswell had sent him. It had the same thin torso and long spindly arms. On each hand were four fingers. Its head was disproportionately large for its body. It had no hair that Mac could see. It seemed to be clothed in a one-piece jumpsuit that matched the color of its skin exactly.

What struck Mac, however, were the two large, elongated, dark black eyes that were the most dominant feature on the alien's face.

The creature jerked its head and looked right at Mac. It seemed distracted by him, like it was bothered somehow by Mac's presence.

Mac found himself staring back.

He shuddered.

Something came at him . . . an invisible force of some kind. It enveloped him but centered in his solar plexus. He felt immobilized, drained. His head suddenly ached and he felt nauseous. He began to feel like he was going to black out . . . horrible images flashed in his mind.

Then Roswell was in front of him and was talking earnestly to him.

"MacKenzie! MacKenzie! Turn around and walk out of here! Do it now! Now MacKenzie . . . Move!"

Mac looked at Roswell but somehow he saw only the alien's eyes. Those awful eyes, so detached, so baleful, so ominous . . . so evil.

He shook his head to try to clear it. *You're Roswell . . . and that's Uri*, he thought. *What was Roswell saying? To move? Move where?* Mac rubbed his eyes and tried to focus on Roswell.

"MacKenzie," Roswell's face was inches away from Mac's and he growled between his teeth. "Move! Now!"

MacKenzie turned around and began to shuffle a few steps. He felt an unexplainable urge to look back at the alien. His legs felt stiff but he kept walking, due primarily to Roswell and Uri who shored him up on either side.

There was a partition a short distance in front of them. Roswell steered them toward it. They reached the partition and walked behind it, finding themselves in a storage area for equipment. Fortunately there was no one in the enclosure.

"Never look at their eyes," Roswell said.

"What?" Mac asked, trying to focus on what Roswell was saying.

"Never look directly into their eyes," he repeated.

"Did you see it . . . Did you see it?" Mac stammered, and he grabbed Uri's arm.

"Yes, Mac, I saw . . . it's okay . . . you're okay . . ." Uri turned to Roswell and asked, "What has happened?"

"I'm not sure," replied Roswell. "There was something that attracted the alien to MacKenzie. It looked to me as if it sensed something. Although I have no idea what." He stared at Mac, frowned, then said, "I've heard about this sort of reaction before, which is why I got us out of there like I did. Did you notice that in this section there are no MPs?"

"What? No, not really," Mac answered, still dazed from the encounter.

"Well, there is a reason for it. The aliens gave us an ultimatum that MPs and, more specifically, weapons are not to be in the area of the craft. Apparently when the craft is activated it can set off ammunition."

"Oh?" Uri exclaimed. "Very dangerous."

"The story I heard, and this is hearsay because I can't substantiate it, is that some Rambo-type MP decided to go into the disk area armed. A confrontation ensued between an alien and the MP, with the result being the MP had his head blown apart by some sort of laser-like weapon."

"Well, I wasn't armed," Mac said defensively.

"And that's what bothers me," Roswell answered. He looked around. "No, there's another dynamic here, but I'm not certain as to what. The alien had an abnormal interest in you. Did you see the way it jerked its head around as if it sensed you were near?"

"What? He did?" Mac said, as he rubbed his forehead.

"Yes," Roswell assured him. "Somehow you drew attention to yourself. Did you do anything that might have caused it to notice you?"

Mac forced himself to think, then replied emphatically, "No, not a thing. I was looking at the disk, making mental notes of the way it was constructed . . . then I found myself staring at the alien. Oh, those eyes." He shuddered and grimaced. "The thing isn't human!"

"You're right there," Uri said.

"No, no." Mac became agitated. "Something . . . a force or something came at me. It hit me here." He touched his stomach. "The thing wanted to kill me. Let's get out of here, for crying out loud. It's evil."

Roswell stared at Mac for a moment, then said, "I want to show you both one more thing before we leave and go topside again. Are you up to it?" he asked Mac.

"As long as it puts me as far away as possible from—"

"It will," Roswell interrupted. He went to the edge of the partition wall and looked back at the craft.

"The alien is gone, although one of the attendants is still there. Can you make it?"

Mac nodded.

"Let's go then and stay close. We'll get back on the train," Roswell said, and led them out from behind the partition.

They walked across the expanse of floor and went back into the anteroom, where the MPs again checked them.

They waited a few minutes for the train, which this time was nearly full of silver-suited technicians who disembarked as Roswell, Mac, and Uri boarded. They rode the train for perhaps ten minutes.

They got off where Roswell indicated and went through yet another clearance procedure. Roswell led them down a corridor and stopped in front of a door. There were two MPs stationed outside. They snapped to attention and saluted as Roswell approached.

Roswell returned the salute and said, "I want access to the document room with these men."

One of the MPs glanced at the I.D. tags on Mac and Uri's jumpsuits. Satisfied, he nodded to his partner, who took a key that was attached by a chain to his belt and unlocked the door. The three of them entered the document room, after which the MP promptly shut the door and locked it.

Mac looked around. It was a plain, unadorned room not much larger than a child's bedroom. A conference table was lined up against one wall with drab-looking upholstered chairs in front of it. Directly above was a row of recessed lights that brightly illuminated the table. On the table were stacks of briefing documents.

Mac looked at Roswell with an expression that asked, "What now?"

"Go ahead . . . take a look," Roswell said, and gestured toward the table. "I've gone through many of them. I think you'll be fascinated. We have a half hour before the MP returns. It's a policy that you only read half an hour at a time. You'll see why, once you dive in. It's a lot to digest."

Mac and Uri sat down. Roswell went to the end of the table and sat on its edge where he could study their reactions while they read.

Mac selected one of the briefing documents. It was bound in a military folder and had Top Secret stamped on the front of it. He opened it and looked at the title page and read, "Genetic Manipulations." He flipped through the pages quickly to get a feel for how much material was contained in the briefing. *About twenty pages, I can read that in half an hour,* he thought. He began to read the document and soon was absorbed in the material.

The room took on the ambiance of a library. Other than occasional page turns, the cloistered room was quiet as the men pored over the material.

Mac was both fascinated and disturbed by what was contained in the briefing. The gist of it explained that a group of aliens from the Pleiades star system had genetically manipulated the evolution of the human race over a period of thousands of years. Sixty-three genetic alterations had affected the evolutionary development of humankind.

Mac recalled what Dr. Elisha had so carefully impressed on him. That if the alien presence was, in fact, the beginning of what he coined the Great Deception, an event that would overtake the planet shortly before the Second Coming of Jesus Christ, then what he was reading would be a part of that deception.

The aliens were saying that *they* were responsible for the creation of the human race. That without their direct involvement, humankind as we know it today wouldn't exist. We would be, at best, in evolutionary terms, still swinging from the trees.

Mac looked at Roswell, who stared back at him stoically, although Mac detected a trace of pensiveness.

"What do you make of it?" Roswell asked Mac in a whisper. "Do you remember when you asked me if I believed in the Second Coming?"

Mac nodded.

"You see why it's impossible to believe now."

Mac pointed to the document. "No. This doesn't prove anything. What if it's a lie?" He stabbed a finger at the document. "What if this is an attempt to actually steer people away from the truth? What if the aliens—or whatever they are—are deliberately lying to us, as Elisha thinks they are?"

"Lie about what?" Uri asked, managing to tear himself away from the briefing document he was reading.

Mac turned to Uri, laid his hand on top of the stack of documents on the table, and said, "All of these may have the same purpose, to deceive and control." He picked up the document he was reading and opened it to the title page. "Look at this, genetic manipulations. What the aliens are saying negates what at least a portion of humankind has believed for thousands of years: the special act of creation by a divine being who designed humans in his own image."

"You should read the document on the crucifixion," Roswell interjected.

"The crucifixion?" Mac exclaimed. "The aliens have a document on the crucifixion?"

"Yes, and briefly put, they claim to have some sort of holographic film of it. They also claim that they directly intervened"—Roswell cleared his throat—"in the Resurrection. It's in one of those somewhere." He pointed toward the stack.

"Do you believe that?" Mac asked.

Roswell stared at Mac with deadpan eyes, then muttered, "I don't know what to believe anymore, but I don't trust them."

Mac looked at Roswell, then Uri, and said earnestly, "You know if you believe this, then the ramifications are of shattering proportions to the fabric of society! But if what Elisha says is right . . . that this is an elaborate deception . . ."

"For what reason . . . this deception?" Uri challenged.

Mac struggled to remember what Elisha had imparted to him. "The reason is this . . . Let's suppose that the prophecies are true, that there is going to be a literal Second Coming of Jesus. Then let's suppose that what the ancient texts, the Bible, say is true concerning him . . . that he is indeed the Son of God. Hold that thought, okay?"

Uri shrugged.

"Now consider you have these supposed alien UFO cosmonauts or whatever you want to call them . . . Why is it that they travel who-knows-how-many light years to get here, and one of the first things out of their mouths is to tell us that Jesus wasn't the Son of God and that the crucifixion was unnecessary and that they assisted in the Resurrection . . . Don't you find that incredible? Doesn't it make you suspicious that here come the aliens and they could talk about a myriad of things, about anything, for crying out loud, and what do they decide to communicate to us? That Jesus wasn't God? Come on . . . why not give us the cure for cancer or something useful?"

Mac brushed the hair off his forehead then started again. "Why is it that the aliens attempt to discredit the story of the Resurrection? They seem to want to negate it in any way possible. If they can succeed, they crush the hope that Jesus has given humankind for the last two thousand years."

Uri frowned and asked, "And what hope is that?"

Mac looked him squarely in the eyes, then firmly answered, "The hope of eternal life!"

They were distracted by the sound of the door opening behind them.

Roswell glanced at his watch. "It's time."

Uri reluctantly closed his folder and placed it carefully on the stack in front of him. The MP stood by the door and the men filed out.

Roswell led them down the corridor, and they came to the doors to the anteroom that led to the elevator. The men went one by one through the small airlocks and regrouped at the elevator. Uri looked over his shoulder one last time, taking it all in.

"The secrets of the universe lie just beyond those doors," he whispered to Mac.

"Or the greatest deceit," Mac retorted.

The elevator appeared, and the doors that separated the anteroom from the elevator shaft hissed open, followed by the elevator doors themselves.

They followed Roswell amidst the usual flurry of salutes and checking of I.D. tags by the MPs. The elevator quickly ascended, stopping at each level on its way to the surface. Finally the doors opened, and they were inside the hangar.

Mac stepped out of the elevator. Sunlight streamed through the gigantic entrance and reflected brilliantly off the polished concrete floor of the hangar. Mac wanted to run and warm himself in the light. His head still ached slightly, and as he looked at the sunlight he realized just how glad he was to be out of the bowels of the earth. A mild breeze blew through the hangar and felt wonderfully refreshing on his face, especially after breathing the conditioned air underground.

Roswell signaled a pair of MPs who ran over, saluted, and waited for his orders. He requested transportation to the base canteen. One of the MPs took his walkie-talkie out and put in the general's request.

Silence prevailed as they waited.

A while later Mac saw a jeep driving toward them. It turned so the front passenger side of the vehicle stopped a few feet from General Roswell. The driver saluted, and one of the MPs stood next to the jeep while Roswell climbed in. Mac and Uri found their way into the backseat. The jeep turned around and sped toward the open doors of the hangar. As it left the hangar and moved outdoors, Mac shuddered. It was like he was shaking off something that had tried to cling to his soul. The further he distanced himself from the hangar the better he felt.

The jeep stopped at a single story, nondescript building that Mac assumed was the canteen. Roswell casually saluted the driver and instructed him to wait until they were finished eating.

They got out of the jeep and went into the building. It was a large one-room cafeteria capable of holding several hundred people at one sitting. What immediately impressed Mac was that most of the personnel ate alone.

There were a few people in the lunch line. Mac watched them slide their trays on the worn stainless steel rail that ran the length of the food tables, helping themselves to whatever they desired.

Mac and Uri got their trays and followed Roswell down the food line, then they retired to a part of the canteen that no one occupied. Mac took a bite of the ham and cheese sandwich. The familiar act of eating felt completely surreal.

Uri, who sat next to Mac, guzzled a large glass of iced tea and started on a second, without touching the food on his plate. General Roswell sat across from them and slowly took a spoonful of soup.

Mac wasn't sure whether it was safe to converse, and he waited for some lead from Roswell.

Roswell lifted the spoon to his lips, held it there, and quietly said to Mac, "In the document room you seemed to be leaning toward Dr. Elisha's theory regarding the aliens." He slipped the spoon into his mouth.

Mac took notice of where the MPs were stationed and then asked Roswell, "It's okay to talk here?"

Roswell rested his spoon on the corner of the bowl and said, "As you both are aware of now, idle conversation is something that doesn't happen here. But you're both with me and as far as anyone is concerned, conversation that takes place between us pertains to the work you will be doing here. We are monitored, so try to talk away from the camera." He looked toward the ceiling in the corner of the room where two surveillance cameras were mounted and moved slowly from side to side monitoring the interior of the cafeteria.

Mac glanced over at the cameras and turned slightly in his seat so he faced away from them. He leaned forward and said to Roswell, "Look, I'm certain of one thing, I've never been so terrified in my life as when that thing looked at me. There was an evil that seemed to emanate from it. I know it sounds crazy, but I literally *felt* hatred directed toward me. It surrounded me and was, as you saw, almost overwhelming. After that and recalling what Dr. Elisha showed me in Israel . . . well . . ." He turned to Uri and said with conviction, "I'm sorry, Uri, but I don't think these guys are here to save our planet or replenish theirs. No. They have another agenda, and I think your grandfather might be right on the money when he equates their presence with what he identifies as the Great Deception."

Uri took a bite of his sandwich, let out a deep breath, and said, "You know what? The experience with the alien was . . . I don't know how to say it . . . nervous?"

"You mean nerve-wracking?" Mac asked.

"Yeah . . . nerve-wracking . . . Maybe it sensed fear and responded to that. What? It seems to work with other humans without incident. Why did it see you?"

"That's not entirely true," Roswell interjected. He lowered his voice so that it was barely above a whisper and said, "People who are exposed to them, the aliens, for any length of time often have disabling emotional and mental incidents."

Mac looked at Uri as if to say, explain that away.

Uri countered, "Yes, yes, but look at their technology! What advanced civilization they come from."

"So they have some high-powered toys that we fall over dead for," Mac argued. "That doesn't tell us anything about them. Not about their morals or ethics—"

"But they evolved in another part of the universe! You expect them to have the same morals as we do!"

Roswell looked at the two MPs, one of whom seemed to be taking an unusual interest in their conversation. "We better hold the chatter until later."

Uri and Mac looked at each other and nodded a truce.

Mac took another bite of his sandwich and looked across the room through the window at the hangar a mile away. Here in the canteen it seemed like none of it had ever happened.

Uri doodled on his napkin with a felt pen as he nibbled at the rest of his sandwich with his other hand. Roswell winced and shifted in his chair. Mac noticed he looked drawn and exhausted. *A man without hope*, he thought. He wondered how all of the people could continue to work under this kind of stress day after day. They seemed to have a commonality about them. It was true that they all worked in the facility together and that alone was a bond, but Mac sensed that there was something else. He couldn't put his finger on it. Abandonment? Isolation? Depression? No, that wasn't the word. He needed to pin it down to define it. *Boil it down*, he thought, *boil it down*.

"We need to leave soon," Roswell said as he glanced at his watch. "I instructed Diebol to pick us up at the Santa Monica Airport. After we land I want to have a look at your friend in the mental hospital. I think there's a link to all of this." And he motioned to the hangar in the distance.

Uri took one last bite of his sandwich and hastily wiped some mustard from his mouth with the napkin he had been doodling on. He crumbled it into a ball and let it fall onto his empty plate.

Their chairs screeched as they got up from the table. They followed Roswell out of the canteen and climbed into the jeep.

"Airstrip," Roswell ordered.

The jeep swung on to the blacktop and headed for the airstrip.

＊ ○ ＊

In the cafeteria one MP thought that the general's companions had been a little too communicative, even if they were new recruits.

"I'm going over to that table where the general was seated," the MP said to his partner.

"Yeah . . . go 'head, Dermot. I'll stay here and guard the place," the other man said in a bored voice that brimmed with sarcasm.

McDermot walked over to the table and looked at the dishes and glasses.

On one of the plates he noticed a crumpled napkin. He thought he saw writing on it, so he reached down and picked it up. He set it on the table and spread it out so he could see what had been written on it.

"Hey, come here." McDermot signaled to his partner.

The other MP slowly walked over.

"Look at this." McDermot pointed at the napkin.

The other MP looked down. "Oh, boy, we got some trouble here," he said.

McDermot picked the napkin up and moved to a quiet corner of the cafeteria. He called his superior on his walkie-talkie.

"Sir, this is McDermot . . . Sir, we got a security breach here . . . a drawing of an alternate life-form." He used the wording he had been instructed to call them. "Yes, sir, right away, sir."

McDermot holstered his walkie-talkie and looked with satisfaction at his partner as he made his way out of the cafeteria to his superior officer.

＊ ○ ＊

Roswell, Mac, and Uri boarded the small jet, buckled themselves in, and waited for the takeoff.

The jet taxied out on the runway, accelerated rapidly, and left the ground. Mac gazed out his small window and looked at the hangar as the jet circled over it. He watched it grow smaller as the jet climbed higher in the air. *The further away the better,* he thought, and he shuddered again, glad for the second time in his life to be on a plane.

＊ ○ ＊

McDermot hopped in the jeep and drove to the office of his immediate superior.

"Here it is, sir," McDermot said as he handed the napkin with the drawing of the alien on it to their commanding officer.

"Good job, I'll see that this is rewarded," the officer said, and he saluted McDermot and dismissed him.

McDermot left the room.

The officer placed the napkin in a manila folder and called in his secretary.

A tall, middle-aged man with a sergeant rank on his sleeve and black circles under his bloodshot eyes walked into the office and awaited his orders.

"Take this to Sec Com and have them run directory for a two-star Air Force general who accessed the pit today. He was apparently accompanied by two silver suits. Get me stills and close-ups. Oh . . . and run a background on him."

The secretary saluted, left the room, and hurried down the hall to the Security and Communications room—Sec Com—a vast enclosure that linked all of the security information both on and off the base.

Twenty people per eight-hour shift staffed Sec Com, which operated continuously twenty-four hours a day. The vast array of computers and data banks were linked to many governmental agencies, including all branches of the armed forces. If you existed they could find you here. They even knew the number of POWs that still were being held in Viet Nam.

The secretary handed the manila envelope with his instructions to one of the operators at Sec Com. A short, thin, bony woman with thick glasses and close-cropped graying hair received the folder. She read the information. *The subject was last seen at the base canteen with two silver suits at thirteen hundred hours.* She typed the information into her computer and stared at her monitor. A few seconds passed and then a picture of the interior of the canteen was on her screen. She fast forwarded the video until she saw the general and two silver suits enter. They went out of the range of the camera. She scrolled ahead and found them sitting in the corner. She froze the frame and keyed in some commands on her computer.

She waited for about five minutes.

The screen on her computer suddenly split in two. On the left side she could see a close-up image of the general. On the right, pages of information pertaining to him appeared.

"Do you want a printout?" she asked.

"Yes," the secretary said.

The woman hit the print icon and the information was transferred. When it was finished, over thirty pages of material were placed in the manila envelope. The secretary left Sec Com and went back to his office. He knocked on his superior's office door and went in.

"Here is the information you requested, sir," he said as he handed the officer the folder. He left the room.

The officer opened the file and perused the information. He took a highlighter from his desk drawer and underlined a few areas. Then he picked up the phone on his desk and called his superior.

"We have a code red."

"Who is it?"

"A two-star Air Force general. General Nathan, sir," the officer replied.

"Thank you, send the information up."

The line went dead and the officer slowly put the receiver back in its cradle. He had worked at the base for three years. Although he had been trained in case of a security breach, he had never actually been involved in one, especially a code red. That meant that someone had accessed areas that they were unauthorized to do so, which was a breach of national security.

General Nathan is going to have to be brought in and debriefed, he thought. His stomach grew queasy. He'd heard rumors of how that debriefing left some of the people who went through it.

27

The round white object sailed through the air in a high, graceful arc. It rotated in the opposite direction it traveled as it intruded on a cloudless deep blue sky.

Jim Cranston stood poised on the ninth tee and watched the ball fly toward the green. It was an excellent shot and it made him feel like a pro. He held his breath and hoped that the ball would roll into the cup, capturing for him the elusive hole in one.

The ball landed a good fifteen feet past the flag and amazingly, spun backward toward the hole. It stopped within less than four feet from the cup, affording Cranston an easy birdie but not the hole in one he'd hoped for.

"A little more and it would have gone in," he lamented.

"Nice shot though . . . huh?" his partner complimented, as he twisted a pinky ring on his chubby finger.

"Thanks, I'll take it," Cranston remarked, letting his nine iron rest on his shoulder as he walked off the tee.

His partner, a short, portly man with slicked-back hair, strode to the tee. He placed the ball on the manicured grass, took a hasty practice swing, then cut at the ball with a fast, choppy backswing. The ball flew toward the hole more like a baseball's line drive than the graceful arc of Cranston's shot. It landed about ten yards in front of the green, bounced hurriedly three times, and then rolled toward the cup. It stopped just inside Cranston's ball, making his ball closer to the hole by a few inches.

"Very nice, John."

"Luck of the Irish." He grinned as he walked quickly back to the cart where Cranston sat. He set his club in his bag, got into the cart, and drove toward the green.

"Any more on MacKenzie?" Cranston asked, as he pulled his cap down on his forehead to keep it from blowing off.

"He's been staying at the Hilton, huh? But you know that."

"How can he possibly afford that? The guy's a bum," Cranston said disgustedly, as the cart stopped in back of the green.

The men got out, grabbed their putters, and stepped onto the green. Cranston went over and fixed his ball mark, which had left an indentation in the smooth, flat surface of the green. He was further away from the cup, so he went to his ball and lined up his putt. He focused on the hole, took two practice putts, and set himself up next to the ball. He wiggled his mustache, a habit that he attributed to good luck before he putted. Then he slowly drew his arms back and tapped the ball, holding his breath as he watched it roll slowly toward the cup.

It was a good stroke, firm and true, with enough force to make sure the ball would roll at least a foot past the hole. To his delight the ball broke slightly, rolled squarely into the hole, and disappeared from sight.

"Nice," John complimented as he squatted behind his ball and lined up. He got back up and then hunched over the ball. He took one last look at where he was aiming and tapped the ball toward the cup using a slower version of the choppy backswing that he had used to hit off the tee. The ball hit the back end of the cup and dropped out of sight.

"Two birds," Cranston said.

"Two birds," John affirmed.

They met at the back of the cart and slipped their putters back into their bags. John grabbed a stubby pencil and marked their score cards.

"Well, what bothers me," Cranston began, picking up the conversation where it had ended, "he's being bankrolled by someone, and you guys don't know who."

"We'll know that soon enough."

Cranston knocked his cleats against the back of the cart. "You said earlier that he shook your surveillance?"

"The BenHassen guy ... huh? ... was in the Israeli army. That could explain why they found the bug so soon," John answered.

Cranston frowned. "Perhaps. But whoever removed it from MacKenzie's car had your men following a truck all over downtown L.A. for half the day before they realized what was going on."

John twisted the ring on his finger. "It's early in the game ..."

"Maybe they're close to putting things together. I don't appreciate the position I'm being forced into."

"I understand," John said.

"I don't think you do," Cranston retorted.

John tossed his golf ball in the air and caught it, then said, "You knew what you were getting into when we first contacted you."

"That's not entirely true," Cranston protested. "It was explained to me that the government wanted a psych ward in the private sector to rehabilitate people from exposure with the extraterrestrials."

"Well, isn't that what goes on there?" John asked.

"Not entirely. We both know there are people being held there against their will," Cranston said.

John tossed the ball in the air again and said, "You don't know that for certain, besides, it's all top secret. Just do your part and don't worry . . . they've got things under control."

Cranston looked at the man. "But what if they don't have things under control?"

John squeezed the ball and answered, "Impossible."

"So what am I supposed to do with MacKenzie?"

"You're still his editor. Use that relationship to find out what he's up to. Draw him in," John suggested, "call his wife. You're friends with her, huh? Use her."

Cranston thought about it, then said, "Okay. I'll call and see if he's contacted her. I'll tell her I'm interested in the story he's working on."

"Good, now you're thinking," John said, and slapped him on the back.

Later, Cranston had missed an easy putt for par, and John was now two strokes up on him. But his mind was distracted from the game.

"Stop for a moment, will you?" he asked.

"What's the matter?" John stopped the cart in the middle of the fairway.

"I want to call Kennedy over at the hospital and have the woman that MacKenzie interviewed moved out."

"It's done . . . already happened . . . she'll be moved today," John said. "But go ahead, call to make sure."

Cranston dialed the number.

A man answered the phone. "Westwood Medical Center."

"Ms. Kennedy, please," Cranston said. He was placed on hold and forced to listen to a syrupy rendition of "I Want to Hold Your Hand," with what sounded like a thousand violins playing the melody. Mercifully Ms. Kennedy picked up before it reached the chorus of the song.

"This is Ms. Kennedy." Her voice was pleasant and professional.

"This is Cranston. I want you to listen carefully. I'm a little worried about a certain patient on the sixth floor. I want her moved out to Camarillo and placed temporarily in the psych ward there."

She lowered her voice to a whisper. "It's been scheduled already."

"When is it going to happen? Immediately?"

"Very soon," she said firmly.

"Good. Oh ... Ms. Kennedy."

"Yes?"

"Call me when the transfer is completed."

"Okay. As soon as it's done I'll ring you."

He clicked off the phone and held it in his hand for a moment before putting it back in his bag.

John grinned. "All under control. Huh?"

Cranston nodded, but inwardly he wasn't so sure.

✳ ○ ✳

The Lear jet carrying General Roswell, Art MacKenzie, and Uri BenHassen touched down on the tarmac of the Santa Monica airport with a perfect three-point landing. There was no bump to the wheels as the pilot glided onto the runway.

The three men had refrained from discussing anything about the base and in fact had continued in their role-playing as General Roswell's new recruits.

Mac looked out the window and saw Roswell's Lincoln parked at the far end of the runway. He recognized Diebol, the general's chauffeur, standing next to the Lincoln.

The jet came to a stop and the men quickly climbed out. As soon as they were a short distance away, the jet wheeled around and started back down the runway. Diebol came forward to meet them.

"Did you have a good flight, sir?" he asked.

"Yes, Diebol. Thank you."

"Your daughter took off half an hour ago," Diebol informed him.

"Good," Roswell said.

She flies? Green Eyes flies, Mac thought and grinned.

They got into the Lincoln and for the first time in hours, Mac relaxed. "Where did the pilot go?" he asked.

"Directly back to the base," Roswell answered.

Mac bent over and held his head in his hands. "Look, I just want a simple answer to this . . . okay? Who's in control, for crying out loud? Are the aliens in control or are we? Simple answer . . . okay?"

Roswell turned away and looked out his window. "It's not so simple . . . we're not certain."

"What do you mean, you're not certain? You're supposed to know that." Mac raised his voice in anger. "There's a bunch of aliens working side by side with American military personnel, and you're not certain who's in charge?"

Roswell faced Mac and said wearily, "Layers upon layers, MacKenzie. The right hand doesn't know what the left is doing." He looked steadily at Mac, then said, "I want to see the woman that you got your initial story from."

"At the hospital?" Mac asked, and he picked his head up and looked at Roswell with a puzzled expression.

"Yes," Roswell replied, "she may know something that will link us to the base. I'll admit it's a long shot, though." He leaned forward in his seat and spoke to Diebol. "Westwood Medical Center."

"Yes, sir," Diebol answered, and swung the Lincoln out of the airport terminal and headed for the hospital.

Uri scratched his wiry hair vigorously and said to Roswell, "I have too many questions, but what about the Maj 12 level?"

"Maj. Is that an abbreviation for majestic? And what does that mean?" Mac asked.

Roswell shifted in his seat. "Right after the crash at Roswell, President Truman formed a committee to deal with the extraterrestrial presence on the earth. The committee—made up of a variety of military and governmental personnel—was named Majestic and later shortened to Maj. Some of those men took matters into their own hands and instigated a rogue element with the Majestic circle. I suspect it has something to do with hybrid engineering between the aliens and us. But the people who have access to that area are unapproachable. They live and work on that level for six months or more. When their replacements come, the entire base goes into such tight security, a mosquito can't get in. The elevator is restricted to Level 12. All extraneous personnel, other than the yellow-hatted MPs, are cleared of the area, and an unmarked 737 delivers the replacements and they fly out the previous group. They install a special tunnel. It's a plastic tube, and the personnel enter and leave through that. No one sees anything. The exchange usually happens right after midnight."

"How do you know the personnel are . . . human?" Mac asked.

"We don't know what comes and goes through that tube."

"Can't you trace where the plane is going?" Uri asked.

Roswell nodded. "We have. That part's easy. But here's the catch—it lands in the People's Republic of China. So we have no way of seeing or identifying who gets on or off."

"What about surveillance satellites?" Uri asked.

"Again, the same thing. We can see where the plane touches down, but a similar tube is in place and the personnel . . . or life-forms . . . are completely hidden from view. The tube even blocks heat sensory detection equipment."

"In China?" Mac asked, surprised.

Roswell nodded and said, "We're certain there's a base located there. Actually there are at least several of these bases that we know about, positioned around the globe."

"Several?" Mac repeated incredulously. "How are you ever going to expose this?"

"Well, our group knows about it, but until we have a plan, until we know for certain . . ." Roswell's voice trailed off, and he stared at Mac before continuing, "Frankly, that's part of what I'm expecting from you. If the public becomes aware of what is going on, they'll put pressure on the government for accountability. The more we can get the story out to the public and do it in such a way as to not sound like a bunch of kooks, the better our chances of revealing the alien presence. Your article in the paper is the type of leaking information I'm referring to."

"Yeah, but to do that we have to get all our ducks in a row first," Mac stated.

"What are . . . these ducks?" Uri asked with a puzzled look.

"It's just another of our expressions," Mac explained. "We have to have the evidence, the witnesses, photos, statements. Hard proof—the ducks. If we take this to the paper, it would be the biggest story of this or the next century."

"And that's why we have to be cautious," Roswell said. "*They* have an uncanny knack for destroying the evidence and concealing the truth."

"And the people who want to expose it," Mac reminded him.

"What? Like the Nephilim's skeleton," Uri said, and leaned back in his seat.

"Exactly," Roswell said. "They're usually a step or two ahead of us."

"Concealing the truth," Mac repeated to himself, "and just what is the truth?" He was confused. He had seen almost more than he could handle. His mind was brimming with questions, but more than anything he wanted to talk to Elisha.

28

――――――――

✦ ◼ ✦

The black Lincoln Continental swung into the Westwood Medical Center parking lot. Roswell, Uri, and Mac emptied themselves from its interior and walked quickly toward the main entrance.

On the way Mac glanced at the construction trailer at the far end of the lot. *I wonder if anyone has questioned Linda or Harry regarding the article I wrote,* he thought as he led Roswell and Uri into the lobby of the institution.

Mac approached the reception desk.

The same man as before—Thomas, according to his name badge—was busy sorting papers. As he lifted his head and saw Mac his expression changed from professional cordiality to restrained distaste. "Mr. MacKenzie, from the *Times,*" he stated dryly. "And how can I help you today?"

Mac leaned forward on the counter. "Listen, Thomas, I'm sure I'm not too popular around here right now, but we"—he nodded over his shoulder at Roswell—"would like to discuss a private matter with Ms. Kennedy. Is she available?"

Thomas looked at MacKenzie without saying a word for a moment then tersely asked, "What is it regarding?"

"It's about a patient."

"I'll check and see if she'll see you," Thomas said and dialed her extension. A moment later he spoke into the receiver. "Ms. Kennedy, this is Thomas at the front desk. Mr. MacKenzie from the *Times* is here with two other gentlemen to see you."

He listened to her reply, then hung up the phone, looked at Mac, and said, "She'll be right down, Mr. MacKenzie. Would you have a seat?" He gestured to the overstuffed couches arranged in a U-pattern by the elevators.

After what seemed like a long wait—over fifteen minutes—Mac heard the elevator doors open behind him.

"Mr. MacKenzie?" He recognized Kennedy's voice.

"Finally," he mumbled.

He hurried to the elevator and began making introductions. "Ms. Kennedy, this is General Black of the United States Air Force," he said, using the name Roswell had instructed him to use. They shook hands. "And this is Mr. Uri BenHassen, an archaeologist from Israel."

"Pleased to meet you both," Kennedy said, as she grasped Uri's hand firmly in her own and looked at the men with a practiced smile.

"What brings you to the Center?" she asked Mac.

"Well, it's somewhat confidential. I was wondering if we could go to your office and discuss it there?"

Kennedy smiled and said, "Sure, right this way, gentlemen," and she pressed the up button on the glass panel in front of the elevator.

A short time later they were settled in her office. The door was closed and the three men sat in a semicircle around Kennedy's desk, which, other than a neatly piled stack of folders next to a leather blotter and a phone, was uncluttered.

She rested her hands on the blotter, drummed on it with her fingernails, and smiled reassuringly. "Now what can I do for you, gentlemen?"

Mac looked at Roswell who, with a nod, deferred back to him.

"Well, Ms. Kennedy," he began, "first, let me thank you for seeing us without an appointment. I know you have a busy schedule, thanks for fitting us in."

She flashed another of her inexhaustible smiles.

He continued, "Well . . . I'm not sure exactly how to put this. It . . . ah . . . has to do with one of your patients. More specifically we . . . General Black, that is, would like to talk with one of your patients . . . on the sixth floor."

Ms. Kennedy fixed him with her gaze, her face suddenly serious. "That floor is operated solely by personnel from the United States military. It's completely outside my jurisdiction. I'm only a liaison between the hospital and the military establishment. They have their own staff; you need to ask them." She paused a moment, then began tersely, "Since we're on the subject of the sixth floor, Mr. MacKenzie, your carelessly written article alleging a clandestine military psych ward for UFO abductees has made my life incredibly difficult. I've had a barrage of calls from what seems like every UFO nut in the country."

"The article didn't implicate anyone directly," Mac said.

"Perhaps, but really, Mr. MacKenzie . . . you have an overactive imagination. I would think that you, as a journalist, would be more discerning regarding your sources of information."

"What I wrote can be substantiated," Mac argued.

Roswell straightened in his chair. "Ms. Kennedy, I can assure you that I have at my disposal the means to access the sixth floor. That authority comes directly from the secretary of defense."

Kennedy shifted a little in her chair and folded her hands in front of her. "*The* secretary of defense?" she repeated, trying her best to conceal her astonishment.

"Yes, ma'am," Roswell answered quietly. "We have reason to believe that a woman who is interned as a patient here may be able to provide us with valuable information."

"In this hospital?"

He cleared his throat and said, "Yes, in this hospital . . . on the sixth floor."

Kennedy frowned. "I don't have any information pertaining to patients on the sixth floor."

Mac's eyes darted over to Roswell and waited to see how he would respond.

"Ms. Kennedy," Roswell began slowly, "in a matter of hours I can have this hospital shut down and quarantined because of the threat of a deadly virus . . . say Ebola . . . found in one of your patients. The quarantine would be extended to all staff and personnel as well as patients. I'm sure you don't want to trouble yourself with that."

She looked at Roswell steadily, her blue eyes holding his without blinking. Finally she said tersely, "I'll have to call my superior and defer to his judgment on this." She picked up her phone and dialed quickly. "Yes, this is Ms. Kennedy. Is the director there?" A moment passed, then, "Sir, there is a General Black in my office, and—"

Mac watched as she stopped midsentence. He could hear a man's voice on the other line.

Kennedy tried her best to conceal her astonishment which quickly turned to controlled anger. "Oh, then it won't be a problem . . . right . . . thank you, sir." She put the phone back in its cradle, avoiding eye contact for the moment.

Mac watched as she pulled herself together and faced Roswell.

"Well, General, I'm sure a quarantine won't be necessary. The director has instructed me to escort you gentlemen to the sixth floor myself. Just let me inform them we're coming."

Roswell cracked the faintest hint of a smile and replied, "Thank you."

Kennedy made the call and asked for a Captain Myers. She informed him that an Air Force general was in her office and wanted to locate a patient on the sixth floor.

"All set, gentlemen," she said as she put the phone down.

They followed Ms. Kennedy out of her office and walked down the hall to the elevator used strictly by personnel who worked on the sixth floor. Kennedy pressed the button and waited.

A minute passed and the doors opened. A uniformed man saluted General Roswell and introduced himself as Captain Myers. They stepped into the elevator and ascended to the sixth floor.

"How can I help you, General?" Myers asked as they got out and moved into the dimly lit amber-colored corridor.

"What kind of work are you involved in here?" Roswell asked.

"Sir, we primarily are engaged in the rehabilitation of patients who are suffering from severe psychoses." He shot a nervous glance at Kennedy.

"Will you show us some of your patients?" Roswell asked.

"Sir, I would need special clearance to allow any direct contact between you and our patients, but you could observe them in their rooms from the doorways."

"Very well, Captain, proceed."

They walked down the corridor and stopped in front of one of the rooms.

Mac recognized the patient he had seen before—the woman with the scar on her temple. He pulled Roswell away and whispered, "I think the one we want was in the next room on the right."

They went to the next room and found it empty. "Try the next one," Mac whispered.

They went to that one and found it empty also.

"I'm sure she was in one of those two," Mac said, frustrated.

The group continued down the corridor, stopping at each room. Mac saw a variety of patients, all of whom appeared to be heavily sedated, but the woman he had interviewed was not among them.

"Will you excuse us for a moment?" Roswell said, and he motioned to Mac and Uri as he walked a short distance away.

"They must have anticipated we'd come here so they've moved her," Roswell stated.

"A step in front," Uri added.

"She was in the room back there. I'm positive. What are you going to do?" Mac whispered.

"I want to talk to Kennedy again."

They rejoined the group and Roswell said, "Captain, why are all the patients sedated?"

Myers fidgeted and looked down at his shoes. "Sir, we deal with severely psychotic individuals. The people you see here are part of an experimental group. We sedate them for long periods of time as part of their therapy. It's called Project Deep Sleep."

"And when do you awaken them?" Roswell asked.

"Sir, that varies in each individual's case."

"Oh." He stared at Myers for a moment, then said, "Well, I think we have seen enough. Thank you, Captain."

Myers looked relieved and led them back down the corridor toward the elevator. They entered and rode to the fifth floor, where they got off and walked back to Kennedy's office.

"Did you find what you were looking for, General?" Kennedy asked, and Mac could detect her gloating as they seated themselves around her desk.

Roswell remained silent, allowing her question to hang in the air for an inordinate amount of time.

Kennedy drummed her nails nervously on her blotter.

"Ms. Kennedy," Roswell began so softly that Mac and Uri could barely hear him, "if you're involved in a cover-up in any way it could be very debilitating for you . . ."

His statement caught her completely off guard. "I don't have the faintest idea what you're talking about," she said, but the tension on her face belied her words.

"You moved a certain patient, didn't you, Ms. Kennedy?" Roswell's voice took on an accusatory tone.

Kennedy frowned and folded her arms in front of her. "General, we get a lot of patients in here every week. I can't possibly keep track of every single one—"

Roswell interrupted, "Yes, but you knew about *this* patient, didn't you."

She didn't respond.

"I could have you brought in for interrogation, Ms. Kennedy," Roswell threatened.

She trembled slightly and blurted out, "The woman was moved recently . . . to another location. I don't know anything more than that."

Roswell pressed closer and said, "And *where* is that location?"

"I . . . I honestly don't know. I only know she was moved, that's all."

Roswell's eyes bored into hers.

Mac could hear her breathing in little pants. *She's scared,* he thought. *How much does she really know? What is she hiding from us?*

She lowered her head and her hair fell in front of her face, concealing it. "They moved her to another hospital."

"And where might that be?" Roswell repeated.

She took a deep breath, lifted her head up and glared at MacKenzie, then turned to Roswell and answered, "Camarillo State Hospital."

"I don't know what you're involved in, Ms. Kennedy, but if I were you I'd think about informing me about what you know. In the long run, doing so will serve you well," Roswell said gently.

She lowered her head and didn't answer him.

Roswell rose from his chair and left the room. Mac and Uri followed, leaving Kennedy at her desk.

They boarded the elevator, rode to the first floor, and hastily exited the building.

"They deliberately moved the woman," Mac yelled, once they were outside. "They knew we were coming."

"A step in front, always," Uri said angrily.

"Not always," Roswell said. "Let's go see if your friend the security guard is in."

They crossed the parking lot and stood in front of the trailer. Mac knocked on the door.

"Yeah," an annoyed voice answered from inside.

"Harry . . . it's MacKenzie, the reporter from the *Times* . . . can I talk to you?"

"Huh? Oh, all right, give me a minute, be right there."

They heard a small commotion from the inside of the trailer as Harry made his way to the door. Roswell looked at Mac and raised his eyebrows.

The trailer door swung open and Harry appeared. His eyes opened wide when he noticed Roswell standing next to Mac. "Hey now, I didn't have nothin' to do with that . . ."

"It's all right, Harry," Mac assured the man. "This is General Black. He wants to talk to you for a minute." Mac lowered his voice and winked. "About the sixth floor."

"Well, come on in. Place is a mess though."

"That won't be necessary," Roswell said.

Harry walked down the steps of the trailer. "Oh? Well, hey, you know somethin'?" he said. "Your article set some things straight about what's been going on round here."

"Yeah, like how?" Mac asked.

"Well, like those special ambulances I see come in here in the middle of the night."

"What's special about that?" Mac asked.

"Those ambulances aren't marked. There's no company name on 'em. They just roll on in here and there's all this hurrying while they take some poor soul out of the back and roll 'em into the hospital. Other times they bring 'em out and load 'em into one of those ambulances and off they go. No sirens, either. They just vanish into the night." He whistled and moved his hand like a bird.

"So?" MacKenzie prodded.

"So?" the guard repeated. "So them's the peoples that have some connection . . ." He paused, looked around, and lowered his voice. ". . . With the aliens and all." He looked at Mac, then at Roswell, then at Uri.

"Okay . . . so go on," Mac prompted.

"Well, remember that woman who'd lost her baby? The one Linda got you in to see?"

"What about her?" Mac played dumb.

"That's what I'm trying to tell you . . . they wheeled her out and stuffed her in one of those ambulances a little while ago."

Mac shot a glance at Uri, then at Roswell, then asked the guard, "You saw it happen?"

"They took her out of there and drove her off real fast, couple of hours ago."

Roswell shook his head.

"Did you see anything else?" Mac asked.

"Well, she was struggling pretty much. They had her tied to one of those roll-around bed things."

"A gurney," Mac offered.

"Yeah, and like I said, she was struggling bad. They gave her a shot of something and she passed out. But here is the weird thing—and you understand that I was peeking out the back window of the trailer so nobody saw me seeing all this. They gave her a needle or a shot of something in her eye. Then she got real still and stopped struggling."

Roswell stepped forward and asked, "Did they look as if they were putting drops in her eyes?"

"Yeah . . . that's what it was. Drops. Some kind of drops. I knew that. I knew they wouldn't be shooting nobody in the eye with a needle." He grimaced.

"Any idea where the ambulance went?" Mac asked.

He shook his head. "Nah. Like I said, they just vanish. Hey, but this was the first one I ever seen in the daytime. And I've been here since the first day the place opened."

"Thanks," Mac said.

Roswell extended his hand. "Thank you very much for your help. Your country appreciates it."

Harry shook General Black's hand. "Thank you, sir."

"Let's go," Roswell said, as he spun on his heel and started toward the car.

They climbed in and Diebol drove them out of the parking lot.

"Now what?" Mac asked. "Kennedy wasn't telling us everything."

"I'll deal with her later, but more importantly, we've got to get to Camarillo immediately," Roswell said.

"What do we do when we get there?" Mac asked.

"I'm thinking we rescue the woman," Uri offered.

"And then?"

Roswell sighed and said, "Get her someplace that's safe and far away. Diebol, see if you can reach Laura, will you, please?"

"Yes, sir."

Diebol picked up the cell phone and dialed Laura's pager number. He punched in a code indicating that it was urgent she speak with her father.

"It's done, sir."

Wincing with pain, Roswell shifted in his seat. "Thank you, Diebol," he said as he slipped another pill in his mouth.

"General, I want to speak to Elisha," Mac began. "Actually, that's not accurate . . . I *have* to speak with him. What happened a few hours ago . . ." He shook his head and sighed. "I have to speak with him today . . . now."

Roswell looked at Mac. "I understand. Why don't we go to Camarillo and you can call after we locate the patient?"

Mac shook his head vigorously. "No, it can't wait. It's got to be now."

Roswell looked at Mac. "If I drop you at the hotel, how am I going to identify the woman?"

Mac slapped his hand on his thigh in frustration. "All right, so I guess I'm going to Camarillo . . ."

"I'm sorry, MacKenzie. Your questions for Dr. Elisha are going to have to wait."

29

* O *

The Lincoln was caught in a snarl of rush-hour traffic on the 101 freeway.

"Will you look at this, for crying out loud," Mac exclaimed as he looked out the window at six freeway lanes of parked automobiles. "Welcome to the land of gridlock."

"I'm not believing this," Uri agreed, "too many cars."

"That's an understatement," Mac said.

Uri leaned forward in his seat to make eye contact with Roswell. "What about Kennedy? She is knowing more than we think."

"Yes, a wild card, and she probably knows a great deal more than what she's letting on . . . a lot more, but our focus must be on the woman MacKenzie talked to. She may be able to tie her abduction to the underground base. Abductees often report military personnel working alongside the aliens."

"Do you realize how nuts that sounds?" Mac exclaimed.

"You saw them with your own eyes," Roswell said gravely.

"Yeah, don't remind me," Mac replied.

The car phone rang and Diebol picked it up.

"It's your daughter, General." He passed the phone over the seat.

"Thank you, Diebol," Roswell said as he grabbed it. "Laura, what is your position? Good, I want you to fly into the Camarillo airport ... That's correct. I'll send Diebol to get you ... Probably not more than an hour from now after we get through this traffic ... Okay, over." And he passed the phone back to Diebol.

* ◇ *

Feeling uneasy, Mac stood next to General Roswell at the admittance desk of the Camarillo State Mental Hospital. There was an overwhelmingly oppressive feeling to the building, even though it had obviously been recently renovated. New computers, telephones, linoleum floors, counters, desks ... fresh paint on the walls. But the original shell of the old building had been left untouched. And it seemed to Mac that all the paint in the world couldn't cover the feeling that had bled its way into those walls over the years.

Mac watched four severely mentally retarded adults, led by an orderly, shuffle through a set of double doors and disappear down the hall.

He and Roswell waited for an attractive black woman with beautifully braided hair who was talking on the phone behind the admittance desk. She raised a long purple fingernail indicating she'd be just a moment.

Roswell nodded.

The woman finished the call and started toward the counter. A small fan, directly behind her, blew her perfume toward Mac, the smell of which preceded her arrival.

She laid one hand on the counter and tapped its new Formica surface lightly with the end of a pen. "How can I help you, gentlemen?" she asked pleasantly.

"My name is General Black from the United States Air Force. I'm here to see a patient that you may have just admitted from the Westwood Medical Center ... specifically from the military psychiatric ward."

Her demeanor suddenly became very professional and she answered, "Yes, someone was admitted just a short time ago from there," and she stopped tapping the pen.

Roswell moved a little closer to the counter and said, "I would like to see the woman."

"Are you part of the Conservatorship?" she asked.

Roswell waited a moment before replying tersely, "No, I am not."

"Are you related to the patient?"

Again he answered, "No, I am not."

"I'm sorry, sir, but I can't let you see the patient unless you're part of the Conservatorship."

Roswell frowned. "I understand."

"Would you like to speak to her doctor?"

He nodded.

"You're in luck, he's coming down the corridor just behind you. I'll call him for you . . . Dr. Jones?" And she raised her hand and waved.

Jones was reading a chart as he walked. When he heard his name he stopped and looked up.

"Dr. Jones," she called again and waved the pen.

Jones walked over to them. "Yes, Ms. Burross?" he replied, but his eyes were fixed on Roswell.

"This gentleman, General Black from the United States Air Force, is requesting to see a patient that was just admitted from the military psychiatric ward at Westwood. He's not part of the Conservatorship, however."

Jones pursed his lips together and addressed Roswell. "Are you a member of the woman's family?"

"No." Roswell folded his arms in front of him. "Dr. Jones, it's important that I at least see the patient. Is she still sedated?"

"I'm sorry, sir, but that is private information. I'm not at liberty to discuss the patient's case."

Roswell compressed his lips and looked at the man. "What is it going to take to allow us access?"

"I'm sorry, General, but unless you're part of the Conservatorship there really isn't anything you can do. May I see some I.D., please?"

Roswell unfolded his arms. "That won't be necessary, Doctor. Thank you for your time. I'm sure you're very busy here." He nodded to Mac and they left.

"Now what?" Mac asked as soon as they were out of earshot.

"I think a phone call is in order," Roswell said. On his way out he stopped in the lobby and noted the name of the executive director of the hospital. Mac wondered what Roswell had in mind to clear the red tape.

Mac saw Uri and Diebol standing beside the Lincoln as he walked into the parking lot. With them was Roswell's daughter, Laura, who was clothed in a faded orange jumpsuit. As worn out as Mac was, he perked up when he saw her.

"Glad you made it," Roswell said to Laura as they all climbed into the Lincoln.

She turned around in the front seat. "How are you feeling?" she asked her father.

Roswell was clearly perturbed at her question. "I'm fine," he grumbled.

Laura looked at Mac and smiled. "Hello, MacKenzie."

Mac smiled. "I didn't know you could fly."

"Since I was a child. He taught me." And she glanced lovingly at her father.

"Oh . . ." Mac exhaled.

"Let's get down to business . . . shall we?" Roswell interrupted. "Diebol, make the necessary call so we can get to the woman. The name is Edward Heggins, he's the executive director here."

"Yes, sir, General, give me a minute, sir." And he typed in a command on his laptop, which was plugged into the cell phone of the car.

Mac leaned forward, rested his elbows on the seat, and looked at the screen of the laptop.

"What's he doing?" Mac asked.

Laura turned so that she faced him. "Trying to find a link between the executive director here and one of our contacts. There are other military personnel who have pledged their lives to defending our country from what many believe is an imminent invasion."

"What invasion?" Mac asked.

Laura smiled at him with interest dancing in her eyes. Mac felt butterflies in his stomach.

"The day they reveal themselves," she answered.

"I'm thinking that would be a very interesting day," Uri added.

"A very unstable day," Roswell corrected.

Mac shook his head. "A very terrifying day if they are who your grandfather believes they are."

Diebol interrupted, "Got it, sir. We need to contact Major Lewis and brief him. He knows the executive director of the hospital. They're old personal friends."

"Okay, do it," Roswell ordered.

Diebol reconnected the cell phone, dialed the number, and handed the phone to Roswell.

"I need privacy for this, please," he said.

Mac, Uri, and Laura exited the Lincoln.

Mac could see the silhouette of Roswell through the tinted glass. He turned to Laura and asked, "Why wouldn't your father let me use the laptop to call Dr. Elisha?"

She tossed her long loose ponytail over her shoulder and said, "I don't know . . . I suppose he has his reasons. He can be very stubborn."

Mac stared at the ground. "Do you really think they're going to reveal themselves soon?"

She nodded. "I think whatever agenda they have is accelerating. So does he." And she pointed to her father.

The window went down and Roswell said with satisfaction, "We'll be able to see the patient as soon as the executive director arrives. He should be here in less than a half hour."

Who are these people? Mac wondered. The day was proving to be too much for him. All he wanted was to call Elisha and process some of what he'd observed. He had questions that needed answers. But what troubled him was the realization that he didn't fully trust Roswell. There was a gap between them. He thought about Roswell's comments in the document room, that he didn't believe in the Second Coming anymore ... Not that Mac was sure about all the details of it either, but that was another reason why he wanted to talk to Elisha. He remembered what Roswell said, that he had almost embraced the idea of the Second Coming until his ongoing involvement with the alien presence. Then everything changed ... something died in him. Hope? Isn't that precisely what Elisha said would happen ... that the deception would be great ... people would be deceived and believe the lie?

Roswell looked at his watch and said, "I was told the executive director was on his way. We're to wait for him in his office. Let's see what kind of welcome we generate now. Let's go." And he opened his door.

* ○ *

Mac, Roswell, Laura, and Uri had waited in the executive director's office for almost half an hour. Ms. Burross had brought in a fresh pot of coffee and some crumb cake. Mac had eaten three pieces of the cake and was reaching for a fourth when the door to the executive director's office opened and a tall, lanky man with stringy gray hair and a slight limp entered the room. He held a hospital file in one hand.

Mac and Uri stood up, following Roswell's lead. The man walked straight to Roswell and announced, "I'm Edward Heggins, the executive director of this hospital." They shook hands.

Roswell made the introductions.

"I'll get right to the point, General," Heggins said. "A good friend of mine ... and apparently yours, Major Lewis, called a short while ago. Carl—sorry, Major Lewis. We go back a long way . . . high school wrestling team . . . Well, no matter. Major Lewis informed me of the situation. I came as quickly as I could."

Roswell put his hands behind his back and said, "Thank you for your cooperation, Mr. Heggins."

"Here." Heggins waved the file. "Ms. Burross handed me the woman's file as I came in. There are some things here . . ." He opened the file and turned a few pages. "Well, it's not exactly clear as to why she's being held in lockup."

"What's lockup?" Mac asked.

Heggins appeared startled by the question. "Well, the lockup area is usually reserved for the criminally insane. Essentially it's a jail. Every room has a keyed entry. All areas in that wing of our facility have to be entered with special keys . . . even to use the toilet."

"Why is she being held there?" Roswell asked.

He held up the legal file in front of him. "There really isn't a good reason, except it was requested by the military psych unit for security purposes."

"Can we see her now?" Roswell asked.

"Yes, of course . . . follow me." Heggins showed them out of his office.

They arrived at the entrance to the lockup wing. An orderly opened the door, which had a heavy wired meshed glass window in it, and they entered the area. Heggins asked the man to escort him to where the woman was being kept.

The group walked down the hall. Suddenly someone screamed. A high, wild wail . . . like that of a crazed animal.

Mac froze and looked at Laura. She appeared startled as well.

"It's all right," Heggins reassured them. "Some of them do that, you know . . . when they get excited."

The orderly, who sported two solid silver crowns for front teeth, came close to Mac. "They see things we don't," he said, and winked.

They continued down the hall and arrived at the door of the patient that Roswell had requested to see. The orderly fitted his key into the lock and opened it.

Mac recognized the woman he'd seen days ago. She lay asleep on a bed with her hands bound at the wrists to the stainless steel side guards that were lifted in place. She appeared noticeably thinner and her hair was matted in clumps next to her face. Her eyes were swollen shut and the lids had a peculiar red color to them.

"Oh no . . ." Mac groaned, turning to Roswell. "It's her. She looks terrible."

"Are you sure?" Roswell asked.

Mac nodded. "Yeah, I'm sure. What have they done to her, for crying out loud?"

Roswell ignored the question. Instead, he turned to Heggins and asked, "How soon before we can have her moved?"

Heggins frowned. "Major Lewis didn't say anything about having the patient moved . . . it's not something—"

"Director Heggins," Roswell interrupted, "let me assure you that it's important that we move this woman to a safe location . . . her life may be in danger."

"Here?" Heggins looked shocked.

"Yes, here," Roswell stated grimly.

"Well, I suppose as soon as she regains consciousness, but I'll have to contact the Conservatorship and have it cleared."

"I'm afraid you will be unable to do that . . . at least for the time being," Roswell said. "This is a matter of national security, and I need your cooperation on this to the fullest."

Heggins shifted uneasily. "Well," he answered, "Lewis said to do whatever you asked . . . but her chart indicates she was given an experimental drug which induces long periods of sleep."

"Thank you for your cooperation. Now I want her cleaned up and given a change of clothes," he said to Heggins. Then he turned to Laura. "When she wakes up see that she gets some real food to eat, and I want you to stay with her until we transport her." Roswell took from his pocket a small black plastic device that was no bigger than a credit card and pushed a button.

Diebol's voice, sounding thin and tinny, came from the card. "Yes, sir?"

"Make a call for a special transportation unit . . . Laura will accompany it when it moves the patient."

"Yes, sir. Anything else, sir?"

"No, that's all. Thank you." Roswell hit the button and slipped the communicator back into his uniform pocket. He turned to Heggins. "Thank you for your cooperation, Mr. Heggins. My daughter Laura will remain with this woman until the transportation unit arrives."

"That's fine. The orderly can stay with her in case she needs assistance."

"Thank you, Mr. Heggins."

Uri held Mac's arm and whispered with genuine concern, "I'm thinking it's a good thing we found her."

"Yeah, it's a good thing," Mac agreed.

"Well, let's go. Laura, stay in touch," Roswell said, and he put his hand on her shoulder just before he left the room.

"Are you going to be all right?" Mac asked her as he was leaving.

She grinned at him and said confidently, "I can take care of myself, MacKenzie . . . even in here."

They started back up the corridor. They got to the main entrance and another orderly opened the door and let them out. Just as Mac stepped over the threshold the screaming started again.

He looked back at the room Laura was in and hoped she'd be okay.

* ○ *

Mac sat in the front seat of the Lincoln as it sped down the 101 freeway toward Los Angeles. Diebol had turned on his headlights and eased the Lincoln into the fast lane. Roswell,

Mac, and Uri were conversing about what they had encountered at the secret base.

"Who's going to believe anything that we've seen in the last twenty-four hours?" Mac said. "We have no proof."

"You know what? I almost don't believe it, and I was there too!" Uri agreed.

"More people than you would like to know what is going on," Roswell said. "We're just waiting to find out what the alien agenda really is before we go in and shut it down . . . Or try to," he added.

Mac's jaw dropped. "Do you mean you're deliberately allowing all of this to continue unabated, until you discover what *their* agenda is?"

Roswell nodded. "We're allowing it in order to discover their weakness."

"Their weakness? What about that woman who was locked up in the loony bin? The aliens with their agenda ruined her life! How about the zombie scientists at the base? Not to mention the who-knows-how-much of the public's tax dollars that have been dumped into that hole in the ground. You don't even really know what it is you're dealing with. Whether their intentions are good or evil. And that Kennedy woman was holding back something, that's obvious. How crazy does this all have to get before someone stands up and cries time out, for crying out loud!"

Roswell held up his hands and motioned for Mac to calm down. "It's not as simple as it sounds. We have moles that have infiltrated some of the secret bases."

"Moles?" Uri asked.

"People who have erased their past lives and taken a new identity. They work their way slowly into an organization or a government agency or in this instance a secret base and remain there. They provide us with an incredible amount of information."

"So what do moles have to do with going public?" Mac asked.

"We have to protect them and get them out first before we go in. Their lives are at stake." He paused for a moment, stared at Mac with a poker face, then continued, "Mac, I want you to contact your editor and start to leak bits of the story. I have an outline that I want you to use to guide you, but I want you to make the story your own. You have enough information that you've seen firsthand, and what you don't know can be filled in later."

Mac shook his head doubtfully. "I don't know. Unless you come forward and I can get a television crew down into that hole in the ground in the desert, I don't think we have much of a story."

Roswell shook his head. "You have the DNA evidence from Fineberg's lab, plus the sample Uri brought back is being tested by our people. Start with that. There's also something else, another link I want you to investigate. It's tangible evidence. You'll be able to write a good story with it."

"And what's the new evidence?" Mac asked.

"It's here." He handed Mac a file. "It has to do with cattle mutilations. Apparently, cows are drained of their blood. Certain parts of their anatomy are cut away by what appears to be something like a laser, and the carcasses are found without any visible signs of struggle around the dead animal. It's like they were dropped from the sky."

"What does that have to do with the aliens?" Mac asked.

"There are the usual UFO sightings before the carcasses are found. We think it has something to do with their genetically producing some sort of human-alien hybrid."

Mac put his head in his hands and groaned. "Evil. They're just plain evil! What has Elisha been saying? It's the return of the Nephilim! Can't you guys see that?"

"What? Because they take cows?" Uri asked.

"No," Mac moaned, "they could take anything they wanted with what we've seen of their spacecraft. But they *deliberately* leave the carcass so that it will be discovered! What's the point in that? It's like waving the whole thing right in our faces, taunting us!"

"There's a fresh carcass in Arizona, with a very unusual addition, if I can use that term. It's in the file," Roswell said quietly. "I want us to go out there tomorrow and take pictures, do interviews, the whole nine yards. Laura will fly us out after she's finished helping with the transport. I'll be going with you but in civilian clothes, as your assistant."

"Tomorrow?" Mac asked. "Which reminds me—my jeep is still somewhere outside of Palmdale. How am I going to retrieve it?"

"You're not going to. It's too conspicuous. Diebol has a car in the garage at the Hilton for you. Another thing—I'm dropping you off about a block from the hotel and I'm giving you cash, about ten thousand dollars in small bills. Use the cash for everything."

Mac was dumbfounded.

"I also have a new computer I want you to use. It works off any phone line. It can be linked up with Dr. Elisha in Israel. It has a scrambling device on it to insure privacy, but it also enables you to talk to each other and have visual images. Also a cell phone with a special scrambling device on it . . . make all your calls on it."

"I can't wait," Mac said.

Roswell smiled faintly, then said, "But first I want you to call your editor and whet his appetite. Mac, listen carefully. Cranston serves on the board of directors at the Westwood facility . . . He may be connected to all of this."

"Cranston?" Mac repeated. "I can't imagine that."

"And that's why I want you to be careful. Now listen, after you contact him, *then* you can call Elisha. Afterward, I want you both to get some sleep. We'll leave for Arizona in the morning."

"Why don't we all stay together?" Mac asked. "Don't you think that's safer?"

"No. I have some other people further up the ladder that I have to report to. I'll see you in the morning."

Diebol slowed the Lincoln and pulled up next to the curb. Mac and Uri got out of the car. Diebol let the engine idle in park, went to the trunk, opened it, and handed them a briefcase. "The money and the computer are in here," he said as he handed it to them.

Uri took the briefcase and gripped it firmly.

The tinted glass window slid down and Roswell poked his head out. "Read the briefing. I'll see you tomorrow."

Diebol got back in the car, and Mac watched as it slowly wove its way into the traffic. "What a day it's been," he said as he rubbed his forehead with his fingers. "I've got a splitting headache."

"What, like one that you have on the TV? An Excedrin headache?" Uri teased.

Mac looked at him and shook his head. "Your brain has been corrupted by American television. Let's get out of here," he said, and they walked up the street toward the Hilton.

30

Jim Cranston was eating a wonderfully succulent dinner of filet of swordfish served in a wine sauce. He took a bite and savored the flavor.

"What did she say?" John asked with a knowing look on his face. He cracked his knuckles, which produced a disapproving glance from Cranston.

"Kennedy said they were there. MacKenzie and that tagalong BenHassen and . . . someone else." He took a deep breath and added, "An Air Force general."

"It's heating up, huh?"

"The general wanted to speak with one of your patients."

"Well?" John pressed.

"Thanks to your foresight the woman was moved, but just barely in time. They almost got to her," Cranston said angrily and took a sip from his wine glass.

"Like I keep telling you, it's under control, huh?"

"Yes, so did you know about the general?" Cranston asked, anxious to see John's response.

John grinned and his eyes narrowed. "General Nathan. He's responsible for taking MacKenzie and BenHassen out to the base. Apparently, one of them did something foolish which attracted the attention of security. They're sending a team out to bring Nathan in for debriefing."

"What about MacKenzie and BenHassen?"

"They have other plans for them." John made a face, then said, "I sure wouldn't want to be in their shoes right about now. I'm sure it will be a very unpleasant experience . . . if they can remember it."

* ○ *

Mac and Uri were inside their hotel room. Because of their Do Not Disturb sign, the beds were unmade. The tape on the suitcases was still in place, and it looked as if no one had entered their room while they were gone.

Uri went over to the bed, stood on the mattress, and unscrewed the heating duct grill that was just underneath the ceiling. He reached in, retrieved his gun, and stuck it in the back of his pants. He then pulled out the manila folder containing the Roswell artifact. "Here it is," he said as he refastened the duct.

Mac set the briefcase Roswell had given him on a small table. He opened it and took the computer out. "Where should we put all this cash?" he asked, taking a stack of twenties out and slapping his hand with the wad of bills.

Uri stepped off the bed. "We each take some, put more in the trunk of the car Roswell has got for us, and put the rest of it up there"—he threw a thumb over his shoulder toward the air duct—"when we get to the new room."

"Sounds like a plan," Mac said, and he started to split up the money. "I'm going to call my editor," he said, as he handed Uri a stack of bills.

"Yeah, this is good, but call from the lobby. Use the phone Roswell gave you, and we can switch the rooms while we are there," Uri instructed.

"But what about all of this?" Mac gestured toward the computer and money.

"We take it, is nothing to pack up, easy like one, two, three," Uri said as he slipped the money into his rear pocket.

Mac put the computer back into the briefcase and closed it. "One, two, three, ready?" he mimicked Uri.

Uri slapped Mac on the back. "Let's go."

They made their way to the lobby of the hotel. Mac stepped into the walnut-veneered phone booth and pulled out the Roswell phone. "How does the scrambler work?" he asked Uri, who positioned himself with his back toward MacKenzie so that he could survey the lobby around them.

"It works on the frequency; it modulates it," Uri answered.

"Oh . . . Okay, whatever," Mac replied, not understanding Uri's answer.

Mac dialed Jim Cranston's number. "He's hardly ever there," Mac explained as he listened to the phone ring. "Plays a lot of golf, among other things." Mac thought about his last meeting with Cranston out at Paso Robles and his stomach flipped.

Cranston's secretary picked up the phone.

"Hey, this is MacKenzie. Is he in?"

"Hi, Mac, how are you? I heard you were in Israel," a female voice responded.

"Hi, Lee, news travels fast. Yeah, it was a nice vacation."

"A nice vacation, what?" Uri smirked. "You almost got shot!"

"Shhh," he said, trying to quiet Uri, then said into the receiver, "Oh nothing, Lee. Is he in?"

"No, but I can give you his voice mail."

"Okay, put me through."

MacKenzie heard the prerecorded voice of Cranston.

"Blah, blah, blah," he mimicked as he listened. Finally the tone came and he said, "Cranston, this is Mac. I've been covering a very interesting story, an exclusive. Big stuff! You could even say giant stuff! I'm almost ready to go to print. I'll call again in the morning." He hung up the receiver.

"Giant stuff?" Uri repeated, looking doubtful.

"I'm setting him up. You know, underground tunnels, hidden rooms, giant skeletons. The whole thing."

Uri looked confused.

"Cranston doesn't know beans about any of this and besides, it's how you sell papers. Trust me."

* ○ *

Roswell's Lincoln Continental was stopped at a traffic light. The general sat in the rear seat and tried to find a comfortable position. The pills weren't working. Every time he went out to the base it felt to him as if the excursion had aged him another year. He felt exhausted.

Maybe MacKenzie is right, he thought as he sifted through the events of the day. *Perhaps they really are evil.*

At one time he had tried to embrace that idea. Once he had studied the prophecies . . . the return of the Messiah . . . the Second Coming. Now, he knew too much. *If I could only think like MacKenzie,* he mused. *Everything is so simple, so black and white.*

He heard a thump on the glass next to him, followed by a hissing noise.

"Diebol, what's that?" he asked as he sat up and turned in the direction of the noise.

"I don't . . . General?"

He saw Diebol slump onto the steering wheel.

No time, he thought. *Gas!*

He watched as Diebol's door suddenly flew open. His seat belt was unbuckled and he was yanked from his seat.

Roswell's vision began to narrow quickly, becoming tunnel-like. Everything began to slow down.

I've got to reach it before the darkness. His hand groped for his watch. *They've come for me at last!* His hand found the button and he somehow managed to turn it and then press it into the timepiece before he crashed against the door, unconscious.

* ○ *

Mac and Uri sat at the small table in their new hotel room conversing with Elisha BenHassen on the computer that General Roswell had given them.

Elisha's face appeared in high resolution on the screen. "So one of the aliens looked at you?" he asked.

"Yeah, if looks could kill . . . I had the distinct impression that it loathed me. And that's not a strong enough word to describe what I felt," Mac answered.

"But, what? So it looked at you, you don't know what it was thinking," Uri protested and leaned toward the computer so his face would be picked up by the small remote camera.

"No, I don't know what the thing was thinking, but I know what I felt, for crying out loud. It was like waves of hatred were directed at me," Mac argued.

"Or directed at *he* who resides and dwells in you," offered Elisha.

"What do you mean?" Mac asked.

"Although it may be hard for you to comprehend and I admit this is a great mystery, the spirit of the living God dwells within you," Elisha stated firmly.

Mac glanced at Uri and saw that he had immediately assumed his not-another-religious-lecture posture, as he folded his arms on his chest and knitted his brows together defiantly.

"I'm not sure I understand," Mac said, trying his best to ignore Uri.

Elisha adjusted his wire-rim glasses on the bridge of his nose and said, "The promise that Yeshua gave his disciples before he ascended to heaven." At this Uri rolled his eyes and shook his head, but out of the computer's camera range so that Elisha saw none of his antics.

"Yeshua promised that the Comforter, the Holy Spirit, would come and fill them with power. He not only promised this to his disciples but to all those who would come after them. Do you understand the importance of that, MacKenzie?"

Mac nodded and said, "Yeah, I think so."

Dr. Elisha continued, "That same promise applies to you and me. Once we accept the Messiah we are filled with the Spirit. Mac, you have opened your heart to him again, and he resides in you. What the alien—or I prefer to use the term 'fallen angel'—sensed in you, repelled him! It angered him, for he knows that he will be separated from that Spirit for all eternity. The waves of hatred were real, Mac. What you felt in your spirit was the power of the Enemy, one of the many fallen ones who knows his time is short."

Uri turned the computer so it faced him. "What? These fallen angels make spacecraft?" he asked sarcastically.

Elisha slowly shook his head. "Uri, Uri. Do you remember in the book of Enoch it specifically stated that these fallen angels instructed mankind in the making of weapons?"

"Yes," Uri reluctantly admitted.

"If the account in the text is true—and surely we can at least agree that it is a historical work, yes?—then this would imply that these fallen angels had developed the technology to produce those weapons."

"Yes, but the text is saying that these were spears and shields ... big difference from the disk in the cavern we saw," Uri countered.

Elisha rubbed his bearded face and said, "I'll admit it is a jump, a leap of faith here, but look how far we have advanced since the Industrial Revolution. In the last hundred years or so, knowledge has increased exponentially! Remember these beings, these fallen angels, are thousands of years old, perhaps millions ... no one really knows. Why is it that you find it so hard to attribute advanced technology to them? Especially when we have a historical model to compare to."

Mac turned the computer back so it faced him and said, "From what I've read in the sixth chapter of Genesis and the little I've read from the book of Enoch, there seems to be a pattern established. They reveal themselves, dazzle us with technology, then begin to crossbreed with us. Doesn't that sound strangely familiar? And by the way, what happened to Roswell? I get the feeling that he used to believe."

"Yes," Elisha said, "at one time he was very close. He studied the prophecies, he knew about Yeshua but . . . he has been deceived. And that is why you must guard your thoughts, Mac. Turn them over when they come at you. Take each one captive. Remember the passage I told you to read in Ephesians?"

Mac remembered. "About the armor of God?" he asked.

"Yes. Stand firm, Mac, because you know the truth! And pray. It is your weapon. Nothing can touch you when you pray."

"I will. I'll pray. But when that . . . fallen angel stared at me it was as if . . . I couldn't remember my own name. My mind went blank," Mac blurted.

"And that is why you have to build yourself up. You must always be on guard! I cannot stress this enough. You are in a battle! Arm yourself, shield yourself, wash your mind with prayer. And be strong in the Lord and *know* that he loves you and that his Spirit resides in you."

Mac was stirred. Hearing Elisha made him feel as if he could face anything. In contrast, Uri slumped in his chair.

"Let's pray together now," Elisha said. Mac closed his eyes and bowed his head as Elisha prayed for them.

When Elisha was finished he asked, "Where are you going with Roswell tomorrow?"

Uri stirred and slid the computer so that the camera faced him and said, "To investigate a very bizarre cattle mutilation."

Mac turned the computer back to himself and said, "Roswell thinks it's a good place to start leaking the story."

"He should know, if anyone," Elisha admitted. "I'll leave you with a sobering thought. If this is the beginning of the Great Deception, then you must remember: 'The coming of the lawless one will be in accordance with the work of Satan displayed in all kinds of counterfeit miracles, signs and wonders, and in every sort of evil that deceives those who are perishing. They perish because they refused to love the truth and so be saved. For this reason God sends them a powerful delusion so that they will believe the lie and so that all will be condemned who have not believed the truth.'"

Mac said, "Laura—Roswell's daughter—thinks that the fallen angels are accelerating their agenda. What do you think about that? What's stopping them from landing on the White House lawn?"

"He that restrains continues to do so," Elisha said.

"God's Spirit?" Mac asked.

"Yes." Elisha nodded. "God's Spirit will not allow it until the time of the end, and then . . ."

"The coming of the lawless one," Mac repeated.

"Yes, precisely," Elisha said. "You're beginning to grasp the order in which these events may take place."

"I have something else to ask you," Mac said. "Who is responsible for the Web site? Is it one person, a group of people, a consortium of some kind?"

Elisha rubbed his beard. "An enigmatic old man who goes only by the name of Johanen is responsible. I've never met him. He's very wealthy, but more than that, he has certain gifts . . . although I have only heard about them secondhand."

"What kind of gifts?"

"Apparently he has the ability to heal people by the laying on of his hands."

"Miracles?"

"As I said, the story came to me secondhand, but yes, they're what I would call miracles."

"Miracles," Mac repeated. "And he believes the Second Coming is soon?"

Elisha chuckled. "No one knows the day or the hour, Mac, but yes, Johanen thinks Jesus' return will be in our lifetime."

"For crying out loud," Mac whispered.

"Anything else?" Elisha asked.

"Yeah, I've got about a thousand more questions, but let me chew on what we've just discussed for a while."

"That's probably a wise decision. Well, good night, gentlemen." Elisha's face disappeared from the screen.

Mac turned the computer off and slumped in his chair. "Pretty heavy stuff, huh?" he said, looking at Uri, then repeated again softly, "Heavy stuff."

31

✦ ○ ✦

Laura sat on an uncomfortable metal chair and studied the sleeping woman who was lying before her. She and a female orderly had given the woman a sponge bath, changed her clothes, and combed out her matted hair. Then they had released her wrists from the restraints and rubbed lotion on her raw, chapped flesh. Laura had lifted one of the woman's eyelids and saw that her eyeball was rolled up toward her forehead. Whatever they had drugged her with was very powerful stuff.

She looked at her watch. It was seven-thirty and still the transport unit hadn't arrived. She hadn't eaten a thing since morning and along with her hunger she was in desperate want of a hot shower. But she folded her arms in front of her and continued her vigil.

She felt a lump in her jumpsuit and realized she'd put a power bar in one of the suit's pockets. She unzipped the pocket, took out the power bar, and began to eat. At least one of her needs had been met.

Her mind alternated between concern for her father and her growing interest in Art MacKenzie.

It was true that she had a tendency to be like a mother hen when it came to her father, but after all he had cancer and it seemed to be spreading. She also knew that he'd just as soon die before he'd admit any pain. She'd learned to watch him for the slightest indications of discomfort. She did her best to be ready with his medicine or pain pills.

How long does he have, six months or a year maybe? she wondered.

Her thoughts turned to MacKenzie. From the first time she saw his picture on her father's desk she'd thought him handsome. She smiled as she remembered his reluctance to board the plane at LAX. And what was the nickname he'd called her when they met again? *Green Eyes.* She took another bite of the power bar and crossed her legs in front of her. It seemed he was interested. Hadn't he perked up when he saw her in the hospital parking lot? And when he left the hospital room he reached out and touched her and asked if she was going to be all right. She liked that . . . he was caring.

She took the last bite of the power bar and realized it had made her thirsty. She also needed to use the bathroom.

She went to the door of the room and looked out the wired mesh glass window. The corridor was empty. The orderly had promised he'd check in on her every half hour. The man had been fairly punctual. She looked at her watch again. Roughly another ten minutes before he'd be back.

She decided to pace around the small room rather than sit again, walking slowly, taking long strides and holding them to stretch her leg muscles. After a few minutes passed, she was relieved when she heard the door being opened. It was the orderly. A little early this time.

"Everythin' all right?" he asked.

"Yes, she's still out cold though," Laura said, and nodded toward the sleeping woman. "Look, I have to use the bathroom, and I could use something to drink."

"Thought you might. I bought you a soda but regulations say I can't bring anything down into lockup. You got to come up to my post."

"Okay, just take me to the bathroom first."

"Yeah, all right . . . come on."

Laura looked over at the sleeping woman.

The orderly followed her gaze and said, "Oh heck, she ain't going nowhere, she'll be all right."

"Okay, let's go, but we'll make it quick," Laura said, as she left the room.

"I'm the only one with the key," he assured her.

She followed him up the corridor. They stopped in front of a bathroom, where the orderly fitted his key in the lock and let her in. "It locks from the outside, so you'll have to knock or call me when you're done," he said. "I'll be right here so you go 'head."

Laura flipped the light switch on and entered the bathroom. *At least it's clean,* she thought as she closed the door behind her.

*   *   *

A short distance away in the same area of lockup, Bobby sat like he always did in his little cell, on the balls of his stocking feet on the cell floor, with his knees tucked into his chest and his chin resting on them. His palms lay flat on the floor and helped him to keep his balance.

He was mildly retarded and had been institutionalized for as long as he could remember. He was prone to unpredictable violent outbursts of behavior, which was the reason he had spent most of his life in lockup. He was nicknamed "the Screamer" by the orderlies. It was his wild, wailing scream that had sent shivers down MacKenzie's spine a few hours ago.

Sometimes he would just go on screaming. It was the only thing he knew how to do to get attention. He would scream, and if he kept it up long enough, someone would come in to quiet him and give him his medicine. And then he would try to bite or scratch or kick or anything else he could do to hurt . . . he liked to hurt. And if he hurt he would get more medicine and then he would disappear . . . for a while.

Bobby sensed things other people, normal people, didn't. He sensed something now, although he wasn't sure what it was. It made him very frightened, though. He rocked slowly on the floor of his cell. He suddenly threw his head back and let out a long wail . . . almost like that of a wolf.

Whatever it was, it was getting closer to him.

Using his hands and feet to propel him, he slid on his butt to the corner of the cell and pressed his bony body as far as it would go against the wall.

He began to shake all over.

Something bad was here . . . and he didn't want it to find him.

* ○ *

Laura wanted to look at her face as she was about to leave the bathroom but she realized *this* bathroom did not have the luxury of a mirror. She knocked once lightly on the door and called out for the orderly.

Suddenly she was plunged into darkness. She groped for the light switch and flipped it, on and off, on and off, on and off . . .

"Hello?" she called out.

She heard the same wailing scream she'd heard earlier that day. Alone in the darkness it terrified her.

"Miss Laura?" It was the orderly's voice.

Another scream echoed down the corridor and entered unwanted through the crack between the bottom of the door and the floor.

She didn't know the orderly's name so she just said, "Is that you . . . the orderly?"

"It's me. Listen, something's happened to the electricity, that's all."

"Get me out of here, please." She pounded the door with the palm of her hand.

"I'm tryin'. Hold on, the lock has to be here somewheres."

Another scream, this time starting with a long low note which slowly crescendoed to a high shrill where it oscillated deafeningly.

Laura held her ears.

"I got it, I got it," the orderly said, as he finally found the keyhole. He opened the door. Laura groped her way slowly from the interior of the bathroom. The corridor was just as dark.

"I can't see a thing," she yelled, almost in a panic.

The screaming stopped suddenly and almost as if by cue started again, but this time the other patients began. And the laughter started, wild, insane laughter along with the shrills and shrieks and groans chorused in chaotic confusion. It was nightmarish.

She held her hands to her ears and yelled above the cacophony, "What's going on?"

"Electric's off. It's got 'em all riled up. They're afraid of the dark. Let me have your hand and I'll get you out of here."

She reached out, groped for the orderly's arm, and followed it down to his hand.

He grabbed her tightly. "It's all right, miss, I know the way, we just follow the wall. I got a flashlight back at my post," he said reassuringly.

They started to make their way slowly down the corridor.

Then an explosion of light . . . blinding light that came violently from the room where the sedated woman lay.

Laura looked at the orderly's face, illuminated by the sudden light. "What's that!" he cried.

The inmates screamed louder. She could hear some of them hurl themselves against the doors of their cells, at the peak of madness.

The light grew in intensity.

Laura felt the orderly let go of her hand. She glanced at him and watched as he began to inch away from her with his back pressed against the wall.

Laura shielded her eyes and started toward the light. She knew what it was . . . what its source was . . . and why it had come.

She staggered down the hall to the room where the woman was and realized she didn't have the key to gain entry. She peered in and what she saw terrified her. The small steel reinforced window that was placed high in the wall was gone. Through the opening the blinding light poured into the room. Floating above the bed was the woman . . . but now she was awake.

Laura pounded on the glass and screamed.

The levitating woman managed to look once at her. It was a helpless, wide-eyed, terrified stare, crazed with fear.

The woman's lips moved and Laura could read them. "Help me, help me!"

There was a noise, like the rush of a freight train. The woman's body quivered, and like a leaf going over a waterfall, she was sucked out the window.

A moment later the light was gone.

Laura slumped to the floor. All she was aware of was her breathing. Then she realized the screaming and crazed laughter had suddenly stopped.

The hall was dark again.

She wiped her forehead with a trembling hand and started to cry.

32

+ O +

Mac was startled out of a sound sleep by the ringing of the telephone. On the bed across from him Uri had tossed the covers off, clicked on the light, and motioned for Mac to pick it up.

"What do I say?" Mac asked.

The phone rang again and Uri said, "You pick it up and say hello." He motioned vigorously toward it.

Mac reached out and slowly took the receiver off the hook and held it to his head. He cleared his throat and said, "Hello."

The voice was that of a man but sounded hollow and metallic. "You won't be meeting Roswell tomorrow," it said.

"Who is this?" MacKenzie demanded, caught off guard by the statement.

"And if you walk away and just forget about everything you've seen, we'll make sure nothing happens to your wife and children in Paso Robles."

Mac looked at Uri, covered the mouthpiece, and frantically said, "They've got Roswell and now they're threatening my wife and kids."

"Keep talking to him," Uri said.

"Look, I don't know who you are or what you're talking about, but—"

The man cut him off and said angrily, "You know exactly what I'm talking about. Get out of town. And leave all of this alone! You have till morning. We're watching you."

Mac started to yell, "You can't . . ." but the phone went dead.

He held it away from him and stared at it, not believing that such a short conversation could have such a disastrous effect on his state of mind.

"What did he say?" Uri pressed.

Mac put the phone gently into its cradle and said, "That I should leave everything where it is and get out of town . . . I have until morning."

Uri raised his eyebrows. "They are saying they got Roswell?"

"Yeah." MacKenzie stood up and paced the room. "If they got Roswell, we don't stand a chance! He's got connections, he's big time! And if they got to him . . ."

"And the caller said we had to be leaving by morning, yes?" Uri asked quietly.

"Yeah, I've got to call Maggie and warn her."

"Use the cell phone that Roswell gave us, the one with the scrambler," Uri said.

"Right." Mac walked over to the nightstand, picked up the phone, and dialed her number.

"Hello," came Maggie's sleepy-sounding voice.

MacKenzie tried to calm himself, took a deep breath, and began, "Maggie, this is Mac, and—"

She cut him off. "Mac? What time is it?"

"Maggie, listen, I've got to talk to you. It's impor—"

She interrupted again. "Mac, it's three-thirty in the morning! Can't this wait?"

"Maggie, listen to me." His voice took on an urgency. "I just got a phone call, a threatening phone call. You're not safe where you are. You have to take the kids and leave!"

"Mac ... have you been drinking?" she asked slowly.

"Maggie, listen, please! I don't have time to explain all of this now, but I want you to take the children and get out of the house."

"What are you talking about!" she exclaimed, fully awake now. "And where am I supposed to take them?"

Mac began to regret the call, but what other choice did he have? Not call her? Not try to warn her?

He took another deep breath. "Listen, just listen, okay? Some of the people I have been associated with recently are pretty important in the government—"

"Mac," she yelled, "I don't care if you're playing tennis with the president. It's three-thirty. No, make that three-thirty-two, in the middle of the night, and whatever nonsense this is, it's going to have to wait until morning."

"Maggie, please listen to me ... Please!" Mac pleaded.

There was silence. He barreled ahead. "I just received a call threatening my life, yours, and the kids'. You've got to believe me and take this seriously."

"Mac ..." She hesitated. "Is this something to do with the trip to Israel Jim warned me about?"

"What?" He raised his voice.

"Mac, I don't have time for this, call me when you're sober." And she slammed the receiver down.

Mac groaned, looked at Uri, and said, "She thinks I'm drunk."

"What can you do? I'll call Elisha, and we go to the Web site," Uri said as he sat down at the table and typed on the computer's keyboard.

"Yeah, good idea ... I wonder if anyone else knows Roswell's been taken out?" Mac said.

"I'm thinking someone like Roswell disappears and some people are going to be knowing about it. Look." And Uri pointed to the screen.

Once again Mac saw the feet about to touch the Mount of Olives. The screen changed, and they were on Roswell's page.

"Look at all of this!" Uri exclaimed.

There were pages of information, most of it in code.

Mac leaned over Uri's shoulder. "Wow . . . Roswell must have some sort of warning system. He must have anticipated something like this."

"Yeah, look here, at this," Uri pointed to a map of the United States which showed a red line from Los Angeles to Nevada where a small green dot flashed.

"Some kind of tracking device?" Mac asked.

"Yeah, and look where it's flashing from," Uri added.

"That's the base in Nevada. I remember from the map he showed us."

On the top right corner of the screen Dr. Elisha BenHassen's face appeared. "Uri . . . MacKenzie," Elisha addressed them.

Uri typed a command and the screen divided so that half of it showed Elisha's face and the other was the information from Roswell's page on the Spiral of Life site.

"They got Roswell," Uri stated.

Elisha stared from the screen. "Oh no, when?"

Uri used the mouse and scrolled to the top of Roswell's page. "Here." He pointed and showed Mac, then said to Elisha, "Seventeen hundred hours is what it says."

"It's the first bit of information on his Web page; it's flashing in green letters," Mac added. "After that are pages of information."

"Most in code," Uri said.

"Let me see," Elisha responded. "Give me a moment." His head bent down and he began to type on his keyboard. "There it is. Yes, I see it," Elisha said.

"What should we do?" Mac asked.

Elisha's voice was somber. "We must pray for Roswell's safety and also our own."

Uri was incredulous. "What? We get the call telling Roswell is taken, MacKenzie's wife and children threatened, and you say to pray? I'm not believing this . . . I'm thinking we should be doing something else. Getting more guns maybe."

"Uri." Elisha's voice was insistent. "No, Uri, listen. First we must pray. What we fight against is not of flesh and blood—"

Elisha was interrupted by something that began to flash on his screen. "Do you see it?" he asked.

"Yes," Uri replied. "What is happening?"

"I'm not sure," Elisha replied.

"Maybe someone's hacked into the site?" Mac suggested.

Elisha adjusted his trifocals. "No, something else is happening . . . Wait, let's see."

The map of the United States showing the pulsing green dot at the secret base flashed on the screen.

"What is happening?" Uri asked again.

"Look, the flashing dot has stopped," Mac said.

"And it is changing color to red, " Uri added.

"They must have found the transmitter," Elisha said.

"Now what?" Uri asked.

Elisha looked tiredly from the screen and said, "I'm not sure . . ."

* ○ *

Maggie had tried to go back to sleep after Mac's call but tossed and turned for half an hour. Finally she decided to get up and check the children. As she walked down the hall toward their rooms, she chided herself for not listening to Mac. She excused her hastiness by telling herself, *He's been drinking again.*

She gathered her bathrobe around her and fastened it with the silk ribbon that was sewn into the lining.

She knew she was being deliberately obstinate . . . it was a pattern she had fallen into after Art's death. One she was never able to break, and coupled with Mac's drinking eventually led to their divorce.

When they sold the house she got the lion's share of the proceeds. Mac didn't get much; he never even bothered to hire the services of a lawyer. By that time he didn't care much about anything. He'd been living in Venice for a few months and bingeing on the booze pretty hard.

When the final papers for the divorce came in the mail, she cried. Everything caught up with her . . . she was devastated. She realized too late she'd made a mistake, but the thread of their marriage was a disjointed tangle of frayed ends . . . impossible to put together again.

She moved back with her mother in Paso Robles and tried to give Sarah and Jeremy a life. They were what she clung to, her anchor.

She got to Jeremy's room first, slowly opened the door, and peeked into his room. The child was sprawled so that one leg hung out over the mattress. His head rested jointly on the pillow and an action figure. She went to the bed and gently moved his leg. Then she slipped her hand underneath his head, recovered the toy, and set it on top of the dresser.

She went over to the window and drew the curtains closed, then tiptoed out of his room and closed the door behind her. She crossed the hall and entered Sarah's room.

Her daughter was curled in a little ball with just her head peeking out from between the covers. Maggie smiled.

Standing at Sarah's window, she stared out at the night sky. She was about to close the curtains and leave when something caught her eye.

In the distance she looked at a light that was moving very quickly toward her. She watched, fascinated, as it grew larger.

What is that? she wondered as she saw it veer suddenly at a sharp angle, to the left. The object accelerated, moved over the range of hills bordering her family's vineyard, and dropped out of sight.

Probably a meteorite, she thought as she drew the curtains closed in Sarah's room. She went back to her room and picked up a novel she had started a year ago but had lost interest in.

She tried to read, but her mind kept going back to what had disappeared over the hill and what Mac had said.

* ◊ *

Uri closed the connection on the computer with his grandfather, looked wearily at Mac, and said, "He will do what he can. He can give us documentation we need from the Department of Antiquities and Fineberg's report on the genetic anomalies. So you call your editor. He is going to protect us."

"Okay," Mac said, grabbing the cell phone with the scrambler on it. "Besides, it will be fun to wake him."

33

General Nathan stared at the dimly lit bare walls, ceiling, and floor of what he knew was an isolation cell. He had been stripped of his clothes, his jewelry, and his dignity. He sat in a corner of the cell with his back against the wall and his legs gathered underneath him so that the soles of his feet rested on the floor while his arms wrapped around his knees.

His back hurt, the cancer . . . he wished he had his medicine. He forced himself not to let the pain dominate him. Instead, he attempted to retrace how he'd gotten here. First the abduction from the car . . . the gas . . . then fading in and out of consciousness. He remembered being wheeled on a gurney through what seemed like an endless labyrinth of passageways. Voices had sounded distant and echoed. His vision blurred, and he continued to black out without warning . . . then he awakened here, in this cell.

He ran the palm of his hand slowly over the material that was used to construct it. There were no seams or joints. The walls and ceiling melded into each other as if they were fashioned at the same time from a mold. It was alien technology and therefore he was probably being debriefed at the base in Nevada . . . but he wasn't positive.

Because of his capture and subsequent internment he also knew that MacKenzie's and BenHassen's lives were in danger, as well as a host of others ... and what about Laura? The thought of something bad happening to her made him sick to his stomach.

He wondered how long his watch had sent out its homing signal before it was deactivated ... that was his one hope.

He rubbed his eyes. They still burned slightly from the drops that were put into them.

He remembered being wheeled into what looked like an operating room. There were surgeons, nurses, and ... aliens. They worked together on him. He had tried to move but found that he couldn't ... tried to scream but no sound left his throat. A metal harness was attached to his head, holding it in place. He remembered something grabbing his eyelid and holding it so that it remained open. Then the drops ... then nothing.

How long had he been sitting here? Judging from the lack of hunger pains, probably not long. But what if they had fed him intravenously? Then maybe he wouldn't have hunger pains. Had he been there for days, weeks, months? He wasn't sure.

The cell was suddenly plunged into darkness. Darkness like he had never experienced, the complete absence of any light. He held his hand in front of his face, inches from his eyes, and couldn't make out the faintest silhouette. There was a hissing noise from the opposite corner of the room. Struggling and pressing his back against the wall, he tried to hold his breath. There was nothing he could do, nowhere he could go. He clawed at the smooth surface of the floor. He realized that even with all his training he was terrified. He screamed. And as he sucked the gas down his throat, he mercifully began to lose consciousness.

* ◊ *

Mac sat on the bed opposite Uri and stared at the floor in front of him, lost in his own thoughts.

He was numb. He couldn't understand why Maggie had hung up on him. *Have we grown that far apart?* he wondered.

He tried to capture the thought, as Elisha had instructed, and pray about it, but found he couldn't, or more exactly didn't have the strength of will. He was burned out, scared, threatened, and just wanted to be left alone.

Unfortunately the call with Cranston had made him feel more hopeless.

Uri shifted his weight on the bed, looked up at Mac, and asked, "So what did Cranston tell you again?"

Mac let his breath out slowly and sighed. "To meet him, first thing in the morning." Mac fell backward on the bed and stared at the ceiling. "He's not taking any of this seriously. He wants hard proof, solid evidence. Frankly, I get the feeling he thinks I've gone over the deep end. It seems like he's placating me." Mac put his hands behind his head and closed his eyes. "What's frustrating about all of this is to think that no one will believe us."

Uri slouched a little lower and said, "You know what? Why should anyone? And Roswell has the last bone from the skeleton."

"Well, at least his people have it . . . it's safe," Mac added.

"Who is what? We don't know what anything is for certain," Uri lamented. "It could have been destroyed."

There was a brief silence, then Uri said, "Elisha is right, I'm thinking we go to the cattle mutilation, where Roswell told us."

"Yeah, I guess," Mac said, still staring at the ceiling. "I wonder if they got Laura and the woman at the hospital."

Uri shrugged. "Who knows?"

"I feel like a trapped cockroach," Mac admitted.

Uri reached over and tapped Mac's leg. "Almost morning, we should be ready."

They were startled by a knock on the door. Before Mac regained an upright position on the bed Uri had grabbed his gun that was next to him and moved quickly toward the side of the door to their room.

The knocking came again, this time a little louder and more insistent.

Uri motioned for Mac to move into the bathroom and then answer. Mac hurried into the bathroom and called out, "Who is it?"

A woman's muffled voice answered, "MacKenzie, Ben-Hassen . . . It's Laura."

Uri's eyebrows lifted on his forehead. He looked at Mac, waved the gun, and whispered, "Don't talk."

"Are you there, MacKenzie? Let me in. It's important."

Uri shook his head and mouthed the word, "No."

Mac looked at him, grimaced, and whispered, "It sounds like her. What are we supposed to do?"

Uri moved back away from the door, crouched down, and fixed his gun on the spot where the woman's head should have been on the other side. He looked at Mac for approval.

Mac's eyes practically popped out of his head. "You can't just start shooting people," he whispered angrily.

"MacKenzie," she started again. "It's me . . . open up."

Mac looked at Uri nervously, wiped his mouth, and answered, "I don't know what you're talking about. There's no MacKenzie here. I'm going to call hotel security."

"Listen to me." She was angry now. "It's Green Eyes, open up."

"It's her," Mac said, and he walked out of the bathroom.

"It might be a trap," Uri said, and kept his gun aimed at the door.

"I'm going to let her in," Mac stated and glared at Uri with determination.

Uri nodded. "Okay . . . Open from the side, and then out of the way. If it's a trick somebody is going to start to shoot." He aimed the gun with both hands.

Mac walked toward the door. His hands shook as they reached for the latch. "God, please help me. Protect us!" he whispered out loud. He threw back the bolt, opened the door, and stepped out of the way.

He held his breath and watched the trigger finger of Uri's right hand.

Uri slowly lowered the gun. "Laura ..." Mac exhaled with relief, and he got up and went to her.

"They got the woman ... at the hospital," Laura cried as she ran into the room.

Mac closed the door and bolted it. "What? How?"

"They sent a ship ... and they short-circuited all the power, and everything went crazy ... She levitated out of the room."

"Who levitated?" Mac asked.

"The woman ... The aliens did it ... I was so scared ..."

"What about security, and what happened to the transport unit?" Mac asked.

She shook her head. "Everything fell apart ... there was none."

"You saw the ship?" Uri probed.

"No. By the time I got outside to look, they were gone."

Mac gave an acknowledging grunt. "How did you get here?"

"I had the orderly drive me back to my plane. I landed at Santa Monica and got a cab here."

Mac looked at Uri. "She doesn't know."

"Doesn't know what?" Laura asked with immediate suspicion.

"They got your father," Mac said slowly.

"They also threatened his kids and ex-wife," Uri added, pointing to MacKenzie.

Laura went to the bed and sat down. "If he doesn't have his medicine ..."

"Always one step before us ... What now?" Uri asked.

She collected herself and answered, "I know he wore a special watch. If he pressed one of the buttons a certain way, it would activate backup support of some kind. It's also supposed to send a homing signal for twenty-four hours."

"That explains what's on the Web site," Mac said.

"Yeah, but who else does it contact?" Uri asked.

"I'm not sure exactly," Laura said.

"So what happens now?" Mac asked.

Laura played with the ends of her hair and bit her lower lip again. "We follow what he outlined yesterday. We go and look at the cattle mutilation. In my plane."

Mac ran his hand through his hair, scratched the back of his head, and said, "In your plane? The guy on the phone said we had to leave by this morning. That only gives us a few hours."

"They can't be everywhere," Laura countered.

"We go to his editor first," Uri redirected, "then after, the dead cow."

"Okay, okay, but I need a shower ... I've got to have a shower," Laura said, and got up from the bed and headed for the bathroom, shaking her hair loose as she walked.

"You want to take a shower with all of this going on?" Mac asked.

She stopped at the bathroom door, turned, and said, "I can't think when I'm this dirty."

Mac and Uri looked at each other.

Without any further comment she disappeared into the bathroom.

34

* ⬤ *

Cranston swiveled his chair so that he looked out of the window in his office at the expanse of the city below him. He said into the phone, "MacKenzie called early this morning."

"And," John pressed.

"And, he's coming here to discuss this story of his. What am I supposed to do?"

There was a pause, then John said, "See what he's got and do nothing, huh?"

Cranston tapped his manicured finger on the desk and repeated, "Nothing."

John cleared his throat. "Nothing . . . No one is going to believe MacKenzie. Let him write his story, he has no evidence."

"What about the woman in Camarillo?"

"She's been picked up. She's no concern of yours."

"The sixth floor?" Cranston asked.

There was silence on the other end. Cranston was used to this by now so it didn't agitate him the way it normally would have. Let the silence hang in the air, he didn't care. He stared out his window and watched a red sports car weave in and out of the early morning traffic.

"Files have been moved and patients reassigned; everything's been covered in miles of military red tape."

"Oh?"

John continued, "By the way, we contacted MacKenzie last night and gave him an ultimatum." A slight pause, then he added, "We also apprehended General Nathan. He won't be leading MacKenzie around anymore."

Another long pause. Cranston waited. Finally John instructed, "Call me after your meeting with him. Remember, do nothing, just play along. He'll discredit himself, huh?"

The line went dead.

Cranston shook his head with disdain. He didn't like where this was going. He was becoming more involved and he didn't want to be. He had other things to do, a paper to run, committees to report to, and meetings to plan. He turned his attention toward the upcoming meeting with MacKenzie. *If he's been to the base then he must know a good deal.*

He pondered the short conversation he had had with MacKenzie a few hours ago. *He may have a story but no proof,* he thought, *and without proof who will believe him?* He leaned back in his chair and reminded himself to do nothing.

* ○ *

General Nathan slowly awakened. He was lying facedown in the interior of his cell. He opened one eye and stared at the floor a few inches in front of his face.

Where am I? he asked himself.

His mind was fuzzy. Strange images floated in and out of his consciousness. He moved his hand in front of his face and slowly moved his fingers.

Who am I? he asked himself.

Images exploded in his mind.

He saw himself in an airplane. Flying and shooting other planes in aerial combat. He shot a burst of machine gunfire at an oncoming German warplane. He braced himself as the bullets found their mark and the aircraft burst into flames. His body cringed and jerked on the floor of the cell, responding to the all-too-realistic scene in his mind.

He heard something slide open behind him and instinctively tensed.

"General Nathan?" a voice whispered. A dim light swam above his head.

He remained still. His mind swirled in a series of jumbled pictures, like a movie rearranged so the viewer can make no sense of the plot or the characters in it.

"General Nathan . . ." The voice whispered again.

Nathan moved his hands underneath his chest and was startled to realize he was naked. He pushed himself into a sitting position, rubbed his burning eyes, and tried to focus on where the voice was coming from.

"General, over here."

Nathan tried to stand, but a searing pain shot through his lower back. The room began to spin. He sat down again, then slumped against the wall.

Through eyes slitted against the light, he watched as someone approached him. The man held a syringe out in front of him.

Nathan instinctively recoiled. "Get away," he murmured with slurred speech.

"This will help you, General," the man whispered as he reached out and took Nathan's arm. "It will clear your mind, trust me."

"Whas are you doin'?" Nathan slurred as he tried in vain to pull his arm away.

"Shhh," the man whispered as he slipped the syringe into a vein.

Nathan stared as the man withdrew the needle, rubbed the place where the needle had entered, and hurriedly left the cell.

Moments later Nathan passed out.

* ○ *

A man exited from General Nathan's cell . . . the same man who had injected the general. He looked cautiously down the hall in both directions.

I made it, he thought, *at least this far.*

His attention focused on the surveillance camera above the door to the cell. He reached up and took a special lens from the camera's eye. He quickly put it into his lab coat pocket and walked away from the cell.

He pretended to be lost in his own thoughts and so gave no hint of recognition as two aliens passed him in the corridor.

Mustn't turn around and see if they're going to go into the cell, he told himself.

He ground his teeth together and began to walk faster.

* ○ *

Mac, Uri, and Laura sat in overstuffed leather chairs in the comfortable expanse of Jim Cranston's office.

Cranston sat in his favorite chair, a high-backed leather throne that wrapped itself around him, encasing him like a shell. He turned his chair so he faced them. "And you're going to fly to Arizona and take photographs of a rotting cow's carcass?" he asked.

Mac and Uri looked at Laura and waited for her to respond.

"Mr. Cranston," she began.

"Call me Jim," Cranston said, and smiled broadly.

"Mr. Cranston," she continued, ignoring his attempt at informality, "are you aware of the ongoing cattle mutilation phenomena?"

Cranston looked at her with a bored expression and said, "Old news."

"This recent mutilation in Arizona apparently happened only a day ago. Mr. MacKenzie and Uri agree it's good to start breaking the story. It also provides you with at least some of the hard evidence you need."

"Not to mention what Dr. BenHassen will send to us shortly," Mac added.

Cranston glanced at Mac, then scoffed, "A cow carcass is hard evidence? These things have been going on for years . . . even Geraldo doesn't cover them anymore."

"That might be true," Laura admitted, "but something is different with this one."

"Very different," Mac added in support.

"I'm waiting," Cranston said impatiently.

Laura began, "About a week ago a rancher in Billings, Montana, saw a mysterious object in the sky. When he went to investigate it he saw one of his cows floating upward into the belly of a UFO."

"That certainly is newsworthy," Cranston quipped sarcastically.

"Don't be so quick to judge," Mac said. "Now go to just outside Biloxi, Mississippi, the same day. A farmer there witnesses the same type of thing. Sees his prize cow floating upward toward—"

"Let me guess," Cranston interrupted, "a flying saucer. Really, Mac, you'll have to do better than this."

"You haven't let me finish," Mac said, an edge rising in his voice. "As I was saying, the same phenomena happened in Biloxi and Billings. Right? So guess what shows up in Arizona a week or so later?" Without allowing Cranston a word, Mac continued, "They find a mutilated cow on this ranch, but here's the kicker ... The head of the cow is from the missing cow from Billings while the body is from the cow from Biloxi. They're two different cows put together ... and that's impossible."

"And the sheriff there believes that the operation was successful and the cow was alive before it was mutilated," Laura interjected.

"How do they know—" Cranston started.

Laura interrupted. "The cow's head had an I.D. tag on the ear and the body of the other had a brand on its flank. The sheriff did his homework. That suggests something of an enigma, wouldn't you think?" And she folded her arms across the front of her jumpsuit.

Cranston frowned and said, "Oh, it's probably some sort of grizzly ritual performed by a Satanic cult or something," and waved his hand as if dismissing the subject.

"No," Laura stated emphatically, "it's not a satanic cult."

"Well ... I'm sure there's a rational explanation," Cranston huffed.

"I'm surprised you're balking at this," Mac said. "Normally you'd be jumping out of your skin to get a story like this."

"I need proof, Mac," Cranston said. "I am concerned for the safety of your family. But what if you just had a crank call?"

"It wasn't a crank call," Mac said wearily.

"No matter," Cranston said. "I'll admit, although somewhat reluctantly, that you do have the beginnings of something here ... This cow story. But it's too much to swallow, and the pieces don't fit together, pardon my pun, at least not in my mind."

He leaned back in his chair and looked at them like a father looks at his teenage children who still believe in Santa Claus.

"I know what it sounds like," Mac said, "but you've been my editor now for how many years?"

"It will be a decade this coming summer," Cranston replied.

"When have you ever known me to exaggerate or slant a story to fit my own personal agenda?" Mac leaned forward and bored a hole into Cranston with his eyes.

Cranston looked away and swiveled in his chair so Mac saw only his profile. "Actually, Mac, you never did, and this is why you were the best. But ever since your son's death . . . well—"

Mac interrupted him. "I know what you're going to say and I agree with you, but things have changed. I haven't had a drop to drink since I got off the plane in Israel."

"That's not a very long time, is it, Mac?"

"Maybe not, but I swear on my son's grave that all of what we've told you is true! Why do you think Laura and Uri are here? Look at them! Heck, look at all of us! We're sitting on an incredible story. We've got the possibility of collecting some very bizarre hard evidence in Arizona, and you're stalling! I can't believe you, for crying out loud!" Mac got up from his chair, walked around to the back of it, and curled his hands into the leather padding. "Do I have to take this to another paper? Is that what you want me to do?" he threatened.

"Mac," Cranston said, using his best fatherly tone, "I'm not saying that at all, and you know it. Just sit back down and we'll talk this over some more. Okay?"

"Mr. Cranston," Uri said, "in Israel, I am archaeologist. Now what? I have come all this way for a wild goose?"

Mac leaned over and whispered, "You mean a wild goose chase."

"A goose chase." Uri shrugged. "What MacKenzie is telling is true. Something is going on and whatever, it's hardball." And he looked at Mac, who grinned at him.

Cranston knew his control of the situation was slipping and felt he was rapidly losing credibility with MacKenzie. He mentally shifted gears. "Okay, why don't Laura and Uri fly out and look at the cow carcass . . ."

"Mutilation," Laura corrected.

Cranston looked annoyed but continued, "Whatever . . . and Mac and I will go and make sure Maggie and the kids are all right."

Mac shook his head and replied, "No, I'll go with Laura. I'm the guy that's going to write the story. I want to see the mutilation. Besides, Uri's the ballistics freak."

Do nothing, Cranston reminded himself.

He swiveled his chair so that he faced them again, folded his hands on his polished desktop, and said, "I guess I can't argue with you. After all, it's your story." He looked at Uri and said, "Uri and I will go out and protect Maggie and the kids."

Mac walked over to the desk. "Why are you so interested in protecting Maggie?"

Cranston did his best to look offended. "Mac, I've known Maggie a long time. I'm just concerned, that's all."

Mac stared at him. "Why do I feel like it's something more?"

Cranston stroked his mustache. "Really, Mac, we're just friends. Besides, you are"—and he lowered his voice—"divorced."

Mac let his breath out. "Okay, I'm sorry. See you get them all someplace safe, okay?"

Cranston pushed his chair away from his desk and stood up. "I'll see to it personally, Mac. Don't worry, I understand."

Mac said, "I'm sure you do."

Cranston turned to Laura. "When do you leave to see the cow car—sorry, mutilation?"

"Immediately," she said, and let the faintest hint of a smile crease her lips.

"We'll hook up with you tonight, through the computers," Mac said.

"Computers?" Cranston asked.

"Yeah, the people I'm working for loaned them to us."

"Very sophisticated." Cranston feigned surprise.

* ○ *

A quarter hour had passed with Laura and Mac showing Cranston where the mutilation was located on a map that Laura produced.

Laura smoothed her faded jumpsuit like it was a tailored dress and looked at Mac. "Ready?" she asked.

Mac nodded. "In a minute. Jim, let me use your phone. I want to call Maggie and let her know what's going on."

Mac grabbed the cordless phone and walked over to the corner of the office. He dialed Maggie's number, then leaned on the large tinted plate glass window with one arm. He let the phone ring at least twenty times.

She must have left the ringer turned off, he thought with dismay.

He hung up the phone and stared out the window, completely detached from the antlike activity far below him on the busy city streets.

He took a deep breath, closed his eyes. His mind was swirling, but the one thought that recurred and dominated him was fear for his children's safety. *Here goes,* he thought as he tried his best to take the thought captive. He said a short prayer. Then he faced the thought and told it: *You have no power here. In the name of Jesus, you have no power here.*

It was a telling moment for him, like a man who tests his sword for the first time in battle . . . but to his astonishment the thought began to dissipate . . . fall away of its own weight . . . and leave his mind.

Wow, it worked. I brought it to prayer and it worked, he realized much to his surprise. *I wish I could tell Elisha.*

"Are you ready?" Laura called from Cranston's desk where she had watched him the entire time.

"Huh? Yeah, let's go." Mac quickly strode across the office floor. He held out his hand to Uri, looked him squarely in the eyes, and admonished, "Be careful!"

"You, too," Uri answered and grabbed Mac's hand in both of his. "We'll talk . . . the computer."

"Got it," Mac said, and he gave a thumbs-up sign to Uri. He looked at Cranston and said, "We'll get the story."

"Go get it then," Cranston replied.

"All set?" Mac asked Laura.

Laura nodded.

Mac held the door for her as they left Cranston's office.

Cranston turned to Uri and said, "Mr. BenHassen, I have to make a private call. Could you wait outside for a moment?"

"Not a problem," Uri answered, and got up from his chair and left the office.

Cranston picked up the phone and hurriedly dialed a number.

35

✱ ◯ ✱

This is different, Mac thought as the small aircraft dipped its wing toward his side of the plane, which caused the ground and horizon to assume crazy relationships to one another.

His stomach lurched toward his mouth. He gripped his seat belt with one hand and the edge of his seat with the other and closed his eyes.

"Are you all right?" Laura asked.

Mac opened one eye, looked over, and saw her giggling.

"You really *don't* like to fly, do you?" she chided, but mercifully leveled the plane.

Mac relaxed a little. "Thanks. I thought I was getting better at this, but now I'm not so sure. What kind of plane is this, and why do you have all the gear fastened down with bungee cords?"

She gave the faintest hint of a smile, slapped her hand affectionately against the stick, and replied, "A Decathlon. It's also a Citabria. And the bungee cords keep the gear in place . . . in case of rough weather." She looked at him mischievously.

"Oh," Mac replied, not wanting to pursue *that* subject in a hurry.

"I learned to fly while most kids were still riding their bikes," she boasted.

"Aren't there laws to protect the citizenry from that kind of fanaticism?" Mac kidded.

She laughed and said, "There are, but when your father's a general in the Air Force, rules don't always apply."

"You love this, don't you?" He gestured to the interior of the plane.

"Flying?"

Mac nodded.

"I do. Always have. It's been my surrogate mother since I was seven. That's when she died. I'm the youngest of five kids, separated by eight years from my closest sibling. I was the accident." She smiled.

"Sorry about your mother," Mac offered.

"It was a long time ago." She checked one of her gauges and clicked the glass case with her finger to make sure the needle wasn't stuck. "After she died, Daddy would take me up almost every weekend. It was his way of dealing with his grief and keeping our family together. It bonded us. I suppose it made us closer than we would have been had my mother lived."

Mac glanced out the window, thought better of it, and quickly looked back at her.

"My father died when I was young too," he mumbled. "He was stationed at Roswell, New Mexico, at the same time your father was there."

"Yeah." She nodded. "Dad mentioned that to me. I'm sorry." She looked out the front windshield, pointed, and said, "That's the Colorado River up ahead."

Mac peered out and saw the river wind across the land like a carelessly tossed ribbon.

"It's beautiful." He smiled at her. *And you are too*, he thought. "Remember back at the airport when you helped me get on the plane to Israel?" he asked.

"Yeah, great disguise," she teased.

"Yeah, Green Eyes," he said with mock annoyance. He turned in his seat so his back pressed against the door of the plane, grew serious, and said, "You asked me if I wanted to know the truth about my father . . . about the whole UFO phenomena . . . remember?"

"I remember."

"I think I know what's going on . . . the truth."

She shook her head. "Nobody knows what's going on."

"Before I went to Israel and the base with your father, I would have agreed, but not now . . . not after what I've seen . . . and felt."

"My father would never take me out to the base . . . said if I went it might change me into something he didn't want to see." She frowned. "It changed him . . ."

"How?" Mac asked.

"Well, he was different before. He smiled a lot more. I've watched him slowly deteriorate; it's like he's been drained of his emotions."

"Yeah," Mac agreed, "he's one of the most unreadable persons I've ever met, and I consider myself fairly adept at reading people."

"That's what he's become, Mr. Deadpan."

"At the base, he collapsed against the wall. I could see he was in pain, real bad pain. He just popped a pill and pulled himself together and went on like nothing had happened."

"That's my father."

"He's sick, isn't he?" Mac asked.

Laura bit her lower lip and gripped the stick tighter in her hands. "He's got cancer of the prostate . . . and it's spread to his back."

"I'm sorry," Mac said softly.

She nodded and there was a moment of awkward silence.

Mac changed the subject. "Have you ever spoken to Dr. Elisha, Uri's grandfather?"

"Some, what of it?"

"I think he knows what's *really* going on."

"And what's that?"

"Do you know about the Second Coming?"

"Yeah, I know about that from the Web site. There's a group of people who believe Jesus is going to come back. My father toyed with the idea for a while. I think he almost believed it." She shrugged indifferently. "I don't know, I've thought about it. But it's a lot to embrace."

"Elisha thinks that there is going to be a great spiritual deception, one that will overtake the entire planet just before Jesus' return."

"Really?"

Mac nodded. "Yeah, he showed me certain passages in the Bible and I've read and reread them. Elisha believes it will be so powerful that the world's major religions will crumble in the wake of it."

"And he thinks the aliens have something to do with it?" she asked, following his lead.

"Everything to do with it," Mac corrected. "And by the way, they're not aliens."

"I've heard the theory, from Elisha and my dad, *fallen angels returning*, right?"

"That's it."

She looked at him and frowned. "I don't think that's what's going on."

"Oh, so what's your take on it?"

"I think the aliens are just that, aliens, and they're producing a hybrid to repopulate the planet ... our planet ... to invade us."

"Do you know how nuts that sounds?" he said.

She grinned and said slowly, "Yeaaah."

"I don't understand something though."

"What's that?"

"Why are they sharing their technology with us if they're planning to invade us?"

"I know. I've asked my dad the same question."

"Did he give you an answer?"

"He compared it with us giving another nation airplanes from World War II and then having them fight a war against modern jets."

"No contest."

"That's right. But if you don't have any planes to begin with, then it becomes a big deal."

"Another deception," Mac huffed. "It seems as if they're pulling all the strings. You know one thing really bothers me, though. I can't seem to get it out of my mind."

"What's that?"

"When your dad and I were in the document room at the underground base, he said that the aliens were responsible in some way for the Resurrection of Jesus . . . at least that is what *they* claimed."

"Do you believe that?" she asked.

"No way. I mean, why come millions of miles to say that? There's something really strange here . . . more deception. It seems they twist everything. They lie, and they're masters of deceit."

"I agree," she said.

"If they had noble intentions, why not give us the cure to one of our more horrible diseases, like your dad's cancer? Or if they're so powerful and all-knowing, why not give us a plan to end world hunger or put an end to war?"

"That would be nice."

Mac continued, "No, they malign Jesus' divinity and attempt to drive home that they, the aliens, will show us who God really is. You see, spiritual deception."

"So you believe that this is what's going on?"

Mac nodded and looked at her solemnly. "Yeah, right now it makes the most sense to me, especially after my encounter with one at the base."

"Tell me what happened," Laura said.

Mac recounted his journey from seeing the bones of the Nephilim in Israel to what had transpired at the underground base. He elaborated on his experience when the alien had looked at him. How it had made him feel and what it had done to him mentally and physically.

He finished and was silent, allowing Laura time to digest what he'd told her.

"And you think the return of the Nephilim is happening ... now?"

Mac nodded. "Yeah. Remember the woman in Camarillo?"

"How can I forget?" She shivered.

"That woman was abducted, impregnated, and the child that she claimed was shown to her later by the aliens was not entirely human. I agree with you that they are creating a race of hybrids, but I believe the seed is demonic in origin."

"I used to believe that the aliens had come to help us, usher the inhabitants of earth into a time of global peace."

"Uri believes that too, but I think he's changing his opinion after what he's been through," Mac said.

They flew in silence for a while longer. Mac relaxed a little and even managed to look out the window at the earth streaking by below.

"Hey, we're almost there," Laura said, and she banked the plane to her side. Mac responded by holding onto the seat again.

She glanced over, saw him all tensed, and shook her head. "You've got to relax and enjoy it. Here, let me show you."

"You don't have to do that, you know," Mac said nervously.

"No, really, look," she said confidently. "I'm going to dip the wing on your side, and we're going to do a circle. Just relax and pretend you're an eagle and those are *your* wings, not the airplane's!"

"That's easy for you to say."

"Try it, we'll do a nice little circle," she insisted and dipped the wing on Mac's side. The plane began to turn.

"I'm an eagle!" he shouted, then moaned. "I don't think it's working."

"Just let go . . . you're not going to die, you know! Look down at the ground . . . get into it."

Mac stared at the ground and quickly closed his eyes. Then he opened them again but only halfway so that the terrain below looked a little fuzzy. He pretended he was a soaring eagle. With his eyes closed it wasn't too bad, almost like being a bird . . . almost.

"I'll circle the other way now. Ready!" Before he could answer she dipped the other wing and the plane began to circle to the left.

"Remember when you asked me what kind of plane this was?"

"Do I have to answer you right now?" Mac mumbled.

"I said it was a Decathlon," she continued, ignoring him.

"Yeah."

"Also that it was a Citabria."

"Yeah, so."

She giggled. "Well, Citabria is airbatic spelled backwards."

The pun was not lost on Mac. "You mean like a stunt plane?" he asked.

"Well, in the purest sense of the word, yes, and a whole lot more."

"Oh."

"It's got an inverted fuel and oil system so it can fly upside down."

"Really?"

"How about a barrel roll?" she asked.

"No, I don't like the sound of *that*."

"Hold on!" Before Mac could protest any further she put the plane into a roll.

"Ahhhhhhh!" Mac screamed as the plane rolled over twice. She stopped the roll, but now they were flying upside down.

"Hi there." She looked over at him and laughed.

Mac felt like he was facing a firing squad. His eyes were tightly shut and he had a death grip on his seat with both hands.

"Turn it over," he groaned.

"What?" she pretended not to hear him.

"Please," he pleaded.

She flipped the plane so it was right side up. "Whew!" she shouted, "I love doing that!" She took her hands off the stick and quickly put her hair back in place.

"I think I'm going to throw up," Mac said.

"No eagle?" Laura asked, as she stuck out her lower lip and pouted.

"No, and don't do any more barrel rolls, for crying out loud!"

She laughed. "You don't know what you're missing."

"How much farther?" Mac asked angrily, still holding his seat.

She checked her gauges, looked out at the terrain, and said, "It's not far now. Maybe another twenty minutes before we land, which reminds me that I should radio our contact there—the local sheriff."

"The local sheriff?"

"Jim Huffman. He's the authority that did the follow-up on the tag and brand found on the mutilated cow; he'll take us out to the ranch where it was found."

"How far is it from the airstrip?"

She glanced at him. Her eyes lit up and she smiled slyly. "Well, it's not exactly an airstrip."

Mac studied her face and said slowly, "What do you mean . . . not exactly?"

She turned her head so it faced her window and mumbled quickly, "It's more of a landing field . . . I think."

"What!" Mac shouted. "A field! *You think?*"

She peeked at him from the corner of her eyes, saw that he was mad, and giggled. "Well, I've never landed there, but Sheriff Huffman said that once in a while planes use it to make an emergency landing."

"Emergency landing?" he groaned.

She reached over and punched him in the shoulder.

"Ow." He grabbed his throbbing arm.

"Well, you deserve it," she laughed. "Maybe I should fly upside down or do another barrel roll." And she wiggled the rudder.

Mac raised his hands in the air and cried, "Okay. Okay. I'm sorry. Only no more barrel rolls!"

* ○ *

The plane passed low over the landing field that Sheriff Huffman had assured her was an adequate place to touch down. At the far end of the field she throttled down the plane and circled so she could land into the prevailing wind.

"You're going to land this plane on that?" Mac cried as he strained to get a better look at the field through his window.

"Actually it looks pretty good," she said. "Just a few ruts from where a car got stuck after a rain. No tree, no poles, no wires, plenty of room to maneuver! I can do it with my eyes closed."

"That's okay . . . you can keep them open. But are you sure you don't need more . . . ah . . . runway?"

She looked at him and proudly stated, "I've landed this plane in half this space."

"Okay," Mac said, and pressed himself into the back of the seat.

She brought the plane in about twenty feet or so above the field, turned her flaps up, and cut the throttle. She leveled the wings with the horizon and tilted the nose up a little by pulling back on the rudder. Mac had never seen anyone actually land a plane and in spite of his fear, he found it fascinating. Laura made it look easy. He watched as she concentrated on the field in front of her. The wheels lightly touched the dirt and picked up dust. She braked the plane, and in less than half the distance of the field, it came to a stop. She turned off the engine and looked over at Mac.

"Well?" she asked.

"You made it seem more like parking a car than landing a plane."

"Thanks," she said. "Daddy was big on landings. Sometimes that's all we'd do. Circle the field and touch the rubber. Over and over again."

"Touch the rubber?" Mac asked.

"It's when you bring the plane in and the wheels first hit the runway, but instead of landing you bring it back up, circle, and do it all over again. Most people call that a 'touch and go,' but Daddy always said 'Touch the rubber.' He told me that's what his flight instructor used to call it way back in World War II days."

"You had a good teacher."

"The best," she replied, and squinted her eyes. "Hey, look, there's a car coming." She pointed out the window.

Mac eyeballed the country surrounding him. It stretched out from him in all directions, mostly flat land with clumps of sage and a few Joshua trees scattered in the distance. He saw the car kick up a trail of dust as it moved across the otherwise still landscape. "What did you say his name was?" Mac asked.

"Huffman. Yeah, it looks like it's him. I can see the lights on the top of his car." She shielded her eyes with her hand to get a better look. "Let's get the gear."

They climbed out of the plane, and Laura grabbed a video camera case with a worn Air Force decal pasted on the cover.

"Should I take the computer?" Mac asked.

"Yeah, grab everything; you never know what we might need."

Mac wrestled with a crisscrossed tangle of bungee cords, retrieved the gear, and set it on the ground in front of the plane.

Huffman's car turned off the road and slowly made its way onto the field toward them. It stopped about twenty feet from the nose of the plane. Through the car's windshield Mac could see a middle-aged man with graying hair, a round face, and a neatly trimmed mustache.

"Howdy, folks, I'm Jim Huffman," the sheriff bellowed as he got out of the car. He walked over and offered Laura his hand.

"You must be Miss Nathan," he said. "Thanks for coming out here. Hope the field was okay?" he said, and nodded toward the plane.

"More than adequate, and call me Laura," she replied, then turned to Mac. "This is Art MacKenzie, the reporter from the *Times* I told you about."

"Pleased to meet you, Mr. MacKenzie," Huffman said, and took his hand and pumped it vigorously.

"Thank you, nice to meet you, Sheriff."

Huffman stepped a pace backward, stuck one hand in his pocket, and said, "I'm glad you folks came. The Parras brothers called early this morning. They're really spooked by this thing."

"How far is it from here?" Laura asked.

"Not far. Maybe half an hour drive," Huffman said. "Let's get your gear stowed and we'll get over to the Parras brothers' ranch."

"What do the brothers think is going on?" Mac asked.

Huffman looked at the immense spread of land that fanned out in every direction. "Sure is pretty country, isn't it?" He moved some loose dirt with his boot and looked at Mac, then answered, "They have a Spanish name for it . . . call it the *Chupacabra*."

"How's that again?" Mac asked.

"Chupacabra. Roughly translated it means 'goat sucker.'"

"Goat sucker?" Mac repeated.

"As the tale goes, the Chupacabra goes out in the cover of darkness and sucks the blood out of goats, cattle, even chickens."

"Has anyone ever seen it?" Laura asked.

"There are reports from time to time. We follow up on 'em, but we never see anything. No tracks, nothin'."

"And the Chupacabra is what you think is responsible for the cattle mutilations?" Mac asked.

Huffman grinned. "Well, that's why you folks flew out here, isn't it? Whatever it is, it's got most of the local ranchers spooked. I've seen quite a few of these . . . mutilations, but never nothin' like this . . . I'm anxious to see what you two make of it."

"Well, let's get out there then," Mac said, as he picked up the camera case and walked over to Huffman's car.

They loaded the rest of the gear, climbed into the car, and left the landing field.

After a half hour of driving dusty roads, Huffman turned the car onto a gravel driveway and passed by two large whitewashed wooden gates. "Here's the entrance to the Parras ranch," he said. They crested a small hill, and a low, sprawling ranch house came into view. There were cattle pens and horse corrals, with freshly painted whitewashed fences. Hay bales were stacked on top of each other, creating a mound the size of a small house. A large tractor with a trailer attached to it drove out of the barn and headed toward the cottonwoods. There were two dust-covered jeeps parked near the house.

"The Parras brothers have a real nice spread," Huffman said. "They own close to ten thousand acres."

Mac whistled through his teeth. "That's a lot of land."

"You need that much out here to make a go of ranching," Huffman replied. He parked the car and they all got out.

"Hey! Alfredo, Bob!" Huffman called, and he waved to two men who had just walked out of the barn. They were dressed alike in jeans, sun-faded flannel shirts, and battered cowboy hats. Huffman chuckled and said fondly, "They're always together, those two, practically inseparable."

The Parrases waved back.

Huffman made the appropriate introductions, then Laura stated, "Sheriff Huffman informed us that you'll be taking us to where the mutilation is."

The Parras brothers looked at each other. Their faces, which moments ago had smiled warmly during the introductions, now looked worried, even fearful.

"The Chupacabra," Alfredo said, somberly.

"Yes, he was here again," Bob added.

"I understand," Sheriff Huffman said in a consoling tone, then added, "Look, boys, I promise I'll do everything in my power to get to the bottom of this thing."

"Thank you, Sheriff," Alfredo replied. "We'll take the jeeps. The land gets rough out there."

"Our foreman will take us to the spot," Bob added, "but from where he says the carcass is, you are going to have to walk some of the way."

"Get your stuff and we'll meet at the jeeps," Alfredo said. "Bob and I will get Julio, our foreman, and meet you there."

"We'll do just that," Huffman replied.

"Well, what do you think?" Laura asked Mac as they walked back to Huffman's car.

"They seem frightened," Mac answered.

"I agree. They're scared, all right," Laura said, as she picked up her camera bag from Huffman's car trunk.

Mac opened his suitcase and brought out a small tape recorder, which he held in his hand. "Glad I brought this," he said, as he tested it to make sure the batteries were working.

"Ready?" Huffman asked.

"All set," Laura answered as she fixed the camera bag strap over her shoulder.

"Yeah," Mac replied. "Ready as I'll ever be." He slipped the tape recorder into his shirt pocket. And they walked over to the jeeps and waited for the Parras brothers.

* ○ *

A while later, Mac found himself bouncing along in the back of one of the jeeps. Laura sat next to him and punctuated the more rough spots with a boisterous, carefree, "Yahoo!" Alfredo drove and Bob sat next to him. From Mac's view their bodies jerked and jumped like nervous puppets as the jeep sped down the rough, hole-infested dirt road.

Huffman and Julio were in the jeep ahead. Julio swerved around small boulders and deep potholes. The drive seemed to Mac more like a qualifying run for the Baja 500. They streaked by clusters of cattle, who stared at them with big unblinking eyes while they slowly chewed their cud and twitched their tails.

"It's not far now!" Bob yelled over the noise and swirling dust. Mac nodded and held onto the roll bar that was in front of him.

Julio slowed his jeep and pulled up next to an outcropping of large boulders. Alfredo pulled up in back of him and shut his motor off.

At least that's over, Mac thought, as he got out of the jeep and dusted himself off.

"Down here," Julio said, as he pointed down an embankment to a dry creek bed. He made the sign of the cross over himself.

They gathered together at the side of the dirt road and looked in the direction Julio pointed. "There it is," Bob said in a whisper.

Mac could see the cow lying on its side about fifty yards away.

Laura nudged Mac. "Let's check it out." She started down the embankment.

"Watch for snakes," Alfredo cautioned. "There are big rattlers out here."

Laura reached the dry creek bed first and started off at a slight trot to where the carcass lay. Mac and Sheriff Huffman came next, followed by the reluctant Parras brothers.

Julio would not come down. He stood and watched them for a moment, made the sign of the cross over himself twice, and then walked back to the jeep.

Laura reached the carcass first and stopped about ten feet from where the animal lay. She took the camera off her shoulder and set it down on the ground. Mac came up next to her and the two of them stared at the dead cow, which lay with its back facing them so they couldn't see its underside or the front of its head.

Sheriff Huffman arrived and stood next to Laura and Mac for a moment, then proceeded to the carcass.

"Look here," Huffman said, pointing to the head of the cow. "Different color than the rest of the body."

"Could it be dyed?" Mac asked.

Huffman shook his head. "Nope, had it tested. The hair is the animal's own. Look here where they joined it to the body." He pointed to a large scar that encircled the animal at the neck. "No sign of infection or even sutures," he continued. "It has the appearance of old scar tissue. Heck, there's even hair beginning to grow."

"Are you sure it's the same cow that was reported missing from Montana?" Laura asked.

He knelt down near the cow's head. "Here's the tag," Huffman said as he pulled on the cow's ear. "Numbers check out all right." He pointed toward the cow's hindquarters. "And the brand on the rear flank corresponds to the cow from Mississippi."

Huffman wiped his forehead with the sleeve of his shirt and said, "You'd better come over and take a look for yourselves. I'm warning you, though. It's not too pleasant."

Laura grabbed her video camera, inserted a new cassette in it, and started to film as she walked over to where Huffman was. Mac took the tape recorder from his pocket and pushed the record button down as he followed her.

"Look here," Huffman said, as he pointed to where the cow's sex organ should have been. "They've been cored out. Notice how clean the incision is. No jagged edges or torn flesh. Just like the others. The blood vessels have been cauterized by something that produced a high temperature."

"Like a laser?" Laura suggested.

"Something like that," Huffman agreed.

"Grisly," Mac whispered with astonishment as he got his first look at the cow.

"Look where the eye should be." Laura pointed.

"It's not there," Mac said.

The Parras brothers stood shoulder to shoulder where Laura had left her camera bag but would come no further.

"There's no sign of any blood," Huffman reported.

"Chupacabra," Alfredo muttered and took a step backward from his brother.

"Are you sure about the blood?" Laura asked.

Huffman took a small knife from his pocket. He opened the blade and pushed it into the gaping hole where the animal's sex organs should have been. "If there was any blood left in this animal, we would see some evidence of it now," he said grimly.

"Not a drop," Mac affirmed.

"No footprints, other than ours," Huffman said, motioning to the ground around him.

Laura peeked her head out from behind the camera and added, "No apparent signs of a struggle."

"It's like it was just dropped out of the sky," Mac said as he looked overhead at the expanse of cloudless blue sky.

"It's deliberate, that's for sure," Huffman announced somberly, as he put his knife back in his pocket.

"What do you mean, deliberate?" Mac asked.

"Well, if I wanted to scare people or make them spooked, this is one heck of a way to do it." Huffman stood back up on his feet and then kicked the carcass. "Whoever is doing this is just rubbing our noses in it. Saying to us, 'Hey, we can do whatever we want, and you can't do a thing about it.'"

"It's the devil!" Bob called out.

"I'm not sure what it is, Bob," Huffman answered. "Truth is, I'm not sure I want to know!"

Mac bent down and examined the carcass. Being a reporter, he had been to the morgue and seen his share of corpses. But this was different. He turned to Huffman and said, "Why go through all the trouble of joining two cows together and then do this to them?"

Huffman shook his head. "Beats me."

"Are you sure it's not a hoax of some kind?" Mac asked.

"We're going to do further tests on the animal, but from what I can determine the cow was alive before it was mutilated," Huffman said.

"And no one knows about this?" Laura asked.

"I can keep things pretty quiet out here, but once we get the animal into town there's no telling what is going to happen."

Mac turned to Laura. "What if they're using the blood for the incubation of the hybrids, like Dr. Elisha suspects?"

Laura stopped the camera and said, "It's a strong possibility, and leaving it here like this sends us a message, and it's an ominous one."

"Yeah, like Sheriff Huffman says, they're just rubbing our noses in it," Mac agreed.

"My men won't touch it," Alfredo called out.

"The coyotes don't even bother it and they'll eat anything," Bob added.

"It's the Chupacabras," Alfredo said, and he mumbled something in Spanish to his brother. They turned and walked back down the dry creek bed.

"You need to get anything else?" Huffman asked.

"Yeah, let me take some still shots with the camera," Laura answered. She went over to her bag, put the video away, and brought out her Nikon.

"I can't get over the way it's been joined together. It's a precise surgical operation," Mac said, as Laura began to take some close-ups of where the animal was joined at the neck.

"But the coring into the animal and removing its organs is no less astonishing," Laura added.

"I've seen more than two dozen mutilations and I still can't get used to it," Huffman agreed.

Laura snapped another picture. "Makes me nervous," she added.

Mac looked at the carcass one last time then went and stood by Laura's camera bag. Laura took a final shot, joined Mac, and put the camera away.

"Let's get out of here," Mac said. "This place feels evil."

Huffman looked at Mac curiously and asked, "You feel it too, don't you?"

Mac searched his eyes and saw that the man was sincere. "Yeah, I feel it." He recalled the way he felt down in the underground base when the alien had looked at him.

They walked quickly back down the dry creek bed and climbed the embankment. The Parras brothers were already sitting in their jeep, anxious to leave. Mac and Laura climbed in while Alfredo fired the engine.

Julio had turned his jeep around so it faced the same direction that they had come from. Huffman climbed into the front seat next to him. Julio then drove over and stopped so that he was directly across from Mac. He stared at him with searching, dark brown eyes and said one word.

"Chupacabra!"

Then he gassed the jeep and drove away.

36

◻

Mac and Laura sat in front of Sheriff Huffman's desk. They scrutinized a selection of documents and files that he had spread out for their review, all dealing with the burgeoning phenomena of cattle mutilations. There were pictures, reports, signed affidavits, and a list of names and dates corresponding to each file.

Although Huffman may have been the sheriff of a small town, he took his job very seriously. The man had a passion for details.

"Look at this," Huffman said as he pointed toward the wall at a map of the surrounding area. "These colored pins show where each mutilation was found. They're numbered, so they correspond with the files you're looking at."

"Is there a discernable pattern?" Laura asked.

Huffman shook his head and moved his hand around the perimeter of the map. "No, not really, not that I can make out anyway. They seem to be random occurrences."

"You're very thorough," Mac said. "Can I get a copy of this? I can use it in the article."

"Sure thing," Huffman replied, and he opened a drawer in his desk, pulled out a file, and thumbed through it. He handed

Mac a smaller version of the map. "I've even talked to other law enforcement officials in neighboring states, especially New Mexico, about mutilations in their jurisdiction."

"Any luck in finding a common link?" Laura asked.

Rubbing his jaw, Huffman went back to the big map. "The only link seems to be in the actual mutilation itself. The cattle are left without any blood in the carcass. There's also a similarity in the organs which are taken. But of course the one we just came from is a first."

"What are the similarities of the organs that are extracted?" Mac asked.

Huffman looked out his office window at the expanse of range that stretched for miles and allowed his eyes to wander for a moment. He looked at Mac and stated, "Mostly the sex organs, eyes, and tongues."

"You know, the draining of blood might be used in the reproduction of the hybrids," Mac offered.

"Hybrids? You mentioned that earlier," Huffman responded.

Laura set one of the photos back on the desk and said, "In the course of our investigation we have developed a theory that this phenomena might be caused by extraterrestrial involvement. And that the harvesting of blood and organs might be used in some sort of crossbreeding between the aliens and us. A hybrid."

Huffman paled. "Extraterrestrials? Breeding with humans?" His face grew dark. "It's downright evil!"

"Why do you say that?" Mac asked and shot a knowing glance at Laura.

"Well . . . I'll tell you. I usually make it a point not to mix my personal beliefs with my job, but with this cattle mutilation thing . . . well, it goes against the grain of everything I believe in!"

"Oh, and what's that?" Laura probed.

"Well, like most folks around here, I'm a God-fearing man, and I think what's happening out there on the range is from hell itself." Huffman walked over to the worn wooden chair behind his desk and sat down. "Miss Nathan, I believe all these cattle being torn up is the result of some sort of supernatural occurrence. I'm not saying I can prove it, mind you. But I find it funny that almost every rancher who finds one of these mutilations on his ranch first attributes it to some sort of Satanic cult. Heck, the FBI was even called in to try to infiltrate it, in order to find out who was responsible. You know what they found?" Huffman paused and looked at them. "Nothin'. There wasn't any Satanic cult, didn't exist . . . but a lot of folks reported seeing strange lights, or what you'd call UFOs, just before a mutilation occurred. Well, all this got me thinking . . . maybe it's old Slew Foot himself. One thing is for certain, I don't see nothin' good coming from all of this."

Laura crossed her legs, grinned, and asked, "Who's old Slew Foot?"

Huffman chuckled. "Sorry, that's a nickname around here for the Devil."

"Oh." Laura glanced at Mac.

Huffman ran his fingers on the edge of his worn horseshoe belt buckle, then continued quietly, "I'm a simple man. I've seen a lot of bad things in my twenty-odd years in law enforcement. I've also kept up with big-city crime, serial killers, and such. People can surely do some horrible things. But I got to tell you, this is right up there with the strangest of 'em in my book. Call it what you like, Chupacabra or whatever, but I think it's just plain evil."

Laura picked up another one of the pictures and examined it. There was silence in the room.

Mac cleared his throat. "Remember when you asked me if I felt it, when we were at the mutilation site?"

Huffman nodded.

"Well, I did feel it . . . the presence of evil. I know it sounds weird. But I felt it."

Huffman stared at Mac and nodded slowly. "I used to think I was imagining it too, until the ranchers told me that the coyotes didn't bother the carcasses. I figured they were scared of something. Something that lingers around the dead animal."

"It might be some sort of lingering gas associated with the technology used in the surgery itself," Laura suggested.

"Anything's possible, I suppose." Huffman shook his head slowly. "But I don't agree. When we were out there looking at it . . . what was it you said to me? You put into words what I've been feeling every time I go out to one of those . . . there is a lingering presence of evil."

Mac picked up another picture from Huffman's desk. It showed a bloated cow whose stomach had been surgically cored out. He threw it down on the desk. "You know, it's funny."

"How's that?" Huffman asked.

Mac leaned forward in his chair. "You know the way the movies portray these aliens. Friendly guys like E.T. or the benign overlords in *Close Encounters*. All you have to do is look at one of these pictures and that whole scenario goes right down the tubes."

Silence again for a moment, then Huffman let out a sigh. "Well . . . I'm anxious to read your story. It seems like you got a good line on where you're going with all of this. By the way, I'll make sure none of this leaks to the media until your article comes out."

"Thanks, I appreciate that," Mac said.

Huffman gathered some of the material in a pile on his desk, then slapped his thighs with the palms of his hands and rose from his chair. "I suppose we better be getting you folks back to your plane."

Laura smiled at Mac. "Yeah, a good idea, he's got a deadline to meet."

"Always a deadline," Mac agreed.

Fifteen minutes later the sheriff dropped them off at the landing field. Standing near their plane, he shook their hands. "Well, it's been good working with both of you," Huffman said.

"Likewise," Mac replied.

"Thank you for your time, Sheriff. You've been a real help to us and because of that, Mr. MacKenzie has a good foundation for his story," Laura added.

"Well, I'm only glad I could help you folks out," Huffman replied. "Maybe if others read about some of this, somebody might be able to figure out what the heck's going on."

They transferred their gear to the aft section of the plane, and Laura fastened it down with the bungee cords. Mac reluctantly boarded, fastened his seat belt, and wondered woefully if he'd be made privy to more aeronautical tricks on the way back.

He looked out his window and saw Huffman gazing in the direction from where they had come. Then Mac saw a dark car speeding down the road toward the airfield.

"Hey, Laura, take a look," he said, and nodded toward the car.

Laura was busy checking the gauges and fuel levels, but she stole a quick glance out the window.

"Maybe it's the Parras brothers," she offered and returned to her pre-takeoff punch list.

"No, it's not them, at least I don't think it is," Mac mumbled. He watched as the car turned toward the landing field and stopped on the road directly across from Huffman's car a short distance away.

The sheriff looked at Mac with an expression that said "beats me" and headed over to the parked car.

"Who is it?" Laura asked, as she started the engine and the propeller whirled to life.

"I don't know," Mac yelled over the noise.

Laura throttled the plane and taxied slowly toward the end of the field.

Mac leaned forward to get a glimpse of Huffman. He was a half dozen feet away from the car when a tinted window opened. Mac saw the barrel of a gun protrude from it and almost simultaneously a small gray puff of smoke. Huffman reached down and pawed at something. Mac saw a thin wire that led from Huffman's body back to the gun. Suddenly Huffman's body went into a spasm and shook violently, then collapsed to the side on the dirt.

"Laura!" Mac cried. "Somebody shot Huffman!"

"What?" She looked at Mac, then over to where Huffman had left his car. "I don't—"

"There!" Mac yelled. "Over by that other car. It's like he was electrocuted."

Laura screamed, "Oh no! Oh no! They've shot him!"

"They're coming this way!" Mac yelled as he saw the rear end of the car slide and tires smoke as the driver accelerated.

"We've got to get out of here!" Laura yelled.

"We just can't leave Huffman!" Mac protested.

"He's just stunned. Didn't you see the wire? It's a taser. They used a taser on him!" she screamed as she slammed the throttle down. The plane lurched violently forward.

"What?" Mac shouted.

"He'll be all right," she yelled, as she reached the end of the field. She eased off the throttle, spun the plane around, then slapped the throttle down again and started to take off.

The dark car fishtailed onto the field spewing a cloud of dust and dirt behind it as it raced for the plane.

"We're not going to make it!" Mac shouted as he watched the car gain on them.

"Come on!" Laura pleaded.

The car swerved toward the plane and nearly smashed into it.

"They're coming again!" Mac yelled.

The car closed in on them. Mac could see two men. The guy in the passenger seat leaned out of the window and over the roof of the car and aimed a gun at him. To Mac's horror he realized it was the same guy that had punched him at the airport . . . the guy with the pinky rings.

"They're going to shoot us!" he yelled.

Then everything slowed down, and he felt the inward hand on him. *Is this God's Spirit touching me again, now, while this is happening?*

His fear fell away and he knew that somehow they were going to make it out of this. *Help us . . . Jesus, help us now,* he prayed.

Then everything exploded again. He heard a shot from the gun and a bullet tore into the cockpit close to his head.

"We don't have enough speed!" Laura screamed. "He's going to ram us!"

She moved the plane toward the car and at the last second yanked back on the stick. The plane lurched into the air for just a moment. The car slid underneath it. Laura pushed the stick away from her and brought the plane down. One of the plane's landing wheels hit the windshield and it exploded inward, covering the two men inside with glass.

She pulled back on the stick and the plane hopped off the car and landed back on the dirt, bounced once, and started to gain momentum.

"They've lost control!" Mac shouted, as he looked behind him and saw the car skid to a stop in the middle of the field.

"Come on! Come on!" Laura coaxed, as the plane accelerated.

"They're getting out of the car!" Mac yelled. "They're going to shoot!"

"Come on . . ."

"Laura!" Mac shouted. "He's aiming at us!"

Laura yanked the stick back. The plane sprang into the air and quickly gained altitude. She banked it to the left away from the field.

"Wow! That was amazing!" Mac yelled and slapped his thigh.

"Thanks . . . we were lucky," she said. "We didn't have enough speed to hop into the air like that."

"What do you mean?"

Mac noticed her hands shake as she wiped a wisp of hair from her eyes. "I know my plane, and we didn't have enough speed to lift off the ground like that . . . it was like something picked us up at the last moment . . ."

Mac sat very still and realized that something incredible had happened. *It's not coincidence,* he told himself. *He was here and I prayed and he helped us . . . I know it.* He looked back at the two men standing in the field. They were far away, out of range for a handgun. "I know one of those guys."

"Yeah?" Laura asked.

"The guy that shot Huffman is the same guy who roughed me up at the airport. How could he possibly know I was out here?" Mac asked.

"I don't know," Laura replied. "Only five of us knew where we were going. But they could have found us by checking our flight log at the airport, in Santa Monica."

"Yeah, but they would have had to know we were flying, and as you just said, Uri, Cranston, Nathan, the sheriff, and the two of us were the only people who knew we were going to fly out here."

"They could have been monitoring our radio," she said.

Mac frowned and said, "Yeah, I suppose, these guys seem to pop up everywhere . . . and at the most inopportune times."

"Yeah," she agreed. "But what do we do now?"

Mac thought for a second, then said, "We fly directly to Paso Robles. To the vineyard."

Laura pondered that for a moment. "Okay. At least it's a plan. But I'll have to put down to refuel somewhere en route. One more thing . . . Is there a place to land near the vineyard?"

"I don't know," Mac replied, and he racked his brain trying to remember what the terrain was like around Maggie's vineyard. "I think there's a field nearby. Could you land there?"

"Is it planted with anything?" she asked.

"No." Mac shook his head. "I seem to remember that most of the time it lies fallow. Do you think you could land there?"

She nodded. "I can put this plane down just about any-where." And she wiggled the wings.

He ignored her antics and his thoughts turned to the wounded sheriff. "Do you think Huffman is okay?" he asked.

Laura bit her lower lip. With a worried expression on her face she answered, "They could have killed him if they had wanted to. But they used a taser. It served their purpose though. It got Huffman out of their way."

"Yeah. But out of whose way?" Mac asked.

"Probably the same people who abducted my father. The same people who are linked to the alien agenda and want to help carry it out."

"Your father's right about something—there's always another layer . . ." He closed his eyes and offered a quick prayer for Huffman. Opening them again, he saw the bullet hole in the window.

"That was too close," he said, putting his finger in the hole.

"Yeah. Hey, there are some rags under the seat. Grab one and stuff it into the hole."

Mac found the rag and worked an end of it into the hole. "Did you really mean it when you said that your plane didn't have enough speed to get airborne?" Mac asked.

She nodded. "Yeah, that was really weird. It's like we hit a sudden updraft from nowhere. I've never experienced any-thing like it before."

Mac listened and kept his feelings to himself, unsure of how to respond to what he *knew* had happened. Once again he needed to call Elisha and hear what the old man would say.

"You said you had to land to refuel?" Mac asked.

She nodded. "There's an abandoned Air Force base . . . George Field. It'll be a good place to land because it's an uncontrolled field."

"What do you mean?" Mac asked, taking particular dislike to the word *uncontrolled*.

"You know how airports have a control tower?"

"Yeah."

"Well, George Field has a tower, but it's unmanned. Nobody is controlling the air traffic coming and going, so all we have to do is announce ourselves on radio just before we land."

"Planes flying around without a traffic controller. Is there anyplace else . . . safer?"

"Nothing close enough." She noticed his consternation and said, "Don't worry, it's safe. Honest."

"How far is George Field?"

She looked at the low hills she was flying over, got her mental bearings, and answered him, "Maybe an hour . . . a little more perhaps."

They continued to talk about the guy with the pinky rings that had shot Huffman with the taser and also taken a shot at them. It was obvious he was shadowing Mac. Mac figured he was the guy who trashed his apartment while he was away in Israel.

"Who do you think the guy works for?" Mac asked.

"I'm not certain, but like I said earlier, there are people who *want* to be part of the alien agenda. They're committed to it."

"Your dad briefed Uri and me about certain rogue elements of the government being involved."

"Yeah, but he's never confided in me as to the specifics. But I know this, that very powerful people want the alien technology. My father said it was the reason we won the cold war."

"Alien technology?" Mac asked incredulously.

"I'm only repeating what he told me, but yeah. We had the alien technology, some of it recovered from Roswell, and the Russians didn't."

"Why us and not the Russians?"

"Dad said at the time in 1947, we had the bomb and they didn't."

"That's it?"

She nodded. "Yeah, we were contacted because we were the most powerful nation on earth."

Mac rolled his eyes. "Incredible."

"Yeah, if it's true . . . but something else happened. My father along with others came to believe in the very real threat of an alien invasion."

"Layers of deception," Mac said.

"Yeah," she repeated, "deception."

Mac nodded. "You know, I remember something President Reagan said, in a speech . . . He used that same scenario. That the threat of an alien invasion would unite the countries of the world . . . that we would drop our petty differences and bond together to fight a common enemy."

"I know the one. Daddy has it on video tape."

"So Reagan knew about the possibility of invasion?"

"Yes, he was aware of it. He gave that speech you mentioned at the United Nations . . . just read between the lines."

"But what about guys like Pinky Rings?"

She shrugged. "Who knows? Some people want power and feel that if they side with the aliens they'll get it."

"Your father thinks—"

"I hope he's all right," she interrupted.

"Your dad?"

She nodded and took a deep breath. "Yeah, I know he can take care of himself, but without the pain medicine . . ."

"I'm wondering the same about my kids. I hope Uri got there by now."

"We'll call as soon as we set down." She looked out her side window. "Hey, we're almost at George Field."

In the distance Mac could see a huge landing strip. *At least it's not dirt,* he thought with some comfort.

Laura banked the plane and started a gradual descent. She looked out of the cockpit in all directions as she got closer to the airstrip.

"There's a biplane at nine o'clock and a small jet at eleven. Other than those two aircraft, I don't have any other visuals."

Mac confirmed the two aircraft she had spotted. "Yeah," he said, "I see them."

Laura descended lower and cut the speed. She flew just on the outskirts of the airstrip and looked for a good place to put the plane down.

"Over there's a hangar. It's open and I see a fuel truck. Let's head for it," she said.

Mac nodded, spotted the truck, and held onto his seat as Laura banked the plane and circled. She radioed her position, then came in low to the runway and made another perfect landing. Mac hardly felt the transition.

"Nice! Thank you," he said gratefully.

She flashed a smile and then taxied the plane near the entrance to the hangar.

"Well, let's gas her up," she said, and shut the engine off. The propeller whirled a few more seconds, then came to a halt.

Mac reached behind him, loosened the bungee cord, and got the laptop. They climbed out of the plane and walked toward the hangar.

Laura untied her hair and shook it out with several tosses of her head. Her long, silky brown locks spread like a dark fan across her back. Mac looked at her admiringly. Their eyes met for a moment. There was a poignant silence as they walked toward the hangar.

Mac felt a mixture of emotions. He wanted to say something to her to take the first step and was about to when she suddenly called out, "Can we buy any fuel here?"

The moment was lost.

Mac redirected his attention to a mechanic on a metal scaffold who was bent over the engine of a small plane.

A middle-aged man lifted his grease-smudged head, squinted through heavy-lens glasses, then answered, "Sure thing. I'll be right with you." He climbed down off the scaffolding and took an oil-stained rag from the back pocket of his coveralls and wiped his hands on it as he came over to where Laura and Mac waited.

"That your Decathlon?" he asked and nodded toward the plane.

"Yes, it is," Laura answered proudly.

"Nice wings. I'll bring the truck around. Cash or card?" he asked as he started for the fuel truck.

"Cash," Laura answered. "Is there a phone we can use here?"

"Yeah, it's in the office. If you're calling long distance be sure you use a calling card," he shouted over his shoulder as he turned the corner of the building.

Laura pointed toward an office that protruded from the wall of the building. It was enclosed on three sides with dirty, grease-smudged windows.

"I'm going to see if I can get a hold of Maggie," Mac said as they entered the cluttered office. He dialed Maggie's number and waited. After ten rings he gave up. "No answer."

Laura picked up on his anxiety. "Maybe Cranston and Uri moved them to a hotel."

Mac shrugged. "Maybe . . . how long before we can get there?"

Laura glanced at her watch. "If we're lucky we can get there before sunset."

Mac sighed. He took the laptop out of its case and moved aside a stack of invoices to allow a space for the computer. He unplugged the phone jack and inserted it into the back of the laptop.

"I want to talk to Elisha," he said, as he accessed his number. He typed in a greeting and waited for Elisha's response.

Nothing happened.

"He's not there," Mac said, and stared vacantly at the screen.

"I guess we're on our own ..." Laura answered softly.

"Yeah, but I'll bring him up to speed on what happened."

Mac typed in a quick message detailing the incident on the landing field, then folded the laptop and put it back in the traveling case. He reconnected the phone, and they left the office.

They walked back to Laura's plane. The fuel truck was alongside of it and Mac could hear the whir of the electric motor pumping the fuel into the tanks of the plane.

The mechanic looked up from the fuel gauge and said, "Another couple of minutes and you're on your way."

"Great," Laura said.

"Where are you folks headed?" the mechanic asked.

"Paso ..." Mac began, but Laura cut him off and answered quickly.

"Colorado."

"Denver?" he asked, as he topped off the tank, turned off the pump switch, and jiggled the nozzle so that the last few drops of fuel dribbled into the tank.

"Yep," Laura said.

"Kind of tricky landing there in the dark?" he probed.

"I've landed there before." She smiled and asked, "How much do I owe you?"

The man looked at the fuel tank gauge. "Make it forty-two even."

Laura paid for the fuel and thanked him.

Five minutes later they were airborne.

37

＊◉＊

Dr. Elisha BenHassen made his way slowly toward the Via Dolorosa. He stopped at an ancient house, which overlooked the Way of the Cross, and waited.

It was twilight and the streets of Jerusalem were growing quiet as the heat of the day mercifully began to subside. As he leaned against the whitewashed stone, he could smell fresh garlic and olive oil from the evening meals being prepared in houses throughout the old city.

Elisha was anxious.

He had never spoken to the man he waited for, and so when a few hours ago the message had come over his computer to meet with him, he was stunned.

Now here he was at the place he had been instructed to go.

His mind turned for a moment to MacKenzie. *Protect him, Lord. Watch over him. Give him the power of your Spirit. Strengthen his mind and keep his heart steadfast . . .*

Elisha sighed like a worried father and looked around.

A group of tourists were starting up the Via Dolorosa. A vendor pushed his cart wearily while two teenage girls giggled as they walked quickly by. A young Jewish man with a yarmulke and prayer shawl draped around his shoulders mumbled prayers on the other side of the street.

What will he look like? Elisha wondered.

His mind turned to MacKenzie again. *Shelter him, Lord, under a rock that is mightier than himself. Give him wisdom. Let him learn to rely on you and not his own strength. As he goes through the valley of the shadow of death, be his protector. Strengthen him and draw him to you, Almighty Lord . . .*

In the distance a lone figure appeared.

Elisha knew instinctively that this was the man he waited for.

He watched as the man drew nearer. The man walked under a street lamp, and Elisha was able to get his first look at him. He was stout of build with broad shoulders and short sturdy legs. A great mane of white hair, combed straight back from his forehead, hung almost to his shoulders and contrasted with his deeply tanned, weathered face.

But then he looked at the eyes. Even from that distance they drew his attention. Deep blue like the ocean. They looked right at him, a piercing look of bold assurance.

The man walked up to Elisha and stopped a few feet away from him.

Elisha felt something powerful suddenly surround him— a wave of peace that preceded this man.

"I am Johanen," the man introduced himself.

"Elisha BenHassen. It is an honor to meet the founder of the Spiral of Life Web site."

Johanen smiled broadly and his eyes danced playfully as he looked at Elisha.

"Why have you come . . . why call me?" Elisha asked.

Johanen's face grew serious. "You had a dream that he, MacKenzie, was coming to you."

Elisha was taken aback. "How . . . how did you . . ."

Johanen smiled knowingly. "The Spirit of the Living God whispers many things. But of MacKenzie—he has been chosen to warn of the coming deception and to fight against it. You, Elisha, are to mentor him in the Way. I have come to strengthen you and to assure you that God knows of your work . . . of your holiness . . . and he is well pleased."

Elisha was dumbstruck. He couldn't believe what he was hearing.

"Who are you?" he managed to ask.

"A sojourner like yourself. A little old and sometimes weary, but always ready to serve him who is the Ancient of Days."

Elisha stared in bewilderment. Without warning, suddenly his cough erupted. He leaned against the wall and braced himself. His chest heaved spasmodically as he tried to clear his lungs and give them air.

Johanen stepped closer and placed his hand over Elisha's chest. Elisha felt a burning heat that emanated from his hand, then worked its way deeper into his muscles and bones. For the first time in over forty years, Elisha began to breathe easier.

He was being healed. He had heard about this, the rumor that this man Johanen could heal . . . that miracles happened when he was present.

He straightened up, tears welling in his eyes. "I can breathe . . . like when I was a young man . . . before the camps."

He reached his arthritic hand out to thank this man. Johanen took it and then gathered Elisha's other hand and held the bony, twisted fingers firmly, then cupped them between his own.

Again Elisha felt the warmth. He heard the bones in his fingers snap as they began to straighten out. He felt the constant ache, which for years he had numbed with aspirin, lessen until all the pain was gone.

Johanen slowly released his hands. Elisha held them up and stared at them. His fingers were straight. He flexed them a few times to make sure it was true.

"My God . . ." he whispered and began to fall to his knees.

Johanen reached out and grabbed him and pulled him upright again. "No, I am a man like you. Give God the glory. It is he who has healed you through his Son, Jesus, and his mighty Spirit."

Elisha nodded dumbly.

"Listen now, I haven't much time. I am in need elsewhere. You must pray for MacKenzie and when he contacts you, you must impress upon him that he use the weapons of the Spirit to fight that which he will go against. You must instruct him, warn him that the battle will take place in his mind. What he goes against will try to destroy him and others who are with him. Remind him that God's Spirit has gone before him to prepare a way. Tell him to be bold and strong in the Lord."

Johanen's eyes blazed as he instructed Elisha, to the degree that Elisha could not look at them for long. He turned away and gazed at the ground below him.

"Elisha," Johanen called softly, and he placed his hand upon Elisha's head. "Go now, and may the peace of the Lord be with you, and may his Spirit guard your heart."

Elisha's eyes were closed and he felt Johanen's hand leave his head. Tears streamed down his cheeks and gathered in his beard. He heard Johanen leave. Heard his feet walk quickly, deliberately, back the way he had come.

He breathed deeply, enjoying the air rushing unhampered into his lungs. He folded his hands on his chest and began to give praise and thanksgiving.

38

$*\ \bullet\ *$

The sun cast an orange ember glow on the low rolling coastal hills of Paso Robles, as it dipped behind the horizon.

Mac studied Laura's aerial map book and tried to determine where the fallow field was situated in relation to the vineyard. They had crisscrossed the area several times trying to find it.

"Are you sure that's it?" Laura asked impatiently.

Mac held the map book in his hands, then turned it at an angle as he looked out the window. "Yeah, I think so . . . It just looks really different from up here," he said.

"I'll do a flyby and you can see if you recognize anything."

She maneuvered the plane and passed low over what looked like a vineyard.

"I think that's it," Mac said. "Yeah, I can see the farmhouse and the barn . . . but it looks like nobody's home."

"Maybe Uri and Cranston got them out of there," she offered.

Mac shrugged and said hopelessly, "I don't know. I hope you're right."

"It's getting dark quickly. We've got to land soon or we'll have to go to a conventional airport. Where's the field?" she pressed.

Mac looked out his window and tried to get his bearings. He saw the creek and the long gravel driveway pass beneath him. "I think it's over to our right on the other side of the creek." He pointed out the window.

"Let's hope you're right," Laura answered, and she banked the plane in the direction Mac had pointed.

"I think I see it . . . that's it, there!"

"I thought you said this land wasn't used. It's all planted! I can't land in that," she protested.

"Are you sure?" Mac asked. "Let's get a closer look."

"Let me check it out," she said, and she cut the throttle and flew in low, over the cornfield.

"Look over there." She pointed out her window. "There's a dirt service road that runs next to a drainage ditch. It looks like it goes the length of the field. It looks wide enough. I might be able to land on it . . . depending on how high the corn is."

"What does that have to do with landing?" Mac asked anxiously. "It's just a cornfield."

"If the corn is taller than the wing, it will rip it apart and cause resistance, right?"

Mac nodded.

"And if there's no resistance on the other wing because it's slicing through the air unimpaired at eighty miles an hour, what do you think happens?"

"The plane flips?"

"Something like that . . . how bad do you want to land here?" she asked.

"How high do you think the corn is?" he replied

"I don't know," she sighed. "Let's have another look."

She passed over the field again. "It might work," she admitted, and bit her lower lip nervously. "I'll try."

Mac looked at her, smiled, and gave her the thumbs-up sign, then held onto his seat belt.

Laura banked the plane and flew to the far end of the field. "The road looks really rough!" she stated.

Mac looked nervously out the window and remained mute.

She turned the plane and eased it toward the earth.

The field grew closer and finally Mac could see the tassels crowning the tops of the corn stalks.

The plane's wheels touched the road.

Thump!

Mac jerked his head toward the sound and asked, "What was that?"

"What you don't want to hear any more of! A corn stalk hitting the wing!" she yelled.

Mac heard a hissing sound as the wing passed just over the tops of the silky tassels, making them rustle.

Laura guided the plane along the service road, and struggled to keep the wings level.

Thump!

"Oh no! It can't take too many of those!" she cried.

The plane careened down the service road with the cornfield on the left and the drainage ditch on the right.

It fell into a dip in the road, which made it veer toward the drainage ditch.

"Nooo!" Laura yelled as she yanked the rudder over and braked as hard as she could. The plane shuddered violently and rocked from side to side. The service road narrowed at one point so that one of the wheels ran precariously along the lip of the drainage ditch.

The plane slowed and finally stopped. Laura slumped back in her seat.

"Nice going!" Mac said softly and looked at her with admiration.

She let out a deep sigh. "Thanks."

"The house isn't far from here; if we run we can make it in about ten minutes."

"What about the gear?" Laura asked wearily.

"We'll get it later. All I want is to see if the kids are all right."

"Okay, let's get going."

They climbed out of the plane, and Mac led the way down the last part of the service road. They came to the edge of the vineyard and were stopped by a deer fence—an eight-foot chain-link fence surrounding the entire vineyard to keep out the deer, rabbits, and other wild animals that would eat the grapes.

"We'll have to climb over it," he said, and he started to scramble up the fence.

Laura took a few steps back and then ran at the fence and jumped. She landed with her feet first, then her hands, which managed to hold on to the chain-link very near the top. She then climbed up the rest of the way, swung her leg over, and perched on top for a moment, then launched herself off. She landed catlike, on the balls of her feet.

"Very nice!" Mac called. "Were you in the Marines?"

"Gymnastics," she retorted and folded her arms in front of her as she waited for him.

Mac clambered to the top of the fence, balanced himself for a moment, then pushed off and landed next to her. He looked around at the long rows of trellised grapevines, got his bearings, and said, "This way." He set off at a trot between the rows.

They came to the end of the row and Mac turned to the left and headed down a slight hill. They came to the bottom and Mac recognized the spot.

"Over there," he said, panting now from the run. "The house is over there."

They ran down the road and came to the backside of the barn. It was dark now and the silhouette of the old building loomed in front of them.

They ran around the side of it and followed the gravel driveway to the house.

"I don't see Cranston's car," Mac said.

"Maybe they were already here," Laura offered hopefully.

"We'll find out in a minute," Mac said. The furrows deepened on his forehead.

They climbed the stairs to the front porch and got to the screen door. Mac flung it open and they ran in.

"Hello? Maggie? Sarah? Hello? Jeremy? It's Dad! Is anyone here?" he yelled as they entered the foyer.

He flipped the light switch but found to his surprise that it didn't work.

"That's strange," he said, as he flicked the switch on and off a few times. "I wonder why the power's off?"

Laura stepped into the living room and tried to turn on a lamp. "The power's not working in here either," she said. "I don't like this . . . it's just like at the mental institution. The same thing happened."

Mac entered the living room. "What, the power being off?"

"Yeah, right before that poor woman got sucked out the window."

Mac walked to the mantelpiece where he grabbed a candle and some matches. He lit the candle, then returned to Laura.

"Maggie!" he yelled desperately.

A muffled voice came from the hallway.

"Maggie!" Mac called again.

He heard the closet door beneath the stairwell open.

"Dad?" a voice answered timidly.

"Jeremy . . . is that you?" Mac cried.

He rushed out of the living room and went over to the stairwell.

He held out the candle and saw a visibly shaken Maggie, who held Sarah in her arms. Behind her Doris cradled Jeremy protectively. They all looked terrified.

He knelt down and took them in his arms. "Maggie, what's going on?"

She looked at him with wild, pleading eyes. "Something's out there."

"What? Come on, let's go into the living room," he said, and he helped them get out of the closet.

Maggie clutched Sarah to her as they walked into the hall-way.

"What are you afraid of?" Mac asked, as he slipped his free hand around Maggie's waist, something he hadn't done since their divorce. He helped her into the living room, then gently eased her down onto the sofa. He knelt in front of her and asked softly, "What happened?"

Maggie twisted a lock of her hair in her fingers. Tears streamed down her face.

"I don't know . . ." she stammered. "We saw something in the sky, bright lights, then the power went off . . . and then . . . we heard strange noises . . . so we hid."

"Dad, I'm scared," Jeremy said.

Mac looked at his son and held his hands out to the boy. Jeremy ran and buried his head in Mac's shoulder.

"Are you all right?" Mac asked gently.

"No, Dad, Mom's right, something's out there . . . something weird."

"It was bright and it made the whole room light up," Sarah exclaimed.

"Maggie?" he asked, gently.

Maggie looked at Laura then back to Mac and asked, "Who is she?"

"She's helping me with the investigation I'm on . . . She's a pilot," Mac answered.

"Oh," Maggie replied. "What are you doing here, Mac?"

"I told you, you might be in danger, right?"

She nodded.

"Didn't Cranston get in touch with you?"

"No."

"He didn't call?"

"There's something wrong with the phone; it's been out all day."

"Dad?" Jeremy interrupted.

"What?" Mac answered.

"Something's coming in here," Jeremy stammered and backed into his mother's arms.

Suddenly the room was filled with a brilliant light, the source of which came from behind Mac.

"Oh . . . Oh no. Not again," Laura yelled, as she snapped her head toward the source of light.

As Mac turned he caught a glimpse of Maggie's face . . . a mixture of awe, wonder . . . and fear.

Then he saw it.

He gasped, for on the other side of the room stood a tall, magnificent-looking, angelic being. He had long, shoulder-length blond hair and fierce, fiery eyes. The light seemed to emanate from his very presence. He wore a long, tunic-like garment, which along with his hair swayed slightly as if being blown by a gentle breeze.

Mac was awestruck, frozen in a state of fear and wonder.

Thoughts came at him . . . penetrating his mind . . . but they were evil thoughts and he knew that their source was from the shining intruder.

What's happening? he wondered. *This is wrong, how could something so beautiful do this? Isn't this an angel?* Coupled with those thoughts he suddenly felt the same hatred toward him as he had experienced at the underground base.

He heard Laura mumble something. Her voice seemed like it came from another room. It sounded hollow and distant. Mac's attention was transfixed. His mind seemed locked in a whirl of horrible images that he was unable to shake or alter. He heard Laura strain to speak.

"Mac, do something."

A wave of hatred came at Mac, overwhelming his mind. The force of it made him stagger on his feet. Mac took a deep breath and managed to shout, "Leave . . . leave us."

The room shook for a moment, almost like an earthquake had hit it. The light from the angel changed and grew dark and yet somehow inexplicably was still brilliantly white.

Mac watched in horror as the being changed shape. It was like it had been clothed in a costume or a disguise, for it shed its benevolent appearance. What floated at the far end of the room was wraithlike, tall, and gray, with thin spindly arms and legs. Its skin was scaly like a lizard. Its head was large and elongated with two black slanted eyes that glared with unrestrained rage and hate.

A voice exploded from the creature. "Who are you to address me! You have nothing to do with me." It extended one of its arms and pointed a clawlike finger at Laura. She was hurled against the wall behind her. She looked at the creature and called out weakly, "Mac, kill it."

The creature raged. It snarled and spat something vile from its mouth and then flew across the room at her, clawing at her head.

Laura covered her face and hollered for Mac. Maggie screamed in terror and hid the faces of her children in her bosom. Doris clutched her chest, gasped, and slumped unconscious to the floor.

Pandemonium surrounded Mac as he stood up and tried to move toward Laura to help her. Then it happened again. The hand of the Lord came upon him and everything slowed down. For a moment the thoughts that the alien had put in his mind were gone. He felt peace and assurance and then the thought, *Your weapons are not carnal . . . trust in me for your strength.*

Then everything rushed back.

Maggie and the children were screaming. Laura was crying out, nearly unconscious now as the creature mauled her. It picked her up from the floor and pressed itself against her, pinning her to the wall, where its clawlike fingers cut at her clothes and flesh.

Mac saw her scream once more and then she passed out. Her head banged against the wall like a rag doll, from the force of the creature.

He forgot what he had just heard about his weapons not being carnal ... earthly ... of himself. Instead he grabbed a lamp that was next to the couch and hurled it at the thing, trusting in his own strength.

The lamp slammed into its back.

It screamed in rage, spun around, and glared at Mac.

Then a commotion at the entrance of the living room. He looked and saw ten or so small gray alien beings swarm into the room. They came toward him. He grew sick in his stomach and felt as though he would vomit.

Some of them swarmed toward Maggie and the children. Mac changed directions and tried to reach Maggie. One of the small gray aliens grabbed Sarah and pulled her from Maggie.

"No!" Maggie screamed and began to fight with the creature, wildly throwing punches at it with her closed fists.

Other grays swarmed over her. Two of them grabbed her while others latched onto Jeremy.

Both children were now unconscious and floated above the floor.

"No!" Mac yelled. He picked up the coffee table and was about to hurl it at the new intruders when the creature that had pinned Laura turned and pointed its finger at Mac. Mac was hurled through the air. His body slammed against the wall with such force that the back of his head smashed a hole in the plaster. He crumpled to the floor.

He thought he heard the sound of a helicopter. Or was it Maggie screaming? Or the children . . .

He tried to fight the blackness which began to overtake him. His body grew numb and he could no longer feel it. Then darkness closed in. He tried to pick his head up, to remain in the here and now.

"Maggie!" His lips moved but no sound came from them as he tumbled into the oblivion of unconsciousness.

39

＊ ▢ ＊

Mac heard voices in the distance as he hovered on the verge of consciousness. He felt something cool on his forehead. His thoughts passed in abstract, dreamlike forms, a twisted jumble of images, people, and events surreally mixed together. A cacophony of undefined noises rushed into his ears.

"MacKenzie, hello . . . you hear me?"

He slowly opened his eyes and saw Uri BenHassen sitting in front of him. It was he who had placed the damp towel on Mac's forehead.

"Hey, Uri," Mac mumbled as he tried to sit up. "Ohh, my head." He collapsed back into the chair. As he did, his memory flooded with images of aliens and screaming women and children.

"Maggie? Where's Maggie?" he called out.

In spite of the pain he willed himself to pick his head up. He was astonished at what met his eyes. He was in the living room of Maggie's mother's house. At least that was recognizable. But the place teemed with uniformed men in black jumpsuits. They had set up what he assumed could only be a command base of some sort. Couches, chairs, end tables, and other furnishings were bunched in a heap in one corner of the room and replaced with an array of computers, maps, radios, and other sophisticated equipment.

"What's all this?" He looked at Uri for an explanation.

Uri shook his head. "You know what? You have been out for hours," he said.

Mac nodded grimly, closed his eyes, sorted through his thoughts, and tried to remain objective.

Uri continued, "This is the military team that Roswell is connected to. They found you next to the wall."

"And Maggie? Where are the children? Where's Laura?" Mac pressed anxiously and grabbed the handrails of the chair and tried to lift himself. Pain exploded in his head and he collapsed back in his seat.

Uri looked away, then cautiously said, "Maggie's with her mother. They have a medical unit here. Laura's in shock, they have her upstairs . . ."

"Yeah, okay, but what about the children?" Mac asked, losing patience.

Uri stared at the floor. "They were taken."

"Oh no," Mac exclaimed, and he covered his face with his hands. "I thought for a moment that maybe I had dreamed that part." His stomach knotted as he asked, "Taken where?"

Before Uri could answer, a bulldog of a man wearing a black beret and a special insignia walked into the room. He glanced in Mac's direction, noticed he was conscious, and strode vigorously toward him.

"Mr. MacKenzie," he addressed Mac in a way that exuded authority. "I'm Colonel Austin. How's that nasty bump on the back of your head? I had one of our medical team look at it. Glad you're okay." He patted Mac's shoulder.

"Yeah, thanks, but where are my children?" Mac asked.

Austin glanced at Uri then back at Mac and said, "Mr. MacKenzie, I believe your children have been taken to an underground base in the Nevada desert . . . the same base where General Nathan is being held. We've been monitoring it constantly." He gestured toward the men and equipment in the room.

"The alien base?" Mac groaned. His worst fears had come true.

Austin looked him squarely in the eyes and said with confidence, "Mr. MacKenzie, we are going to do everything in our power to get your children out of there as soon as possible."

Mac touched the back of his head gingerly, then turned to Uri and asked, "Why weren't you here earlier? Maybe you could have helped us."

Austin responded crisply, "I'll answer that, Mr. MacKenzie. I had orders to bring you, BenHassen, and Nathan's daughter in. We discovered that you and Laura had flown to Arizona, so we sent a team of men to intercept you there. Unfortunately, you had left only minutes before our team arrived. We did, however, manage to apprehend the two men that we assumed assaulted you on the landing field. And we also attended to the wounded police officer."

"Then Sheriff Huffman's all right?" Mac asked, relieved that at least Huffman was safe.

"He'll be fine," Austin assured him. "It's my fault that we didn't get here sooner. We had orders to intercept BenHassen and Cranston. Bring them in for their own safety."

"We didn't know what was happening!" Uri added.

Austin grinned at Uri. "He was ready to fight four Air Force helicopters with his handgun. It was only after we were able to relay specific details about his grandfather and General Nathan that he accepted we were on the same team."

Mac saw Maggie enter the room. Her face was tear-stained and she looked drained and broken. Mac struggled up from the chair. He felt lightheaded and swayed on his feet. Uri reached out and steadied him.

"Maggie?" he called tentatively.

He saw her lip quiver, but she stood motionless. Mac took a couple of steps toward her; the spell was broken. She ran to meet him and they embraced. Mac held her tightly, caressing her head with his hand.

"They've taken the children . . . What were those horrible creatures?" she cried.

"Shh," Mac whispered gently, "it's not like with Art, Maggie, we won't lose the children this time. I won't let it happen, I promise you." Mac realized he was reassuring himself as much as he was Maggie. For a moment he was overwhelmed, like when he had watched the failed operation of his oldest son. As he held Maggie he closed his eyes and prayed for help . . . something he hadn't done in the operating room years ago.

Finally Mac looked up at Austin. "Why didn't you get here sooner?"

Austin cleared his throat. "After we picked up Uri and Cranston, our orders were to rendezvous at a prearranged site and proceed with our operative to secure the base. Uri was adamant about us coming here first. If it hadn't been for his constant persuasion and refusal to go anywhere else, we wouldn't be here at all. I only wish it hadn't taken so long to clarify the switch in orders."

Maggie picked her head up from Mac's shoulder. "Colonel Austin, can you get my children back?"

Austin clasped his hands behind his back, his face solemn. "Mrs. MacKenzie, I can assure you that all the manpower and every piece of equipment at my disposal will be used to rescue your children. You have my word on that."

"Colonel Austin, sir?" someone called from the front porch.

Austin looked at Maggie. "Will you excuse me?" Without waiting for a reply he spun on his heel and headed out the front door.

Mac looked out the large bay window and saw Austin approach a group of black helicopters on the front lawn. The entire area was lit up by two spotlights powered by portable generators. He watched as Austin began to talk to a cluster of men that were gathered around one of the choppers.

"He's a good soldier," Uri said, with a look of approval. "I'm thinking we're lucky he's on our side."

Mac saw the confusion on Maggie's face and said by way of introduction, "This is Uri BenHassen. I stayed at his house in Israel . . . he's a good judge of this sort of thing."

Mac gently pulled Maggie toward him and held her in his arms for a moment. Then he eased away from her and said, "Is your mother okay?"

"They're not sure, but they think she suffered a mild stroke."

"Is she awake?" he asked.

She shook her head. "No, they gave her something. She's sleeping. Mac, who are these people?"

Mac rubbed the back of his head, then gently touched the lump protruding from his skull. "It's a long story, Maggie." He sighed, then asked, "Where's Cranston?"

"I don't know. I think he's in the kitchen," Maggie said.

Their eyes locked together, and for what may have been the first time in years they really *looked* at one another. Looked past the old hurts, past the drone of day-to-day routine, that through the sheer monotony of repetition had slowly desensitized them to the importance each played in the other's life. It was like meeting one another for the first time and yet knowing the other intimately because of a myriad of shared experiences. The crisis had removed every trace of petty ego and fighting between them.

To Mac's amazement he found himself leaning forward to kiss her. It was natural, familiar. She raised her head up to meet him, closed her eyes, and parted her lips. Afterward, Maggie leaned her head on Mac's shoulder and gave a little sigh.

Mac thought of how much he had really missed her. How much of life they had shared together, how he wanted to be back with her . . . and his children. He also realized how stubborn he had been, and so self-centered. Everything he ever wanted in a woman was nestled in his arms, but it had taken all of this to bring them back together.

As he held her he saw Laura enter the room. Her arm was in a sling and her face had several bandages on it. She still wore the same faded jumpsuit, although it was ripped in several places.

She looked at Mac holding Maggie and managed a wan smile. The look reminded Mac of someone who graciously loses a contest, but would have preferred another outcome or an ending other than the one presented.

Mac held Maggie tighter and winked at Laura.

"Maggie, I want you to meet one of the greatest pilots in the air today," Mac said, as he let go of her.

"How would you know? You hate to fly!" Maggie retorted.

"He's been a good passenger, even likes barrel rolls now," Laura said, managing a weary smile as she walked slowly over to them.

Mac shook his head. "No more barrel rolls, Laura. Maggie, you met her before but—"

"I know, I know," Maggie interrupted.

Laura reached out and the two women survivors embraced.

"Are you all right?" Maggie asked.

Laura bit her lower lip. "I'll live, but I'll have nightmares the rest of my life."

"Me too," Maggie agreed.

"Colonel Austin will get the children back," Laura whispered.

Maggie gave her head a few quick nods as she started to tear up again.

Mac grabbed her hand and pulled her to his side and held her.

"Uri?" Mac said. "I need to get Elisha on the computer, talk to him about what's happened here."

Uri nodded. "It has been done already." He motioned to a portable aluminum table where a group of men sat monitoring information at the terminals. "He's online, very anxious to be talking with you."

"Did you tell him anything of what happened here?" Mac asked.

"Only what your wife . . . oh, sorry," Uri said.

"It's okay, Uri," Mac assured him.

"Only what Maggie told us," Uri concluded.

"Did you tell him about when the alien changed shape on us?"

Uri shook his head, then rubbed the dark stubble of beard and said, "No. That you explain. You saw what happened."

Mac whispered in Maggie's ear, "Why don't you and Laura look after your mother?" He kissed her lightly on the forehead. "It's going to be okay," he said reassuringly.

"I believe you," she said, and took a few steps, looked at Mac one last time, then called, "Laura?"

Laura came up next to her and grabbed her arm, and the two women left the room.

Mac turned back to Uri. "He's online now?"

"Over here," Uri said, and he escorted Mac to the table where several computers were. "This is Mr. MacKenzie," Uri said and introduced Mac to the soldier operating one of the computers. The man rose from his chair and offered it to Mac.

The soldier reached in front of Mac with one hand and punched in an access code. The screen cleared and the face of Dr. Elisha suddenly appeared on it.

"Dr. Elisha." Mac exhaled with relief, and in spite of his own traumatized state he smiled broadly.

"Shalom, shalom, MacKenzie," Elisha greeted in return.

Mac stared at Elisha's face on the computer and said, "You look great."

Elisha laughed. "Yes, I'm feeling better than I have in years, but Uri tells me that you had an encounter and your children have been taken."

Mac's smile fell and he became grim-faced. "Yes . . . and I wish the latter weren't true."

"What happened?" Elisha asked.

"Laura and I arrived at the house in the early evening. It was completely dark—the lights wouldn't work. I discovered Maggie, my mother-in-law, and my two children hiding in the closet under the staircase. What happened after was terrifying." He paused and took a deep breath. "We were in the living room and my son, Jeremy, screamed that something was coming into the room. I saw . . ." He paused and gathered his thoughts. "Well, it looked like an angel—not that I've ever seen one before—but it was breathtaking."

Elisha nodded slowly and then asked, "Why did you think it was an angel?"

Mac thought a moment and said, "Good question. I guess I don't know what else to call it."

"So what happened next?" Elisha asked.

"Well . . . I told it to leave us . . . pretty lame, huh? But the creature went crazy. It suddenly changed shape. No, let me rephrase that. It reverted to what I think is its true form."

"Like shedding a disguise," Elisha suggested.

"Yeah, exactly. It screamed at me, yelled it had nothing to do with me. Then it pointed toward Laura and she was hurled against the wall."

Elisha frowned. "I believe it was a fallen angel or demon that you encountered, and I will not hesitate in using those terms interchangeably from this point forward. You challenged it, at least you tried to, and it fought back, unleashing its fury on you and everyone else. The next time this happens—"

"Wait, wait," Mac stammered, "what do you mean, the next time?"

Elisha was silent for a moment. "There will be a next time, MacKenzie," he spoke softly. "And when that time comes you will be ready to take authority over it."

"Authority?" Mac asked.

"There is a passage in Scripture that deals with an exorcism. Briefly told, a man is possessed by a demon. Seven brothers go and try to exorcise it. But the demon taunts them and actually beats them and throws them out of the house."

"Sounds similar to what happened here," Mac replied.

"Yes," Elisha agreed, "and when the next encounter happens, you must fight with the weapons of the Spirit. You must command it in the name of Jesus to leave and you must tell it to remain quiet. But there is something more. In the story, the demon gives us a clue as to why the men who came to exorcise it were powerless. The demon says to them, 'Jesus I know and Paul, but you I do not!'"

"What does that mean?" Mac asked.

"It means that those seven brothers were not infused with the Spirit of the Living God. And without that Spirit they were powerless. But you have God's Spirit dwelling in you, Mac. You have the authority—you need to use it."

"How?" Mac asked, dumbfounded.

Elisha grew passionate. "Who you are in your flesh, Art MacKenzie, has no power or authority whatsoever . . . but he that resides in you does. The Spirit of the Living God. It is he who will fight for you."

"So I command it to leave in the name of Jesus and it will go?" Mac asked incredulously.

"It's not as simple as that," Elisha said. "The demon will project thoughts into your mind, he will forbid you to speak, choke your words, try to make you utter things you would never say. He will try to terrify you. He will prey upon your fears—things you can't even imagine he will put into your mind." Elisha leaned closer to the camera and his face filled the screen. "MacKenzie, this will be the hardest thing you will ever do in your life."

Mac turned and saw that Colonel Austin was next to him and was listening intently to the conversation. He glanced to his other side and saw Maggie and Laura standing in the foyer. The room had grown quiet, and Mac realized that everyone's attention was riveted on what Dr. Elisha was saying.

"MacKenzie, I know you will overcome the Evil One. There are many who are praying for you, even now. Remember these aliens are the fallen ones, demons. They are unclean and can never again be in the presence of the Holy God. They are evil, malevolent, and doomed to eternal darkness! Drive them out, MacKenzie."

The room was still with every eye turned on Mac.

Mac glanced at Maggie. She smiled at him and nodded encouragingly, although tears streamed down her face.

Elisha continued, "What beings of any good would take two small children against the will of their parents?"

Silence in the room.

Elisha began again and his voice rose and he shouted, "When you encounter the demon again, command it by the power of the Living God to return to the Abyss!"

Mac nodded.

The tension in the room was broken as one of the soldiers called out to Colonel Austin. "Colonel, we have word that the doors at the end of the tunnel are opening!"

Austin strode over to where the man sat at his terminal. He looked at the screen where a satellite view showed the huge doors of the tunnel slowly beginning to open.

"Let's move out!" Austin yelled. "Move out! Proceed with Operation Magic! I repeat, Operation Magic is a go!"

Mac had never seen so many people move with deliberate precision. Equipment was folded, packed, and moved from the living room and onto the helicopters in minutes.

Mac went to Maggie and pulled her to his side. They stood in the foyer of the house and watched the flurry of activity.

Austin was busy poring over a map with one of his pilots. He glanced up and spotted Mac, finished his conversation, and walked over to him.

"MacKenzie, I want you in my chopper. All of you, Ben-Hassen, and Laura if she's up to it."

"Wait a minute," Maggie protested, suddenly coming to life. "If you think I'm going to stay behind wringing my hands and crying into a handkerchief, you're greatly mistaken! I carried those kids for nine months, and I'm going to be there when we get them back." She stared defiantly at Austin.

Austin glared at her for a moment, then his look softened and he asked, "Who will stay with your mother?"

Maggie began in earnest, "Your medical people said she's stabilized. Besides, the ambulance will be here shortly, and one of your men could stay with her until they arrive—"

"I could do that!" a voice interrupted. It was Jim Cranston.

"How's that?" Austin replied.

"I'll stay with her . . . until the ambulance arrives. Then I have a paper I have to get back to and run."

Mac couldn't believe what he was hearing. He looked at Cranston, trying to figure out why he wanted to stay and miss the action, much less watch over an older woman. *Is that fear in his face?* he wondered.

"All right!" Austin said. "I'll leave a radio with you, and I want you to check in when the ambulance arrives."

"Got it," Cranston replied.

Maggie went over to Cranston. "Thank you for staying with her. You've been such a big help to us." And she hugged him.

Mac took Maggie's hand and left the house. Uri followed just behind and assisted Laura.

Mac walked out onto the front porch and stopped. On the wooden decking of the porch lay his daughter's book of David and Goliath. Mac reached down and picked it up. He opened it and in the light, powered from the generators, he saw the picture on the next page of Goliath lying on the ground with David holding a sword over the giant's head, ready to hack it off.

"What are you looking at?" Uri asked.

"Part of your history . . . the offspring of the fallen angels . . . the Nephilim . . . Goliath the giant."

Uri reached out and grabbed Mac by his arm. "You know what? Seeing all this has made me thinking that my grandfather is right . . ."

"About the aliens," Mac offered.

Uri nodded. "I'm thinking they might just be what my grandfather believes . . . evil . . . but my mind is having still great trouble accepting this."

Mac looked at him and was about to reassure him when Colonel Austin boomed, "Let's move out!" He waved them to the chopper he was about to board.

They ran over to the chopper. Its blades picked up speed, fanning the air in wide circles. Mac instinctively ducked and pulled Maggie after him. They boarded the chopper, and Austin motioned for them to buckle in along with ten other men. Uri and Laura sat toward the rear. One of the soldiers fitted all of them with helmets that were equipped with internal headsets and mouthpieces, which enabled them to listen and talk to Austin and one another over the whine of the jet engine.

"We're about to take off! Hold on!" Austin yelled as he slipped his helmet on.

He climbed into the seat next to the pilot and gave the thumbs-up sign. Instantly four choppers rose from the ground, sending a cloud of dust and debris which whirled madly about the house, cyclone-like.

Powerful searchlights from the choppers swung wildly, illuminating the house and casting garish shadows over the vineyard. Suddenly they switched off, plunging the area into the natural darkness of the night.

* o *

Cranston shielded his eyes and hurried back into the foyer. He watched as the silhouettes of the choppers grouped into a formation and headed southeast toward the direction of the secret base in Nevada.

Cranston waited until he couldn't hear the sound of the choppers.

This was more than I ever bargained for, he thought.

He hesitated for a moment, trying to figure out what to do. *Whose side is going to win? Who has the power and who will wield it in the future?* he wondered. He took his cell phone from his jacket and stared at it. Finally he dialed a number.

40

Four black helicopters flew in tight formation low over the expanse of desert near the Nevada and California border.

Colonel Austin checked his watch and then looked at the digitally displayed location grid on the chopper's control panel. He adjusted his headset and barked an order into his mouthpiece. "We're to rendezvous with the fuel trucks at checkpoint delta. Let's set 'em down and do it quick."

The choppers hovered for a moment and then descended onto an area that ground forces had marked with flares. The choppers landed on the dry desert floor, their propellers billowing clouds of desert dust. As the blades slowed, men swarmed over the choppers and began to refuel them.

Austin was the first to leave the chopper. He gave a thumbs-up to the commanding sergeant of the ground forces, who snapped to attention and saluted Austin in return. A voice crackled over his headset confirming that refueling had begun. Satisfied, he went to the cargo door of the chopper and climbed into the hold to talk to MacKenzie. He found him holding his wife close to him with both arms wrapped around her.

He inspected the other men seated along the length of the aircraft. "Sergeant, take your men outside for a moment and have them stretch their legs," he ordered.

"Yes, sir," the sergeant answered and repeated the orders to his men. A dozen men shouldering automatic weapons and outfitted with survival gear left the rear of the chopper.

Austin found a seat directly across from Mac and Maggie. He motioned to Laura and Uri to move up and join them.

He took off his helmet. "MacKenzie, I have a question I'd like to throw at you."

Mac managed a weary smile. "Fire away."

Maggie opened her eyes but remained wrapped in Mac's arms.

Austin took off his beret, revealing a bald head. He scratched it vigorously and asked, "Do you believe what Dr. BenHassen said about these aliens ... that they might be fallen angels or demons?"

"Yes, I do, Colonel, especially in light of my firsthand encounter with one," Mac replied.

Austin frowned. He lowered his voice, then asked in a frustrated tone, "Then how am I supposed to fight them?"

Mac loosened the chin strap on his helmet and answered, "I'm not so sure myself ... Before you came in I was praying for protection. And that we would have the strength to fight when the time comes."

"And how do you think we are to do that?" Austin growled.

"One thing I learned from my encounter, both at the base and at the vineyard, is that the demon—"

"Hold on," Austin growled, "I wish you wouldn't call it that. It makes my skin crawl."

"It is what it is," Mac replied, "and it's unsettling to think that's what we're going up against. But the demon can communicate telepathically. It can put thoughts inside our heads. He can try to force us to think about whatever he wants us to. I found it overwhelming ... terrifying."

"Who is what with all of this business?" Uri pointed to his helmet. "I don't want to be thinking what something else is putting into my head."

Mac laughed grimly. "I know, Uri, it sounds like something from the *Twilight Zone*, but it projected thoughts . . . horrible thoughts into my mind. The thing that abducted our children was vile and loathsome. It was also violent. You should have seen the way it tore at Laura. The thing's a demon," he stated emphatically.

"You were there, tell him," Mac said to Laura.

Laura folded her arms in front of her and leaned forward slightly. She looked over at Uri and said softly, "Look, I'm not religious and I'm not certain what the thing was . . . but it was evil . . . horribly evil."

Maggie didn't move from the shelter of Mac's arms but agreed. "It was filled with hate."

Uri shook his head. "How are we to fight something like this?"

"Well," Mac said, "Dr. Elisha told us that all the bullets in the world won't stop this creature. I believe him. Prayer is the only thing that is going to have any effect against it. It's just simply too powerful to master otherwise."

Austin stared at MacKenzie and drew his lips together tightly. "Well, MacKenzie, that's something I haven't done in so long that I think I've forgotten how."

Mac hesitated for an instant, then said firmly, "We could try it now."

Austin fidgeted and Uri cleared his throat and stared down at his boots. Finally Maggie suggested, "We could try. It can't hurt, can it?"

"I suppose not," Austin replied. He chuckled and said, "I always thought that real men didn't pray . . . now I'm not so sure. Will you do it, MacKenzie?"

They closed their eyes and Mac began to lead them in prayer.

* ○ *

Deep in the underground base on the level that was known as Maj 12 the man who had given General Nathan the injection sat dejectedly in a chair. Beside him stood two MPs. He wanted to reach up and grab the wire noose which was held tightly around his throat by a third MP, but didn't dare. He had learned all too quickly that any movement brought reprisal, by way of a baton across the back of his hand. He looked at his swollen, bleeding flesh and shuddered.

The man known to him only as Abaris sat in front of him. He inhaled deeply from a cigarette, held the smoke in his lungs for a moment, then exhaled a long, thin stream of smoke into the man's face.

Abaris was the commander of Maj 12. He was in almost constant contact with the aliens. Rumor had it that he had been underground since the early sixties. He should have been an old man, maybe eighty or so. Yet he looked deceptively younger, like a man in his early fifties. Oddly, the pigment of his skin was a strange light gray color, perhaps caused from decades of dwelling in the subterranean level. Abaris's eyes had a yellow tint where the white should have been. His aquiline nose had been broken and was set off center beneath bristled eyebrows and a protruding forehead. On his head, thin white hair was combed straight back from a deep receding hairline.

"Well, Dr. Gleason," Abaris began in a raspy voice, "I'm amazed that you attempted what you did. Surely you knew the risk you were taking . . . yes?"

Gleason remained silent.

"Nathan is a detriment to our entire project here. And do you know why?"

"No," Gleason managed to answer.

"Because he doesn't understand what we're doing. He doesn't comprehend the importance of our work here. The great benefit to mankind that will result from it." He paused, then asked, "What about you, Doctor? Surely you've seen enough to understand the importance of our work?"

Gleason stared at the man. "I suppose interrogating a man with a noose around his neck is one of your more cogent examples of that."

Abaris pounded the desk in front of him with his fist. "Doctor, you're here because of aiding and abetting an intruder."

Gleason stared silently at the desk in front of him, avoiding Abaris's icy stare.

Abaris calmed himself and continued, "Dr. Gleason, Nathan's actions are reprehensible. Are you aware that he exposed classified top-secret information to two civilians?"

Gleason lifted his eyes but remained silent.

Abaris scowled and asked, "Dr. Gleason, how involved are you with General Nathan?"

Gleason fidgeted in his chair. His training had included a mock interrogation similar to this, but it had been just that, a mock interrogation. This, unfortunately, was the real thing. He felt his heart beating wildly in his chest. He remained mute mostly out of fear.

Abaris looked at him, slowly put out his cigarette, and said, "Take him to the court."

Gleason moaned as the MPs on either side of him grabbed his arms, picked him up from the chair, and escorted him out of the room.

＊ ◊ ＊

Jim Cranston thanked the ambulance driver again as the man closed the rear door. He peered in the window at Doris.

"She'll be fine," the paramedic said reassuringly.

The elderly woman lay asleep on the gurney. An oxygen mask was over her face. Another paramedic sat beside her and monitored her heart rate and pulse.

Cranston was satisfied. He'd done his part for Maggie—now it was time to go. "Thanks, see that she gets to the hospital quickly," he instructed.

"We're on our way," the driver said. He climbed behind the wheel and started the engine.

Cranston moved to the front porch and watched the ambulance turn around and head down the driveway. For a moment, he savored the stillness of the house and grounds. It was hard to imagine that just a short time ago the place had served to facilitate a highly trained military entourage.

Cranston closed and locked the front door. Then he bounded down the steps of the porch and headed to where his BMW was parked. He was glad he was leaving. Relieved that he was returning to Los Angeles, to his paper, to his work.

He'd made the call and done what he thought was the right thing. But he wanted no more of the Agency. He would be firm in distancing himself . . . and somehow he would find a way of dealing with the repercussions.

Cranston slipped into the front seat and started the car. He would be driving for a few hours, and he wanted to relax. He selected Bach's Brandenburg Concertos and started the CD player. Putting the car in gear, he started down the long gravel driveway. He looked once in his rearview mirror at the silhouette of the big dark house. He was glad to be leaving.

At the end of the driveway he turned the car onto the two-lane road that led to the Pacific Coast Highway. He adjusted the temperature control, relaxing as his mind followed the musical dialogue. He had rounded a bend in the road and started into a sizable stretch of straightaway when suddenly his lights went dead, the CD stopped, the steering wheel locked up, and the engine quit.

In a panic he pressed on the emergency brake and the car came to a stop in the middle of the road.

"What the heck," he said angrily, realizing that he was miles from anywhere and getting a tow truck this late at night would be difficult. He grabbed his cell phone and began to dial a number.

"What?" he said out loud.

There was no dial tone. The phone was dead.

Frowning, he shook the phone. *Must have forgotten to charge it,* he thought, annoyed with himself.

He climbed out of the car and started to go toward the hood to check the engine when suddenly he was immersed in a brilliant white light beaming down from above. He looked up, terrified. Directly above him was a disk, pulsating a deep orange color.

"Oh no," he moaned and took a step backward. Every nerve in his body began to tingle. He had the sensation of floating upward toward the belly of the ship, and when he looked down he saw, to his amazement, that that was precisely what was taking place.

He closed his eyes and screamed, "No, not me! No . . . *no!*"

His body shook from fear and his mind reeled in terror at the thought of what they might look like and what they might do to him.

He looked up and saw an open portal above him. His body floated up into the ship, and he felt something cold and metallic grab him and pin him to a coffinlike opening that conformed to his body. Pain pierced the base of his neck, but when he tried to touch his neck he found that his arms wouldn't respond. He was paralyzed. His eyes darted wildly as he saw two small gray creatures coming toward him.

They had large heads and slanted black eyes . . . ominous eyes. He tried to scream . . . but found he couldn't.

41

✦ O ✦

The 737 is on time, sir." Mac heard the voice in his headset.

"Good. What's the status of the doors?" Mac heard Austin ask.

"They're still open, sir."

"What's our ETA?" Austin demanded.

"Less than twenty-five minutes, sir."

"Radio to have the drones launched," Austin ordered.

There was a pause, then Mac heard the reply, "Drones away, sir."

Austin chuckled. "That will give them something to deal with."

Mac put his arm around Maggie and she snuggled closer to his side. Across from him he saw Uri examining the rifle Austin had issued him. He checked the magazine, unloaded a clip of ammunition, inspected it, and pushed it back into place. He laid the rifle across his lap and threw Mac a thumbs-up. Mac smiled wearily back at him and turned his thoughts toward the safety and whereabouts of his children. He clasped Maggie's hand tightly in his own and began to pray.

✦ O ✦

Once again in his uniform, General Nathan stood before someone whose facial features were concealed in darkness. His mind was still a jumble of disjointed thoughts. MPs stood on either side of him.

"How are you feeling, General Nathan?" the man asked. "You may call me Abaris."

Nathan looked around him and almost succeeded in figuring out where he was, but the thought eluded him.

Abaris chuckled. "Having trouble remembering where you are? Who you are?" he taunted.

Nathan rubbed his eyes and blinked them a few times. He struggled to put his thoughts in order, took a deep breath, then mumbled, "I'm at . . . in . . . Level 12 . . . Nevada."

"Good," Abaris said. "You know, General, it's good to see your memory coming back. You do remember that you are being treated for . . . cancer?"

A series of thoughts flashed rapidly in Nathan's mind. Hospital, doctors, chemotherapy, pain . . . always the pain. He began to remember—granted it was slow and at best jumbled—but it was memory, his memory.

He looked at the shadowy figure of Abaris and answered, "Yes . . . I remember the cancer, it's here." He placed his hand near the small of his back.

"General," Abaris said, "what if I were to tell you that I could cure your cancer? That you would be free from pain . . . forever?"

Nathan looked at him and wondered why Abaris was baiting him with promises that he knew were impossibilities. "How can you do that?" he asked.

"If you'll follow me I can show you. Please escort General Nathan," he called to the MPs as he began to walk down a corridor.

Nathan followed behind him, his arms held by the MPs. He noticed that the construction of the corridor was the same as that of his cell.

A flood of memories came with the thought. Diebol, his driver. Gas through the window. Aliens. Drops in his eyes. Gleason entering . . . He stopped walking for a moment as he remembered Dr. Gleason. He was the mole that Nathan had positioned to infiltrate Level 12. Where was he now?

The MPs remained at the entrance as Nathan entered a strange-looking room. It was oval shaped and looked at first like a small theater that could accommodate perhaps fifty people. Benchlike seats molded out of the floor created a semicircle which tiered down toward a small stagelike area.

Abaris led the way down the narrow aisle and took a seat several rows from the front. "If you'll sit here." He motioned to Nathan to sit in the front row.

General Nathan reluctantly sat where he was instructed. He looked at the stage and saw nothing. He glanced back at Abaris, who motioned to him to look at the stage again.

Nathan looked again and gasped in wonder. In front of him, floating slightly above the floor, appeared a being of such beauty and strength that the sight of it made him almost forget to breathe.

"This is Ramiel," Abaris called from behind him. "He can heal you of your cancer. All you need to do is to ask him and he will do it."

"He looks like an—"

"Yes, General, you see how myths are started now, don't you? But I assure you he is not an angel as you are so ready to label him. No, he is a very evolved being from another planet."

"Where, the Pleiades star system?" Nathan asked as another part of his memory jerked loose.

"Yes, you're correct . . . you're beginning to remember, aren't you, General?" Abaris said. "The Pleiades star cluster. Are you aware that the door to the great pyramid at Giza points to the Pleiades constellation?"

Nathan nodded. He heard Abaris, but his voice sounded far away.

He was overcome by the entity that floated in front of him. A sharp pain shot through his lower back. He pressed his hand against it, hoping to ease the hurting and wishing for his pain medicine.

"You can be rid of that horrible pain forever," Abaris said. "All you need to do is ask. How simple it is, just ask and you will receive . . . Oh yes, you will."

Nathan shifted his weight, trying to ease the pain. Wincing, he looked up at the alien. Another stab of pain doubled him over.

"General, ask and it shall be given," Abaris encouraged.

Nathan mumbled, "Will you help me? Heal me?"

"Good, General, very good." Abaris laughed. "Ramiel is willing, look."

The room slowly began to fill with a wondrous light. Nathan felt a warmth in his back where the prostate cancer had spread. He touched his back with his one hand. Already it felt better. The pain was diminishing. He twisted at the waist, something he hadn't dared do since the onset of the cancer. To his amazement, there was no pain.

"Now you know the secret," Abaris said. "Now you are ready to understand why you must join us."

Nathan choked back tears. "How did he . . ."

"Ramiel rearranged the cell structure in your body, but it's more complicated than that," Abaris answered. "That's one of their secrets . . . They can also slow down the aging process to where it's almost imperceptible. Can you imagine the possibilities? Einstein or Mozart could have continued their work for centuries. Think of the benefits to mankind."

Nathan looked at Ramiel and said, "Thank you . . . thank you."

Abaris called again, "But there is more. Yes . . . Yes, there is more. So much more. General, do you know what happens when we crossbreed their species with ours?"

Nathan shook his head dumbly.

"Wonderful things. And you, General, will appreciate some of what we do here. I want to show you."

Abaris got up quickly and began to exit the room. "Hurry, General," he called.

Nathan got up and started after Abaris. He looked behind him and saw that Ramiel was following him. As he came to the door, he noticed the MPs struggling to hide their fear as Ramiel approached.

"Nothing to be afraid of," Abaris called over his shoulder.

Nathan exited the room and started down the hallway.

"I want to show you the man of the future," Abaris called excitedly. "You of all men will appreciate him . . . accept him, embrace him."

Nathan nodded and moved his hand to his back again, amazed that there was no pain. He glanced over his shoulder and saw that Ramiel still followed. He felt uncomfortable but he didn't know why. The alien had healed him. Shouldn't he be grateful? Overwhelmed at the benevolence of his act of mercy? He thought again of the MPs' faces . . . fear that was so easily readable . . . but fear of what?

Abaris stopped in front of a large set of doors. They were jet black with a sleek surface. He put his hand into a scanning device and the doors slid open.

Nathan followed Abaris through the doors and into the room. He found himself in a glass-enclosed walkway that overlooked a space below which was about the size of a basketball court. The walkway continued around the perimeter of the area, allowing the viewer the advantage of observing from every angle. The court had a sand floor, much like that of the desert high above them. There were huge boulders and rock formations that were interspersed throughout the court. Felled trees of sizable girth were in haphazard stacks on the floor.

"Where are we?" Nathan asked.

Abaris stood apart from Nathan and managed to keep his face hidden in the shadows of the room. "Where are we?"

Abaris echoed the question. "This is our observation room where we can see the man of the future. We can watch as he demonstrates his abilities, his power, his might." Abaris gestured toward Ramiel who now floated between the two men. "We can see him in all his glory . . . the end product of our eugenics, if you will . . . Yes, the superman."

Abaris called to one of the MPs who had remained by the door. The man took his walkie-talkie from his belt and mumbled something into it but remained outside the observation room.

"Yes, now look there," Abaris pointed excitedly toward a hidden door that was revealed for an instant as it slid open.

Out of it came an ordinary man. A man of no great physical consequence, somewhere in midlife, overweight, balding, muscles weak and unused.

Nathan looked at the man who, except for a loincloth, was naked. But what he noticed most was the weapon that the man carried. A lightweight automatic weapon that he seemed to clutch in wild desperation.

"I don't understand," Nathan said.

"Oh, you will soon. Yes, yes, you will soon," Abaris chortled with genuine delight.

The man began to walk cautiously into the open area of the court which was several stories beneath Nathan's vantage point. On the opposite wall of the court a panel slid open. Something dashed out from it and hid in a group of rocks several yards away.

"What was that?" Nathan asked.

Abaris motioned toward the court. Nathan looked below.

The man who held the gun pointed it at the rock grouping where whatever had just entered hid itself.

Suddenly something streaked out from behind them. Something large and humanlike that was crouched over as it sprinted to a stack of tree trunks then disappeared.

To Nathan's amazement the man with the gun fired a short burst at the intruder. He watched as sand splayed upward from the bullets. One of the bullets hit a rock, ricocheted, and found its way to the glass a few yards from where Nathan stood. Instinctively he shied away from the impact.

"Bulletproof . . . nothing to fear," Abaris assured him.

Nathan looked again at the court below.

A large object exploded from the tangle of logs and smashed into the floor, sending a wall of sand and dust billowing toward the man with the gun.

"That's a tree trunk," Nathan yelled.

"Yes, yes, that's what it is," Abaris replied.

The man dived out of the way and in doing so lost his gun. He landed in a heap and looked frantically for the misplaced weapon. He spotted it and began to crawl toward it. He grabbed it, stood upright, and moved to a pile of boulders.

Nathan's head began to clear and he started to feel more like his old self. Whether this was due to the excitement of his healing from Ramiel or what he was viewing, he wasn't sure, but he was becoming more lucid by the moment.

Nathan looked below at the man with the gun. He stared at the man's profile. *He looks familiar,* he thought. *Who is he? Why do I think I know him?*

Again something darted out from behind the tree trunks. This time it ran more upright, offering a better target. Nathan looked at it. Even with the barest glimpse he could see that the humanoid figure was large, very large.

Another burst of gunfire.

Surely some of the bullets had to have hit the running figure. But it disappeared behind a large rock formation.

Silence below.

The man stalked the creature, holding his gun in front of him, clutching it tightly so that Nathan could clearly see the man's knuckles turn white. He saw the man tremble.

Another period of silence.

Abaris called, "Now watch, yes, watch."

There was a small ledge on the topmost rock that was twenty feet above the sand floor. Something began to appear on it.

Nathan watched, fascinated, as an enormous hand gripped the rock's edge and was followed by a thick and muscular forearm. Then the top of the head showed—long strands of white hair that stuck out from the gray, scaly skin. Next the shoulders, massive and round, followed by the rest of the body, which gathered itself into a tight ball on the topmost rock. The man didn't see it. He was looking much lower, waiting anxiously, glancing furtively. Slowly the curled mass rose up from the rock and stood upright, revealing its full height.

Nathan's mouth dropped open and he instinctively stepped backward.

To call it a giant would be misleading, for it certainly was that but so much more. It was fearsome to behold, horrible and commanding. Human and yet not human. From this earth but not entirely of this earth. Nathan stared at its face, a marriage of arrogance and fury.

The man below still did not see it. It seemed as though he was blinded to its presence in some way. The giant looked down at the pitiful little man, opened his mouth, and let out a sound that almost stopped Nathan's heart. A tumultuous war cry, a deafening roar of ear-splitting intensity.

The man jerked his head upward. His face grew terrified, then blanched, and he dropped his gun.

The giant crouched low and then like a beast of prey leaped from the rock ledge and landed inches from the man. He reached down and with one huge six-fingered hand grabbed the man around the waist and hoisted him high over his head.

"Yes, oh yes," Abaris exclaimed.

Ramiel moved toward the glass and then did something completely baffling. He passed through it as if it wasn't there and floated over the inside of the court.

The giant saw him and he lifted the man, kicking and struggling, toward Ramiel, almost like an offering.

There seemed to be a sort of telepathy between Ramiel and the giant that Nathan was not privy to. The giant slowly set the man down in front of him and pinned him to the sand with an enormous boot.

Nathan looked at the man's face. He rubbed his forehead. *I know him,* he thought, *I know him. That's . . . Gleason.* The realization made him sick to his stomach.

Abaris gestured excitedly. "You see before you the new man, the man of the future. Unstoppable in battle, uncompromising in loyalty. This was for your benefit, General. You see what we have accomplished . . . Yes, how important it is, how glorious. The new man has emerged. Embrace him."

Nathan looked back down at the court. The giant and Ramiel had disappeared, leaving the little man lying like a crushed worm on the sandy floor.

42

"We're going in! Hold on!" Austin's voice boomed in Mac's headset.

Mac looked over at Uri and gave a nod of recognition. He gave Maggie an encouraging hug, then leaned forward expectantly in his seat.

"MacKenzie," the voice of Colonel Austin crackled in his headphones, "you better brace yourself. We'll be entering the outermost perimeter of the base in about two minutes. We're not sure what kind of welcoming committee they've prepared for us."

"Got it," Mac answered. He looked to the rear of the chopper and saw that the men were making a last-minute check of their gear. They were ready to go. Mac listened to the chatter in his headset.

"We've just crossed the perimeter."

"Sir, the drones are slightly ahead of us. Radar shows the base has sent out intercepts."

"Touchdown in three minutes, thirty seconds."

"Steady, men," Austin encouraged.

"They barely seem to be responding, sir. I think we caught them off guard."

"Let's not be too sure," Austin replied. "Stay focused and keep alert. Less than two minutes . . ."

"Sir, the 737 is on the landing strip. All points are hitting together . . ."

* ○ *

Sec Com, short for Security and Communications, was alive with activity. Captain Marshall stood with his hands clasped behind his back and listened to a barrage of information directed at him.

"Sir, I have the Pentagon, and they've ordered us to stand down."

Another voice shouted, "Sir, our rockets were launched before that order."

Still another voice, "Sir, no response from Maj 12. They're not answering on that level."

A young woman blurted, "Sir, we have what appears to be unauthorized personnel deboarding from our 737."

Marshall, the captain of the watch for that eight-hour shift, remained calm. "Order the base on red alert."

"Sir, I have a direct order from the secretary of state to prepare for an immediate inspection."

"Can you verify that?" Marshall asked.

"Yes, sir, decoding and authorization is complete. It's authentic."

Everyone looked at Marshall and waited for his answer.

"Sir, another order from the Joint Chiefs of Staff. We are being told to stand down, sir."

Marshall clasped his hands behind his back. "Nothing from Maj 12?" he asked.

"Nothing, sir."

The captain swore. "Order our people to stand down. Have all personnel evacuate to the lowest level as if they were preparing for a nuclear assault." He stomped angrily from the room.

* ○ *

The chopper was almost at the designated landing area. A soldier slid the door open and the cold morning desert air rushed in. Mac peered out and saw the first light of dawn streak across the desert sky.

Moments later Austin's voice boomed. "This is it! Touchdown! Let's move it! Move it! Move it!"

The chopper set down fast and hard. Mac heard Maggie give a stifled cry as it jarred her in her seat.

"It's all right," he encouraged.

"Move it! Move it!" Austin shouted.

The men poured out of the belly of the chopper and set themselves in a defensive circle around it.

"This is it," Mac yelled to Uri.

Uri gave a thumbs-up.

"You going to be all right?" Mac yelled to Laura above the noise.

She nodded.

"Stay with me close," Uri said, and he grabbed her hand and led her out of the chopper.

"Come on, Maggie," Mac coaxed as he took her hand and helped her to the door of the chopper. They jumped out together.

Mac looked around and saw the three other helicopters on the ground a short distance away. The men deboarding those fanned out, crouched defensively, and awaited orders.

Austin opened the cockpit door and jumped out. He swung his hand around his head and pointed toward his right. The men began to trot in the direction he indicated. Forty men and two women ran toward a gaping hole in the side of a mountain.

Mac assumed it to be the other end of the tunnel that he had seen when he was underground with Nathan. It was a huge opening over two hundred feet in diameter. They gathered at the mouth of the tunnel.

Mac saw Austin crouched low next to a soldier who was equipped with a mobile communication device. Uri and Laura were next to him. Mac reached them and overheard Austin say, "They got the drones, but there doesn't seem to be any resistance at the main hangar."

"Sir, the doors are beginning to close," a soldier cried who was closest to the mouth of the tunnel.

"Use the grenades. Move it! Quick!" Austin ordered.

Mac watched as half a dozen men ran to the mouth of the tunnel. The huge doors were slowly beginning to close. Mac saw that the surface of them was camouflaged to resemble the terrain on the side of the mountain.

The men ran behind the doors. In less than a minute they were back out again. Smoke billowed out from the tunnel.

Mac caught Austin's eye and threw him a confused look.

"Thermite grenades," Austin answered. "They don't blow everything to kingdom come . . . just melt the metal together. Let's move into the tunnel, men," he ordered, and he led the way past the gigantic doors that were now frozen in place, leaving the entrance still over ninety percent open.

Following Austin and a group of his men, Mac, Maggie, Uri, and Laura entered the tunnel together and moved rapidly over the smooth, wide floor. The sound of their boot-clad feet reverberated off the walls.

Mac looked down the length of the tunnel until it disappeared in a black pinpoint far in the distance, in the depths of the earth.

One of the soldiers walking next to Austin informed him, "Sir, we've lost contact with our main force above ground."

"Okay," Austin replied, "we thought that might happen. Let me know if we reconnect."

"Yes, sir."

Another of Austin's men using a laser range finder informed him of their progress in the tunnel. "We're about halfway down, sir," the man announced.

Mac watched as Austin divided the men into two groups. One hugged the right side of the tunnel—this included Uri, Laura, Maggie, and himself. The other group proceeded down the left side.

Trotting along to keep up, he was awed by the enormity of the tunnel. It towered over his head and dwarfed the entire company.

"Where are we?" Maggie whispered.

"This leads to where the saucers are kept," Mac answered and then put his finger to his lips.

Mac kept his eye on the soldier who held the range finder and ran next to Austin. The man signaled Austin, who then held his hand up and ordered the men to stop. The soldier took a reading.

"It's just up ahead, sir. We should make a visual soon," he said.

Austin said, "Okay, men, this is it. Remember, do your job and secure the area. Let's move out!"

They continued at a brisk pace toward the end of the tunnel.

Mac realized he was about to enter the underground cavern again—the now infamous area where the alien had bored into his soul with its baleful eyes. The thought made him nervous. He gripped Maggie's hand tighter as they walked side by side.

The soldiers crouched low at the end of the tunnel in the dim greenish light. Mac saw Austin signal the group opposite him to move out into the cavern. Four men ran out of the tunnel and after fifty feet dove to the ground and stayed in a covered position. One of them signaled, and the rest of the men ran out and joined them.

Someone gasped as he saw the disk hovering just above the cavern floor.

The men fanned out in a succession of movements. A team of four men activated the caged elevator and ascended into the web of scaffolding attached to the cavern's roof.

This is weird, Mac thought. *This place should have been crawling with personnel, and yet there's nobody here.*

Mac spotted Uri and Laura, who had remained with a cluster of men in the initial assault. They stood with them near the saucer. Laura made eye contact with Mac and shook her head in disbelief.

"Maggie, I want to talk to Uri. Stay close, okay?" He led the way as they trotted over to where Uri was.

As they approached, Uri threw a glance at the saucer and said, "They've evacuated the area . . . at least their personnel."

Mac looked over at Maggie and saw her stare wide-eyed at the disk. He watched as she timidly reached out and touched it.

"Mac?" she called softly. "This is amazing!"

"I can't believe it either," Laura said.

"I know, fancy toys . . . but don't let this fool you," Mac warned.

They were interrupted by a soldier calling from the roof of the cavern, "Nothing up here, sir. The area is secured."

The same cry echoed from other areas. Austin strode over to the saucer. He stretched his hand, touched the disk, then shook his head and muttered, "Of all the things . . . will you look at this, MacKenzie?"

"It brings back some very unpleasant memories, Colonel," Mac replied.

Mac watched as Austin took a folded map from the inside of his jacket and walked over to a tool cart a few feet away. He unfolded the map and his point men gathered around him.

He announced, "We're at this location but we need to get to this area . . . here," and he showed them a cross section of the underground base, which illustrated the tiered levels stacked one on the other. "We believe this area is under tight security. If the map is accurate, it can be reached through the air filtration system or an emergency exit shaft that runs from the surface to the lowest level. The shaft was installed as a safeguard in case the main elevator or one of the levels collapsed. We'll enter it here," he said, and he stabbed the map with his finger.

"We know very little about the area we are going into." Mac received an uneasy look from him before he continued, "We believe that this is the level that the aliens use to house their genetic experiments." He paused, letting the men digest his words. "Men, remember your briefing. Don't use force unless absolutely necessary."

Mac watched Austin survey his men. He could see Austin's admiration and pride of the force he commanded.

"Let's move out, men," Austin ordered as he folded the map and stuck it in his jacket pocket.

They headed toward the anteroom and elevators which shuttled personnel throughout the complex. At the doors two soldiers unscrewed the access panel. After a moment they spliced the wires together and the doors slid open. Mac braced himself, sure that there would be MPs behind the doors. The room was empty. The soldiers entered it and hit the controls, which opened the other set of doors that led to the train tracks.

Austin and a few of his men walked toward the platform's end and peered down the tunnel in both directions. "This way, men." He jumped down and landed next to the miniature tracks. His men followed suit, and soon they were running single file down the length of the tunnel. As they neared the first platform, Austin stopped and waved four soldiers up and ordered them to secure the area just ahead.

The men ran single file toward the platform. As they arrived there, two of the four remained at the platform's edge and aimed their weapons at the closed doors. The other two lifted themselves up onto the platform floor and cautiously approached the doors. They removed the access panel as before and spliced the wires. They flattened themselves against the wall as the doors slid open.

"Clear," one of the soldiers shouted from the tracks.

The men who were against the wall spun toward the open doors and secured the room as two others hopped onto the platform and backed up their position. One of them signaled to Austin, and the rest of the team ran down the tracks and occupied the platform and anteroom.

Six soldiers knelt in front of the closed sliding doors with their weapons ready, while six more stood behind them.

"Open them," Austin ordered.

A soldier pressed the red button and the doors slid open with a slight hissing sound. There was a moment of tension, then everyone relaxed, for the corridor was empty.

Uri leaned over and whispered to Mac, "I'm not understanding why no one is here."

"It's strange," Mac agreed.

They entered the corridor and proceeded toward the main elevator. Austin held up his hand and the company stopped. "There's a room up ahead. Take four men and secure it," he ordered one of his point men.

The men moved quickly to the room's entrance. One man kicked open the door while another darted past him into the room. He came out a moment later and gave the all-clear sign.

The company moved past three other rooms the same way. All were empty. In the last room one of the soldiers came out holding a cup of coffee and gave it to Austin.

Austin took the cup and frowned. "It's still warm," he remarked. "Move out and use extra caution."

The soldiers spread out in the corridor and came to the anteroom, which connected that level to the main elevator shaft.

Austin took his map out and spread it out on the floor. "The main elevator lies just behind this last set of doors. I want one man to jam the doors open, then the rest of us will follow. We'll open one portal first and see if the area on the other side is clear. If it is, we'll jam the other doors and proceed to the emergency elevator shaft. Any questions?" Austin waited a moment then said, "Let's get it open, men."

One soldier went through the first portal. He jammed the door open and looked into the interior of the elevator anteroom.

"All clear," he called, and knelt facing the elevator while men began to cross through the jammed doors of the portal.

The other portals were accessed in a similar manner, and the rest of the force poured through the openings.

Mac scrambled through with Maggie close behind him.

"Over here, sir," a soldier called. The man was standing next to the wall on which a large square plate was attached.

Austin walked over and examined it.

"Get it open, lower the ropes, and prepare for descent to Level 12," he ordered.

Two soldiers took out electric screwguns and began to unscrew the panel from the wall. Others set their packs on the floor and unloaded rope and tackle.

The plate came off and was handed to two men who leaned it against the wall. A soldier peered down the shaft and sent a coil of rope down it. He handed the other end to a soldier who took it and relayed it to yet another man, ten feet away, who fastened it to a ring that he set into the floor with a special gun.

Ten men knelt with their weapons pointing toward the elevator, while small groups guarded the portal entrances.

"Down the hole," Austin ordered.

One soldier wearing a mountain-climbing harness climbed into the shaft and sat for a moment on its edge. He snapped a ring which was attached to his harness to the rope and positioned himself for the descent.

"Hold it! Hold it! The elevator's started and it's coming this way!" a soldier yelled.

The soldier scrambled out of the shaft.

The entire group of men reformed themselves into three rows. They focused their weapons on the doors of the elevator.

"Hold your fire until I give the order!" Austin yelled.

Mac grabbed Maggie's arm. "Get down here," he said, and pulled her to the floor.

Uri positioned himself in front of Maggie and Laura and pointed his weapon at the elevator.

Everyone tensed. Mac felt a slight vibration to the floor as the elevator stopped. The outer doors opened with a loud hiss. Then the inner doors slowly opened. Mac sucked his breath in and looked.

A lone figure stepped out. It was General Nathan. Behind him were ten MPs standing at attention.

"Hold your fire, men. Hold your fire," Austin bellowed as he ran toward the elevator. "General Nathan, sir?" he asked.

Nathan nodded. "Alive and well, Colonel Austin."

"Dad!" Laura ran through the soldiers toward her father. She threw her good arm around him and hugged him. "I'm so relieved, you're alive, you're alive!"

Nathan frowned as he saw her bandages. "What happened to you?"

"It's nothing, what's important is that you're alive. How's your—"

"Sir," Austin interrupted, "we are under orders to secure the base."

Nathan gently moved Laura from him. "I'm aware of that, which is why I'm here. I've been sent here to make an offer." He gestured toward the MPs behind him. "This is all of security from Maj 12 . . . sort of a good-faith gesture. They're not armed."

Austin looked perplexed.

"MacKenzie?" Nathan called out.

Mac looked at Maggie, squeezed her hand, and moved forward.

"MacKenzie, I just saw your children a short while ago. They're well and no harm has come to them."

Maggie let out a stifled, "Oh!"

Mac nodded, waiting for the *but* that he knew was to follow.

"The deal is this." Nathan shifted his weight, eyed Austin then MacKenzie, and said, "Colonel Austin is to move his men from this level and go topside. All of us are to go with him." Nathan reached into his pants pocket and held up a metal card with coding over it. "You, MacKenzie, are then to proceed to Level 12 alone. Once you're there, your children will be released. It's an exchange, you for them."

Maggie started to cry. Uri put his arm around her.

"But General, why are we allowing this?" Austin asked.

Nathan frowned and said, "Because all of your forces will be destroyed if you try to invade Level 12. I don't like this any more than you, but I've been assured that if MacKenzie goes alone, his children will be released."

"I'll do it," Mac said without hesitation.

Austin looked at him. "Are you sure, MacKenzie?"

Mac nodded, then turned and looked at Maggie.

"General, what do you want me to do?" Austin asked.

"Get your men topside and do the trade for the children," Nathan said.

"And if something . . . goes wrong?"

"Ask me when that happens, Colonel," Nathan replied.

Austin saluted and shouted, "Let's move into the elevator, men."

The commandos collected their gear and moved quickly into the elevator.

Maggie worked her way over to Mac so that she stood beside him as the elevator doors closed. Nathan stood at the control panel and slipped a key he had been given into it and pressed the topmost button. The elevator made the ascent quickly, gliding smoothly to the surface.

The doors opened and the MPs exited, flanked on either side by Austin's commandos. They were met by the surprised look of the rest of Austin's force.

Mac remained in the elevator with Maggie by his side.

"Here is the card that will let you access Level 12," Nathan said.

MacKenzie took it and glanced at the circuitlike surface of the card.

Nathan said, "MacKenzie, listen, you'll be meeting Abaris, the commander of Level 12. I'm not sure what he's up to, but I don't trust him. For some reason he's obsessed with you, which is why you're going down to meet him. You're on your own . . . Be careful and good luck."

Uri tried his best to smile and called from just outside the doors, "I'm thinking you are going to be okay with this."

Mac nodded.

Laura gave him a thumbs-up.

Nathan escorted Maggie out of the elevator. Mac looked at Maggie as he slipped the metallic card into the slot. The doors began to close. Maggie grabbed Uri and held his arm.

"I love you," Mac mouthed the words at her just before the doors separated them.

43

⚫

Mac held his breath as the doors to the elevator slid open. Stepping out into the anteroom, he slipped the metallic card into the control panel, stood back, and waited for the inner doors of that level to open. They slid to the side, and to his delight he saw his children standing a few feet away accompanied by an Asian man.

"Daddy," Sarah yelled and ran to meet him.

Jeremy followed and Mac caught both of them in his arms. He held them out in front of him to make sure they were whole in body and mind.

The Asian man stepped into the anteroom, the door sliding closed behind him. "I've been with children since arrival here," he assured Mac.

"Oh?"

"Abaris wants to assure you, they remember nothing of what happened."

Mac rose to his feet holding his children close to him. He wanted to smash the guy in the nose, but he forced the impulse aside and said, "I'm going to put them on the elevator now," as he moved the children behind his back.

"Very good. Do that. But please, I go with the children."

"How do I know they'll reach the hangar? Why should I trust you?"

"You watch here," and the man pointed to a series of security monitors that were recessed above the elevator.

Mac glanced behind him and saw monitors representing the anterooms on all the levels. The one farthest to the left showed the hangar area. Mac could make out some of Austin's men.

"Okay, let's do it. What do I do?" he asked.

"Go there," and the man pointed to a black wall behind him.

Mac bent down on one knee. "Jeremy, are you all right?"

Jeremy nodded a couple of times. "Where are we, Dad? Where's Mom?"

"Listen closely," Mac said, and he held the boy in front of him. "Mom's waiting for you. Hold Sarah's hand and in a minute you'll be with her, all right?"

Jeremy nodded and reached for Sarah's hand.

Mac stood up and kissed them both. The Asian man motioned them toward the elevator, and Mac did his best to look like nothing was amiss as the doors began to close before them. The last thing he saw was Sarah's hand waving goodbye.

He looked up at the monitor and waited.

Moments later he saw the children run into Maggie's outstretched arms. Mac could see Uri and Laura next to her. He also saw Austin deploy some of his men around the Asian man. Then, to Mac's dismay, the entire group moved out of the range of the camera.

Mac turned around and took his first careful look at Level 12.

It looked similar to the other level he had been on with the exception that the lighting for the area was from an unseen source. It seemed to emanate simultaneously from the walls, floor, and ceiling.

He took a few cautious steps toward the black wall that separated the anteroom from the interior.

He waited. Nothing happened.

He walked up to the edge of the wall, reached his hand out, and tried to touch it. To his surprise he watched his hand disappear. Jerking his hand back, he looked at it and balled his fingers to make sure it wasn't damaged.

He reached out again and saw it disappear into the wall, but this time he extended his hand as far as it would go, almost to his shoulder.

He withdrew it, examined it, then slowly put out his leg. He watched, fascinated, as it also vanished. He put both arms out in front of him and said out loud, "Here goes," and moved the rest of his body into the wall.

He reappeared on the other side and found himself in a beautiful garden. Tall, green ferns fanned out around him. Exotic flowers were in full bloom. A variety of grasses bordered a small stream that flowed by, almost at his feet.

Mac didn't know what to make of it. It seemed completely out of context with everything else that he had seen at the base. He looked high overhead and to his amazement saw a glowing orb similar to a small sun which lighted and warmed the area.

There was a small bridge that straddled the stream. He went over to it and crossed it.

The path led to a corridor, which intersected a larger hall. Directly in front of him was a great black door. Mac was about to walk past when the door split into four sections. A panel disappeared into the ceiling, one fell into the floor, and two more slid to the sides. Yet moments ago the door had appeared seamless.

Mac entered and found himself in a circular room.

"Well, well, MacKenzie. Yes, Art MacKenzie," a man's raspy voice called.

Mac saw the silhouette of a man sitting at a circular table. "Who are you?" he asked.

"Come closer," the man answered. "Yes, I want to see you."

Mac walked toward the man.

"Sit here," and he pointed to a chair next to him.

MacKenzie sat down.

Light seemed to filter through the wall's ceiling and floor in a steady source of illumination, but for some reason the man who had called him was masked in darkness. His face remained featureless in the shadows. "What do you want with me?" Mac asked.

"MacKenzie, MacKenzie," the man whispered through his lips, "I knew you would come . . . that is why I cleared everyone out, all the personnel. Yes, we don't want anyone hurt now, do we? There was no resistance, was there? No bothersome MPs, yes?"

Mac frowned, not trusting what he heard. "You mean that all of this was staged for my benefit?"

The man laughed. "We know everything, MacKenzie, oh yes, everything. Here, look." Next to him on the table was a control panel in the shape of a hand that was molded into the table. The man put his hand in it, and suddenly the room exploded with a series of different holographic images which encircled it.

Mac jumped from his chair and turned around so he could glimpse the pictures. The images were vivid, like looking through windows.

There were African villages that appeared to be in the midst of severe drought and famine. Withered infants clung lifelessly to their mother's skeletal frame. In another, uniformed men moved through a bombed-out street, ducking sniper bullets and returning fire with their weapons. In what looked like India thousands of homeless people fled the swirling waters of the monsoon rains. In Iran, Muslims marched down a street chanting and smashing their foreheads with rocks in religious ecstasy. In Burma a mass grave was being exhumed, revealing the bodies of over a thousand murdered men, women, and children. In a dirty, garbage-strewn alley in an American city a wild-eyed crack addict was giving birth to a baby, already addicted to the nightmarish drug. A line of Chinese student protesters marched arm in arm toward their country's militia in riot gear.

Then the images changed faster, scenes juxtaposed from different parts of the twentieth century ... Nagasaki. Hiroshima. The human skeletons of the concentration camps. The killing fields of Cambodia. JFK's head exploding in Dallas. The human carnage lying dead on the battlefields of World War I. Hitler gesticulating wildly as he delivered an impassioned speech of racial hate. The Bolsheviks running through the streets of St. Petersburg. The gulags in Siberia.

Mac was overcome as still more images came. Each so real, like looking into a window in time.

The pictures suddenly stopped and the room grew quiet.

"You see, MacKenzie, I want you to understand what we humans are ... Yes, it isn't a pretty picture, is it? All the butchery ... the pain and misery ..."

Mac was speechless.

"What the aliens ... our brothers have to offer us is peace, security, and a world that will be governed fairly, justly, benignly. Yes, all of what you saw will be a thing of the past. Gladly a thing of the past. All the isolated fiefdoms warring in Africa. The fractured provinces of the former Soviet Union. The Bosnias and Pakistans that are so volatile ... yes, all the chaos, uncertainty, instability. The aliens will change that. Yes, a thing of the past it will become."

"So why tell all of this to me?" Mac asked, completely bewildered.

The man reached toward the control panel next to him and let his hand rest a moment in the indentation. A light began to illuminate the man's face, lifting it from the shadows, and the man began to hum a song. Mac heard the familiar strains of "Home on the Range."

"I used to sing that song with my . . ." Mac's voice trailed off.

"Your father?"

The light grew and the man's features became recognizable. Every muscle in Mac's body tensed and froze. His stomach tightened and he tasted bile rising in his throat. He felt as if his mind was about to snap.

He stared in fear, in disbelief, at a lost man . . . a dead man . . . his father.

44

Art MacKenzie walked slowly down the dimly lit corridor. He fought to keep his hands from trembling as he listened to the bizarre tale his father told.

"They renamed me Abaris," he began, "after a Greek sage who had the power to heal. It was I who communicated with the one alien that remained alive after the Roswell crash. When his shell began to die I allowed him to enter into me. To the aliens it was the most noble act, the highest calling, to allow one of them to share my body."

"Is he still with you now?" Mac asked hesitantly.

"You have been talking to both of us, for we are now one. It has been the most valuable experience of my life."

"So that's why you left us and faked your murder . . . so that the alien could share your body?"

"Yes, that and more. I want you to understand that my shell is beginning to die . . . That is why I brought you here. You, my son, are the person to carry on. To help change the misery on this planet. If you will allow us to enter . . ."

Mac grew suddenly afraid. "I can't do that."

Abaris stopped in front of a large black panel. He set his hand into an indentation and the door split into four sections and opened.

He gestured for Mac to enter. "Don't be so sure. You need to see for yourself. You must understand that the time of their revealing to all mankind is almost at hand, and they are here to usher us into the new millennium. A world of peace and understanding. Harmony and love. The true brotherhood of man realized to its fullest potential."

Mac was overwhelmed, his emotions and thought processes derailed.

"This is Ramiel, the leader of our alien brothers," Abaris said, indicating with a nod that Mac should look.

The room was bathed in a brilliant white light as Ramiel appeared from an entrance off to the side. He was magnificent, powerful, and splendid to behold. Mac gasped with wonder. He looked similar to the angel at Maggie's house, but seeing him here was somehow different.

A thought crossed Mac's mind. Just a subtle whisper. "I really *am* an angel. Trust me." Mac let the thought go unchecked.

Ramiel floated above Abaris and Mac. He then began to change his appearance slowly. He became Ghandi, looking serene and holy with a white dhoti wrapped around his otherwise naked, brown-skinned body.

Then he changed into an image of the Buddha, silent and detached, with a beam of light streaking from the center of his forehead.

Then he turned into the image of Jesus, and he was hanging on the cross, his arms outstretched and pinned horribly through the wrists to the rough, wooden cross beam. A crown of thorns rested on a bloody head, marred almost beyond recognition. He was in his final stages of death. His head was lowered. Mac watched in stunned silence as he breathed his last.

Then the image changed again and became a small point of light that swirled and became a primordial cloud of spinning galaxies. A universe unto itself.

Then it disappeared.

Mac's head ached and he rubbed his forehead vigorously with both hands. He looked around and realized his father had left him.

Abaris called from an adjacent room. Mac followed and entered a large room illuminated with a strange reddish glow. He saw hundreds of glasslike containers. Inside the jars hybrids rested in a thick liquid in different stages of incubation and development. They were set in tiered rows, the lowest of which began at the entrance where he stood.

Abaris began to speak from the topmost tier. He pointed to the rows of hybrids and said proudly, "This is the future . . . Their seed and ours joined together to create a race of supermen. Our genes mixed with theirs to replenish their dying race and evolve ours."

Mac stared in shock.

Abaris chuckled. "The aliens are here to enlighten us. It was they who stimulated the creation of the world's major religions in the first place. Krishna, Muhammad, Jesus, Moses. All genetically engineered. Soon their time of dwelling with us will be revealed, and the kingdom of heaven will be on earth."

Mac's mind whirled in contradiction. *No, I don't believe that, it isn't true . . .*

He recalled the woman in the hospital. Her life was ruined by these creatures. He remembered the cattle mutilation, the carcass of which had its sex organs removed . . . for what? This? He gazed at the creatures curled in their containers, suspended in an alien liquid solution made partially of . . . cow's blood? The thought made him sick.

One of the hybrids in a container close to him turned slightly in the jar so that its eyes looked out at Mac. Its face twisted in what Mac could only associate as a look of hatred.

He recoiled and stared back at it. Reaching out a clawlike hand, it scratched the side of the container. The thick liquid moved around it.

Mac was transfixed. *A monster,* he thought, and he took a step away.

"You see," Abaris said, almost as if he could read Mac's thoughts, "this all might seem strange to you now, but I assure you it is mankind's future."

Mac listened and wanted to believe his father . . . in everything he had said . . . in all that he was part of. He struggled with the thought . . . and almost embraced it.

Then Mac felt the hand of God's Spirit upon him. *Where have I been?* he thought, and the realization made him shiver. He closed his eyes and said two words, "Help me."

Even before he could finish asking, a thought rocketed at him. *What was the alien trying to say? That Christ and Ghandi and Buddha were the same? Or that they were part of a greater force? No, it was a trick, an illusion deliberately contrived to manipulate and control.*

He looked at the creature in the container and let the word roll off his tongue. "Nephilim."

Images whirled in his head. The bones in the sarcophagus, Sarah's book of David and Goliath, Dr. Elisha earnestly exhorting him to pray, the encounter at Maggie's house, the way the creature changed its form and lunged at Laura . . .

"Nephilim," he repeated the word, only this time louder.

"What did you say?" Abaris said.

Mac ignored him and took another step toward the container.

"What are you thinking of, my son?" Abaris asked in a paternal tone and moved down to the next tier.

Mac made his way slowly toward the jar that held the hybrid which glared at him. He reached out and rested his hand on the jar.

"What are you doing?" Abaris demanded.

Mac didn't look at his father. Instead, he stared at the developing hybrid. He could feel the warmth from the container work its way into the palms of his hands.

The hybrid turned so that its face was pressed against the jar.

Mac wanted to recoil from it.

"Are you embracing it?" Abaris asked.

The thought made Mac sick. "What?"

Abaris took a step down to another tier and said, "Yes, oh yes, embrace him, for he is your brother."

Mac closed his eyes and ground his teeth together. Then he pushed the jar with all his might so that it toppled off its shelf and tumbled to the floor with a loud crash. The creature spilled out of the jar and began to writhe on the floor in the midst of the foul-smelling liquid.

"Nephilim!" Mac yelled, suddenly coming alive. "It's all a lie. You're a lie." He pointed at Abaris. "You're not my father."

"What are you doing?" Abaris demanded.

At the same time Ramiel reappeared. His countenance became angry as he saw the contents of the containers spilled before him.

Mac looked up at Ramiel. He felt dizzy. It seemed as if his throat was beginning to close on itself. He closed his eyes for a moment and yelled in his mind, "Jesus." Then he opened his eyes and looked at Ramiel, tried to speak, but his throat closed tightly. He gasped for air.

"What are you trying to do?" Abaris shouted. "Destroy the future of mankind?"

* ◇ *

"Sir, I have a Captain Marshall on the radio," one of Austin's men informed him.

"Who's he?" Austin asked.

"Sir, he wants to talk to you, sir."

Austin grabbed the receiver. "This is Colonel Austin, United States Air Force Special Forces."

"Sir, this is Captain Marshall, the base commander of Sec Com. We have been ordered to report to you and relinquish control of this base to you, sir."

"By whose orders?"

"Sir, the Pentagon for starters."

"Have your personnel report to the hangar, Captain."

"Sir, most of our personnel is underground . . . lowest level. They have orders to remain there."

"Do you have access to Maj 12?" Austin asked.

"Sir, we do not . . . it has always been an independent area under the direct command of the extraterrestrial biological entities."

"I don't like it, sir," Austin said to General Nathan.

"Not me too," Uri added.

"Tell him to report back to the Pentagon that the base is secured . . . at least the human portion of it," Nathan ordered.

Austin relayed the information, then awaited Nathan's orders.

General Nathan glanced at the two men, then looked over at the elevator. "I'm not sure what or who to believe at this moment." He looked at his daughter who was sitting with Maggie and her children at the mouth of the hangar. "Laura will attest to the degree my cancer spread . . . she knows only too well. But whatever it is down there, it healed me. And because of that it can't be all bad."

"General, sir," Austin began, "Dr. BenHassen thinks it is, sir. He seems pretty confident that this . . ."

"Is the work of the devil?" Nathan finished his sentence.

Austin looked at the ground, embarrassed, then admitted, "Yes, sir."

"No, I don't think so. But I will say this. The aliens are thousands of years ahead of us mentally and spiritually."

"Sir, if I may," Austin began.

"Go ahead, Colonel."

"Sir, Dr. BenHassen strongly suggests that these beings are posing as aliens in an elaborate deception."

Nathan shook his head. "That may be, Colonel, and if it is, just what am I supposed to do?"

Austin was silent.

Nathan continued, "Have your second in command relocate the women and children to the Sec Com; they'll be safe there. Position your men near the elevator and remain there."

"Yes, sir."

"General," Uri said, "you know what . . . somebody is playing big games with us. What they are doing with the children and you and MacKenzie is not making sense. I'm thinking somehow we are to be fooled by all of this."

Nathan nodded in agreement. "They're up to something, but believe me they could have blown us out of the water if they'd wanted to. You won't believe what's down there."

* ○ *

Thousands of miles away Johanen knelt in a cave once used as a retreat by Christians in the first century. He was praying.

The air in front of the cavern wall began to shimmer. He had seen this countless times but always beheld the phenomena with wonder. He watched as the veil that separates this world from the world of the spirit opened. A man clothed in brilliant raiment appeared where moments before a cold cavern wall had been.

Johanen bowed his head. "My Lord and my God, Ancient of Days," he proclaimed.

"It is almost time," the shining figure stated.

Johanen slowly lifted his head and gazed into the eyes of his Lord. He beheld what, for him, was almost unbearable to witness. A holiness, righteous and awesome in its splendor, radiated and burned like a thousand galaxies from the noble face. Johanen bowed his head again and felt hot tears stream from his eyes and fall to the cavern's floor. But these were tears of joy. He felt as if his very being would burst with the emotion.

"Yes, my Lord, it is almost time," he managed to repeat.

"You have labored long, faithful one," and his Lord raised his hand and blessed Johanen.

Johanen felt a surge of joyous energy ripple through his body.

"Yes, Lord, for many decades."

"Soon your tasks will end . . . and in my Father's house are many rooms."

For a moment Johanen thought about the first time he'd heard those words. *So long ago*, he mused. He raised his hands in front of him and began to worship.

* ० *

Dr. Elisha BenHassen knelt by his bed. He had remained so since the last time he had talked with Art MacKenzie. He now felt a stirring in his spirit. He prayed in earnest . . . he knew the battle had begun.

* ० *

"What are you doing?" Abaris demanded, and took a step toward Mac.

Mac's hands went to his throat as he tried desperately to breathe.

"I am strong in the Lord," Mac muttered. Then again more boldly, "I am strong in the Lord."

He looked at the hybrid writhing on the floor. To his horror he saw it change to the body of his son Art, twisting in agony. He gasped and was about to run toward it when he again felt the hand of God upon him. He stopped and looked again. The illusion had vanished . . . the hybrid was back on the floor.

Mac looked toward Abaris and Ramiel. "You're a lie," he shouted. "You are filled with lies!"

The room shook and the angel shuddered and shed its appearance, like a costume. Suddenly it became a thin, gray, wraithlike creature that floated above him menacingly.

Mac steeled his mind and faced the demon.

The creature glared at him.

Mac's mind was suddenly overwhelmed with horrible images. He held his hands to the side of his head and shut his eyes.

Mac staggered backward. The images were replaced with an impression of Jesus hanging on the cross, in death, in hopelessness. For a moment his mind went blank ... then he thought despairingly, *Is that all there is? A dead man on a cross?* He felt abandoned, surrounded in a fog of dark hopelessness. Then he was hammered again as twisted perverse images sought a foothold in his mind. He opened his eyes and with a great act of will he pushed the images away and managed to utter the one word that was a lifeline to his sanity ... "Jesus." He repeated the name, again and again. Each time he said the name he felt the doubting thoughts and grotesque images retreat.

The wraithlike creature glared at Mac and rose up, ready to charge him and claw him like it had Laura.

* ✿ *

A powerfully built angel appeared and bowed low to the Ancient of Days, who raised his hand and blessed the emissary of light.

"I am ready, Lord," the angel said.

"The time is now," the Ancient of Days said, and his words echoed like thunder in Johanen's ears. "Go swiftly and do the Father's will."

Johanen marveled as he watched the angel disappear in what he could only describe as a chariot of fire.

The air around the cavern began to shimmer.

"It is time for us to part, faithful one."

"Yes, my Lord," Johanen said, and he reached out and touched the hem of the Lord's shining garment.

* ○ *

Elisha clasped his hands together tightly and felt his heart race as he prayed for Mac's protection and victory.

The calls had gone out to those connected to the Spiral of Life Web site. In different parts of the world, men and women were on their knees in prayer, interceding for what they knew to be the first of many battles.

The time of the Great Deception had begun.

* ○ *

Mac's head cleared. His heart was strengthened and he felt a righteous boldness. A holy fire burned within him. This was the power of the Living God, the protection of the full armor of God.

He gathered himself, set his will against the demon, and with a mighty shout cried, "By the Blood of the Lamb spilled on Calvary, you are commanded to return to the Abyss!"

The creature let out a hideous, tortured scream. Abaris stepped back, his face filled with bewilderment.

A loud, cracking sound filled the room. Mac had never heard anything like it. It was as if the air around him and every atom in it were being torn apart. He saw a gaping hole being rent in the center of the room, between himself and the demon.

A large hand seemed to create the opening. A huge hand, a hand the size of a grown man. It moved something that Mac couldn't see with his human eyes. It tore away the fabric that separates the visible from the invisible. The seen from the unseen.

Before Mac appeared an ominous black pit descending as far as he could see.

The Abyss.

Mac suddenly found himself in a deafening, whirling hurricane, a maelstrom. The force of it struck him and he fell to the floor. His hair flew wildly about his head. His eyes teared and his clothes felt as though they were being blown off his body.

He tried to scramble away from the pit. He glanced at the demon above him. Its face was a twisted mask of rage and fear as it tried desperately to move away from the Abyss.

Mac watched horrified and yet fascinated as suddenly a tentacle of wind, like a small tornado, lashed out from the Abyss and enveloped one of the containers that held a hybrid. The container was violently torn from its shelf and pulled by the tentacle into the Abyss. He watched as it tumbled out of site and was lost in the darkness of that great maw.

Another container near it was picked up and hurled in the same manner.

More tentacles appeared from the pit and fastened themselves to containers which were spun into a frenzied helix and drawn into the depths.

Mac watched as the demon tried with all its strength to escape as one of the tentacles began to wrap around it . . . a shroud of whirling fury.

The demon desperately clawed at one of the shelves and managed to hook its clawlike fingers on its edge. For a second or two it held against the supernatural force that pulled at it, and then its body was torn from the arm that held it to the ledge. The demon was hurled shrieking into the pit, followed moments later by its severed arm.

Mac watched in horror as one of the tentacles whipped its way toward him. For a desperate moment he thought that he too would be ensnared by it and plunged into the dark depths. The thought terrified him. He pressed his body close to the floor and tried to back away from it.

The tentacle moved closer.

Mac yelled but his voice was lost in the frenzied cacophony.

Suddenly a magnificent angel appeared near him. Mac recoiled at the sight of it and for a moment thought it might be yet another demon posing as an angel of light.

But as he looked he saw the difference.

There was holiness in this being. A fierceness and determination shone from his eyes. The angel drew a sword that gleamed and burned with what looked like fire and brought it down on the tentacle that was reaching out to Mac. The whirling tentacle recoiled back into the pit. The angel then placed himself between Mac and the entrance of that great maw.

Mac looked around to see if he could locate Abaris . . . his father. He spotted him at the edge of the room. In the midst of the thunderous turmoil.

Abaris shouted wildly, "My son, my son, why have you forsaken me?" Then, before he too could be pulled into the Abyss, Abaris opened a hidden door and vanished from the room.

Abaris's words echoed in Mac's ear and tore at his heart. He staggered back to the wall.

The only thing left of the alien presence in the room was the hybrid that Mac had knocked to the floor. The hybrid reached out a clawlike hand and flicked its hideous tongue.

Suddenly three tentacles appeared and snatched the thing and hurled it into the pit with such force that it spiraled down and was instantly lost from sight.

To Mac's terror the angel moved toward him. Mac found himself being pressed close to the angel's side. He felt himself rise into the air as the angel floated over the Abyss to the other side of the room. He let go of MacKenzie at the topmost tier.

Mac collapsed on the floor, shaking all over. The angel reached down and touched him on his forehead. The shaking subsided, and he slowly sat up and took a deep breath.

He watched as the angel moved away and hovered over the Abyss. He began to close the tear that had opened into the unseen world of the spirit, and the black opening of the Abyss slowly began to close.

Mac watched transfixed as the room returned to normal except for the angel now floating over the place where the Abyss had been. The angel's sword flashed as he pointed to the secret corridor through which Abaris had escaped.

Mac staggered to his feet in obedience.

He watched the room explode into a brilliant shower of colored light as the angel disappeared.

Mac rubbed the back of his neck and entered the corridor wondering about Abaris and how many of the aliens were left and, more importantly . . . where were they?

* ◊ *

In the darkness of his mind, the giant heard Ramiel yelling, and he knew something was very wrong.

He strode across the room he was in, past a dozen small gray beings who attended him. Near the door, he cocked his monstrous head.

He felt fear . . . this emotion was new to him. He had never experienced it. It wasn't fear of men. He had faced many in the court, and to him they were simply playthings. This was different. Something he couldn't see. He found no words to describe what he felt . . . but it was more powerful than he was.

He straightened to his full height and sent a message telepathically to Ramiel. What returned to him were twisted thoughts of mayhem. And then nothing.

The giant lifted his hand and slammed the huge door as he strode from his room. He darted down the length of a corridor, dwarfing the aliens who followed closely behind. He pushed his way through the black wall and went to the elevator.

He paid little attention to Abaris who slipped something into the wall and made the elevator doors open.

"Yes. Yes, you go now and show them," Abaris coaxed.

The giant looked down at Abaris and bellowed, "I will crush them like worms." He bent low and climbed into the elevator. The doors shut and it began to ascend.

✳ ○ ✳

Mac found himself in a tube that was carved from solid rock. *A connecting tunnel,* he thought, *but to where?*

He ran madly and reached the end of it. There was an outline of a door carved from the rock. He paused and tried to get his breath, then he slammed his body against the door and hoped that it would open. It didn't budge. He looked to where a handle or lock should have been and saw nothing. He frantically searched the area and found, lower than expected, an imprint in the shape of a hand. He thrust his hand into the impression and the door swung open. He ran ahead and found himself in the huge cavern that housed the disk. But now the disk had been activated.

To his astonishment another disk flew in from the tunnel at the far end of the cavern and hovered near the tunnel's mouth. It pulsated with a deep orange glow. Mac heard a low-frequency hum coming from it. He looked up at one of the portals and saw the face of an alien glare down at him. The disk slowly rotated and came toward him. Mac moved back toward the connecting tunnel, pausing at the opening to stare at the new disk.

To his horror Jim Cranston stared out of one of the portals at him. He looked terrified. Mac saw his mouth move. He could read the man's trembling lips. "Help me!"

Cranston was suddenly jerked from the window.

The other disk began to move, and this time Mac saw his father glare at him through one of the portals.

Both disks slowly began to turn. The disks tilted at an angle and headed toward the entrance to the tunnel at the far end of the cavern. Mac watched as the first disk entered the tunnel's mouth, where it vanished instantly. The other stopped for a moment, then suddenly shot into the opening and whisked out of sight.

Mac gasped for breath and collapsed to the floor of the cavern. He closed his eyes and thanked God that it was all over.

45

＊◇＊

He's been down there over an hour, sir," Austin said as he paced nervously.

Nathan nodded but remained silent.

Austin took off his beret and scratched his bald head. "Sir, are we going to go down? I mean, sir, if we don't hear something from him soon."

Nathan started to say something when he was interrupted by one of Austin's men. "Sir, the elevator is moving this way," the commando shouted.

Austin slipped his beret back on. "Move back . . . find cover if you can and keep your weapons at the ready."

The commandos moved back quickly and took up positions next to one of the tall partition walls in the hangar.

"Sir, I'd feel a lot better if you'd move directly out of harm's way," Austin suggested.

"I'll take up a position by the hangar doors with some of the men from Sec Com," Nathan replied.

Austin used his index finger and ticked off four men who escorted Nathan to the large entrance.

"It's almost here, sir," a soldier yelled.

Uri came up next to Austin, who acknowledged him with a grunt. "There might be some action, BenHassen. We'll find out in a moment or two," he said, and squinted toward the elevator.

The elevator arrived.

The commandos clicked the safeties on their weapons off and took aim at the doors.

Nothing happened. The doors remained closed.

"Colonel?" one of the men shouted. "Should we approach, sir?"

Austin shot a glance at Uri. "What do you make of it, Ben-Hassen?"

"I'm thinking to wait and see what happens," Uri offered.

Austin grumbled something unintelligible then shouted, "Sergeant, move forward and investigate with four of your men."

"Yes, sir."

Four men moved cautiously forward following their sergeant. He signaled his men to fan out so that the area that made up the front of the elevator would be covered . . . and in case it was some kind of trap, his men were dispersed far enough apart to be a more difficult target to hit.

The sergeant was in the middle with two men on either side of him. He crept toward the center of the large elevator doors. The elevator rested level with the hangar floor, its walls creating a rectangular room ten feet overhead.

Austin held his breath as he saw the sergeant reach the doors. The man turned back to him and shrugged his shoulders. Austin heard a loud tearing sound come from the top of the elevator. Something had pushed its way out of the interior of the elevator and onto the roof.

"What is that?" Austin yelled as he saw something fall down onto the sergeant who was nearest the elevator. The man buckled under the weight of it.

"Look at the size of that thing . . ." Austin said under his breath.

He heard the man yell for help as he suddenly tumbled through the air, smashing into a cluster of men fifty feet away and sending them scattering like bowling pins.

Before anyone could react, the giant had moved away from the front of the elevator, sprinting in a low crouch. He reached out and smashed the chest of one soldier as he flew by him, sending the man sprawling. He hit the second man in his legs, breaking one of them at the knee.

"Kill it!" Austin roared.

A burst of machine-gun fire hit the concrete floor but missed the giant. He darted behind one of the partition panels that almost reached to the ceiling.

"Did you see that?" Austin yelled to Uri.

Uri glanced at the Colonel. "He's too big, isn't he?" Uri whispered.

Austin's men ran toward the partition. Suddenly the metal panels flew off the wall, one after the other in rapid succession. They were being pounded loose from the other side, acting like shrapnel. Austin's men scrambled to get out of the way.

"It's the giant!" Nathan yelled from the mouth of the hangar.

"The what?" Austin yelled. He grabbed his radioman and barked, "Get the choppers up here."

"Yes, sir." And the man frantically talked into his phone while he kept a fearful eye on the battle in the hangar.

"Where is it?" someone yelled.

"I don't know. It's moving too fast . . . I can't get . . . *ahhhhhh!*" a soldier screamed as a metal panel ripped into his chest.

Austin's men began to fire where the last panel had come off. Bullets tore into the partition wall. Metal shards flew in all directions.

"I think we got it," one of the commandos yelled.

"Don't be sure ... stay back," Austin yelled.

Five commandos approached the wall. The soldiers moved in cautiously, a step at a time. Then they waited, listening.

"See it?" someone asked.

Before anyone could answer a banshee-like cry echoed through the hangar. It came from high above the men ... from the roof.

The men jerked their heads upward.

Hurtling down on them from the top of the hangar was the giant. It landed on one of the men, crushing his shoulder bones, then rolled on the floor toward Austin.

The giant was between the soldiers and their commander. One man raised his gun. Before he could fire the giant picked up a twisted panel and tossed it at the man. It sliced into him just above his knees. The man screamed in agony and dropped to the floor.

Someone below activated the elevator, and it descended into the earth.

"We've got to kill this," Uri yelled, and he fired his weapon at the giant.

The giant moved away with such speed that Uri missed completely.

"Where is it?" one of Austin's men yelled.

Nathan raised his handgun and moved back into the hangar. He spotted the giant crawling on top of another partition wall at the ceiling of the hangar. "There it is." He took aim and squeezed off several shots.

The giant disappeared.

A crashing sound came from the other side of the partition wall. "I think you hit it, sir," a commando shouted.

Suddenly an experimental jet engine came crashing through the wall. It hit the floor of the hangar and slid toward some of Austin's men, who scrambled desperately to get out of the way. One man was bowled over.

"Watch out!" someone yelled.

The entire partition wall began to collapse. The metal buckled and the wall collapsed on Austin's men, burying most of them.

The elevator reappeared. The doors opened and out ran Mac.

"There it is," Austin yelled, who had dived away from the crashing wall.

The giant stood for a moment and roared at Austin, "I will bury you."

Austin momentarily froze.

Uri aimed his gun at the creature and it jammed. He reached into his back pocket and produced his own handgun.

The giant grabbed a piece of debris and hurled it at Uri's head. Uri ducked and fired a shot. His bullet struck the giant in the upper arm. The thing gnashed its teeth and roared at Uri, then leaped the thirty feet that separated them.

It knocked the gun from Uri's hand and it slid across the floor toward the elevator ... toward MacKenzie.

Mac grabbed it, then ran at the giant, shouting. The giant wheeled around at the sound of Mac's voice. Uri took advantage of the moment, grabbed a metal pipe, and brought it down on the creature. The giant threw its head back and roared in rage. Mac was only a few feet away. He raised the gun, aimed, and fired.

The bullet struck the giant in the forehead, between the eyes. The giant looked stunned ... as if it weren't sure what was happening. It reached toward its forehead, but before the six-fingered hand ever got there, it fell forward and crashed onto the floor.

A hush fell over the hangar and no one moved.

Mac remained in a crouched position, the handgun still held out in front of him ... except that now he realized he was trembling. He stared at the fallen creature that lay before him. Its eyes were already beginning to glaze over.

Uri slowly got to his feet. He was the first to break the silence. "Hey, Mac, you all right?"

The other men began to stir slowly.

"What . . . what is that . . . thing?" one of Austin's men stammered.

Several uninjured commandos grouped themselves around the fallen giant.

"Make sure it's dead," Austin growled.

"Yes, sir." One of the men slowly checked the giant at the neck, searching for a pulse. "It's gone, sir," the man called out.

Mac found his voice. "I'm okay . . . Uri. Where's Maggie . . . the kids?" he asked.

General Nathan answered, "Over at Sec Com." Then he addressed Austin, "Colonel, radio and have them join us, but I want the body moved first," he ordered.

"Where do you want it moved to?" Austin asked.

"Call ground transport and have it moved somewhere where a medical team can conduct an autopsy."

"Yes, sir," Austin responded.

Mac stood at the feet of the giant. He looked up and saw Uri at the giant's head . . . fourteen feet away.

"Nice shooting, MacKenzie," Uri said. "You saved us."

Mac shook his head. "Just lucky, that's all . . ." Then he mumbled, "And God was with me."

Uri heard him and added, "Yes, MacKenzie, I believe God was with you."

Mac gave Uri a tired grin.

A truck pulled up and personnel from Sec Com scurried out of it.

"Over there, men," Nathan ordered as he pointed to the fallen giant.

Mac took a step back and looked out over the expanse of tarmac. A jeep was barreling toward the hangar. A hand shot up from it and waved. Mac recognized it.

"Maggie!" he yelled, and took off toward the jeep.

They met on the tarmac. Maggie bounded out of the jeep before it had come to a complete stop. She ran to Mac, who picked her up and whirled her in the air, then set her gently on her feet and kissed her.

"Oh, Mac, you're safe . . . you're okay." She started to cry.

"Daddy . . . Daddy," Sarah and Jeremy chorused as they jumped out of the jeep and ran toward their father. Mac and Maggie held their arms out and the children tumbled into them.

Uri ran up next to them. He smiled broadly and gave Maggie a quick hug. "I'm thinking that it is good to have a family." He laughed and slapped Mac on the back. Mac nodded and gave Sarah a big squeeze.

"Mac," Uri began, "General Nathan and Colonel Austin want to talk to you. They are saying it will be a few minutes only."

"All right," Mac replied. He leaned forward and kissed Maggie again. "Don't go anywhere. I'll be right back."

He followed Uri back to the mouth of the hangar. The massive doors were almost closed, and Mac and Uri could only pass single file through the opening. Mac looked at the spot where the giant had fallen.

Nathan came up to them. "MacKenzie, all of us are going to have to be debriefed. It could take a couple of days . . . you know military reports."

Mac nodded. "Did you know it was my father . . . down there . . . all this time?"

Nathan looked Mac in the eye for a moment, then turned away from him and said, "Honestly, MacKenzie, I didn't know."

"He got away . . . and I saw Cranston on another ship," Mac added.

"They took him?" Nathan seemed genuinely surprised.

Mac nodded. "Now what?"

Nathan looked out at MacKenzie's family and said, "You can never go back . . . you know that."

Mac stared but didn't answer.

"You know, MacKenzie," Nathan began, "there are other bases . . . and there are probably more of these . . . hybrids . . . giants."

"So what are you saying?" Mac asked.

"I'm saying that you might consider staying on. We need men like you to fight this, MacKenzie."

Mac involuntarily shuddered. "No, you don't understand, General . . . what I saw down there . . ." He shook his head wearily before adding, "The return of the Messiah . . . the Second Coming . . . that's the only hope we have."

* ◊ *

Off the coastal waters of Peru an orange disklike craft hovered for a moment above the deep blue water before it plunged beneath the surface and out of sight.

Epilogue

Dr. Elisha BenHassen sat at a small folding table on the shore of the Sea of Galilee. He had driven there himself in spite of the protestations of both his daughter-in-law, Rebecca, and his driver of the last several years.

He looked out at the shimmering sea, took a deep breath, and relaxed for the first time in many weeks. He nibbled at a cold fruit salad that Rebecca had prepared for his lunch. That morning the worried look had departed from her face at the news of Uri's impending arrival.

Elisha speared a piece of cantaloupe and popped it into his mouth. He looked again at a small fishing boat a few hundred yards away. A lone fisherman cast his net expertly into the water. Elisha continued to pick at the melon as he watched the fisherman go about his work.

A short time later the man began to pull in the net. Even from Elisha's vantage point he could see that it was a big catch. The fisherman hoisted the full net to the side of the boat.

Much to Elisha's amazement the man began to release the fish, taking them out of the net one by one and throwing them into the water. He struggled with a particularly large fish. Elisha heard him laugh as he tossed the fish just before he lost his balance and fell back into the boat.

He continued to empty the net except for two of the choicest fish, which he threw toward the bow. He tied the net to the gun-whale, set the sail, and maneuvered to the stern.

The wind caught the canvas and the little boat angled slightly out of the water. The man steered toward where Elisha sat.

Elisha stabbed at another piece of melon and was about to bite into it when he glanced again at the boat. His fork froze in front of his mouth and the hair stood up on his arms. He recognized the fisherman as Johanen.

As if on cue, the fisherman waved to him.

Elisha was transfixed. He watched as Johanen tacked the boat further down the lake from him and then turned and caught the wind. The boat slid through the water. He held the boat on course and at the last moment jibed the boat down-wind. The boat glided toward the shore where Elisha sat.

Johanen let the prow bottom out on the shoreline. He went forward, retrieved the two fish he had caught, and held them up for Elisha to see.

Elisha rose from the table. "Johanen," he managed to say.

"Here, help with this," Johanen instructed good-naturedly, as he pulled a small brazier from a storage hold near the bow. He handed it to Elisha, then grabbed a sack of charcoal and stepped off onto the shore.

Elisha set the brazier down.

"Get the fire going and I'll clean the fish," Johanen said.

Elisha selected several pieces of the charcoal and placed them into the brazier.

"Here," Johanen said, as he handed several wooden matches to him. "Never have cared for lighters," he commented.

Elisha lit the charcoal and in no time the brazier was hot.

Johanen finished cleaning the fish and placed the fillets carefully on the grill.

Elisha went to the car and brought another folding chair. The two men sat near the brazier and watched the fish sizzle on the grill.

Johanen poked at one of the fillets and said, "How is your grandson, Uri?"

Elisha smiled proudly. "He helped kill the giant . . . it was over fourteen feet tall . . . Did you know that?"

Johanen nodded. "It must have been a formidable sight."

"Yes. Uri told me that he had readied himself for death from the moment he saw it."

"Is he closer now . . . to knowing the Messiah?"

Elisha thought for a moment. "He's still sorting through things. But yes, I think he's closer. He also said that General Nathan's cancer returned."

"So the healing was false just as we knew it would be."

"Yes, and he's a broken, confused man over it."

"We must intercede for him . . . He was exposed a long time to the Evil One, and that without protection. His mind has been twisted, but it can be healed. Laura, also, if she will open her heart." Johanen turned the fillets over, then asked, "And MacKenzie?"

"The debriefing was hard on him. It seems that the higher-ups in the Pentagon didn't believe his story about the alien being hurled into the Abyss . . . They're calling it a psychotic episode due to trauma caused by seeing an extraterrestrial biological entity."

Johanen laughed grimly. "And what does MacKenzie say to that?"

"He submitted himself to a barrage of psychological tests . . . of course the results were negative. Now at least they're reconsidering his story."

"Maggie and the children?"

"Healing slowly. They have nightmares."

"We will ask the Lord to rebuke those," Johanen stated. "When are you going to America to see him?"

"I have a few affairs to put in order first, and afterward I'm off."

"A good thing, too. MacKenzie needs you now. The Enemy knows of his strength and that the Ancient of Days has chosen him as his instrument. They will try to destroy him."

Elisha gazed out at the waters. "It will be a difficult time, won't it?"

Johanen's brow darkened. "Yes, it will . . . The Great Deception will blind the eyes of many . . . and souls will be lost . . . but he whom we both serve shall triumph. Indeed he already has." Johanen lifted the fillets and set them on plates that Elisha had also brought from his car.

The men moved to the table and sat down.

Johanen blessed the meal and they began to eat.

About the Author

L. A. Marzulli lives in a secluded area in the Santa Monica mountains with his wife, Peggy, and their two daughters, Corrie and Sarah. He is also a composer of numerous musical works, his favorite being a two-hour oratorio entitled *The Life of Christ*.

The Highly Anticipated Sequel to Nephilim!

The Unholy Deception
The Nephilim Return

L.A. Marzulli

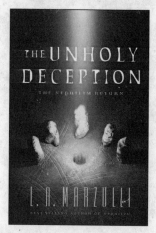

For journalist Art "Mac" MacKenzie, the scenario smacks of an alien agenda. He determines to unearth the truth at any cost. But the Cadre doesn't surrender its secrets easily. Mac's former editor, Jim Cranston, has been found wandering among the ruins of Machu Picchu with burns on his body and in a constant state of fear.

Worse yet, General Roswell, Mac's inside connection in the secret government-alien cooperative, is dead of cancer. However, Roswell has left behind two potential bombshells: a set of files with far-reaching implications, and a link to the aliens that he has kept secret for years.

With Mac hot on Roswell's trail, the Cadre moves forward with its agenda: to convince the world that Jesus was just an ordinary man granted miracle-working powers by the aliens. The Cadre must be stopped before they can publicly unveil the fraudulent body of Christ, an event that could precipitate a global and apocalyptic shock wave. Mac is swept into a race against time in which losing is not an option . . . but winning could cost him all.

Softcover 0-310-24064-6

Pick up a copy today at your favorite bookstore!

ZONDERVAN™

GRAND RAPIDS, MICHIGAN 49530 USA

WWW.ZONDERVAN.COM

We want to hear from you. Please send your comments about this
book to us in care of zreview@zondervan.com. Thank you.

GRAND RAPIDS, MICHIGAN 49530 USA

WWW.ZONDERVAN.COM